"If I give you a home, and all that goes with it—the proper clothes and education, and so forth—I will expect something in return. Are you willing to give what I will demand?"

Thoughtfully, with narrowed eyes, my step-grandfather waited as I stared at him.

"Perhaps you have already found out for yourself that there is a price that has to be paid for everything. First, I will demand complete obedience from you. When I make decisions about your future, you will not argue about them. You will accept without quibbling. And I want no hillbilly relatives of yours showing up, not ever. Nor any of your former friends from West Virginia."

Oh! That was asking too much!

"Yes, Heaven Leigh, I want you to cut off your family ties, forget the Casteels, and become a Tatterton, as your mother should have done."

Like the true Casteel I was, a slithering, sneaky thought squirmed through my brain. Even Tony Tatterton couldn't read my thoughts . . .

Humbly I bowed my head. "Anything you say, Tony." And with my back straight and my head held high I headed up the stairs. Bitter thoughts kept time with my steps. The more things changed, the more they stayed the same. I was unwanted, even here.

**Books by V.C. Andrews**

Flowers in the Attic
Petals on the Wind
If There Be Thorns
My Sweet Audrina
Seeds of Yesterday
Heaven
Dark Angel

**Published by POCKET BOOKS**

# V.C. ANDREWS

## Dark Angel

PUBLISHED BY POCKET BOOKS NEW YORK

Another *Original* publication of POCKET BOOKS

POCKET BOOKS, a division of Simon & Schuster, Inc.
1230 Avenue of the Americas, New York, N.Y. 10020

ISBN: 0-671-52543-3

First Pocket Books printing November, 1986

10 9 8 7 6 5 4 3 2 1

POCKET and colophon are registered trademarks
of Simon & Schuster, Inc.

Simultaneously Published by Poseidon Press

Printed in the U.S.A.

# PART ONE

# ∽ One ∽
## *Coming Home*

ALL ABOUT ME THE LARGE HOUSE LOOMED DARK, mysterious, and lonely. The shadows whispered of secrets, of incidents best forgotten, and hinted of dangers, but said nothing at all about the safety and security I needed most. This was my mother's home, my dead mother's home. The longed-for home that had called to me when I livéd in that mountain shack in the Willies; called loud and sweet into my childish ears so I had been beguiled by thoughts of all the happiness waiting just for me, once I was here. Here in these rainbowed rooms of dreams fulfilled I'd find the golden pot of family love—the kind I'd never known. And around my neck I'd wear the pearls of culture, wisdom, and breeding that would keep me free from harm, from scorn, from contempt. And so like a bride I waited for all those wonderful things to appear and decorate me, but they didn't come. As I sat there on *her* bed, the vibrations in *her* room aroused the troubled thoughts that always crowded into the darkest corners of my brain.

Why had my mother run away from a house like this?

Poor Granny had led me out into that cold, wintry night so many years ago, to visit a cemetery where she could tell me I wasn't Sarah's first child, and show me my mother's grave. My mother, a beautiful runaway Boston girl named Leigh.

Poor Granny with her ignorant, innocent brain. What a trusting soul she'd been, believing her youngest son Luke would sooner or later prove himself worthy enough to lift up the scorned and ridiculed name of Casteel. "Scumbags," I seemed to hear ringing like church bells in the darkness all around me, "no good, never will be no good, none of 'em . . ." and my hands rose to my head to shut out the sound.

Someday I'd make my granny proud, though she was dead. Someday when I had my string of degrees I'd go again to the Willies, to kneel at the foot of her grave, and I'd say all the words that would make Granny happier than she'd ever been in life. I didn't doubt in the least that Granny up in heaven would smile down on me, and she'd know at last one Casteel had made it through high school, then college . . .

What an ignorant innocent *I* was to arrive with so much hope.

It had all happened so fast: the plane landing, my frenzied scramble to find my way through the crowded airport to the luggage carousel, all the worldly things I'd thought would be so easy, but they weren't so easy. I was scared even after I found my two blue suitcases that seemed amazingly heavy. I looked around and floundered, filled with trepidation. What if my grandparents didn't come? What if they had second thoughts about welcoming an unknown grand-daughter into their secure, wealthy world? They had done without me this long, why not forever? And so I stood and waited, and as the minutes passed I became convinced they'd never show up.

Even when a strikingly handsome couple advanced toward me, wearing the richest clothes I'd ever seen, still I was nailed to the floor, unable to believe that maybe, after all, God was at last going to grant me something besides hardship.

The man was the first to smile, to look me over really carefully. A light sprang into his light blue eyes, bright, like a golden candle seen through a window on Christmas Eve. "Why, you must be Miss Heaven Leigh Casteel," greeted the smiling blond man. "I would know you anywhere. You are your mother all over again, but for your dark hair."

My heart jumped in response, then plunged. My curse, my dark hair. My father's genes spoiling my future, again.

"Oh, please, please, Tony," whispered the beauti-ful woman at his side, "don't remind me of what I have lost . . ."

And there she was, the grandmother of my dreams. Ten times more beautiful than I had ever pictured. I had presumed the mother of my mother would be a sweet, gray-haired old lady. I'd never imagined any grandmother could look like this elegant beauty in a gray fur coat, high gray boots, and long gray gloves. Her hair was a sleek cap of pale shining gold, pulled back from her face to show a sculptured profile and unlined face. I didn't doubt who she was, despite her amazing youth, for she was too much like the image I saw every day in the mirror. "Come. Come," she said to me, motioning for her husband to sweep up my bags and hurry. "I hate public places. We can get to know each other in private." My grandfather sprang into action, picking up my two bags, as she tugged on my arms, and soon I was hustled into a waiting limousine with a liveried chauffeur.

"Home," said my grandfather to the chauffeur without even looking his way.

As I sat between the two of them, finally my grandmother smiled. Gently she drew me into her arms, and kissed me, and murmured words I couldn't quite understand. "I'm sorry we have to be so abrupt about this, but we don't have much time to spare," said my grandmother. "Miles is heading straight for home, Heaven dear. We hope you don't mind if we don't show you around Boston today. And this handsome man next to you is Townsend Anthony Tatterton. I call him Tony. Some of his friends call him Townie to irritate him, but I suggest you don't do that."

As if I would.

"My name is Jillian," she went on, still holding my hand firmly between both of hers, while I sat enthralled by her youth, by her beauty, by the sound of her soft, whispery voice that was so different from any I'd previously heard. "Tony and I plan to do everything we can to see that you enjoy your visit with us."

*Visit?* I hadn't come for a visit! I had come to stay! Forever stay! I had no other place to go! Had Pa told them I was coming only to visit them? What other lies had he put in their heads?

From one to the other I glanced, so afraid of

embarrassing myself with tears I knew instinctively they'd find in bad taste. Why had I presumed that cultured city folks would want or need a hillbilly granddaughter like me? A lump came to choke my throat. And what about my college education? Who would pay for that if not them? I bit down on my tongue in order not to cry or say the wrong thing. Perhaps I could work my way through. I did know how to type . . .

And in their black limousine I sat for long moments completely stunned by the enormity of their misunderstanding.

Before I could recover from this shock, her husband began to speak in a low, husky voice, using words that were English, but strangely pronounced: "I think it best that you know from the beginning that I am not your biological grandfather. Jillian was married first to Cleave VanVoreen, who died about two years ago, and Cleave was the father of your mother, Leigh Diane VanVoreen.

Again stunned, I felt myself shrink. He was so much the kind of father I'd always wanted, a soft-spoken, kindly man. My disappointment was so devastating I couldn't fully experience the joy I had once upon a time expected to feel when I knew my mother's full name. I swallowed again, and bit down even harder on my tongue, letting go of the image of this fine, handsome man being of my own flesh and blood, and with great difficulty I tried to picture Cleave VanVoreen. What kind of name was VanVoreen? No one in the hills and hollers of West Virginia had been called anything as odd as VanVoreen.

"I feel very flattered that you look so disappointed to hear I am not your natural grandfather," said this Tony, his smile small and pleased.

Puzzled by his voice, by his tone, I turned questioning eyes on my grandmother. For some reason she blushed, and the flood of color into her lovely face made her even more beautiful.

"Yes, Heaven dear, I am one of those shameful modern women who will not put up with a marriage that isn't satisfying. My first husband didn't deserve me. I loved him in the beginning of our marriage, when he gave me enough of himself. Unfortunately, that didn't last long. He neglected me in favor of his business. Maybe you've heard of the VanVoreen Steamship Line. Cleave was inordinately proud of it. His silly boats and ships demanded all his attentions, so even his holidays and weekends were stolen from me. I grew lonely, just as your mother did . . ."

Tony interrupted: "Jillian, look at this girl, would you! Can you believe those eyes? Those incredible blue eyes, so like yours, so like Leigh's!"

She leaned forward to flash him a cool, chastising look. "Of course she's not Leigh, not exactly. It's more than just her hair color, too. There's something in her eyes . . . something that isn't, well, as innocent."

Oh! I had to be careful! I should think more about what my eyes might reveal. Never, never should they even guess what had happened between Cal Dennison and me. They would despise me if they knew, just as Logan Stonewall, my childhood sweetheart, despised me.

"Yes, you're right, of course," agreed Tony with a sigh. "No one is ever duplicated in every detail."

Those two years and five months I spent in Candle-wick, just outside of Atlanta, with Kitty and Cal Dennison, had not given me the kind of sophistication I needed now, not as I had previously thought. Kitty had been thirty-seven when she died, and she'd considered her advanced age intolerable. And here was my grandmother, who had to be much older than Kitty, and she didn't appear even as old as Kitty, and as far as I could see she had a strong hold on confidence. Truthfully, I'd never seen a grandmother who looked so young. And grandmothers in the hills came in very young ages, especially when they married at twelve, thirteen, or fourteen. I found myself speculating on just how old my grandmother was.

In February I'd be seventeen, but that was still months away. My mother had been only fourteen the day I was born; the same day she died. If she'd lived, she'd be thirty-one. Now I was rather well read, and from all the facts I'd learned about Boston blue-bloods, I knew they didn't marry until they finished their educations. Husbands and babies weren't con-sidered essential to the lives of young Bostonian girls as they were back in West Virginia. This grandmother would have been at least twenty when she married the first time. That would put her in her fifties, at least. Imagine that. The same age as I remembered Granny best. Granny, with her long, thin white hair, her stooped shoulders with her dowager's hump, her arthritic fingers and legs, her pitifully few garments drab and dark, her worn-out shoes.

*Oh, Granny, and once you'd been as lovely as this woman.*

My intense and unrelieved study of my youthful grandmother brought two small tears to shine in the corners her cornflower blue eyes so much like my own. Tears that lingered without falling.

Made brave by her small, unmoving tears, I found a voice: "Grandmother, what did my father tell you about me?" My question came out tremulously low and scared. Pa had told me he'd talked to my grandparents, that they would welcome me into their home. But what else had he told them? He'd always despised me, blamed me for killing his "Angel" wife. Had Pa told them everything? If so, they'd never learn to like me, much less love me. And I needed someone to love me for what I was—less than perfect.

Those shining blue eyes swung my way, totally void of expression. It bothered me how empty she could make her eyes, as if she knew how to turn all her emotions off and on. Despite those cool eyes and those tears that defied gravity, when she spoke her voice was sweet and warm; "Heaven dear, would you be a darling girl and not call me 'Grandmother'? I try so hard to retain my youth, and I feel I have been successful in my endeavors, and being called 'Grandmother' in front of all my friends who think I am years younger than I actually am would defeat all my efforts. I'd be so humiliated to be caught in a lie. I confess I always lie about my age, sometimes even to doctors. So please don't be hurt or offended if I ask that from now on you just call me . . . Jillian."

Another shock, but I was growing used to them by now. "But . . . but . . ." I sputtered, "how are you going to explain who I am?—and where I come from?—and what I'm doing here?"

"Oh my dear, sweet dear, please don't look so hurt! In private, maybe on rare occasions, you could call me . . . oh, no! On second thought that just won't work. If I allow you . . . you'd forget and thought-lessly call me 'Grandmother.' So I am right to start us off like this. You see, dear, it's not real lying. Women have to do what they can to create their own mystique. I suggest you start right now lying about your own age. It's never too soon. And I will simply introduce you as my niece, Heaven Leigh Casteel."

It took me a few moments to take this in and to find the next question. "Do you have a sister whose surname is the same as mine, Casteel?"

"Why no, of course not," she said with an efficient little laugh. "But both of my sisters have been married and divorced so many times no one could possibly remember all the names they've had. And you don't have to embroider anything, do you? Just say you don't want to talk about your background. And if someone is rude enough to persist, tell that hateful someone your dear daddy took you back to his hometown . . . what did you say the name was?"

"Winnerrow, Jill," supplied Tony, crossing his legs and meticulously running his fingers down the sharp crease of his gray trouser leg.

Back in the Willies most women competed to become grandmothers at the earliest age possible! It was something to boast about, to be proud of. Why, my own granny had been a grandmother by the time she was twenty-eight, though that first grandson had not lived a full year. Yet, still . . . that granny at age fifty had looked eighty or more.

"All right, Aunt Jillian," I said in another small voice.

"No, dear, not Aunt Jillian, just Jillian. I have never liked titles, mother, aunt, sister, or wife. My Christian name is enough."

Beside me her husband chuckled. "You have never heard truer words, Heaven, and you may call *me* Tony."

My startled eyes swung to him. He was grinning wickedly.

"She may call you 'Grandfather' if she wishes," said Jillian coolly. "After all, darling, it does help for you to have family ties, doesn't it?"

There were undercurrents flowing here I didn't understand. From one to the other my head turned, so I paid very little attention to where our long car was headed until the highways broadened into freeways, and then I saw a sign that said we were heading north. Uneasy about my situation, once again I made my feeble attempt to find out what Pa had told them during his long-distance telephone call.

"Very little," answered Tony, as Jillian bowed her head and seemed to sniffle, from a cold or from emotion, I couldn't tell. Her lace handkerchief delicately touched her eyes from time to time. "Your father seemed a very pleasant fellow. He said you had just lost your mother, and grief had put you into deep depression, and naturally we wanted to do what we could to help. It has always pained us that your mother never kept in touch with us, or let us know where she was. About two months after she ran away, she did write us a postcard to say she was all right, but we never heard from her again. We tried our best to find her; even hired detectives. The postcard was so smeared it couldn't be read, and the picture was of Atlanta, not Winnerrow, West Virginia." He paused and covered my hand with his. "Dearest girl, we are both so very sorry to hear about your mother's

12

death. Your loss is our loss as well. If only we could have known of her condition before it was too late. There is so much we could have done to have made her last days happier. I think your father mentioned . . . cancer . . ."

Oh, oh!

How horrible for Pa to lie!

My mother had died less than five minutes after my birth, shortly after she named me. His lying deceit made my blood run cold and drain down to my ankles, leaving a hollow ache in my stomach so I felt sick. It wasn't fair to give me lies on which to build a solid foundation for a happy future! But life had never been fair to me; why should I expect anything different now? *Damn you, Pa, for not telling the truth!* It had been Kitty Dennison who had died days ago! Kitty, the woman he had sold me to for five hundred bucks! Kitty, who had been so ruthlessly cruel with her scalding hot bath, her quick temper and ready blows before illness stole her strength.

Desperately, as I sat with my knees together, my hands nervously twisting on my lap and trying not to ball into fists, I rationalized that maybe this lie had been very clever of Pa.

If he had told them the truth, that my mother had died years and years ago, perhaps they would not have been as willing to help a hillbilly girl who had grown used to her deprived situation and accustomed to being motherless.

Then it was Jillian's turn to comfort me. "Dearest Heaven, I am going to sit down with you one day very, very soon and ask you a million or more questions about my daughter," she whispered hoarse-

13

ly, choking up and forgetting to blot her tears. "At this moment I am just too upset and emotional to hear more. Indulge me, darling, please."

"But I would like to know more *now*," said Tony, squeezing my hand that he had again captured. "Your father said he called from Winnerrow, and that he and your mother lived there all their married lives. Did you like Winnerrow?"

At first my tongue refused to form words, but as the silence stretched and became uncomfortably thick, I finally found what wasn't truly a lie, "Yes, I like Winnerrow well enough."

"That's good. We would so hate to think that Leigh and her child were unhappy."

I allowed my eyes to meet his briefly before they fled again to stare almost blindly at the passing scenery. Then he was asking: "How did your mother meet your father?"

"Please, Tony!" cried Jillian, in what appeared to be great distress. "Didn't I just say I am too upset to hear the details? My daughter is dead, and for years she didn't write to me! Can I forget and forgive her for that? I waited and I waited for her to write and plead for forgiveness! She hurt me when she ran away! I cried for months! I hate to cry; you know that, Tony!" She sobbed rough and harsh, as if truly sobbing were new to her throat, then touched her eyes again with her lacy bit of cloth. "Leigh knew I was emotional and sensitive and I would suffer, but she didn't care. She never loved me. It was Cleave she loved best. And in truth she helped to kill the father who couldn't put himself back together once she was gone . . . so I have just made up my mind, I *am not* going to let grief for Leigh rob me of happiness and ruin the rest of my life with regrets!"

"Why, Jill, I never thought for one second you would let grief ruin your life. Besides, you have to remember Leigh had seventeen years of life with a man she adored, isn't that so, Heaven?"

I continued to stare blindly out of the side windows. Oh dear God, how could I answer that without spoiling my chances? If they knew—and obviously they didn't know, it might change their attitude toward me. "It looks like it might rain," I said nervously, staring outside.

I pushed backward on the rich suede seat and tried to relax. Jillian had been part of my life for less than an hour, and already I guessed that she didn't want to hear of anyone's problems, neither mine nor my mother's. I bit down harder on my lower lip, trying to keep from showing my emotions, and then, like the blessing white lies could sometimes be, my pride came back in full dress parade. I sat straighter. I swallowed my tears. I vanquished the throat lump. My shoulders stiffened. And to my utmost surprise, my voice came out, strong, honest, sincere:

"My mother and father met in Atlanta and fell deeply in love on first sight. Daddy rushed her to his parents in West Virginia so she'd have a decent house in which to stay that night. His home was not exactly in Winnerrow, more on the outskirts. They were married in a proper church ceremony, with flowers, witnesses, and a minister to say the words, and later they drove away to honeymoon in Miami. And when they came back Daddy had a new bathroom added to our house just to please my mother."

Silence!

A dead silence that went on and on—didn't they believe my lies?

"Why that was very nice, considerate," murmured Tony, looking at me in the oddest way. "Something I never would have thought of, a new bathroom, but practical, very practical."

Jillian sat with her head turned, as if she didn't want to hear any of the details of her daughter's married life. "How many people lived with your parents?" persisted Tony.

"Only Granny and Grandpa," I said defensively. "They were crazy about my mother, so much they called her nothing but Angel. It was Angel this, and Angel that. She could do no wrong. You would have liked my granny. She died a few years ago, but Grandpa still lives with Pa."

"And what day and month were you born?" quizzed Tony. He had long, strong fingers, and his nails shone.

"February the twenty-second," I said, giving the right date but the wrong year—I gave the year Fanny had been born, one year after me. "She'd been married to Pa for more than a year," I added, thinking that sounded better than a birth that came just eight months after marriage, which might have betrayed some frenzied need my parents had had for bedding down with each other . . .

And only when the words were out of my mouth did I realize just what I had done.

I had trapped myself. Now they thought I was only sixteen. Now I could never tell them about my half brothers Tom and Keith, and my half sisters, Fanny and Our Jane. And it had been my solemn intention to enlist the help of my mother's parents so I could put my family back together again under one roof. Oh, God, forgive me for wanting to secure my own place first!

"Tony, I am tired. You know I have to rest between three and five if I am to appear fresh for that dinner party tonight." A slightly troubled look shaded her expression before it quickly cleared. "Heaven dear, you won't mind if Tony and I step out for a few hours tonight, will you? You'll have a TV in your room, and there's a wonderful library on the first floor with thousands of books." She leaned to put a soft kiss on my cheek, smothering me with her perfume that already filled the enclosed space. "I would have canceled, but I completely forgot until this morning that you were due . . ."

Numbness tingled in my fingertips, perhaps because I had my fingers locked so tightly together. Already they were finding reasons for escaping me. No one in the hills would leave a guest alone in a strange house. "It's all right," I said weakly. "I feel a little tired myself."

"There, you see, Tony, she doesn't mind. I told you she wouldn't. And I'll make up for it, Heaven dear, really I will. Tomorrow I'll take you riding. Do you know how to ride? If you don't, I'll teach you. I was born on a horse ranch and my first horse was a stallion . . ."

"Jillian, please! Your first horse was a timid little pony."

"Oh, you are such a bore, Tony! Really, what difference does it make? It just sounds better to learn on a stallion than on a pony, but Scuttles was a dear, a sweet little dear."

It didn't seem so nice to be called "Heaven dear" now that I knew she called everyone and everything "dear." And yet, when she smiled at me, and touched my cheek lightly with her gloved hand, I was so greedy for affection I trembled. I wanted more than anything for her to like me, eventually to love me, and I was going to try to make it happen fast, fast!

"Tell me that your mother was happy, that's all I need to know," whispered Jillian.

"She was happy until the day she died," I whispered, not really lying. She had been happy, foolishly happy, according to Granny and Grandpa, despite all the hardships of a drafty, miserable shack in the hills, and a husband who couldn't give her anything like what she was accustomed to.

"Then I don't need to hear anything more," crooned Jillian, putting her arm around me and pulling my head into the deep fur of her coat collar.

What would they say if they knew the truth about me and my family?

Would they just smile and think soon enough I'd be gone, and what difference did I make after all?

I couldn't let them know the truth. They had to accept me as one of their own kind; I had to make them need me, and they didn't yet know that they needed me. And I was not going to be scared and let them see my vulnerability.

Yet, they spoke a different kind of English than I did. I had to listen very carefully; even familiar words sounded strange in their pronunciation. But I was determined to see that I'd soon be accepted in *their* world, so different from all that I had known. I was smart, quick to learn, and I'd find a way sooner or later to find Keith and Our Jane.

The perfume I'd considered delicate at first was now inundating me with its heavy base of jasmine, making me feel giddy and totally unreal. Thoughts of my stepmother Sarah came fleetingly to mind. Oh, if Sarah could only once in her life have a bottle of Jillian's perfume! A jar or box of Jillian's silky face powder!

The rain that I had predicted earlier began with a soft drizzle, and in seconds sheets of water drummed on the blacktop. The driver slowed and seemed to take more care, as all three of us behind the glass barrier stopped talking and sat each with our own thoughts. Going home, going home, that's all I had in mind. Going to where it's better, prettier, where sooner or later I'll feel truly welcomed.

My dream was happening too fast for me to drink in all the impressions. I wanted to save and savor all of this first ride to wherever they were taking me, and ponder the memories later, when I was alone. *Tonight, alone in a strange house.* Better thoughts came. Oh, wait until I write and tell Tom about my beautiful grandmother! He'll never believe someone so old could look so young. And my sister Fanny would be so jealous! If only I could call Logan, who was only a few miles away, living in some big college dorm. But I had been gullible and naive enough to fall for Cal Dennison's seduction. Logan didn't want me now. He would no doubt hang up if I phoned him.

Then, as the driver made a right turn, Jillian began to ramble on and on about the plans she would soon make to entertain me. "And we always make Christmas a special event, we go all out, so to speak."

Now I knew. She was telling me in her own way I could stay through Christmas. And it was only early

October . . . but October had always been a bitter-sweet month: goodbye to summer and all the bright and happy things; wait now for winter, for all the cold and bleak and stark things.

Why was I thinking like this? Winter wouldn't be cold and bleak in a fine rich house. There would be plenty of fuel oil, or coal or firewood, or electric heat, whatever, I'd be warm enough. By the time Christmas had come and gone, I'd have added so much fun to their lonely household, neither one would want me to go. No they wouldn't. They'd need me . . . oh, God, let them need me!

Miles passed, and to lift my spirits and my confidence, suddenly a brilliant sun peeked through the dreary clouds. Trees in vivid autumn colors lit up, and I believed God was going to shine his light on me after all. Hope sprang into my heart. I was going to love New England. It looked so much like the Willies— only without the mountains and the shacks.

"We'll soon be there," said Tony, lightly touching my hand. "Turn your head to the right and look for a break in the tree line. The first glimpse of Farthinggale Manor is a sight to remember."

A house with a name! Impressed, I turned to him and smiled. "Is it as grand as it sounds, is it?"

"Every bit as grand," he answered somberly. "My home means a great deal to me. It was built by my great-great-great-grandfather, and every first son who takes it over improves it."

Jillian snorted, as if contemptuous of his home. But I was excited, eager to be impressed. With great anticipation I leaned forward and watched for the break in the trees. It came soon after. The chauffeur made the turn onto a private road marked by high, wrought-iron gates that arched overhead and spelled out with ornate embellishments *Farthinggale Manor*.

I gasped just to see the gates, the imps and fairies and gnomes that peeked between the iron leaves.

"The Tattertons affectionately refer to our ancestral home as Farthy," informed Tony with nostalgia in his voice. "I used to think when I was a boy there wasn't a house anywhere in the world as fine as the one where I lived. Of course there are many that exceed Farthy, but not in my mind. When I was seven I was sent to Eton because my father thought the English know more about discipline than our private schools do. And in that he was right. In England I was always dreaming of coming home to Farthy. Whenever I felt homesick, which was most of the time, I'd close my eyes and pretend I could smell the balsam, fir, and pine trees, and more than anything, the briny scent of the sea. And I'd wake up aching, wanting to feel the damp, cool morning air on my face, wanting my home so badly it physically hurt. When I was ten my parents gave up Eton as a hopeless cause, or else I'd be forever homesick, and I was allowed to come back, and oh, that was a happy day."

I could believe him. I'd never seen such a beautiful and huge house, made of gray stone so it sort of resembled a castle, and not unintentionally, I believed. The roof was red and soared, forming turrets and small, red bridges that assisted one in reaching portions of the high roof that would have been inaccessible otherwise.

Then Miles pulled the limo to a slow stop before the tall and wide steps that led to the arching front door. "Come," called Tony, suddenly excited, "let me have the pleasure of introducing you to Farthy. I love to see the amazement on the faces of those who view it for the first time, for then I can see it freshly all over again myself."

And with Jillian following less than enthusiastically behind us, we slowly ascended the wide stone stairs. Huge urns were beside the front door, holding graceful Japanese pine trees. I could hardly wait to see the inside. My mother's home. Soon I'd be inside. Soon I'd see her rooms and her belongings. Oh, Mother, at last I'm home!

## ~ Two ~
## *Farthinggale Manor*

INSIDE THAT HOUSE OF STONE, ONCE MY COAT WAS OFF, I turned in slow circles, my breath caught, my eyes wide, staring, staring, and too late I realized it was bad manners to stare, country and gauche to be impressed by what others took for granted. Jillian looked at me with disapproval; Tony with pleasure. "Is it all that you thought it would be?" he asked.

Yes, it was more than I'd dared hope for! Yet I recognized it for what it was, the object of my mountain wistfulness, my dreamscape.

"I have to hurry, Heaven dear," Jillian reminded, suddenly sounding very happy. "Look around as much as you like, and make yourself at home in the castle of the toy king. I'm sorry I can't stay to witness your first impressions, but I have to hurry on so I can take my nap. Tony, show Heaven dear around your Farthy, then show her to her rooms." She gave me a sweet, pleading smile that took some of the hurt from my heart because she was neglecting me already. "Dearest girl, forgive me for rushing away to tend to

23

my incessant needs. However, you'll see enough of me later on to grow bored with the sameness of what I am. Besides, you'll find Tony ten times more interesting; he never needs to nap. His energy is boundless. He has no health or beauty regimen, and he dresses in a flash." She gave him the strangest look, both of irritation and envy. "Somebody up there must like him."

She was lighthearted now, as if her nap and beauty regimen and the promise of a dinner party later gave her more sustenance than I could ever bestow. Up the stairs she tripped, graceful, swift, not glancing back one time, while I stood staring up, completely in awe.

"Come, Heaven," said Tony, offering his arm, "we'll make the grand tour before going to your rooms, or do you need to wash up, or something?"

It took me a second or two to figure out what he meant, and then I blushed. "No, I'm fine."

"Good. That means we have more time to spend with each other."

At his side I viewed the enormous living room with its grand piano that he said his brother Troy used when he came. ". . . though I regret to say Troy finds little reason for coming to Farthy. He and my wife are not exactly friends, nor quite enemies. You'll meet him sooner or later."

"Where is he now?" I asked, more from politeness than anything else, for the rooms with their marble walls and floors were demanding most of my attention.

"I really can't say. Troy comes and goes. He's very bright, always has been. He graduated from college when he was eighteen, and since then he's been rattling around the world."

A college grad at eighteen? What kind of brain did this Troy have, anyway? Here I was at seventeen with another year in high school to go. And, unexpectedly, a strong resentment against this Troy, with all his blessings, rose in my chest, so I didn't want to hear any more about him. I hoped I would never meet anyone so gifted that he'd make me feel like a dummy, when I'd always considered myself a good student.

"Troy is much younger than I am," said Tony, looking at me with detachment. "When he was a little boy he was sick so much of the time I rather considered him a millstone around my neck. After our mother died, and later on our father, Troy thought of me as his father, not just his older brother."

"Who painted the murals?" I asked, to move the subject away from his brother. On the walls and ceiling of the music room were exquisite murals depicting scenes from fairy tales—shadowed woods with sunlight drizzling through, winding paths leading into misty mountain ranges topped with castles. The domed ceiling arched overhead, causing me to tilt my head so I could stare upward. Oh, how wonderful to have a painted sky overhead with birds flying, and a man riding a magic carpet, and another mystical, airy castle half-hidden by clouds.

Tony chuckled. "I'm happy to see you so taken with the murals. They were Jillian's idea. Your grandmother used to be a very famous illustrator for children's books; that's how I first met her. One day when I was twenty I came home from playing tennis, eager to shower and dress and get away before Troy saw me and demanded I not leave him alone . . . when up on a ladder were the shapeliest legs I'd ever seen, and when this gorgeous creature came down and I saw her face, she seemed unreal. It was Jillian, who had come with one of her decorator friends, and it was she who suggested the murals. 'Storybook settings for the king of the toymakers,' was the way she put it, and I fell for the idea hook, line, and sinker. Also it gave her a reason for coming back."

"Why would she call you king of the toymakers?" I asked, full of puzzlement. A toy was a toy, though certainly the portrait doll of my mother had been more than just a toy.

Apparently I couldn't have asked a question that pleased Tony more. "My darling child, did you come thinking I made ordinary toys of plastic? The Tattertons are king of the toymakers, for what we make is meant for collectors, for wealthy people who cannot grow up and forget their childhood when they had nothing to find under their Christmas trees, and never enjoyed a birthday party. And you would be truly surprised at the number of the rich and famous who weren't given a chance to be children, so that now, in their middle or even old age, they must have what they always dreamed about. So they buy the instant antiques, the winning collectibles made by my craftsmen and artisans—the best in the world. When you step into a Tatterton Toy Shop, you step into fairyland. You step also into any time you desire, be it the past or the future. Oddly enough, the past intrigues my richest clients most. We have a five-year backlog of demands for stone castles built in scale, with the moats, the drawbridges, the bailiwick, the cook houses, the stables, the quarters for the knights and squires, the sheds for the cattle, sheep, pigs, chickens. Those who can afford it can set up their own kingdom, dukedom, or whatever, and people it with the appropriate servants, the peasants, the lords and the ladies. And we make games so difficult they keep the best minds intrigued for hours and hours. For the wealthy and famous after a while become so bored, Heaven, so everlastingly bored, and that's when they turn to collecting, be it toys, paintings, or women. In the end, it is a curse, this ennui, for all who have so much they can find nothing new to purchase . . . and I try to fill the gap."

"There are people who will pay hundreds of dollars for a toy chicken?" I asked, my voice full of awed amazement.

"There are people who will pay thousands to possess what no one else has. So all Tatterton collectibles are one of a kind, and that sort of detailed work is very costly."

It scared, awed, and impressed me to know there were people in the world who had so much money to waste. What difference did it make if you owned the only swan made of ivory with ruby eyes, or the only pair of chickens carved of some semiprecious stone? A thousand starving kids in the Willies could be fed for a year on what one rich potentate paid for his one-of-a-kind chess set!

How did I talk to a man whose family had emigrated from Europe, bringing with them their skills, and right away had begun to increase their fortune tenfold? I was lost in such territory, so I turned to something more familiar.

I was captivated with the idea of Jillian painting. "Did she do these herself?" I asked with awe, very impressed.

"She made the original sketches, then turned them

27

over to several young artists to complete. Though I have to admit she came every day to check on how they were developing, and once or twice I'd come in to see her with a paintbrush in her hand." His soft voice turned dreamy. "Her hair was long and fell halfway down her back then. She seemed a child woman one minute, a worldly one the next. She had her own kind of beauty that was very rare, and of course she knew it. Jillian knows what beauty can do, and cannot do, and at twenty I was not very good about hiding my feelings."

"Oh. How old was she then?" I asked innocently enough.

His laugh came short and hard, decidedly brittle. "She told me right from the beginning she was too old for me, but that only intrigued me more. I liked older women. They seemed to have more to offer than silly girls my own age, so when she said she was thirty, though I was a bit surprised, still I wanted to see her again and again. We fell in love, though she was married and had one child, your mother. But none of that prevented her from wanting to do all the fun things her husband never had time for."

What a coincidence that Tony could be ten years younger than Jillian, just as Kitty Dennison had been ten years younger than her husband, Cal.

"Imagine my surprise when one day I found out, after I had been married to her for six months, that my bride was forty and not thirty."

He had married a woman twenty years older? "Who told you? Did she?"

"Jill, dear girl, seldom refers to anyone's age. It was your mother Leigh who yelled that information in my face."

It upset me to think my mother would betray her own mother in such an important way. "Didn't my mother like her own mother?"

He patted my hand reassuringly, smiled broadly, and then strode off in another direction, beckoning for me to follow. "Of course Leigh loved Jillian. She was unhappy about her father . . . and she hated me for taking her mother away from him. However, like most young people, she soon adjusted to this house, and to me, and she and Troy became very good friends."

I was listening with half a mind, part of me gawking at the luxuries in this marvelous house; I soon found out it had nine rooms downstairs, and two baths. Servants quarters were beyond the kitchen, which formed its own wing. The library was dark and baronial, with thousands of leather-bound books. Then there was Tony's at-home office, which he displayed to me only briefly.

"I'm afraid I'm rather a tyrant about my office. I don't like anyone in there unless I am present to invite them in. I don't even like for the servants to dust when I am not there to supervise. You see, most housemaids consider my organized clutter messy, and right away they want to tidy my papers, return my open books to the shelves, and the first thing I know I can't find anything. A horrendous amount of time can be wasted looking for what you want."

Not for a minute could I picture this kind-looking man as a tyrant. Pa was the tyrant! Pa with his bellowing voice, his heavy fists, his quick temper, though still, when I thought of him now, tears came unbidden to sting my eyes. Once I had needed his love so much, and he'd given none at all to me, only a little to Tom and Fanny. And if he'd ever held Keith or Our Jane I had not seen him . . .

"You are a baffling girl, Heaven. One second you look radiant with happiness, and the next all the happiness has fled and you have tears in your eyes. Are you thinking of your mother? You must accept that she's gone and take comfort in knowing that she had a happy life. Not all of us can say that."

But such a little of it . . . though I didn't express my thoughts. I had to tread warily until I'd gained a friend in this house, and as I looked at Tony, I suspected he'd be the one whom I'd see more than Jillian. At that moment I knew I was going to ask for his help, the moment I knew he liked me enough to give . . .

"You look tired. Come, let's settle you in, so you can relax and rest up a bit." And without further ado, we retraced our steps and soon were on the second floor. Dramatically he threw open two wide, double doors. "When I married Jillian I had two rooms redone for Leigh, who was twelve then. I wanted to flatter her, so I gave her feminine rooms that weren't girlish. I hope you enjoy them . . ."

His head was turned in a way that kept me from reading his eyes.

The sunlight through the pale ivory sheers was misted and frail and gave the sitting room an unused, unreal quality. In comparison to the rooms I'd seen below, this one was small; still, it was twice as large as our entire cabin had been. The walls were covered in some delicate ivory silk fabric, woven through subtly with faint oriental designs of green, violet, and blue, and the two small sofas were covered with the same fabric, the accent pillows soft blue to match the Chinese rug on the floor. I tried to picture myself at ease in this room, cuddled down before that little fireplace, and failed completely. Rough clothes would snag fabric so fine. I'd have to be so particular not to fingerprint the walls, the sofa, the many lampshades. Then I half laughed. Here I wouldn't be living in the hills and working in the garden and scrubbing the floor, as I had at the cabin and at Kitty and Cal Dennison's house in Candlewick.

"Come, see your bedroom," called Tony, moving on ahead of me. "I have to hurry and dress for that party Jillian doesn't want to miss. You have to forgive her, Heaven. She did make the plans before she knew you were coming, and the woman throwing the party is her best friend and worst enemy." He chucked me under the chin, amused at my expression, then headed for the door. "If you need anything, use the telephone there, and a maid will bring it up. If you'd rather eat in the dining room, call the kitchen downstairs and tell them that. The house is yours, enjoy."

He was out the door and closing it before I could reply. I turned in circles, staring at the pretty double bed with four posters and an arching canopy of heavy lace. Blue and ivory. How these two rooms must have suited her. Her chaise was blue satin, while the other three chairs in her bedroom matched those in the sitting room. I wandered on into the dressing and bathroom area, thrilled by all the mirrors, the crystal chandeliers, the hidden lighting that lit up the huge walk-in closet spaces. Framed photographs lined the long dressing table. Soon I was sitting and staring at a pretty little girl sitting on her father's knee.

The child had to be my mother! And that man my true grandfather! Excited and trembling I picked up the small silver frame.

At that very moment someone rapped softly on my bedroom door. "Who's there?" I called.

"It is Beatrice Percy," answered a stiff, female voice. "Mr. Tatterton sent me up to see if I could help you unpack and organize your things." The door opened and into my bedroom stepped a tall woman in a black maid's uniform. She smiled at me vaguely. "Everyone here calls me Percy. You may do that as well. I will be your personal maid while you are here. I have training that qualifies me to do your hair and give you manicures, and if you wish I will draw you a tub now." She waited with an air of urgency.

"I usually bathe before going to bed, or shower first thing in the morning," I said with embarrassment. I was not used to talking about intimate things with a strange woman.

"Mr. Tatterton ordered me to check on you."

"Thank you, Percy, but I don't need anything right now."

"Is there anything that you cannot eat, or shouldn't eat?"

"My appetite is very good—I can eat anything, and like most everything." No, mine wasn't a finicky appetite, or else I would have starved to death.

"Would you like dinner to be sent here?"

"Whatever makes it easier for you, Percy."

Her frown came fast but slight, as if such an easygoing mistress unsettled her. "The servants are here to make life as comfortable as possible for those in this house. If you dine up here or in the dining room, we will be there to serve your needs."

Thoughts of dining alone in that huge room downstairs, seated at that long table with all those empty chairs, washed me over with loneliness. "If you will bring me up something light about seven, that will be enough."

"Yes, miss," she said, appearing relieved she could do something for me, and then she was gone.

And I'd forgotten to ask her if she knew my mother!

Again I turned to complete my search of my mother's rooms. It seemed to me that everything had been left as it had been the day she ran, though it had been freshly aired, vacuumed, and dusted. One by one I began picking up the silver-framed photographs, studying them closely, trying to find the side of my mother Granny and Grandpa had known nothing about. So many snapshots. How beautiful Jillian was, seated with her daughter, her devoted husband standing behind her. Faded and faint, a childishly written caption was on the rim of the photograph: "Daddy, Mommy, and me."

A drawer revealed a fat photo album. Slowly, slowly I turned the heavy pages, staring at the snapshots of a girl growing up, growing prettier through the years. Birthday parties blossomed in full color, her fifth, sixth, seventh, on up to her thirteenth. Leigh Diane VanVoreen, over and over again it was written, as if she delighted in her name. Cleave VanVoreen, my daddy. Jillian VanVoreen, my mommy. Jennifer Longstone, my best friend. Winterhaven, soon to be my school. Joshua John Bennington, my first boyfriend. Maybe my last.

And already, long before I'd turned even half the pages, I was jealous of this beautiful blond girl and her wealthy parents and her fabulous clothes. She'd had trips to zoos and museums and even foreign countries, when I'd had only pictures of Yellowstone Park shown in worn-out, dirty copies of *National Geographic* or in school textbooks. A lump came in my throat to see Leigh with Daddy and Mommy on a steamship heading for some distant port. There she was, Leigh VanVoreen, frantically waving goodbye to someone who took her picture. More pictures of Leigh on board ship, swimming, or with Daddy teaching her to dance and Mommy taking pictures. In London before Big Ben, or watching the changing of the guard at Buckingham Palace.

Somewhere long before my mother changed from child to adolescent, I lost most of my pity for a girl who had died too young. She had experienced in her short life ten times more fun and excitement than I had known, or would likely know in twenty of my years yet to come. She'd had a real father in her most important years, a kind and gentle man from the look of his pictures, to tuck her into bed at night, to hear her prayers, to teach her what men were all about. How had I ever presumed to think that Cal Dennison had loved me? How could I presume now that Logan would ever want me again, when it was more than likely they'd see in me the same thing that Pa had.

No, no, I tried to tell myself. Not to love me had been Pa's loss, not mine. I hadn't been permanently damaged. Someday I'd make a good wife and mother. I wiped at my weak tears and told them never to come again. What good was self-pity? I'd never see Pa again. I didn't want to see Pa again.

Again I studied the photographs. I had never known young girls could wear clothes so fine, when my fondest dreams at nine and ten and eleven had been to own something from the sale racks in Sears. And Kitty had taught me about the K Mart. I stared at photos of Leigh riding a shiny brown horse, her riding clothes showing off her blond fairness to perfection, and with her was Daddy. Always with her was Daddy.

I saw Leigh in school pictures, swimming at the beach, in private swimming pools, proud of her developing figure. Her posture told me she was proud, and all about her were admiring friends. Then, abruptly, Daddy disappeared from the pictures.

With Daddy gone, Leigh's happy smiles also vanished. Darkness troubled her eyes now, and her lips lost their ability to smile. There was Mommy with a new man, a much younger and handsomer man. I knew immediately this very tanned and blond man was twenty-year-old Tony Tatterton. And strangely, the beautiful, radiant girl who had smiled with confident candor into the camera lens before could not manage even a faint, false smile. Now she could only stand slightly apart from her mother with her new man.

I quickly turned the last page. Oh, oh, oh! The second wedding of Jillian. My mother at twelve wearing a pink junior bridesmaid's long dress, carrying a bouquet of sweetheart roses, and, standing slightly to her side, a very young boy who tried to smile, though Leigh VanVoreen made no effort at all.

The little boy had to be Tony's brother Troy. A slight boy with a mop of dark hair, huge eyes that didn't seem happy.

Tired now, drained emotionally, I wanted to escape all the knowledge that was coming at me so fast. My mother had not trusted or liked her stepfather! How could I confide in him now? Yet I had to stay and get that college degree that meant my whole future.

At the windows, I stood looking down at the circular drive that snaked about to become one long, winding road to the outside. I watched Jillian and Tony, wearing evening clothes, step into a beautiful new car that he drove. No limousine this time . . . because they didn't want a chauffeur waiting for them?

Alone, so alone I felt when their car was out of sight.

What to do with myself until seven? I was hungry right now. Why hadn't I told Percy that? What was wrong with me that I felt so shy and vulnerable, when I had determined to be strong? It was being shut up too long, in the plane, in the car, here, I told myself. And I went downstairs and pulled my blue coat from a closet that held half a dozen furs belonging to Jillian. Then I headed for the front door.

# ～ Three ～
## Beyond the Maze

FAST AND FURIOUS I WALKED, NOT KNOWING WHERE I was going, only that I was breathing deeply the "briny scent of the sea," as Tony had put it. Several times I skipped backward so I could admire Farthy as seen on the ground from the outside. So many windows to clean! Such high and wide windows. And all that marble, how did they keep it clean? As I backed away, slowing my walk, I tried to see which windows were mine. Suddenly I collided with something, and quickly turning I confronted not a wall, but a hedge that was almost a wall it grew so tall, and went on and on. Fascinated by what I thought it might be, I followed it until I discovered, yes! An English maze. And with a certain childish delight I entered the maze, not for one moment thinking it could confound me. I'd find the way out. I'd always been good at puzzles. Why, in intelligence tests Tom and I had always known how to send our mice to the cheese, or our pirates to the treasure.

37

It was pretty in here, with the hedges growing as tall as ten feet, and making precise, right-angle turns, and it was so quiet! All the small chirpings of the garden birds sounded distant and faded. Even the plaintive shrieks of the sea gulls flying overhead were muffled, faraway. The house that had seemed so close was lost when I turned to check—where was it? The tall hedges shut off the warmth of the failing sun. Soon it was more than just briskly chill. My footsteps quickened. Perhaps I should have told Percy I was going outside. I glanced at my watch. Almost six-thirty. In half an hour someone would be bringing up my supper. Was I going to miss my first meal in my very own sitting room? And no doubt someone would light those logs already laid on kindling. It would be nice to sit before my very own fire, curled up in a fancy chair, nibbling on delicacies I'd probably never eat anywhere but here. I made another turn, and shortly met another dead end. I turned again. This time I'd take the right turn. But now that I'd turned in circles several times, I'd lost directions and couldn't tell paths I'd already used. That's when I pulled a tissue from my coat pocket, tore off a strip, and tied it to a hedge branch. There, we'd see how soon I was out now.

The sun in its descent to the horizon blazed the sky with vibrant colors, warning me that soon night would fall with a deeper blanket of cold. But what was this civilized Boston area compared to the wildness of the Willies? Only too soon I found out that a coat purchased in Atlanta was not meant for those living north of Boston!

Oh, come now, this was silly! I was wearing the best coat I'd ever owned, bought for me by Cal Dennison.

It had a small, blue velvet collar that only a month ago I'd considered elegant.

Me, who used to roam the hills when I was two and three and was never lost, confounded by a silly maze, meant for fun! I shouldn't panic. There had to be something I was doing wrong. For the third time I arrived at the pink strip of tissue blowing in the wind. I tried to concentrate . . . I pictured the maze, the place where I'd entered, but all the pathways between the high hedges looked alike, and I was almost afraid to leave the comfort of my torn tissue that at least told me where I'd been three times. As I stood there indecisively, straining my ears to hear the surf pounding on the shore, I heard not the ocean waves crashing on the rocks, but a steady tap-tap-tap. Somebody hammering. Humanity nearby. I let my ears guide me forward.

Night settled quickly, heavily, and mists of fog curled on the ground where cold air met the warmer earth and there was no wind that low to sweep it up and out. On and on I followed the sound of the hammering. Then, alarmingly, I heard a window close, bang! No more tapping! The silence stunned me with its frightening implications. I could wander around out here all night, and no one would know. Who would think to check in the garden maze? Oh, why had I walked backward? My mountain habit seemed stupid now.

Crossing my arms over my chest in Granny's way, I made the next right turn, then the next right turn, never making another left turn until abruptly I was out! Not back where I'd begun, true enough, for I didn't recognize anything, but somewhere better than inside the puzzle. It was too dark and foggy to see the house. Besides, before me lay a path of pale flagstones that faintly shimmered in the dark. I smelled the tall pines made faint by fog and dark, and then I saw a small stone cottage with a red slate roof crouched low and surrounded by a stand of pines. It so surprised me a small cry escaped my lips.

Oh, the fun of being rich! Of having money to waste! Such a cottage belonged in a Mother Goose book, not here. A knee-high picket fence that wouldn't keep anything out wound its crooked way around the cottage, giving support to climbing roses that I could only barely see. In daylight all this would have been charming to discover, but at night my suspicions took wing, and I was frightened. I stood still and took stock of my situation. I could turn around and go back. I glanced over my shoulder to see that the fog had closed in, and I couldn't even see the maze!

From the acrid scent of wood burning, smoke must be snaking upward. A gardener's cottage, that's what! An elderly man was inside with his wife, ready to sit down to a simple meal that would no doubt please my appetite more than gourmet dishes prepared in a kitchen Tony hadn't bothered to show me.

The light from the windows didn't stream outside and fall on the path to brighten my way. It was smothered light, anxious to disappear. I headed for those squares of windows before they, too, vanished in the fog.

At the cottage door I hesitated before I rapped.

Three or four times I banged on the solid door that hurt my hands to rap on, and still no one answered! Someone was in there! I knew someone was there. Impatient because whoever it was was ignoring me, and confident now that I was more or less an important member of the Tatterton family, I turned the latch and stepped inside a dim, firelit room.

It was very warm in the cottage. I stayed with my back toward the door and stared at the young man who sat with his back toward me. I could tell from the slender length of his legs, sheathed in tight black trousers, that he was tall. His shoulders were broad, his dark brown, unruly hair held hints of copper where it caught the glow from the fire. I stared at that hair, thinking it was the color of hair I'd always presumed Keith's would be when he was a man. Thick, wavy hair that reached the nape of his neck and curled upward, barely brushing the white collar of his thin blouse that resembled an artist's or poet's smock, with very full sleeves.

He turned a bit, as if my prolonged stare made him aware of my presence. Now I could see his profile. I sucked in my breath. It wasn't just that he was good looking. Pa was handsome in his strong, bestial, and brutal way, and Logan was classically handsome in his own stubborn way; this man was good looking in a different kind of way, a special way I'd not seen before, and behind my eyes an image of Logan rose to fill me with guilt. But Logan had run from me. He had left me alone in the cemetery, standing in the rain, not willing to understand that sometimes a girl of fifteen or sixteen didn't know how to handle a man who had befriended her. Except by giving in, so he'd continue to be her friend.

But Logan was yesterday, and for all I knew I might never see him again. So I stared at this man, more than puzzled by the unexpected way my body responded just to the sight of him. Even without looking my way, he appealed to me immediately . . . as if he sent out his need to me . . . that it was telling me it would be my need too! It also warned me to tread slowly, to be careful, and keep my distance. I didn't need or want a love affair at this stage of my life. I'd had enough of men forcing sex on me when I wasn't ready for it. Yet I stood there trembling, wondering what I'd do when he turned full-faced, when just his profile excited me so much. Cynically I told myself that he'd be flawed when I saw all of him, and maybe that's why he was taking such pains to keep most of his face hidden in shadows. On and on he sat, half-turned away. Even so, he radiated sensitivity, like an ideal romantic poet should—or did he seem more a wild antelope, posed and still, listening, alert, ready to flee if I moved too suddenly or too aggressively.

That was it, I decided. He was afraid of me! He didn't want me here. A man like Tony would never have sat on and on. Tony would rise, smile, take over the situation. This had to be a servant, a gardener, a handyman.

From his very posture, the way he tilted his head a bit to the side, I knew he was waiting, perhaps even seeing me with peripheral vision. One of his dark, thick eyebrows quirked upward quizzically, and still he didn't move. Well, just let him sit there and wonder, for it gave me a marvelous chance to study him.

Again he turned a little, his hammer posed to strike another blow, and now I saw more of his face, and the fact that his nostrils were quivering, flaring wider, even as I sensed he was breathing just as hard and fast as I was. Why didn't he speak? What was wrong with him? Was he blind, deaf, what?

His lips began to curve upward into a smile as he brought down that tiny hammer and delicately pounded on a thin sheet of bright, silver metal—as if to remove from its shining surface small indentations. Tap-tap-tap went his tiny hammer.

I began to tremble, feeling threatened by his unwillingness even to say hello. Who was he to ignore me? What would Jillian do in my situation? Certainly she wouldn't let this man intimidate her! But I was just a hillbilly scumbag Casteel, and as yet I hadn't learned how to be arrogant. I managed a slight artificial cough. Even then he was in no hurry to turn around and make me feel welcome. I thought as I stood there that he was the most unusual looking and acting young man I'd ever seen.

"Excuse me," I said in a low voice that tried to emulate Jillian's whispery way. "I heard you hammering when I was lost in the maze. I'm not sure I can find the right path back to the main house, it's so dark and foggy outside."

"I know you are not Jillian," he said without looking at me, "or you would be chattering on and on, telling me a thousand things I don't need to know. And since you aren't Jillian, you don't belong here. I'm sorry, but I am busy, and have no time to entertain uninvited guests."

It stunned me that he would so willingly drive me away—even before he checked to see who it was. What kind of man was he? Look at me! I wanted to scream. I'm not ugly, even if I am not Jillian! Turn your head and speak, for in a moment I'll run and not care if we ever meet again! It was Logan I loved, not this stranger with his indifferent attitude! Logan who would one day forgive me for something I couldn't have prevented from happening.

A frown put furrows in his forehead. "Please go. Just turn around and don't say a word."

"No, I'm not going until you tell me who you are!"

"Who are you to ask?"

"First you tell me who you are."

"Please, you are wasting my time. Go away now and let me finish what I'm doing. These are private quarters, *my* quarters. Off limits to the servants of Farthinggale Manor. Now scat!" He threw me a quick, surveying glance that didn't linger on any feature or point of my figure that other men stared at, before again I was presented with his back.

He took my breath away! It hurt to be scanned over, then tossed aside as if unworthy of simple good manners. Stupid me and my hillybilly pride! I'd always had too much pride. Pride that had made me suffer unnecessarily many a time, when it would have been so much easier just to let go of something that had no real value. And still that pride rose high and indignant as it always did when someone like him looked down on someone like me! I made myself dislike him. Nothing but a servant, that's what. A hired hand put in a gardener's cottage to repair ancient silverplate! And with the rush of that unlikely conclusion, I spat out in a totally un-Jillian way: "Are you a servant?" I stepped closer to force him to face me and really see me. "The gardener or one of *his* hired hands?"

His head was bowed to his work. "Please, you are in my home, I am not in yours. I don't have to answer your questions. Who I am is not important to you. Just get out and leave me alone. You are not the first woman to say she's lost her way in the maze, and they all end up here. There is a path that follows outside the maze that will lead you back to where the maze begins. A child could follow it—even in a fog."

"You saw me coming!"

"I heard you coming."

I don't know what made me yell. "I'm not a servant here!" I flared in Pa's and Fanny's loud country way, startling even myself. "Farthinggale Manor is the home of my grand . . . my aunt and uncle, who asked me to come and stay." And all the fears crouching in my mind told me to run, and run fast.

This time when he faced me it was fully, so I saw and felt the full impact of his masculinity as I'd never felt it radiate from any man before. His dark eyes were hidden in shadows as they looked me over, this time slowly taking in my face, my throat, my heaving bosom, waist, hips, legs, then back up again, slowly, slowly. And when his eyes had again reached my face, they paused to gaze at my lips before they looked long and deeply into my eyes. I felt drained before he moved his eyes, which had gone slightly unfocused. Oh! I was affecting him, I could tell; something he'd seen made his lips tighten, his hands clench. Turning from me, he picked up that damned little hammer again, as if to continue on and let nothing interfere with what he was doing! I cried out a second time, my voice Casteel loud, Casteel angry: "Stop! Why can't you be civil to me? This is my first day here and my host and hostess have gone to a dinner party and left me alone with servants to entertain myself, and I don't know what to do with myself. I need someone to talk to—and they didn't tell me that anyone like you lived on the grounds."

"Like me? What do you mean by that?"

"Young like you are. Who are you?"

"I know who you are," he said, as if reluctant to speak at all. "I wish you hadn't come. I didn't plan for us to meet. But it's not too late. Just walk out the door with both hands stretched forward, and in fifty steps you will collide with the hedge. Once you feel it before you, keep your right hand on the hedge, let it trail along as you walk to the left, and in no time at all you will be back at the big house. The library has a nice selection of books, if you like to read. And there's a TV there if you don't. And in the closet there are photograph albums on the third shelf from the bottom. They should amuse you. And if all else fails, the chef in the kitchen is very friendly and loves to talk. His name is Ryse Williams, but we all call him Rye Whiskey."

"Who are you?" I shouted, furious with him.

"I really don't see what difference it makes to you; however, since you keep insisting, my name is Troy Langdon Tatterton. Your 'uncle' is my older brother."

"You have to be lying!" I cried. "They would have told me you were here, if you are who you say you are!"

"I don't find it necessary to lie over trifles such as who I am. Perhaps *they* don't even know I am here. After all, I am over twenty-one. I don't send them advance notice when I come to my own cottage and workshop. Nor do I tell them when I go."

I floundered. "But . . . but, why don't you live in the big house?"

His smile shone briefly. "I have my reasons for

liking it better here. Do I have to explain them to you?"

"But there are so many rooms in that house, and this place is so small," I murmured, quite embarrassed now, so much so I hung my head and felt totally miserable. He was right, of course. I had made a jackass of myself. What right did I have to pry into his reasons?

This time he put his small hammer into a special niche on the wall where other tools were placed in neat order. His deep-set, serious eyes were sad, full of something I didn't understand when they met mine. "What do you know about me?"

My knees folded and I sat automatically on a small sofa before the fire. He sighed when he saw me do this, as if he would have liked for me to walk out his door, but I didn't want to believe he really wanted that. "I know only what your brother has told me. And that's not too much. He said you are brilliant, and graduated from Harvard when you were eighteen."

He got up from the table and came to sprawl in a chair across from mine and waved all that I'd said away as if it were annoying smoke that ruined the atmosphere. "I have done nothing important with my so-called brilliance, so I might as well have been born with an IQ of fifty."

My lips gaped open to hear him say something so totally opposed to what I believed. When you had an education, you had the world by its tail! "But you graduated from one of the world's best universities!"

At last I'd made him smile. "I see that you are impressed. I'm glad. Now my education has gained some value, at least seen through your eyes."

He made me feel young, naive—a fool. "What do you do with your education except hammer on metal like any two-year-old?"

"Touché," he said with a grin that made him twice as appealing, and God knows he already appealed to me enough.

I was ashamed to see how easily my physical side could vanquish my intelligence. My anger flared against him. "Is that all you've got to say?" I stormed. "In my own crude way I just tried to insult you."

He didn't even appear offended as he stood up and went back to the table and picked up that irresistible little hammer again. "Why don't you tell me who I am?" I urged. "Give me my name, if you know so much."

"In a moment, please," he said politely. "I've got many tiny suits of armor to make for a very special collector who prizes this sort of thing." He held up a bit of the silver shaped like an S. "These tiny bits will have holes at either end eventually, and when they are fitted one to the other with little bolts, the chain-link mail will move freely, allowing the wearer to be very active, unlike the suits of armor that came later."

"But aren't you a Tatterton? Don't you own that company? Why should you waste your efforts on something others can do?"

"You want to know so much! But I'll satisfy this question, because so many others have asked the same thing. I like working with my hands, and I have nothing better to do."

Why was I being so hateful to him? He was like some fantasy figure I'd created long ago, here in the flesh, waiting for me to discover him, and now that I had, I was making him dislike me.

Unlike Logan, who seemed strong and confident as the Rock of Gibraltar, Troy seemed very vulnerable, like I was. He hadn't said one word to chastise my ugly behavior, and yet I sensed he was hurt. He seemed a violin strung too tightly, ready to twang at the least careless touch.

Then, when I didn't even try to interrupt what he was doing, he put away his hammer and turned to smile at me winningly. "I'm hungry. Would you accept my apology for being so rude and stay to have a snack with me, Heaven Leigh Casteel?"

"You know my name!"

"Of course I know your name. I have my eyes and ears, too."

"Did . . . did Jillian tell you about me?"

"No."

"Then who?"

He glanced at his watch and seemed surprised by the time. "Amazing. I thought only a few minutes had passed since I started work this morning." His tone was apologetic. "Time slips by so quickly, I'm always surprised at how the minutes race by, how soon the day is over." His eyes glazed reflectively. "Of course you're right. I am frittering away my life playing with what amounts to silver Tinkertoys." His hands plowed through his hair and mussed the waves that had arranged themselves neatly. "Do you ever think that life is too short? That before you've half finished what you have in mind, you're old and feeble and the grim reaper is knocking at your door?"

He couldn't be older than twenty-two or three. "No! I never feel like that."

"I envy you. I have always felt I was in a mad race with time, and with Tony." He smiled at me then,

49

quite taking my breath away. "All right, stay. Don't go. Waste my time."

Now I didn't know what to do. I longed to stay, yet I felt embarrassed and frightened.

"Oh, come now," he prodded, "you've got what you wanted, haven't you? And I'm harmless. I like to fool around in the kitchen, though I can't take the time to do more than throw together sandwiches. I don't have a set schedule to eat. I eat when I'm hungry. Unfortunately, I burn up calories as fast as I put them in, so I'm always hungry. So, Heaven, in short order we will have our first meal together."

A meal was due to be served me this very moment in Farthinggale Manor, and I forgot all about that in the excitement of following this man into his kitchen, which resembled the kind of galley they put on yachts, everything close and efficient. He set about opening doors to whisk bread and butter on the table, lettuce, tomatoes, ham, and cheese. Once he had what he wanted from the cupboards, he butted doors closed with his forehead, since both of his hands were full, but not before I had a chance to glimpse the contents. Every shelf was packed neatly, and very full. He had enough food here to last five Casteel children a year—eaten stingily. As he worked putting the sandwiches together, not wanting my help and insisting I be his guest, sit, and do nothing but talk to entertain him, he appeared both tentatively glad to have me and, at the same time, ill-at-ease and self-conscious. I found it difficult to talk, so he suggested I set the table. I did so quickly, then took the opportunity to have a better look at the cottage. It was not so small, seen from the inside, as it had appeared to be from the outside. It had wings jutting out, leading to other rooms. A man's home, sparsely furnished.

Setting the table put me at ease, as keeping busy had always done, so I could turn and watch him without embarrassment. How odd to be here with him like this, in an isolated cottage with darkness and fog shutting us in, as if we were alone in the world. The fire behind me crackled and spat, and sparks sizzled up the chimney. A flush heated my face. I felt too hot and too vulnerable now that making sandwiches had given him something to do. The busy person always seemed more in control than the one watching. I gazed too long at his face, watching the play of the fluorescent lights on his hair, stared too long at his body, astounded at how responsive my body was just to the sight of him. I filled with guilt and shame. How could I feel this way about any man after what Cal had done to me?

I closed off my emotions, clamped down hard on them. I didn't need any man in my life, not now!

"Dinner is served, milady," he called shyly, grinning at me. He pulled a chair for me and I sat before he whipped off a white napkin to expose six sandwiches on the silver platter. *Six!* Parsley, and radishes made to look like roses, garnished the tray; nestled in parsley beds were deviled eggs, and circling around were wedges of various cheeses, an assortment of different crackers, and a silver bowl of shiny, red apples. Polished apples. All this when he had planned to eat alone?

Why, back in the Willies we could have lived a week on all this food, Granny, Grandpa, Tom, Fanny, Keith, Our Jane . . . all of us!

51

Then he brought out two bottles of wine, one red, one white. *Wine!* What Cal had ordered for me in fancy restaurants when I lived with him and Kitty in Candlewick. And wine had fuzzed my brain and made me accept what otherwise might have been avoided.

No! I couldn't afford to make another mistake! I jumped to my feet and snatched up my coat! "I'm sorry, but I can't stay," I said. "You didn't want me to know you were here anyway . . . so I'll pretend that you aren't!"

In a flash I was out the door and racing toward the hedge in a night so black it was frightening. The damp ground fog swirled about my legs, and far behind me I heard him calling my name.

"Heaven, Heaven!"

What a strange name my mother had chosen to give me, I thought for the first time in my life. Not a person, a place; then tears were in my eyes and I was crying. Crying for no reason at all.

# ~ Four ~

## For Better or Worse

"I MUST WARN YOU," SAID TONY THE FOLLOWING MORN-
ing at breakfast, while Jillian was still upstairs sleeping. "The maze is more dangerous than it looks. If I
were you, I'd leave exploring to those who've had
more experience with that sort of thing."

It was just a little after six, and dawn was terribly
similar to twilight, but for the hot blueberry muffins
and the luscious spread of food on the buffet. The
butler was in his place, close to the array of food in
silver dishes, ready to spring into action to serve the
two of us, who sat at a table that could have seated
eight. Unreality had me in a daze. This was the way
I'd dreamed it would be. The naive country girl I used
to be hovered near my shoulder, shivering with delight, enjoying everything ten times more than did the
girl I actually was now—suspicious, nervous, scared
I'd do something so gross neither Jillian nor Tony
would want to see me again. As for Troy, I planned
never to go near him. He was too dangerous.

Tentatively, I tasted each delicious dish Curtis put

53

before me, truly the most wonderful breakfast I'd ever had in my life, and certainly the most satisfying one. Why, with this kind of food inside of me, giving energy, I could have run all the way to school. Then came the sarcastic thought that maybe the food was so good only because I'd had nothing to do with the preparation. And I'd have nothing to do with the cleaning-up in the kitchen.

"Curtis, we won't be needing you anymore," said Tony suddenly. I'd convinced myself he was the most helpless man in the world, unable to do one thing to wait on himself. He seemed to take a curious delight in keeping Curtis always on edge, waiting for his slight signals to do this or that. With the departure of the butler, Tony leaned forward. "How do you like your breakfast?"

"It's delicious," I answered with enthusiasm. "I never knew eggs could taste so good."

"My dear, you have just partaken of one of the delicacies of this world, truffles."

But I'd not seen anything resembling a truffle—whatever that was.

"Never mind," he said, when I stared down at what remained of my eggs, smothered in sauce and served over thin, golden pancakes. "Now it's time for you to tell me about yourself. Yesterday on our way here, it seemed to me I saw something in your eyes that looked like anger. Why did you look so indignant every time your father was mentioned?"

"I didn't know that I did," I murmured, flushing and wanting to shout out the truth, and at the same time afraid to say too much. His brother was on my mind more than Pa; it was Troy I wanted to talk about. And yet I had to think of my plans, my dreams, and of Keith and Our Jane's welfare, too. I knew the first step toward their salvation was not to risk my own.

And, carefully at first, I began to construct a new childhood for myself, built on half-truths; the only lies I told were those of omission. "So you see, the woman who died from cancer was not my real mother, but a foster mother named Kitty Dennison, who took care of me when Pa was ill and I had no one else."

He still sat as if in shock from the news that my mother had died on the day I was born. His eyes turned dull, sad. And then came anger, hard, cold, and bitter. "What are you saying, that your father lied? How could a girl as young, strong, and healthy as your mother die in childbirth if not from neglect? Was she in a hospital? Good God almighty, women don't die giving birth in this day and age!"

"She was very young," I whispered, "perhaps too young to undergo the ordeal. We lived in a fairly decent house, but Pa's carpentry work was never steady. Sometimes our meals were not too nourishing. I can't tell you if she went to a doctor for checkups, for hill people don't believe much in doctors—they believe in taking care of their own ailments. To be honest, old ladies like my granny were more respected than those who had an office in town with an M.D. beside the door."

Was he going to turn against me, too, and for the same reason Pa had? "I wish you wouldn't blame me for her death, like Pa does . . ."

His blue eyes swung to fix on the windows that soared up to the ceiling, framed by deep, rose velvet swags lined with gold. "Why did you sit there yesterday and confirm your father's lies by keeping silent?"

"I was terrified that you would reject me if you knew I came from such a pitifully poor background."

His quick, cold anger surprised me, and told me instantly this man was not another Cal Dennison, easy to fool.

I hurried on, careless now of what kind of impression I was making. "How do you think I felt when I heard that you and Jillian expected me just for a visit? Pa had told me my grandparents were thrilled to have me live with them. And then I learn it is only to be a visit! I have no place to go now. There is nobody who wants me, nobody! I tried to figure out why Pa lied like he did, thinking, perhaps, that you'd be more concerned for my welfare if you thought me still in grief for my own mother. And in a way I am still in grief for her. I've always missed not knowing her. I wanted to do and say nothing that would change your willingness to keep me, even for a short while. Please, Tony, don't send me back! Let me stay! I don't have a home other than this one. My father is very ill with some terrible nerve disorder that will kill him soon, and he wanted to place me with my own mother's family before this world sees the last of him."

His sharp, penetrating gaze rested on me with deep consideration. I cringed inside, so afraid my face would reveal my lies. My towering pride was on its knees, ready to plead and cry and thoroughly humble itself. I began to tremble all over.

"This nerve disease your father has, what did his doctors call it?"

What did I know about nerve diseases? Nothing! My panicky thoughts raced, until I brought to memory something I'd seen on TV once, back in Candlewick. A sad movie. "A famous baseball player died of it once. I find the name of his particular nerve disorder hard to pronounce." I tried not to sound too vague. "It's kind of like paralysis, and it ends in death . . ."

He had his blue eyes narrowed now, suspiciously. "He didn't sound a bit sick. In fact his voice was very strong."

"All mountain people have strong voices. You have to make yourself heard when nobody minds interrupting."

"Who is taking care of him now that your granny is dead, and I believe you said your grandpa is senile?"

"Grandpa's not really senile!" I flared. "It's just that he wants Granny to be alive so much he pretends she's still with him. That's not crazy, just necessary for someone like him."

"I would call pretending the dead are alive and talking to them, real senility," he said, flatly and without emotion. "And I've already noticed sometimes you call your father Daddy, other times Pa, why is that?"

"Daddy when I like him," I whispered. "Pa when I don't."

"Ahh." He looked me over with more interest.

My voice sounded plaintive, as if I had Fanny's way of acting out a role: "My father has always blamed me for my mother's death, and as a result, I have never felt comfortable with him, nor he with me. Still, he would like to see me taken care of for my mother's sake. And Pa can always find some adoring woman to devote herself to his needs until the day he departs this world."

The longest silence came as he considered my information, seeming to turn it this way and that. "A

man who can command a woman's devotion even
when he is dying cannot be all bad, can he, Heaven? I
don't know as there is anyone who would do the same
for me."

"Jillian!" I hastily cried.

"Oh, yes, Jillian, of course." Absently he regarded
me until I squirmed and grew hot. He was weighing
me, judging me, tallying up my assets and my liabilities. Forever and ever it seemed to go on, even as he
gave some small signal and Curtis appeared from
nowhere to clear the table, then disappeared. Finally,
he spoke.

"Suppose you and I strike a bargain. We will not
tell Jillian that your mother died so long ago, for that
information would hurt her too much. Right now you
have her believing that Leigh had seventeen years of
happiness with your father, and it seems a pity to tell
her differently. She is not very stable emotionally. No
woman can be stable when her entire happiness
depends on staying young and beautiful, for it can't
last forever. But while she still has a hold on youth,
fleeting as it may well be, let's you and I do what we
can to make her happy." His piercing eyes narrowed
before he went on. "If I give you a home, and all that
goes with it—the proper clothes and education, and so
forth—I will expect something in return. Are you
willing to give what I will demand?"

Thoughtfully, with narrowed eyes, he waited as I
stared at him. My first thought was that I had won, I
could stay! Then, as he watched me so closely, I began
to feel he was a huge, fat cat, and I was a lean church
mouse ready to be pounced on. "What will you
demand?"

His smile was small and tight. Amused. "You are

right to ask, and I'm glad you have a sense of reality. Perhaps you have already found out for yourself that there is a price that has to be paid for everything. I don't think anything I ask will be unreasonable. First, I will demand complete obedience from you. When I make decisions about your future, you will not argue about them. You will accept without quibbling. I was very fond of your mother, and I am sorry she is not alive, but I won't have you coming into my life to bring about complications. Understand right now, if you cause me trouble, or trouble for my wife, I will send you back from whence you came without the slightest regret. For I will consider you an ungrateful fool, and fools don't deserve a second chance." He opened his eyes and gazed at me steadily.

"To give you an idea of the decisions I will make for you, let's begin with my selecting your school and the college you will attend. I will also select your clothes. I despise the way girls dress today, ruining the best part of their lives with shoddy, common clothes and wild, uncared-for hair. You will dress as the girls dressed when I went to Yale. I will supervise the books you read and the movies you see. Not that I am going to be a prude, I just think when you fill your mind with trash you smother those wonderful ideals and ideas most of us have when we are young. I will have final approval of the young men you date, and when you date them. I will expect you always to be polite both to me and to your grandmother. Jillian will make her own rules, I am sure. But right now I'm going to lay down a few.

"Jillian sleeps every day until noon, her 'beauty rest' she calls it. Don't ever disturb her. Jillian does not like to be around dull and boring people, so you won't bring any into this house. Nor will you speak of any unpleasantness in her presence. If you have school or health or social problems, bring them to me in private. It will be best if you never mention the passing years, or refer to events in time, or sad stories you read in the newspapers. Jillian has managed to condition herself like an ostrich, sticking her head in the sand whenever other people's problems arise. Let her play her little protective games. When it's necessary, I will be the one to pull her head into the here and now . . . not you."

I more than suspected, as I sat there at that long table, that Townsend Anthony Tatterton was a ruthless, cruel man who would use me, just as he no doubt used Jillian for whatever purpose he saw fit.

Still, I had no intention of turning down his offer to keep me here and to send me to college. My heart was racing happily toward that wonderful day when I would have my master's degree—suddenly only that seemed desirable.

Standing, I tried to find a voice that didn't quaver. "Mr. Tatterton, all my life I have known my future lay here in Boston, where I can attend the best schools and prepare myself for a life better than what my mother found living in the hills of West Virginia. I want more than anything to finish high school and go to an Ivy League college that will give me pride in myself. I have a desperate need to feel proud of myself. I want someday to go back to Winnerrow and to let everyone who knew me when I was poor see just what I've become—but I will not sacrifice my honor or my integrity to accomplish any of those things."

He smiled as if he thought me ridiculous to mention

honor and integrity. "I am happy to hear you take those into consideration, though I knew from your eyes that you would. Still, you do expect a great deal from me. I ask only obedience from you."

"It seems to me that a great deal lies beneath the surface of your single demand."

"Yes, perhaps," he agreed, smiling pleasantly. "You see, my wife and I are influential in our own circles and we want nothing to mar *our* reputations. Members of your family could show up here and be embarrassing. I sense that your father and you are not loving, and at the same time, you are protective of him and your grandfather. And from what I already know about you, you adapt quickly. I suspect in the long run you will soon be more Bostonian than I myself am, and I was born here. But I want no hillbilly relatives of yours showing up, not ever. Nor any of your former friends from West Virginia."

Oh! That was asking too much! I had planned, later on when I had won his confidence and approval, to tell him the whole truth! Tell him all about Pa's having had syphilis that terrible autumn when Sarah gave birth to a deformed dead baby, and Granny died, and Sarah moved away and left her four children and me in that mountain cabin to make do the best we could. And then that horrible winter he'd sold us, sold all five of us for five hundred dollars apiece! Sold us to people who abused us! And how could I ever invite Tom here for a visit, or Fanny, much less Keith and Our Jane?—when I found Keith and Our Jane . . .

"Yes, Heaven Leigh, I want you to cut off your family ties, forget the Casteels, and become a Tatterton, as your mother should have done. She ran

61

from us. She wrote only one time, just once! Did anyone down there ever mention why she didn't write home?"

My nerve ends twanged. He was the one to know more than Granny or Grandpa, or even Pa! "How would they know unless she told them?" I asked with some resentment. "From what I've heard, she never talked about her home, except to say she came from Boston, and she was never going back. My granny guessed she was rich, for she brought such pretty clothes with her and a small velvet box of jewelry, and her manners were so elegant." And for some reason I didn't say a word about the portrait bride doll she'd hidden in the bottom of her single suitcase.

"She told your father she was never coming back?" he asked in that strange, tight voice that showed he was affected. "Who did she tell that to?"

"Why, I don't know. Granny used to wish she'd go back to where she came from, before the hills killed her."

"The hills killed her?" he asked, leaning forward and staring at me hard. "I had presumed inadequate medical care took her life."

My voice took on intonations that reminded me of Granny, and the spooked way she used to make me feel. "Some say that there isn't anyone who can live in our hills happily unless they are born and bred there. There are sounds in the hills that no one can explain, like wolves howling at the moon, when naturalists say that gray wolves disappeared long ago from our area. Yet we all hear them. We have bears and bobcats and mountain lions, and our hunters come back with tales of having seen evidence that gray wolves still live in our hills. It doesn't matter whether or not we see the wolves, not when the wind carries their howls and cries to wake us up at night. We have all kinds of superstitions that I tried not to pay attention to. Silly things like you've got to turn around three times when you enter your home, so devils won't follow you inside. Still, strangers who come to live in our hills fall sick easily, and sometimes they never get well. Sometimes there's nothing wrong with them, and still they fall into silence, lose their appetites, grow very thin, and then death comes."

His lips grew so tight and thin a white line developed around them. "The hills? Is Winnerrow in the hills?"

"Winnerrow is in a valley, what the hillfolks call a 'holler.' I tried all my life not to talk as they do. But the valley isn't any different from the hillsides. Time stands still back there, on the hills, in the valley, and not in the way it does for Jillian. People grow old quickly, too quickly. Why, my granny never had a powder puff, much less put polish on her nails."

"Don't tell me any more," he said somewhat impatiently. "I've heard enough. Now why in the world would a smart girl like you want to go back there?"

"For my own reasons," I said stubbornly, lifting my head and feeling the tears sting behind my eyes. I couldn't tell him how I wanted to lift up the name of Casteel and give it something it had never had before —respectability. For my granny I'd do this, for her.

So I stood and he sat. For an eternally long time he sat with his elegant, well-manicured hands templed under his chin, saying nothing, and then he lowered those hands and drummed a mindless beat on the crisp white breakfast cloth, and on my nerves. "I've always admired honesty," he said at length, his blue eyes calm and unreadable. "Honesty is always the best gamble when you don't know whether or not a lie will serve you better. At least you get to state your case, and if you fail, you can keep your 'integrity.'" He flashed me a brief, amused smile. "About three years after your mother ran from here, the detective agency I hired to find her finally traced her to Winnerrow. They were told she lived outside of the city limits, and those who were born or those who died in the county didn't often make it to the city records. But many residents of Winnerrow remembered a pretty young girl who married Luke Casteel. My detective even tried to find her grave for a record of the day she died, but he never found a grave with her name on the headstone . . . but long ago I knew she was never coming back. She made good her word . . ."

Were they tears I saw in his eyes? Had he loved her in his own way?

"Can you truthfully say she loved your father, Heaven? Please, think this question over well. It's important."

How was I to know anything about what she felt, except what I'd always heard? Yes, so Granny had said, she had loved him—because he never showed her his cruel, hateful side! "Stop asking me about her!" I cried, harassed to the point of breaking. "All my life the blame for her death has been put on my head, and now I think you're trying to put something else there as well! Give me my chance, Tony Tatterton! I'll be obedient. I'll study hard. I'll make you proud of me!"

What was it he heard in my voice that made his head bow into his cradling hands? I wanted him to hate Pa for killing her just as much as I did. I wanted

64

him to pledge with me a joint resolve for revenge. And with that expectation I quivered as I waited.

"You swear your obedience to abide by my decisions?" he asked, looking up quickly and narrowing his steady gaze.

"Yes!"

"Then you will never use the maze again, or seek out opportunities to visit my younger brother, Troy."

My breath caught. "How did you know?"

His lips curled. "Why, he told me, little girl. He was very excited about you, how much you look like your mother, what he can remember of her."

"Why don't you want me to see him?"

He shook his head, frowning. "Troy has his own afflictions, which may well be just as fatal as your father's illness. I don't want you to be contaminated with them—not that anything he has is contagious."

"I don't understand," I said helplessly, deeply disturbed to hear he might be ill . . . and dying.

"Of course you don't understand, nobody understands Troy! Did you ever see a more handsome young man? No, of course not! Doesn't he appear remarkably healthy? Yes, of course he does. Yet he's underweight. He's been in and out of illness since the day he was born, when I was seventeen. Now do as I say, for your own good, leave Troy alone. You can't save him. Nobody can save him."

"What do you mean, I can't save him? Save him from what?"

"From himself," he said shortly, waving his hand to dismiss the subject. "All right, Heaven, sit down. Let's get down to business. I will provide you a home here and outfit you like a princess, and I'll send you to the very best schools, and for all that I do for you, you will do just a little for me. One, as I said before, you will never tell your grandmother anything that would cause her grief. Two, you will not see Troy in secret. Three, you will never again mention your father, either by name or by reference. Four, you will do your best to forget your background and concentrate only on improving yourself. And fifth, for all the money that I am investing in you, and for your benefit, you will give to me the right to make all important decisions in your life. Agreed?"

"What . . . what kind of important decisions?"

"Agreed or not agreed."

"But . . ."

"All right, disagreed. You want to quibble. Be prepared to leave after New Year's Day."

"But I have nowhere to go!" I cried out in dismay.

"You can enjoy yourself over the next two months, and then we will part. But don't think by the time you are ready to go you will have won over your grandmother so much she will slip you enough money to see you through college, for she doesn't control the money Cleave left her—I control it. She has everything she wants, I see to that, but she is a fool with money."

I couldn't agree to something as monumental as his making choices for me, I couldn't!

"Your mother was planning to attend a special girls' school that is the best in this area. All the affluent girls cry to go there in hopes of meeting the right young man they can marry later. I expect you will meet your 'Mr. Right' there, too."

Long ago I'd met my Mr. Right, Logan Stonewall. Sooner or later Logan would take me back. He'd forgive me. He'd realize I had been a victim of circumstances . . .

Just as Keith and Our Jane were victims. My teeth came down on my lower lip. Life offered very few chances such as he was extending to me. Here in this big house, with his business in town to take him away often, we'd seldom see each other. And I didn't need Troy Tatterton in my life, not when one day soon I'd see Logan again.

"I'll stay. I agree to your conditions."

He gave me his first really warm smile. "Good. I knew you'd make the right choice. Your mother made the wrong one when she ran. Now, to simplify what might puzzle you, and make it unnecessary for you to go snooping, Jillian is sixty years old, and I am forty."

Jillian was sixty!

And Granny had been only fifty-four when she died, and she had looked ninety! Oh God, the pity of that was numbing. Still, I didn't know what to do or say, and my heart was thudding fast and furiously. Then came the relief, flooding over me, inundating me so I could breathe, relax, and even manage a tremulous smile. It would work out all right in the end. Someday I'd put Tom, Fanny, Keith, and Our Jane together again, under my very own roof. But that could wait until I had a strong, educated grasp on the future.

"Winterhaven has a waiting list yards long, but I'm sure I can pull a few strings and get you in; that is, if you are a good student. You will have to take a test to establish your grade level. Girls all over the world want to attend Winterhaven. You and I will go shopping together and leave Jillian to her own affairs.

You'll need extra warm clothes, coats, boots, hats, gloves, robes, the works. You will be representing the Tatterton family, and we have set certain standards you must live up to. You'll need an allowance so you can entertain your friends, and buy whatever your heart desires. You'll be well taken care of."

I had fallen into a bewitched state, caught up in this charming fantasy of riches, where I could buy anything I wanted, and the college education that had always been so far out of reach was suddenly close, within grasp.

"This woman Sarah that you mentioned, the girl your father married shortly after Leigh died, what was she like?"

Why did he want to know that? "She was from the hills. She was tall and raw-boned, and her hair was bright auburn, and her eyes were green."

"I don't care what she looked like, what was she like?"

"I loved her until she turned against . . . " and I started to say "us" before I stopped abruptly. "I loved her until she ran off because she found out Pa was dying."

"You must strike the name of Sarah from your lips and your memory. And hope never to see her again."

"I don't know where Sarah is," I hastily said, feeling strangely guilty, wanting to defend Sarah, who had tried, even though she had failed . . .

"Heaven, if there's one thing I've learned in forty years, it's the fact that bad seeds have a way of turning up."

I stared at him with forebodings.

"One more time, Heaven. When you become a member of this family, you have to give up your past.

Any friends you may have made there. Any cousins or aunts or uncles. You will set your goals higher than being just another schoolteacher who buries herself in the mountains where nothing will improve until those people decide they want to improve. You will live up to the standards of the Tattertons and the Van-Voreens, who do not turn out average citizens, but exceptional ones. We commit ourselves, not only in words, but in deeds, and that means both sexes."

What kind of man was he to demand so much? Cold, mean, I thought, trying very hard to conceal my true feelings, even as I wanted to stomp and rage and tell him just what I thought of such cruel restrictions.

And I guessed, or so I thought at the time, just what had made my mother run away. This ruthless, demanding man! Then, like the true scumbag Casteel I was, a slithering, sneaky thought squirmed through my brain. Even Tony Tatterton couldn't read my thoughts. He wouldn't know what letters I wrote to Tom and Fanny. He wanted to be a dictator, well let him want. I would play my own game.

Humbly I bowed my head. "Anything you say, Tony." And with my back straight and my head held high I headed up the stairs. Bitter thoughts kept time with my steps. The more things changed, the more they stayed the same. I was unwanted, even here.

## ⌒ Five ⌒
## Winterhaven

THE VERY NEXT DAY TONY TOOK OVER MY LIFE AS IF
neither I nor Jillian had anything at all to say about it.
He set schedules for every minute of my day and stole
some of the thrill I might have experienced if he'd
have gone more slowly toward creating a princess out
of a scullery maid. I needed time to adjust to having
servants at my beck and call; time to learn my way
about a house almost as complicated in design as the
maze outside. I didn't like Percy drawing my bath and
laying out my clothes, leaving me no decisions to
make. I didn't like the order that clearly stated I was
not to use the telephones to call anyone in my family.

"No," he said forbiddingly, looking up from his
study of the stock market page, "you don't need to say
goodbye to Tom again. You told me you'd already
done that."

I felt stunned by events that happened too quickly
to control, and when I murmured a few words of
complaint, he stared at me with astonishment. "What
do you mean, I move too fast? It's what you want,

isn't it? It's what you came for, isn't it? Well, now you have what you've dreamed about, the best of everything. You'll have to begin school right away. And if you think I am sweeping you along in a tidal current, that's what life is all about. It's not my way to tread slowly, or carefully, and if you and I are to establish a nice rapport, my way had better become your way."

When he smiled, and looked me over, I tried not to feel resentful.

While Jillian slept the mornings away and spent another few hours behind closed doors performing her "secret beauty rituals," Tony drove me to small shops where clothes and shoes cost small fortunes. Not once did he ask the prices of sweaters, skirts, dresses, coats, boots, anything! He signed sales slips with the debonair air of one who would never run out of money. "No," he said, when I whispered it would be nice to have colored shoes to match all the outfits. "Black, brown, bone, blue, and one pair of gray-and-red shoes is enough variety in colors, until you need summer white. I'll leave unsatisfied some of your desires. No one should realize every dream all at once. We live on dreams, you know, and when there are none, we soon die." Darkness clouded the clear blue of his eyes. "I made the mistake once of giving too much, too soon, holding back nothing. Not this time."

We drove home that early evening with the back seat loaded down with parcels, enough clothes for three girls. He didn't seem to realize that already he'd given too much, too soon. I, who had dreamed of beautiful, expensive clothes all my life, was overwhelmed. And still he didn't think I had enough. But then, he was comparing my closets with Jillian's.

It hurt many times the way Jillian either ignored me completely or gushed over me with enthusiasm; I was never comfortable in her presence. Often I had the sense that she wished I'd never showed up. At other times I'd see her sitting quietly on her bedroom sofa, playing one of her eternal solitaire games, and from time to time she'd glance my way. "Do you play cards, Heaven?"

Eagerly I jumped to the challenge, happy that she wanted to spend time with me. "Yes, a long time ago a friend taught me how to play gin rummy." That friend had also given me a brand-new pack of Bicycle cards "borrowed" from his father's pharmacy store.

"Gin rummy?" she asked in a vague way, as if she'd never heard of the game. "That's the only game you play?"

"I learn quickly!"

She started that very day to teach me how to play bridge, which was her favorite game. She explained the points of each face card, gave me detailed instructions on how many points you needed to open, and how many you needed to respond to your partner's opening bid; it wasn't long before I realized I'd have to buy a book on bridge and study it in private, for Jillian went much too fast.

But she was enjoying teaching me, and for an entire week she gloated every time I lost. Then came that telling day when we were seated behind our little computerized game board that would play with one, two, or three players (or none at all—it would play against itself), and to Jillian's complete chagrin, I won. "Oh, you were just lucky!" she cried out, her hands rising to her face to press her cheeks together.

"After lunch, we'll play another game and see who wins then."

Jillian was beginning to need me, to want me, to like me. This was the very first time I'd eaten any meal with Jillian but dinner, served in the dining room. Here was one of the richest women in the world, and surely one of the most beautiful, and she lunched on tiny cucumber or watercress sandwiches and sipped champagne.

"But it's not a healthy, nutritious lunch, or even filling, Jillian!" I exclaimed after our third lunch together. "Quite honestly, even after I eat six of your tiny sandwiches, I'm still hungry, and I don't really care for champagne."

Her delicate eyebrows rose as if in exasperation. "What kind of food do you and Tony eat when you lunch together?"

"Oh, he lets me have anything on the menu. In fact he encourages me to try foods I've never tasted before."

"He indulges you, just like he indulged Leigh." She sat for long moments with her head bowed over her dainty meal, and then waved her hand, as if in dismissal. "If there is one thing that really disgusts me, it's to see a young girl eat with a ravenous appetite—and do you realize, Heaven, that's the only way you know how to eat? Until you can control your need for so much food, I think it best that you and I never eat lunch together again. And when we are in the dining room, I will make an effort to pay as little attention as possible to your dining habits."

Jillian was as good as her word. She never asked me to play bridge with her again. We never shared another luncheon, and when we were seated in their elegant dining room with Tony, she addressed all her remarks to him. And if out of pure necessity she had to say something to me, she didn't turn her head my way. Because I wanted so much to please her, I tried to turn down second and third helpings, and I even made my first servings very small. Now I was hungry all the time, so I took to stealing to the huge kitchen, where Ryse Williams, the stout black chef, welcomed me into his domain.

"Why girl, you are just like your mother, sweet Jesus, I never saw a girl so much like her mother—even if your hair is dark."

In that gleaming kitchen, with copper pans and thousands of kitchen tools I'd never seen before, I spent many an hour listening to Rye Whiskey and his tales of the Tattertons, and though I tried many a time to force him to talk of my mother, he always grew uncomfortable and busied himself with his cooking when I asked. His smooth, brown face would go blank, and very quickly he'd change the subject. But one day, one day soon, Rye Whiskey was going to tell me everything he knew—for already I suspected from his expressions of shame and embarrassment that he knew a great deal.

In the privacy of my bedroom I wrote to tell Tom all about it. So far I'd written him three letters and had warned him not to reply until I could send him a "safe" address. (It hurt me to imagine what he had to be thinking.) In those letters I described Farthinggale Manor, Jillian, and Tony, but I didn't say a word about Troy. Troy was naggingly on my mind. Too much on my mind. I wanted to see him again, and was afraid to see him again. I had a thousand questions to ask Tony about his brother, but Tony scowled each time I approached the subject of the man who lived in the cottage beyond the maze. Twice I tried to talk about Troy to Jillian, who turned her head and waved her hand, dismissing the subject. "Oh, Troy! He's not interesting. Forget him. He knows too much about everything else to appreciate women." And, while I thought too much about Troy, I decided it was time to write the most difficult letter, to the one who truly belonged in my future, to find out if he'd let me back in his again.

But how did I write to someone who had once loved and trusted me, and now no longer did? Did I ignore what had brought about the end of our long relationship? Should I discuss it openly? No, no, I decided, I had to see Logan and watch his expression before I went into more detail about Cal Dennison.

Finally I managed a few words that didn't seem adequate.

> *Dear Logan,*
>
> *At last I am living with my mother's family as I always hoped to do. Soon I will be attending a girls' private school called Winterhaven. If you have any feelings for me left, and I hope and pray you do, then please try to forgive me. And perhaps we can start over.*
>
> *Fondly,*<br>*Heaven*

The return address I put on the envelope was the post office box I had secretly opened the day before, while Tony purchased clothes for himself in the shop down the street. I chewed the end of my pen thoughtfully before I finally put that single small sheet into its envelope, with a small prayer. Logan, with all his strength and fidelity, could save me from so much if he would, if he still cared enough.

The very next day I had a chance to mail my letters. I told Tony I needed to use the ladies' room, then I dashed out of the store's side door and ran to drop my letters in a mailbox. There, I sighed with relief. I'd made contact with my past. My forbidden past.

Then back again to Farthy, which was beginning to seem like home, now that I had possessions I could call my own. I was up early each morning to swim with Tony in the indoor pool, and after drying off and changing my clothes, I'd eat breakfast with him, already I had grown accustomed to Curtis the butler, so I could ignore his presence almost as well as Tony did—until I needed something. I saw very little of Jillian, who wasted half her day in her room before she came flitting out, looking gorgeous, on her way to her hairdresser or some luncheon party (where I hoped she ate more substantial meals than tiny sandwiches with champagne).

As for Tony, soon after breakfast he left for Boston to conduct his business at the Tatterton Toy Corporation. Sometimes he'd call from his city office and invite me to lunch in an elegant restaurant, where I felt like a princess. I loved the way people turned to stare at us, as if we were father and daughter. *Oh, Pa, if only you'd had half the manners Tony displayed as second nature.*

Then came the hard days, the surprising days, when I had to drive off with Tony early each morning, while he was on his way to work, and he'd let me out in front of a tall and forbidding-looking office building where I was to take tests that I would have to pass even to be admitted to Winterhaven. "The first tests will get you in to Winterhaven," Tony explained, "the others will determine whether or not you will qualify for the best universities. I am expecting you to receive high scores, not merely average ones."

I sat one evening in Jillian's room watching her put on makeup, wishing I could talk to her as a mother, or even a grandmother, but the moment I brought up the difficult tests I'd taken that day, she flung her right hand out impatiently. "For God's sake, Heaven, don't bore me with talk of school! I hated school, and it was all Leigh could talk about. I don't know what difference it makes anyway, when beautiful girls like you are so quickly snatched off the market they seldom have use for what brains they have."

My eyes widened with shock when she said this— what century did Jillian live in, anyway? Both parents worked in most marriages nowadays. Then, looking Jillian over again with more perception, I guessed she had always believed her good looks would win her a fortune—and so they had.

"And furthermore, Heaven, when finally you enter that hateful school, try never to bring home any friends you might make there—or if you feel you have to, please warn me at least three days in advance so I can make other plans for myself."

I sat silent and stunned and deeply hurt. "You are never going to let me be part of your life, are you?" I asked in a pitifully small voice. "When I lived in the Willies I thought when finally I met you, my mother's mother, that you would love me, and need me, and want us to be a close, loving family."

How oddly she looked at me, as if at some circus

freak. "Close, loving family? What are you talking about? I had two sisters and one brother, and none of us got along. All we did was fuss and squabble and find reasons to hate one another. And have you forgotten what your mother did to me? I have no intentions of allowing you to win your way into my affections, so that I'll be hurt again when you leave."

From the way she kept looking at me, her faint brows raised a trifle, I knew it wouldn't have to be anything earth shattering to put me out of this house —and out of her life. Jillian wanted her life just as it had been before I came. I was giving nothing at all to her. I had never felt so depressed.

But Tony more than made up for Jillian's lack of interest and enthusiasm. I passed my tests with very high scores, the first hurdle overcome. Now all he had to do was grease all the wheels necessary for the faculty of Winterhaven to bypass hundreds of other girls who were on the waiting list.

We were in his posh home office when he gave me the news, his blue eyes watching me narrowly. "I've done all I can to enter you into Winterhaven. Now it's your turn to prove yourself. You scored very high on your tests and will enter as a senior. And we must make your college applications now, and your SAT scores will be forwarded along. Winterhaven is a highly academic school. They'll make you work. They'll supply you with intelligent teachers. They reward their best students with what they consider is good for you, such as special social activities that you may or may not enjoy. If you reach the top of their academic lists, you'll be taken to teas and you'll meet those people who really count in Boston society. You'll be favored with concerts and operas and plays.

Sports are very neglected at Winterhaven I'm sorry to say. Do you participate in any particular sport?"

When I lived in the Willies I'd studied hard to earn good grades. There hadn't been time or energy to play sporting games, when I walked seven miles to school each day and seven miles back to that shack in the hills. Once I reached home there was laundry to do, and gardening, and helping Sarah and Granny. Living with the Dennisons in Candlewick hadn't been that much better, not when Kitty had expected me to be her slave. And Cal had wanted only an indoor playmate.

"What's wrong with you? Can't you answer? Do you like sports?"

"I don't know yet," I whispered, keeping my eyes lowered. "I've never had the chance to play sports."

Too late I realized keeping my eyes lowered wasn't enough when Tony was so observant. I had to keep my facial expressions calm and unrevealing as well. Casting him a quick glance, I saw a glimmer of pity in his eyes, as if he guessed far more about my miserable background than I'd told him. But not in a million years would he be able to guess all the horror of being poor. Quickly I smiled, lest he read too much. "I'm a very good swimmer."

"Swimming is good for the figure. I hope you will continue to use our indoor pool this winter."

I nodded, feeling uneasy.

Directly overhead I could faintly hear the clickity-clack of Jillian's satin mules as she went through her complicated beauty regimen before going out. She had another regimen for getting ready for parties, and the longest and most tiresome was the one she performed before going to bed. "Have you told Jillian yet that I'm staying?" I asked, keeping my eyes on the ceiling.

"No. With Jillian you don't have to be specific or give detailed explanations. Her attention span is short. She has her own thoughts. We are just going to let it happen."

Tony leaned back and templed his hands under his chin. By this time I knew this was his body language to show he was in control of the situation. "Jillian will get used to seeing you around, to having you come and go on the weekends, just as you're getting used to hearing the surf pound on the shore. Bit by bit you'll seep into her days, into her consciousness. You'll win her with your sweetness, with your eagerness to please her. Just never forget you are *not* in competition with her. Give her no reason whatever to think you are mocking her attempts to fool everyone about her age. Think before you speak, before you act. Jillian has a whole entourage of friends who know how to play the 'ageless' game as well as she does, but she's the champion player, as you'll find out. I've written this list of her friends and their spouses and children, also their hobbies and likes and dislikes. Study it well. Don't be too eager to please. Be clever and compliment them only when they deserve it. If they talk about subjects you know nothing about, keep your silence and listen attentively. You'd be amazed how much people like a good listener. Even though you might not say one meaningful thing, if you ask the right questions, such as 'tell me more,' they will consider you a brilliant conversationalist."

He rubbed his palms together, looking me over again from head to toe. "Yes, now that you have the right clothes, you'll be accepted. Thank God you don't have one of those awful country dialects to overcome."

Yet he was making me panic with his long list of Jillian's friends, who represented hurdles I had to jump. It seemed every word he spoke took me farther and farther away from my brothers and sisters. Were they all going to be lost to me now that I'd gained a certain kind of stable ground for myself? Neither Fanny nor Tom could pass for friends I made here in Boston, not with their broad country dialect. Then there was me, I could be triggered into doing something wrong, if I were made to feel too vulnerable. There was only one person from my past who wouldn't raise Tony's suspicions, and that was Logan. Logan, with his strong, clean-cut good looks, and his honest, steadfast eyes. But Logan was not the kind to want to play deceitful games about where he came from. He was a Stonewall, and proud to be a Stonewall, not ashamed as I was of my surname, and my heritage.

Tony was watching me. I squirmed in the wing chair.

"Now, before Jillian comes down and interrupts with talk of where she's going and what she's wearing, study this map of the city. Miles will drive you on Monday mornings to school, and he or I will pick you up each Friday afternoon about four. Later, when you are of age, you can drive yourself to and from. What kind of car would you like, say for your eighteenth birthday?"

It so thrilled me to think of owning my own car, I shivered and was unable to answer for a full minute. "I'd be grateful for any kind you want to give me," I whispered.

"Oh, come now. Your first automobile is a big event, let's make it special. Between now and then, think about it. Watch the cars on the streets. Stop into car dealerships and do some window-shopping. Learn to be discriminating, and most of all, develop your own style. Be yourself with flair."

I didn't have the least idea what he meant; still, I'd take his advice and try to be "discriminating." While I sat on, still thrilled about that day when I'd have my own car, he spread the city map on the desk. "Here is Winterhaven," he said, putting his finger on a spot he'd encircled with red ink. "And here is Farthy."

The hard clack of Jillian's heels could be heard on the marble stairs. Tony began to fold the map. He had it in the drawer by the time she was at the library door. Her perfume preceded her into the room. Oh, how worldly and confident she appeared as she breezed in, smiling at me, smiling at Tony, wearing her black wool crepe suit trimmed with a mink collar and cuffs. From beneath her jacket peeked a black chiffon blouse that glittered. In contrast to all this darkness Jillian's fairness was dazzling to behold. She seemed a diamond set against black velvet.

Perhaps I inhaled too deeply, allowed myself to be too impressed. The sweet waft of her flowery perfume not only filled my nostrils, it seemed to invade my lungs, so that I gasped, almost choked, before I began a violent paroxysm of coughs that racked me and flushed my face with hot blood.

"Why are you coughing, Heaven?" she asked, whipping around to stare at me with wide-eyed alarm. "Are you coming down with a cold? The flu? If you are, please don't come near me! I hate being sick! And I'm not good with sick people, they make me impatient. I never know what to do or what to say. I've never been sick a day in my life . . . except when Leigh was born."

"Giving birth isn't considered an illness, Jill," corrected Tony in a mild, patient voice.

He'd risen to his feet when she came in. I hadn't known men did that for their wives in their own homes. I was so impressed I shivered with the thrill of living with people who had such elegant manners.

"You look absolutely stunning, Jillian," said Tony. "There is no color more flattering to you than black."

Apparently Jillian liked what she was seeing in his eyes. She forgot about my germs and turned to him. Appearing to glide, she entered the embrace he offered, and tenderly she reached to cup his face between her gloved hands. "Oh, darling, where does the time go? It seems you and I see so little of one another. Every time I want you lately, you're not here. Soon Christmas will be making demands on us, and already I'm tired of winter, and planning parties." Her hands slipped from his face and she was embracing him around the waist. "I love you so much, darling, and want you all to myself. Wouldn't it be wonderful to have another honeymoon? Please do try and figure out a way for us to escape the tedium and misery of staying in this hatefully cold house until January." She kissed him twice, and then went on very softly, "Troy can take care of the business end, can't he? You are always raving about his genius for hard work, so give him his chance to prove himself."

It was strange how my heartbeats quickened when she mentioned Troy's name, and at the same time I wanted to scream out my protest. They had to stay! They couldn't leave me here alone, to spend the holidays in some strange school, with students I didn't even know!

And all of what she was doing to Tony brought back Kitty, who had known exactly how to wrap her husband Cal around her fingers! Were all men so acutely tuned to their sexual lives that they lost control of common sense when a beautiful woman flattered them? Oh, it was true, Tony didn't seem like the same man who had templed his fingers under his chin only moments ago. He was studying her with soft intensity, and in some subtle, mysterious way she'd managed to gather his reins, and now she was in control. It scared me, that easy way she had of getting what she wanted from him. "I'll see what can be done," he said idly, plucking from the shoulder of her suit a long, blond hair. Very carefully he dangled it over a wastebasket before he let it fall. And in this small act, I realized no woman would ever control Tony—he'd just allow them to think they did.

He pulled gently away from her hands, which clung to his lapels. "Heaven and I plan to finish our school clothes shopping this afternoon. It would be very pleasant if you came along with us, and we could make a day of it, dinner tonight and then the theater or a movie . . ."

"Ohhh," she murmured, her eyes melting when they met his, "I don't know . . ."

"Certainly you know," he said. "Your friends can do without you. After all, you've known them for years, and Heaven is yet a secret to unfold."

Instant mortification was Jillian's. Her blue eyes swung to me, as if I'd completely faded from her memory. "Oh dear, I've been neglecting you, haven't I? Why didn't one of you tell me in time? I'd really love to go shopping with you and Tony, but I thought you'd finished, and I made my plans. Now it's too late to cancel. And if I don't show up at my bridge club those catty women will rip me to shreds, and they can't do that when I'm there." She started to come closer and kiss me, but just in time she remembered my coughs. She froze and for a second seemed puzzled by something. My long mass of hair, which was difficult to control, drew her critical attention. "You could use a good hairstylist," she murmured absently, bowing her head to delve deep into her purse. She came up with a small card. "Here, love, is just the man you need. He's a genius with hair. Mario is the only person I allow to touch mine." She glanced in a wall mirror, raising her hand to touch her hair lightly. "Never go to a woman stylist; men are so much more appreciative of a woman's beauty and seem to know just what to do to enhance it."

I thought of Kitty Dennison, who had owned and managed a beauty salon. Kitty had considered herself the best anywhere, and in my poor opinion, she had been very skilled. However, Kitty's strong, auburn hair seemed coarse as a horse's tail compared to Jillian's silken tresses.

Smiling, Jillian threw Tony another kiss before she floated through the door, humming that same mindless tune that showed she was happy.

Shadows deep and dark were in Tony's eyes as he sauntered to a window to watch her drive off with Miles, the good-looking young chauffeur.

While his back was still toward me, he began: "One of the things I like best about winter is the snow, and skiing. I was thinking when the season was on, I could teach you how to ski, and I'd have a companion.

Jillian doesn't care for strenuous exercise that could break her bones and give her pain. Troy likes to ski, but he's always occupied with his own comings and goings."

I waited with bated breath for him to say more. He dropped the subject of Troy and went back to Jillian. "Jillian disappointed me in her lack of enthusiasm for anything out of doors. When I first met her, she used to pretend to like golf and tennis, swimming and football. She'd wear the cutest little tennis dresses, although she's never had a racket in her hand, and wouldn't dream of chasing a ball and making herself sweaty."

At that particular moment the vision of Jillian in her black suit was so luminous I couldn't blame her for not wanting to spoil her frail perfection, which certainly couldn't last forever. I wouldn't doubt, or fear, I'd just cling to the dream that had to come true . . . and if I believed hard enough, one day Jillian would really look at me, and her eyes would really smile to say she'd forgiven me for ending the life of my mother . . .

Two weeks after I arrived in Boston I was enrolled in Winterhaven. I had not seen Troy again, but I was thinking of him when Tony opened the car door for me and broadly motioned toward the elegant school that was Winterhaven, nestled snug in its own small campus of bare winter trees with evergreens relieving the bleakness. The main building was white clapboard, gleaming in the early afternoon sunshine. I had expected a stone building, one of brick, not this kind. "Tony," I exclaimed, "Winterhaven looks like a church!"

"Did I forget to mention it used to be a church?" he asked with laughter in his eyes. "The bells in the tower there will chime for each passing hour, and at twilight they play melodies. Sometimes it seems when the wind is right that those bells can be heard throughout Boston. Imagination, I presume."

I was impressed with Winterhaven, by the bell tower, the array of smaller buildings in the same style as the larger one. "You will study English and literature in Beecham Hall," informed Tony, gesturing to the white building to the right of the main one. "All the buildings have names, and as you can see, the buildings form a half circle. I've heard there is an underground passageway that connects the five buildings—to use on the days when snow makes walking difficult. You'll be staying in the main building that houses the dorms and the dining rooms, and the assemblies are held there as well. When we enter, every girl there will look you over and form her opinion, so hold your head high. Don't give them any idea that you feel vulnerable or inadequate or intimidated. The VanVoreen family dates back to Plymouth Rock."

By this time I knew VanVoreen was a Dutch name, an ancient and honorable one . . . but I'd never been a true VanVoreen, only a scumbag Casteel from West Virginia. My background dragged behind me, casting long shadows to darken all my future. All I had to do was make one mistake and those girls with their "right" background would scorn me for what I was. And every inadequacy I'd ever felt was mine began to prickle my skin and heat my blood so I felt so anxious I was sweaty. I had on too many clothes, layers of new clothes, a blouse and a cashmere sweater over that, a wool skirt, and covering it all, a one-thousand-dollar cashmere coat! My hair had been newly styled, so it was shorter than I'd ever worn it, and the mirrors this morning had told me I looked very pretty. So why was I trembling?

The faces pressed to the windows, they had to be it! All those eyes staring out at me, watching the new girl on her first day. I saw Tony glance at me before he left the car to come around and open my door. "Now what's this I see? Come, Heaven, put your pride back on. You have nothing to be ashamed of. Just keep your cool and think before you speak, and you'll do fine."

But I felt conspicuous standing there and letting him haul all twelve pieces of my new set of luggage from the trunk and back seat, and turning, I began to help him.

"How did you explain this to Jillian?" I asked, using both hands to lift out my cosmetic case, which was full to the brim with things I'd never used before.

He smiled, as if Jillian were like a child to control. "It was really very simple. I told her last night I was going to do for you what she would have wanted me to do for her daughter, and she clamped her lips shut and turned away. Now don't take it for granted that everything will work out just because she's more or less resigned to having a granddaughter who calls herself a niece. You still need to win her over. And when you win acceptance in this school, and with her friends, she'll want you to stay, forever stay—as you so poetically put it."

How odd it felt to be standing before the second step of my dream, realizing my first step was not yet completed. My own grandmother didn't truly want me. She felt trapped because I'd come to remind her of what she didn't want to know . . . but one day she'd love me. I was going to see to that. One day she was going to thank God I'd made being with her one of my lifelong goals.

"Come, Heaven," called Tony, breaking into my thoughts, as a man from the school came out to collect my luggage and wheel it away on a cart. "Let's go inside and face the dragons. We all have dragons to slay throughout most of our lives; most of them we create in our imaginations." He caught my hand in his gloved one and pulled me along toward the steep steps. "You look beautiful, did I tell you that? Your new hairstyle is quite becoming, and Heaven Leigh Casteel is a very beautiful girl. I suspect, also, you are a very smart girl. Don't disappoint me."

He gave me confidence. His smile gave me strength to climb those steps as if all my life I'd attended private, ritzy schools. Once I was inside the main building, and I looked around, I shivered. I had expected something like a posh hotel lobby, and what I saw was very austere. It was very clean, with highly waxed hardwood floors. The walls were off-white, and the moldings were elaborate and darkly stained. Potted ferns and other household plants were scattered here and there on tables and beside straight-backed, hard-looking chairs to relieve the starkness of the white walls. From the foyer I could see a reception room that was a bit cozier, with its fireplace and carefully arranged chintz-covered sofas and chairs.

Soon Tony was leading me to the office of the headmistress, a stout, affable woman who shone on both of us a wide, warm smile. "Welcome to Winterhaven, Miss Casteel. What an honor and privilege it is to have the granddaughter of Cleave VanVoreen attending our school." She winked at Tony in a conspiratorial way. "Don't worry, dear, I'll keep your identity secret, and not tell a soul about who you really are. I just have to say your grandfather was a fine man. A gift to all of us who knew him." And in her motherly arms I was hugged briefly before she put me from her and looked me over. "I met your mother once when Mr. VanVoreen brought her here and enrolled her. I'm very sorry she's with us no longer."

"Now let's proceed with the next step," urged Tony, glancing at his watch. "I have an appointment in half an hour, and I want to see Heaven to her room."

It felt good to have him at my side as we ascended the steep stairs, our footfalls cushioned by a dark green carpet runner. The stern and forbidding faces of former teachers lined the wall, drawing my astonished eyes from time to time. How cold they all looked, how Puritan . . . and how alike their eyes, as if they could see, even now, all the evil in everyone that passed.

Behind us, in fact all around us, the faint and smothered giggles of many girls drifted. Yet when I looked behind me, I could see no one. "Here we are!" called Helen Mallory brightly, flinging open the door to a lovely room. "The best room in the school, Miss Casteel. Selected for you by your 'uncle.' I want you to know very few of our students can afford a private room, or even want a private room, but Mr. Tatterton insisted. Most parents think young girls don't want privacy from their peers, but apparently you do."

Tony stepped inside the room, and from one thing to the other he went, pulling open dresser drawers, checking the large closet, sitting in both of the lounge chairs before he settled down at the student desk and smiled at me. "Well, will it do, Heaven?"

"It's wonderful," I whispered, quite overwhelmed to see all the empty bookshelves that I hoped soon to fill. "I didn't expect a room of my own."

"Nothing but the best," he joked. "Didn't I promise you that?" He stood, strode swiftly toward me, and leaned to kiss my cheek. "Good luck. Work hard. If you need anything call my office, or call me at home. I've told my secretary to put your calls through. Her name is Amelia." And then he pulled out his wallet, and to my utter amazement, he put several twenty-dollar bills in my hand. "For pin money."

I stood there clutching the money, watching him stride out the door. To my surprise, my heart sank and my stomach went queasy. Once Helen Mallory knew Tony was out of earshot, her expression lost its softness, her motherly ways abandoned and with hard-eyed calculation she looked me over, weighed me, measured me, guessed at my character, my weaknesses, my strengths; judging from her twisted expression, she found me wanting. It shouldn't have shocked me, yet it did. Even her low, soft voice hardened and became loud. "We expect our students to excel academically and to abide by our rules, which are very strict." She reached and quite matter-of-factly took the money from my hand and quickly counted the bills. "I'll put this in our safe for you, and you can have it on Friday. We don't like for our girls to have cash in their rooms that someone can steal. The possession of money creates many problems." My two hundred disappeared in her pocket.

"When the bells ring at seven each weekday morning, you are to rise and dress as quickly as possible. If you bathe or shower the night before, you won't have to do it in the morning. I suggest you form that habit. Breakfast is at seven-thirty on the main floor. There will be signs to guide you to your various destinations." She pulled a small card from a slit pocket in her dark wool skirt and handed it to me.

"Here are your class assignments. I myself arranged your schedule, but if you find it difficult to follow, let me know. We don't play favorites here. You will have to earn the respect of your teachers and your classmates. There is an underground passageway that connects all of our buildings one to the other. You are to use this underground tunnel only on days when the weather is inclement. Otherwise, you will walk outside where the fresh air will improve your lungs. You arrived here during the lunch hour, and your guardian said he'd see that you ate your lunch before you arrived." She paused, staring at the top of my head while she waited for my confirmation.

Only when she had it did she turn to stare at twelve pieces of very expensive luggage. I thought I saw contempt on her face—or envy, I couldn't tell which. "At Winterhaven we do not flaunt our wealth by wearing ostentatious clothes. I hope you will keep this in mind. Until a few years ago all our students had to wear uniforms. That made everything very simple. But the girls kept protesting, and the patrons of our school agreed with them, so now they wear what they please." Again her eyes swung to me, remote and cautious. "Lunch is served at twelve for those in the lower two grades, and at twelve-thirty for the remaining students. You are expected to be on time for all meals, or you will not be served. A table has been assigned to you, and you will not change your seating unless the occupants at another table invite you to join them, or you invite them to your table. Dinner is at six, and the same rules apply. Each student is expected to wait the tables for one week each semester. We rotate the service, and most students find it not unpleasant." She cleared her throat so she could continue.

"We do not expect our girls to hoard food in their rooms, or to hold secret midnight parties. You are allowed to own a radio or stereo or cassette player, but not a television set. If you are caught with liquor, and that includes beer, you will be given a demerit. Three demerits in one semester and you will be dismissed, and only one quarter of the tuition will be refunded. Study hour is from seven to eight. From eight to nine you may watch television in our recreation room. We do not supervise your reading materials, though we deplore pornography, and we will give a demerit if we find you with the more obvious printed filth. Some of our girls enjoy playing games such as bridge or backgammon. We do not allow our girls to gamble. If money is found on a gaming table, all participants in that game will be punished and given demerits. Oh, did I forget to say that all demerits are accompanied by one form of punishment or another. We devise the punishment to suit the crime." Her smile went from sour to warm. "I do hope it will never be necessary to punish you, Miss Casteel. And lights-out is at ten sharp."

Finished, she spun on her heel and left the room.

And she hadn't shown me where the bathroom was!

The minute she was out of sight, I began my check for the bathroom by testing the door she hadn't used.

It was locked. I sat down to read the small class assignment card. Eight o'clock, English class, in Elmhurst Hall. And then I desperately needed the bathroom.

All my bags I left on the floor of my private room as I took off down the hall, looking for signs. The titters and giggles I'd heard before were gone. I felt totally alone on the second floor. I tried three halls before finally I saw a small brass plaque reading "Lavatory."

With relief I opened the swinging door and stepped inside a huge room where white sinks lined an entire wall, with mirrors above them. The floor was of black-and-white tile. The walls were light gray, softening all that black and white, and when I came out of one of the stalls, I took the time to look it over. Twelve bathtubs were in another compartment, one beside the other. In yet another compartment were shower stalls without doors, all but one. Behind glass doors were shelves where hundreds of neatly folded white towels were placed. Right then and there I decided I would take showers, not tub baths.

Before I left the bathroom, I felt the potted plants and found them dry, and carefully I gave each some water, a habit formed living with Kitty Dennison.

Back in my room I swiftly unpacked, placed my lovely new lingerie neatly in stacks in the dresser, and then glanced at my schedule again. I was due in Sholten Hall at two-thirty for social studies. My first class in Winterhaven.

Easily enough I found Sholten Hall, and wearing the outfit that Tony had suggested for my first class, I hesitated just outside the room; then, pulling in my breath and holding my head high, I pushed the door open and entered. It seemed they were waiting for me. Every girl's head turned my way, and all fifteen pairs of eyes fixed on every detail of my clothes before finally looking up to see my face; then they turned their gazes to the head of the room where a tall, thin teacher sat behind her desk.

"Come in, Miss Casteel. We have been waiting for you." She glanced at her watch. "Please try to be on time tomorrow."

Only the front seats were unoccupied, and I felt terribly conspicuous as I made my way to the closest one and sat down.

"I am named Powatan Rivers, Miss Casteel. Miss Bradley, please give Miss Casteel the books she will need for this class; I hope, Miss Casteel, you came equipped with your own pens, pencils, papers, and so on."

Tony had supplied me with everything, so I could nod and accept the social studies books and top off my neat stack. I'd always taken great pride in books and the paraphernalia that went along with school life, and for the first time I had everything any student could possibly want.

"Would you like to address the class and tell them something about yourself, Miss Casteel?"

My mind went totally blank. No! I didn't want to stand up before them and tell them anything!

"It is customary, Miss Casteel, for our new students to do this. Especially those from other areas of our large and beautiful country. It helps all of us to understand you."

Expectantly the teacher waited, as all the girls leaned forward so I felt their eyes on my back. Reluctantly I stood up and took the few steps to the front of the room, and now that I could see all of the girls, I realized how wrong Tony had been to choose the kind of clothes I was wearing! Not a girl had on a skirt! They wore pants or blue jeans, and their tops were sloppy, too-large shirts or ill-fitting sweaters. My heart sank, for those were the kind of school clothes all the kids back in Winnerrow used to wear! And up here, in this fancy school, I'd expected things to be better, nicer.

Several times I had to wet my lips, which had gone dry. My legs betrayed me and began to shake. Tony's instructions came to me. "I was born in Texas," I began in a faltering, quivering voice, "and later on, when I was about two, I moved with my father to West Virginia. I grew up there. My father fell ill, and my aunt invited me to come and live with her and her husband.

I hurried back to my seat and sat down. Miss Rivers cleared her throat. "Miss Casteel, before you came, your name was given to me to record in our register. Would you mind telling me the origin of your remarkable Christian name?"

"I don't understand your meaning . . ."

"The girls are interested in knowing if you are named after a relative . . ."

"No, Miss Rivers, I am named for that place we all expect to go to, sooner or later."

Several of the girls behind me tittered. Miss Rivers's eyes turned into hard stones. "All right, Miss Casteel. I suspect only in West Virginia are there parents so audacious as to challenge the powers that be. And now, let us open our government book to page 212 and proceed with today's lesson. Miss Casteel, since you join us late in this semester, we will expect you to catch up before this week is over. Every

Friday there will be an exam to test what you have learned. And now girls, begin today's class by reading through pages 212 to 242, and when you have finished, close your books and put them inside your desks. Then we will begin our discussion."

School anywhere was more or less the same, I soon found out. Pages to read, questions to copy from the chalkboard. Except this teacher was very well informed on how our government worked, and she also knew exactly what was wrong with it. I sat and listened, overwhelmed by the passion she displayed for her subject, and when she stopped talking abruptly, I felt like applauding. How wonderful that she knew so much about poverty! Yes, there were people in our rich, abundant land that went to bed hungry. Yes, thousands of children were deprived of rights that should come to them naturally; the right to enough food to nourish their bodies and brains; enough clothes to wear to keep them warm; enough housing to see they were sheltered from the weather; enough rest on a comfortable bed so they didn't awaken with shadows under their eyes, put there from sleeping on hard floors without enough blankets; and most of all, parents who were old enough and educated enough to provide all of that.

"So where do we begin to correct all the wrongs? How do we stop ignorance, when the ignorant don't seem to care whether or not their children will be trapped in the same miserable circumstances? How do we make those in high places care for the underprivileged? Think about that tonight, and when you have found solutions, write them down, and submit them tomorrow in class."

Somehow I made it through the day. None of the

girls approached me to ask questions, though all of them stared, then hurriedly moved their eyes away when mine tried to meet with theirs. In the dining hall that evening at six, I sat alone at a round table covered with a crisp, white linen tablecloth, and in the center of my table was a small, silver bud vase containing a single red rose. The students serving as waitresses took my order from a short menu, then moved on to other tables where four to five girls sat together, chattering in lively fashion, so the dining hall resounded with many happy voices. I was the only girl in the room that had a single red rose on her table, and only when I realized that did I pluck from a small wire the tiny white card that read: "My best wishes, Tony."

Every day until Friday, a red rose showed up on my dinner table. And every day those girls ignored my existence. What was I doing wrong, except wearing the wrong kind of clothes? I hadn't brought jeans or pants or old shirts and sweaters with me. Valiantly I tried to smile at the girls who glanced my way, trying to catch their eyes. The minute they saw my efforts, each and every one of them turned away! And then I guessed what was happening. My thoughts about hunger in America had betrayed me. My own passion for the subject of poverty had given them more information than my tongue ever could. I was too well informed. Too many nights I'd lain awake in a mountain cabin, trying to find answers that would save all the poor from falling into the same desperate plight of their ancestors.

For my theme paper on Poverty in America I was given an A-minus. A very good beginning. But I had betrayed myself. Now everyone knew just what background had been mine, or else I couldn't have known so much. I wished a thousand times I hadn't been so factual and had turned in some solution like that of another girl, who had suggested, "Every rich person should adopt at least one poor child."

Alone in my pretty room, on my back on my narrow bed, I listened to the laughter and giggles that came from other rooms. I smelled the bread toasting and the cheese melting; I heard the clink and clank of glasses, of silverware, the canned laughter played on TV situation comedies. Not once did any girl knock on my closed door and invite me to a forbidden party. Not once were those parties stopped by irate teachers who didn't want their rules broken.

From the wild tales I overheard, every one of those girls had traveled extensively throughout the world, and already they were bored with cities I had yet to see. Three of the girls had been expelled from private Swiss schools for love affairs, two had been expelled from other American schools for drinking, two more for using drugs. All the girls could cuss worse than any drunken hillbilly at a barn dance, and right through the walls I received a different kind of sex education, ten times more shocking than anything Fanny had ever done.

Then one day when I was in the bathroom, in the only shower stall that had a door to close, I heard them talking about me. They didn't want me in "their" school. I wasn't "their" kind. "She's not who she pretends to be," whispered a voice I'd grown to recognize as belonging to Faith Morgantile.

I wasn't pretending to be anything other than a girl

seeking an education. And for that I was resented. I only hoped that when my hazing came, I could survive with my dignity and pride intact.

So here in Winterhaven, despite my VanVoreen ancestors, my Tatterton connections, my fine clothes, my flattering hairstyle, my pretty shoes, and the good grades I worked hard to achieve, I was, as I'd always been, an outsider, scorned for what I was. And the worst thing of all was, right at the beginning, I had betrayed myself, and Tony.

# ～ Six ～
## *Changing Seasons*

It was Tony who came to pick me up that first
Friday when I stood on the front stoop of Winterhaven, with fifteen girls crowded close about me,
pretending to be friendly for his benefit. They
watched him park, ooh'd and aw'd, gasped and whispered and wondered again where Troy was. "When
are you going to invite us to your home, *Heaven?*"
asked Prudence Carraway, whom everyone called
Pru. "We've heard it's fabulous, absolutely fab, fab,
fab!"

Before Tony was out of the car and opening the
door I was down the steps escaping those girls. "See
you Monday, Heaven!" a chorus of voices sang out,
and it was the first time anyone had said my name but
a teacher.

"Well," said Tony, smiling at me and driving off.
"From what I saw and heard, it seems you've already
made lots of friends. That's good. But I hate the
sloppy rags those girls are wearing to school. Why do
they try so to look ugly during the best years of their
lives?"

Several miles passed and I didn't speak. "Come on, Heaven, tell me about it," he urged. "Did your cashmeres create a sensation? Or did they scorn you for wearing the kind of clothes their mothers buy for them, but they leave at home, or trade in for second-hand clothes."

"They do that?" I asked, completely stunned.

"I've heard they do. It's sort of a cause at Winterhaven to challenge teachers and fight parents or anyone in authority. It's like a Boston Tea Party for adolescents, struggling to assert their independence."

So he'd known when he selected all my skirts, sweaters, blouses, and shirts just what he was doing to me, making me stand out, making me different. Still I said nothing.

I could tell from his demeanor he didn't want me to complain about anything that had gone on. I had been thrown into the pot, and now it was up to me to keep from being boiled. He didn't urge me to keep on wearing just what I had. He left it up to me to give in or to fight the peer pressure. And realizing this, I made up my mind never to mention any of my difficulties to Tony. I would handle them alone, no matter what came along.

Tony drove fast toward Farthinggale Manor, and we were almost there before he dropped his bombshell. "Some very pressing business has come up, and I'll be flying to California this Sunday morning. Jillian will be going with me. If you weren't already enrolled in school, we could take you along. As it is, Miles will drive you to school on Monday, and pick you up next Friday afternoon. Jillian and I plan to return a week from Sunday."

His news threw me into a tailspin! I didn't want to

be left alone in a house of servants that I hardly knew. I tried not to let Tony see the sudden tears that sprang to my eyes. What was wrong with me that people found me so easy to leave?

"Jill and I will make up for this week's neglect by really extending ourselves this coming Thanksgiving and Christmas," he said with his rare kind of light-hearted charm, "and I give you my word of honor that we will go to that Pops concert when I return."

"You don't have to worry about me," I said with determination, not wanting him to think I was a burden like Jillian did. "I know how to entertain myself." But I didn't, not really. Farthinggale Manor still intimidated me. The only servant who didn't make me nervous was Rye Whiskey. But if I visited him too often in his kitchen, maybe he'd grow cold and indifferent, too. Once I came home on Friday afternoon, and my homework was finished, what would I do with myself?

Then came that Saturday morning in Farthinggale Manor with servants rushing around in a dither, trying to help Jillian pack for a week's trip. In the upstairs hall she ran to me, laughing, hugging and kissing me, making me feel that maybe I'd been wrong, and she did love me and need me. Then she was clapping her hands together like a happy little girl as we descended the stairs into the living room. "It's a pity you can't come with us, but you were the one who pleaded for a few months of schooling, and dashed all the exciting plans I had for you."

A few months of schooling? Was she planning to push me out of here? Didn't she care for me even a tiny bit? And to fly to California would have been another of my dreams realized, but by this time I was wary of the dreams I'd constructed when I was young, naive, and dumb.

"I'll be fine, Jillian, don't worry about me. This is such a wonderful house, and so big, I haven't had half a chance to look it over."

They were ignoring me, both Tony and Jillian, and deep down I was so hurt I wanted to do some hurting on my own, and so I did something ill conceived and stupid. I decided to go and visit Logan. "Besides," I said, "I have plans to go into Boston this afternoon."

"What do you mean you've made plans of your own for this afternoon?" asked Jillian. "Really, Heaven, isn't Saturday *our* day, when we can do things together?" (This had never been made clear to me before, as I stood around with people much older than I, all talking about subjects I knew nothing about. I had felt as needed as a lamp at noontime.) "I thought tonight we could make it a going-away party in that charming little theater we just had restored, right off the swimming area. We can watch an old movie. I do hate new movies. They embarrass me the way they show naked people making love. We could even invite over a few friends to make it more enjoyable."

But Jillian shouldn't have mentioned inviting friends. Friends would take away the specialness of our last evening together for a week. "I'm sorry, Jillian, but I really thought you'd want to go to bed early this evening, so you'd be rested when you reached California. I'll be fine, and if I get home early, your guests will still be here."

"Where are you going?" Tony asked sharply. He had been browsing through this morning's newspaper; now his eyes above the newspaper were very suspicious. "You don't know anyone in Boston but us, and the few older friends we have introduced you to—or have the girls at Winterhaven suddenly embraced you as a friend? That seems unlikely." He raised an eyebrow. "Or perhaps you plan to meet some boy?"

As always when I was hurt, my pride came rushing to the forefront. Of course I'd made many friends in Winterhaven—or they would be sooner or later. I swallowed first. "One of the girls at school has invited me to her birthday party. It's being held in The Red Feather."

"What girl invited you?"

"Faith Morgantile."

"I know her father. He's a scoundrel, though her mother seems decent enough . . . still, The Red Feather is not the kind of place I'd pick for my daughter's birthday party."

He continued to eye me up and down, until I felt sweat break out in my armpits. "Don't disappoint me, Heaven," he said, turning back to his paper. "I have heard of The Red Feather and the parties held there. You are much too young at fifteen to begin drinking beer, or wine, or to sample any of the other adult pursuits that begin in innocent-appearing games. I'm sorry, but I don't think it is a good idea for you to go."

My heart plunged.

The Red Feather was very near Boston University, where Logan Stonewall went to school.

"And," continued Tony, who was still talking, "I have given Miles instructions not to drive you off the grounds until Monday morning. The servants will take care of your needs. If you grow tired of being indoors, you can always explore the grounds."

At this point Jillian looked up, as if she'd heard nothing about anything but the outdoors.

"Don't go to the stables!" cried Jillian. "I want to be the one to introduce you to my horses—my wonderful, beautiful Arabians. We'll do that when we come back."

For days and days and days she'd been promising that. I no longer believed her.

I had made my play to escape and find Logan, and I had failed. And if they held the party and showed the movie, they'd never miss me, never.

Ten guests would arrive around four for what Jillian called her "Off to California Party." I knew she was still testing me, and a great deal depended on how I went over with this particular group, which included people who had more influence than the ones I'd already met. Then came Tony's information. Everyone had to have a dining partner, and I was the odd one out. "There's a young man I want you to meet," said Tony.

"You're going to like him, darling," said Jillian in her whispery-soft way, while an exceedingly handsome young man arranged her hair in a new style. I perched on a delicate chair, watching the marvel of what he could do with a comb, brush, and hair spray. "His name is Ames Colton, and he's eighteen years old. His father won his seat in the House just last year; Tony expects John Colton to end up in the White House."

That made me think of Tom, and his desire to reach the White House someday. Why hadn't Tom answered even one of my three letters? Was Pa somehow keeping them from him? Didn't Tom care anymore now that he knew I was rich and well taken care of? My family had always given me sustenance, a reason to keep on trying. Now I felt all those dear and familiar ties stretching thin and fading away.

"Be nice to Ames, Heaven," said Jillian with a note of authority in her voice. "And please try not to do or say anything to embarrass us in front of our friends.

It was the first real party of my life, and wearing a brand-new floor-length gown of deep blue with sparkling blue beads embroidered on the bodice, I stood between Jillian and Tony near the door. Tony wore a tux and Jillian had on a glittering white outfit that took my breath away.

"Just smile a lot," whispered Tony as the first guests were shown in by Curtis.

Ames Colton was nice enough, not anything at all like Logan. Not exciting like Troy. In fact I considered him too nice, embarrassingly impressed by someone like me, who was scared half to death, and a fake. If I did anything right that night I couldn't remember it later. I dropped my napkin, dropped my fork, twice! I stammered when I was asked about my past, and how long I planned to stay. How could I answer when Jillian was staring at me with fear in her eyes?

It took so many dishes to have a party like this, so much silverware; and then, when the meal was over, a dainty little bowl with a silver tray underneath was served by Curtis. He stood quietly waiting as I eyed what appeared to be water with a slim slice of lemon on the top. It puzzled me, that small bowl that sat and waited for me to do something with it. I raised desperate eyes to Tony, then flushed when I saw his sarcastic amusement. And very deliberately he dipped his fingertips in that lemon-flavored water, then dried them daintily on his napkin.

Somehow I made it through the evening without any gross mistake to give away my background; I only betrayed my social inexperience. I didn't know what to say when asked for my political opinions. I had no opinions on the state of the nation's economy. I hadn't read any of the recent Hollywood best-sellers that told all, nor had I been to a current movie. I found smiles for answers, and pretenses for getting away, and in my opinion I made a complete jackass out of myself.

"You were fine," said Tony, coming into my bedroom while I was brushing my hair. "Everyone commented on how much you look like Jillian. That is not odd, for her two older sisters are older editions of Jillian, though they are not as 'well preserved,' so to speak." His expression turned serious. "Now, tell me what you thought of our friends."

How could I tell him exactly what I thought? In some ways it seemed all people were alike, despite their fine clothes, and fancy vocabularies. There were some who talked too much, and sooner or later revealed they were fools. There were some there only to make a good impression, and they'd had as little to say as I had. Then there were others who came to eat and drink, and gossip about those they thought were out of earshot.

"If they had played fiddles, banjos, and stomped their feet, and all worn shoddy clothes, they could have been from the Willies," I said honestly. "It's just what they talk about that makes them different. Nobody back home cares about politics, or the nation's economy. Few people read anything other than the Bible or romance magazines."

For the first time since I'd known him, he laughed

with genuine amusement, and when he smiled at me with a great deal of approval my spirits soared.

"So you weren't impressed by fine clothes and expensive cigars—that's good. You have opinions of your own, that's also good. And you are quite right. Behind every successful man is one who has more than a few flaws."

Then as I sat on my dressing room stool and wished again that Pa had been this kind of man, he spoke seriously. "I heard a weather report a few minutes ago, predicting our first serious snow. We expect to fly out very early Sunday, before the snowstorm arrives. You take good care of yourself, Heaven, while we're gone."

His caution made me feel good. Pa had never said anything like that to me—as if he didn't care what happened. "I wish you and Jillian a safe trip," I said, my throat hoarse and hurting.

"Thank you." He smiled again, then stepped close enough to kiss my forehead, and for a moment his hand lingered on my shoulder. "You look so lovely and fresh, sitting there in your pale blue nightgown. Don't let anything or anyone spoil you."

I didn't sleep much that night. The dinner party had revealed to me the great gap between all the friends Jillian and Tony had and the people I'd grown up with. We were all American-born, and yet it seemed we had grown up in different worlds. And all that food that was wasted, enough to feed ten hillbilly families.

Ames Colton would have called on Sunday, if I'd encouraged him at all, but I didn't want him around. I still had plans to find Logan.

Early in the morning, I heard the motor of the limo

driving off with Tony and Jillian. I tried to fall back to sleep. At six I was still awake and waiting for the servants to get up. But they were too far away for me to hear them turning on shower or tub water or flushing commodes. I could sniff and never smell the bacon frying in the kitchen, and the aroma of coffee never drifted this far. Well, I thought, at least I had Rye Whiskey if I got too lonely.

The house at seven seemed bleakly empty and lonely. As I dressed I sniffed the air for the drift of Jillian's perfume that always lingered in the upstairs halls. My breakfast at that long table was a lonely affair, made worse by the presence of Curtis, who stood near the buffet, ready to jump and wait on me, when I wished he'd go away and leave me alone.

"Will you be needing anything more, miss?" he asked, as if reading my thoughts.

"No, thank you, Curtis."

"Is there anything special you would like to order for your lunch and dinner?"

"Anything will do."

"Then I will tell the chef to prepare one of the usual Sunday menus . . ."

I didn't care what was served. Food, when it came on time and in sufficient amounts and always tasted delicious, wasn't the monumental affair that once it had been. Freshly squeezed orange juice was no longer a thrilling treat. Bananas or fresh strawberries on my cereal were to be expected. But it still thrilled me to see the truffles that Tony so adored sprinkled liberally on my omelettes.

In the library I stood for a long time at the windows, gazing out at the maze. The wind began to gust and make faint whistling sounds, scraping the tree branches against the house. Behind me was a roaring log fire, making cozy the library where I intended to spend the day . . . if I couldn't find a way to visit Logan. He hadn't answered my letter, but I knew what dorm he lived in. Already I'd tested the garage door and found it locked. When his wife wasn't around, Cal Dennison had taught me how to drive.

It was Logan who should have run to me, and asked me to explain what happened between me and Cal Dennison. But no, he'd sped away in the rain, leaving me in the graveyard, not even giving me the chance to explain that Cal had felt like a father to me, the father I'd always wanted. And to keep him my father and my friend, I'd have done almost anything! Anything!

A thin curl of smoke spiraled into the air above the walls of the maze. Did that mean Troy was at the cottage today? Without further thought, I hurried toward the hall closet and pulled on my boots and a new warm coat. Furtively I let myself out the front door so none of the servants would report back to Tony that I had broken my word and deliberately set out to see his brother.

It was easy this time to wend my crooked way through the maze, but not so easy to step before his door and knock. Again he was reluctant to let me in, taking so everlastingly long I almost turned around and left. Then, suddenly, the door was open and he was there, not smiling to see me again, but looking at me sadly, as if he pitied someone doomed to do the wrong thing time and time again. "So you are back," he said, stepping aside and motioning for me to come in. "Tony assured me you would stay away."

"I have come to ask a favor," I said, embarrassed by his indifference. "I need to drive into town today, and Tony has ordered Miles not to take me anywhere. If I might use your car . . ."

Already he was seated and beginning to work on small objects he had on his workbench. He threw me a look of surprise. "You, a sixteen-year-old, want to drive into Boston? Do you know the way? Do you have a driver's license? No, I think for your own safety and that of others, you should stay off of icy highways."

Oh, it did hurt to keep letting him believe I was only sixteen, when I was really seventeen! And I was a good driver, at least Cal had thought so. Back in Atlanta they had given girls my age driver's licenses. I sat down without an invitation, still wearing my coat, and tried not to cry. "They are fall cleaning in Farthy," I said in a small voice. "Getting ready for all the festivities coming up. Cleaning windows and sills, scrubbing and waxing floors, dusting and vacuuming, and even in the library where I planned to stay all day, the odors of ammonia seep under the door."

"It's called holiday cleaning at this time of the year," he informed me, looking up, and showing amusement. "I hate a house all torn to pieces as much as you do. One of the pleasures of having a small house like this is that there is no need for servants to invade my privacy. When I put something down it stays there until I pick it up again."

I cleared my throat, pulled myself together, and then approached the object of my visit again. "If you won't allow me to drive your car, would you be so kind as to drive me into town yourself?"

He was using a tiny screwdriver to fasten miniature legs to tiny bodies. How intense he was about his toymaking! "Why do you need to go into town?"

If I told him the truth, would he report it to Tony the minute he was back? I sat tense and considering as I studied his face. It was one of the most sensitive faces I'd ever seen. And from all past experiences, only those completely insensitive were cruel. "I have a confession, Troy. I am very lonely. I have no one to share in my successes but Tony. Jillian doesn't care what I do, or don't do. There is a friend of mine who attends Boston University that I would like to visit."

Again he glanced my way, appearing guarded, as if somehow I was getting to him, and he didn't want that to happen. "Can't you wait until some other day, when you are in Winterhaven? B.U. isn't so far from there."

"But I need to see someone who understands me! Someone who remembers the way it used to be with me."

He didn't say anything, just sat thoughtfully while the light snow drifted by his wide windows. Then he smiled. The smile lit up his dark eyes and made them glow.

"All right, I will drive you where you want to go, but give me a half hour to finish up what I'm doing, and then we'll be on our way—and I won't tell Tony that you are breaking one of his rules."

"He told you?"

"Yes, of course he told me he forbade you to visit me. And I am not welcome to visit Farthy much, because of Jillian."

"Jillian doesn't like you?" I asked, thinking she had to be crazy not to like someone as fine as Troy.

"I used to care a great deal about what Jillian thought of me, then I found out that no one really knows what goes on in Jillian's head. I don't even know if she's capable of loving anything as much as she loves her image. But she is clever. Never underestimate her cleverness."

I was stunned, and yet he had made so much clear. "But why doesn't Tony want you and me to become friends?"

He gave me a wry, self-mocking grin. "My brother thinks I am a bad influence on anyone who grows too fond of me, and of course, I am. So don't grow too fond of me, Heavenly."

My heart seemed to skip a beat when he called me Heavenly as Tom had always done.

"Oh, you are much too old for me to grow fond of!" I cried with happiness in my voice. "I'm going to dash back to the house and change my clothes!"

Before he could speak again and perhaps change his mind, I was out the door and racing through the maze back to the big house. The roar of cleaning machines inside disguised my footfalls as I darted up the stairs. In my room I quickly changed into what I thought were my most becoming clothes. I touched my nose with face powder, added lipstick, and sprayed on perfume. Now I was ready to meet Logan Stonewall. Not once in the whole time he'd known me had he seen me dressed as I was now.

Troy took no notice whatsoever of what I wore. He drove his Porsche with a casual ease, seldom speaking, but I had lost my shyness and was brimming with happiness. I was on my way to Logan. Despite his disappointment in me, he'd forgive and forget, and remember only the sweetness of our young romance, when we walked in the hills and swam together in the river and shared so many plans for our future together.

It was only when we reached the entrance to B.U. that Troy spoke: "I am presuming this friend is male, right?"

Startled, I glanced at him. "Why presume that?"

"Your clothes, the perfume, and the lipstick."

"I didn't think you noticed."

"I'm not blind."

"His name is Logan Stonewall," I confessed. "He's studying to be a pharmacologist because that will please his father most, but what he really wants to be is a biochemist."

"I hope he knows you are on your way to meet him."

My heart lurched again, for Logan didn't know.

As chance and good luck would have it, we no sooner pulled to a stop in front of his dorm than I saw Logan sauntering by with two other fellows his age. I hurried out of the car, not wanting to lose sight of him.

"Thank you for driving me here!" I called back through the window. "You can drive on home; I'm sure Logan will drive me back."

"Does he own a car? He was walking."

"I don't know."

"Then I'll hang around and wait until I am sure you have a way to get home again." He nodded toward a small coffee shop. "I'll be in there. As soon as you know he'll drive you back, let me know."

Troy headed for the coffee shop, and I strolled in Logan's direction, hoping to surprise him and delight him with the way I looked now. He went into the drugstore across the street to make a purchase. I watched him pay for it, not knowing now quite what to do. He was just the same, standing tall and straight, with his broad shoulders squared, not turning to stare at every girl who passed, and a great many passed. He accepted his purchase, then headed for a side door that would let him outside.

"Logan!" I cried, running forward slightly. "Don't go! I need to talk to you."

He turned to look my way, and I swear to God he didn't know me! He looked at me and through me, and a look of annoyance was in his sapphire eyes. Perhaps it was my shorter, smarter hairstyle and the makeup I'd learned to apply with skill, or perhaps it was the beaver coat Jillian had given me that made his eyes scan over me twice without knowing who I was.

And before I could decide just what to do, he had the side door open, letting in the strong wind that ruffled the magazine covers, and then he was outside in the snow, walking so fast I knew I'd never be able to catch him. And maybe he'd only pretended he didn't recognize me.

Like the fool that I often was, I went to the counter at the drugstore and ordered a cup of hot chocolate. I took my time sipping the steaming brew and nibbling on two vanilla wafers. Only when I thought enough time had passed for me to have had a long and serious talk did I pay my check and prepare to leave.

It was nice the way Troy immediately jumped to his feet and broadly smiled at me. "You took forever. I was beginning to believe this man from your past was going to drive you home after all."

He pulled a small chair for me, helped me off with my fur, then sat me down. "It would have been nice if you had brought him over and introduced me."

My head bowed. "Logan Stonewall is from Winnerrow, and your brother has ordered me to have no contacts with any of my old friends."

"I am not my brother. I would like very much to know your friends."

"Oh, Troy," I half sobbed, bowing my head and really beginning to cry, "Logan stared straight at me. He had the nerve to pretend not to even know me! He looked me squarely in the eyes and then he turned and walked away."

His voice came softly and kindly as he reached for my gloved hands and held them in his. "Heaven, has it occurred to you that you have changed a great deal? You are not the same girl who arrived here in early October. You have had your hair styled differently. You wear makeup now and you didn't then. And those high-heeled boots you wear add a few inches to your height. And Logan may have had other thoughts on his mind, other than meeting an old girlfriend."

"Here," he said, pulling out a clean, white handkerchief and handing it to me. "And when you've finished crying—soon, I hope, for I hate seeing a woman cry—then perhaps you can tell me more about Logan."

When I had dried my tears and put his handkerchief in my purse, intending to wash and iron it later, another cup of hot chocolate had arrived. I saw so much kindness and understanding in Troy's eyes that before I knew what I was doing, I was telling him everything, right from the very beginning, when Logan had seen me in his father's pharmacy, and Fanny had been sure he was admiring her, not me; then how we met in the Winnerrow schoolyard; how he insisted on buying lunch for four starving Casteel children. "And when he became my regular boyfriend and walked me home from school, I was the happiest girl in the world. He wasn't like the wild boys who hung around Fanny. He was the most different boy I'd met, decent and never fresh. We were planning to be married as soon as we finished college—and now he doesn't know me." My voice rose in slight hysteria. "And it took so much nerve to do what I did. Did I overdo it, Troy? Am I too overwhelming in Jillian's beaver coat, and wearing so much jewelry?"

"You look beautiful," he said softly, reaching to take both of my hands in his. "Now let's put today in perspective. Logan didn't expect to see you, did he? You were here, out of the element he'd grown accustomed to seeing you in. Nor did he expect to see you dressed as you are. So give him a telephone call later on, and tell him what happened. Then you two can plan a meeting, and you'll both be ready for each other."

"He won't forgive me! He'll never forgive me!" I sobbed, hotly and passionately. "For I haven't told you everything. When Pa sold all five of his kids to strangers for five hundred dollars apiece, something bad happened to me. First Keith and Our Jane were bought by a lawyer and his wife. Then Fanny was sold to Reverend Wayland Wise, and unlike Keith and Our Jane, Fanny was delighted to be sold to such a wealthy man. Then a burly farmer named Buck Henry showed up at our place, and he went straight to Tom and felt him over like he was an animal. Pa and Buck Henry dragged Tom away.

"I was sold to Kitty and Cal Dennison in Candlewick, Georgia. Their house in Candlewick was the nicest, cleanest house I'd ever been in before, and there was always plenty to eat. But Kitty wanted a kitchen slave, a housekeeper to keep everything spotless while she ran her beauty shop. She worked five days a week there, and on Saturdays she taught a ceramics class, and that meant Cal saw more of me than he did of Kitty. Oh, it was complicated, for I used to think Cal was twice the man Pa could ever be. I began to think of Cal as my own father, the kind I'd always wanted and needed. He was someone who saw me, liked me, needed me. When he bought me new clothes, new shoes, and a lot of little things I didn't even know I needed, I'd sometimes go to bed hugging those dresses to my heart.

Like a river undammed, started by my tears, my story gushed forth in full, horrible detail. I think the only area I left clouded was the exact year of my birth, and somehow, long before my tale was told, I knew Troy had forgotten his plans for today, and soon we were headed for the road that took us back to Farthinggale Manor. Under the high, arching iron gates he drove, closing them with his automatic control. Then on a road I'd never noticed before, he wended his way toward his stone cottage. The gray autumn afternoon touched me with sweet melancholy for the hills, for the innocent and trusting girl I used to be.

Not a word did Troy speak until we were both in his cottage, and he had his fire renewed and burning brightly. Then he said his meal would be ready in a jiffy. "The chef from the big house keeps my larder full," he said, as he began to ready a snack. It was four o'clock by this time, and I'd already missed lunch. I didn't doubt for one moment that that would be reported to Tony by Percy.

"Go on, don't stop," he urged, handing me a chopping board with raw vegetables to slice. "I have never heard anything like your story before. Now tell me more about Keith and Our Jane."

Only then did I realize I should have held on to caution and been more discreet, but it was too late, much too late. But what did I care about anything now that Logan had cut me out of his life? I had already told Troy every last thing about the Christmas Day when Pa began to sell us off one by one, repeating it all again because he had to hear it twice in order to believe it. I was even careless enough to let out the reason Logan didn't trust me anymore, and not once did Troy look my way, or comment, or hesitate in what he was doing.

"I didn't know that those trips to the movies, and those wonderful dinners in fine restaurants, and all the gifts he gave me were part of Cal's seduction. I grew more and more dependent on him. He gave me my best times when I lived there, and Kitty gave me my worst times. I used to pity Cal when every night she'd find one reason or another to say 'no' to him, and when she finally did agree to accept his advances, he'd come to the breakfast table looking so happy. I wanted him to look happy all of the time. And when he began to touch me too often, with odd lights in his eyes, and his kisses became not so fatherly, I'd lie on my bed at night and wonder just what kind of signals I was subconsciously sending out. I never blamed him. I kept right on blaming myself for putting wicked ideas in his head. How could I hold on to him as a father figure, and not submit to what he wanted to do?"

I paused, gasped for more breath, then went on.

"So you see, I have no one now! Tony has ordered me to cut my family out of my life, even out of my thoughts, and he doesn't even know about Tom, Fanny, Keith, or Our Jane. Tom hasn't responded to my letters. Fanny is expecting the Reverend's baby, and she never writes to me. I don't even know if she wants to. And someday I have to find Our Jane and Keith!"

"Someday you will find them," said Troy with the kind of sincerity that made me trust him. "I have a great deal of money. I can't think of a better way to spend some of it than to help you find your family."

"Cal promised me the same thing, and nothing ever came of it."

He turned to give me a chastising look. "I am not Cal Dennison, and I don't make promises I don't keep."

My tears began again. "Why would you do that? You don't know me. I'm not sure you even like me."

He came to sit beside me at the table. "For you and for your dead mother I will do this, Heaven. Tomorrow I'll see my attorneys and put them on the trail of this lawyer whose first name is Lester. You should bring me the studio portraits of Keith and Our Jane that you told me about. Photographers are always proud to display their names somewhere on their photos, or on the back. In no time at all, you will know the full names of the couple who bought your younger brother and sister."

I sat spellbound, breathless with the hope that flooded me. Hope that soon simmered down to nothing, for hadn't Cal Dennison promised the same thing? And I didn't really know Troy.

"Now tell me what you'll do when you know where they are?"

What would I do?

Tony would put me out of his life. He'd stop his support of my education.

I was on my way now toward the goal I had to have . . . but I'd think of the answer later, when his attorneys found the little boy and girl who belonged with me. I'd find some way to get them back and to hold fast to my goals too. I was determined, now that I'd come this far, never to slip back again.

Oh, if only things had been different! If only I could have grown up like a normal girl! I felt tears begin to well up in my eyes again. Shoving my memories away and taking a deep breath, I said, "There, now you know everything about me. And I'm not even supposed to be talking to you. Tony has ordered me to leave you alone, never to come to your cottage. In fact he told me before he left that you were not here at all. If he knows I've broken one of his rules he'll send me back to the Willies. I'm terrified of going back there! There's no one in Winnerrow who cares what happens to me. Pa lives somewhere in Georgia or Florida, and Tom is living with him, but Tom never writes, nor does Fanny! I don't know how to live without someone who loves and cares about me." I ducked my head so he couldn't see those irrepressible tears that began to fall. "Please, Troy, please! Be my friend! I need someone so desperately."

"All right, Heaven. I'll be your friend." He sounded reluctant, as if he were committing himself to something that was going to be burdensome. "But remember that there are good reasons why Tony doesn't want you to become involved with me. Don't be too harsh on him. Before you decide that I am just the friend you need, you have to realize that Tony rules here, not me. We are at different ends of the pole in personality. He is strong, and I am a weak dreamer. If you arouse Tony's disapproval and displeasure, he will send you out of his life, and out of Jillian's, straight back to the Willies! And he'll do it in such a way I'll not have the chance to save you, or even to give you money."

"I would not take money from you!" I flared, my pride rearing high.

"You take it from my brother," he said wryly.

"Because he is married to my grandmother! Because he told me he manages the money Jillian inherited from her father and her first husband. Money that would have gone to my own mother if she had lived. I feel perfectly justified in taking from Tony."

He turned his head away so I could no longer see his face. "Heaven, your passion exhausts me. It is much later than I thought it was, and I'm tired. Would you mind if we continue this discussion next Friday when you come home from Winterhaven? I'll still be here."

He touched me deeply as he sat there, looking totally vulnerable, and I suspected he was terribly afraid of letting someone like me into his well-organized life. Slowly I got up from the floor, reluctant to leave the cozy warmth of his cottage.

"Please, Heaven, I have a thousand things to do before I go to bed tonight. And don't cry because Logan Stonewall didn't recognize you. His thoughts could have been elsewhere. Give him another chance. Call him up at his dorm. Offer to meet him somewhere you can talk."

Troy didn't know Logan's stubbornness. Logan was like his name, a stone wall!

"Good night, Troy," I called at the door, "and thank you for everything. I'm looking forward to next Friday."

Softly I closed the door behind me.

No servants were around when I slipped inside the door of the big house, and in the dining room, when I checked, I found food in silver chafing dishes: wonderful, thin slices of meat covered with French sauce. Before I knew what I was doing, I'd put a little of each dish on a plate and then sat down to eat again. All by myself, at a table big enough for all the Casteels.

## ～ Seven ～
### Treachery

THE GIRLS OF WINTERHAVEN WERE NOT AS DISTANT my second week there. Boldly they eyed me up and down, staring at the lovely knit dress I wore, for I'd be damned before I'd go back to wearing clothes not so much better than what I'd worn in the Willies. To my delight, that very Monday when I sat down to eat my lunch, Pru Carraway smiled my way, then invited me to eat at her table. Three other girls were seated there. Happily I gathered up my silverware, my plate and napkin, and carried them over. "Thank you," I said, as I sat down.

"What a pretty pink dress," said Pru, batting her pale eyelashes.

"Thank you. The color is mauve."

"What a pretty *mauve* dress," she corrected, as the three other girls tittered. "I realize we have not been very nice to you, *Heaven*," and again she put stress on my name, "but we try never to be nice to any new student until we are sure she's worthy of our approval."

What had I done to gain their approval? I wondered.

"How do you know so much about poverty and hunger?" asked Faith Morgantile, a very pretty, brown-haired girl in a clean but ratty-looking white sweater and pants.

My heart skipped a beat. "You all know I am from West Virginia. That is coal-mining country. There is also a cotton mill there. The hills are full of very poor people who think an education is a waste of time . . . so naturally, I know about the people who used to live around me."

"But you described the pangs of hunger so well in your theme paper," persisted Pru, "it's almost as if you knew hunger from firsthand experience."

"When you have eyes and ears, and a heart that feels compassion, you don't really need firsthand experience."

"How nicely you put that," said another girl, smiling at me warmly. "We've heard that your parents divorced, and your father won custody of you . . . isn't that unusual? Most of the time the mother wins custody, especially when the child is a girl."

I tried to shrug nonchalantly. "I was too young to remember the details of the divorce. When I was older my father refused to talk about it." And with that I dismissed the subject as my fork stabbed into my tossed salad and speared the tomatoes and lettuce I liked most.

"When will your father be coming to visit you? We would just love to meet him."

You bet they would love to meet him! Luke Casteel would shock them into instant old age. I resented Pru Carraway, who was like a thorn constantly trying to draw blood. I felt the power of her background, her family, her heritage, the friends she had and I didn't, forming a barricade around her, while I was defenseless, with only my wits and new clothes to shield me. I finished my lunch with determination, eating every strand of spaghetti, relishing every morsel of the meatballs, and wanted in the worst way to sop up the spicy tomato sauce with what remained of my Italian bread, but I didn't dare. And they were watching me with such fascination I felt I was doing everything wrong; showing too much enthusiasm for an ordinary dish like spaghetti. Made hostile and angry from their insinuations, I decided to blast them with a little truth. "My father will never come to see me, for we don't like each other, and he is dying."

Each one of those four girls stared at me with lips agape, as if I were an apparition straight from the cemetery of bad taste. And even as I'd said the words, the thought of Pa being dead filled me with strange, uneasy guilt. As if I had no right to hate him or wish him dead because he was my father. There was no reason why I should feel ashamed. None! He deserved every mean thought I gave him.

Again Pru Carraway spoke, carefully: "We have in this school certain private clubs. Now, if you could arrange, somehow, for one of us to have a date with Troy Tatterton . . . we would be very appreciative."

Thoughts of Pa had come between me and them. I was caught off guard. I sat with the last of my Italian bread held halfway to my mouth. "I really couldn't manage that," I said uneasily. "He's a man who makes up his own mind, and he's much too old and sophisticated for the girls of Winterhaven."

"Troy Tatterton turned twenty-three only two weeks ago," stated Faith Morgantile. "Some of the students here are eighteen, and just right for a man of his age. Besides, we saw him with you on Sunday, and you are only sixteen."

It stunned me that in a giant city like Boston I'd be spotted with Troy!

So that was it! The reason for their sudden interest in me! They had seen me, or one of their friends had, in the coffee shop with Troy. I stood up. I dropped my napkin on their table. "Thank you for inviting me to your table," I said with real pain in my heart, for I'd so hoped to have friends here. All my life I'd never had a girlfriend, only Fanny, who had been kind of a family cross to bear. At my own table I picked up the books I'd left there and stalked from the dining room.

From that moment on I sensed a difference in their attitudes. They had been suspicious of me before just because I was new and different. Now I had challenged them, and without any effort at all, I had made enemies.

The very next morning I selected from my dresser drawer a beautiful cornflower blue cashmere sweater to wear with its matching skirt, and to my utter horror, my brand-new sweater had begun to unravel. And the wool skirt I'd laid out on my bed, brand new, was losing its hem, and very carefully someone had picked at the rows of stitches that held a front box pleat neatly in place. In the Willies I would have worn the sweater and skirt anyway, but not here, not here! Not when I knew that just yesterday both sweater and skirt had been perfect!

One sweater after another I took from the drawer

and inspected! Five of my sweaters were ruined! I ran
to the closet to check on my skirts and blouses and
found them hanging as I'd left them, still in good
shape. Whoever had done this hadn't had time to ruin
everything I owned. That Tuesday morning I didn't
have time to eat breakfast. I went to class wearing just
a blouse with my skirt, and no sweater. None of the
girls ever wore topcoats to class, scorning thoughts of
colds and chills, even though most of them sat with
their arms crossed over their breasts and shivered
from time to time. Hardy, puritanical souls ruled
Winterhaven, seeing that none of us experienced too
much luxury. The classroom was not much warmer
than the cabin in the hills had been in late October.
All morning I shivered, thinking I'd run to my room
at noon and pick up a lightweight jacket.

I ate my lunch so fast I almost choked on it, then I
dashed upstairs to my room; the door was never
locked. I ran to the closet to snatch from the rod one
of the three warm jackets Tony had chosen for me.
Two jackets were missing! The one remaining jacket
was sopping wet!

Were they so rich and powerful they thought they
could get away with vandalizing my possessions?
Shivering as much from anger as from cold, I ran
down the hall with the wet jacket extended before me.
I barged into the bathroom. Six girls were in there
smoking and giggling. The moment I came through
the door a deadly quiet descended, while the cigarettes burned and created the worst kind of choking
smoke. Using both hands I held up the wool jacket.
"Did you have to put it in *hot* water?" I asked.
"Wasn't it enough just to ruin my sweaters? What
kind of monsters are you, anyway?"

"Whatever are you talking about?" asked Pru Carraway, her pale eyes innocently blank.

"My new sweaters are unraveled!" I yelled. I shook the water from the jacket so some of it flew into their faces. They drew back and formed a tight bunch. "You have taken two of my jackets and ruined the third! Do you think you'll get away with this unpunished?" I glared, with what I hoped was menace, into each pair of eyes that stared back at me. The very fact that they didn't seem intimidated by me or my puny threats made me even angrier. Their confidence grew as I hesitated, not knowing how to defeat them.

Turning, I thrust the sopping-wet jacket into one of the two clothes chutes. The heavyweight metal door had a very strong spring that slammed shut. There was a multisectioned bathroom on each one of the three floors. With two hundred girls bathing or showering daily, hundreds of white towels were used. Each day maids brought up stacks and stacks of clean white towels and put them neatly behind the glass doors of the linen closets. The chutes took the wet, soiled towels quickly to the basement, where they fell into huge baskets.

"Now," I said, whipping around and trying to build some fear into them, "that jacket will be found and reported to the headmistress. You can't take the evidence from me and destroy it, for the cellar is off limits to all of you."

Pru Carraway yawned. The other five girls followed suit.

"I hope they dismiss each and every one of you for willful destruction of property that didn't belong to you!"

"You sound like a lawyer," moaned Faith Morgantile. "You scare us, really you do. What does a wet jacket prove? Nothing but your own carelessness for being dumb enough to wash it in hot water."

I suspected as I stood there in that bathroom that no matter what I said they would not accept blame for what they had done. Then the sweet, pretty face of Miss Marianne Deale flashed behind my eyes, and her soft voice came to whisper in my ears: "It is better to champion a losing cause that you believe in than to keep your silence and risk nothing. You can never tell what effect your argument will have later on."

"Right now I am going to the office of Mrs. Mallory," I stated with fire. "I am going to show her the tears in my brand-new sweaters, and I am going to tell her about the jacket you just ruined."

"You can't prove anything," said a small, plain girl named Amy Luckett, her hands moving in an agitated, betraying way. "You could have snagged your own sweaters, accidentally ruined your own jacket."

"Mrs. Mallory saw me wearing the jacket Monday morning, so at least she will know its former condition. And when it is found in the wet towel basket, that will also prove what you've done."

"You talk like a *second-rate* lawyer," sneered Pru Carraway. "The faculty here can't touch us. Two years ago we told our parents not to continue donating cash gifts to this school, which would go under without them. They didn't even appreciate all the money we saved them when we stopped wearing those crappy French schoolgirl uniforms. We always win when we unite and fight. We have our parents behind us. Our *rich, rich* parents. Our influential, *political* parents. You have no friends here. You are not one of us. No one will believe what you say. Mrs. Mallory will look down her nose at you and think you mean-spirited and spiteful because she knows we will never make you one of us. She will believe you damaged your clothes yourself, just so you could put the blame on us."

What she said made shivers race up and down my spine! Could anyone believe such a thing? I wasn't wise or experienced in the ways of the world. I hadn't been to school in Switzerland, and learned how to handle a situation like this. Still, I had to believe they were bluffing, and I had to bluff as well. "We'll see," I said, turning and leaving the bathroom.

With my arms full of ruined sweaters, I entered the dean's office. Mrs. Mallory looked up with annoyance clearly written on her round face. "Aren't you supposed to be in your social studies class, Miss Casteel?"

I dropped the sweaters on the floor, then picked up what had been a lovely blue one, and held it high for her to see. A finishing thread had been pulled so the neckline was half raveled. "I have never worn this sweater, Mrs. Mallory, and yet it is full of holes and raveling."

She frowned. "You really should take better care of your clothes. I hate to see money thrown away on ungrateful children."

"I take very good care of my clothes. This sweater was neatly folded in my second dresser drawer, along with others that are also falling apart because threads have been pulled or cut."

For the longest time she was silent. One by one I displayed the sweaters. "The jacket you commented on Monday morning when I checked in was soaked in hot water while I was in my morning classes today.

Her red lips pursed. She adjusted the half-glasses

she wore on the tip of her nose. "Are you making accusations, Miss Casteel?"

"Yes. I am not liked here because I am different."

"If you want to be liked, Miss Casteel, you don't tattle on schoolmates who play tricks on all the new girls."

"This is more than a trick!" I cried, dismayed by her indifference. "My clothes were ruined!"

"Oh, come now, you make too much out of what appears to me just careless packing. Sweaters catch in zippers, in luggage locks. You tug to pull them free and holes appear, and threads ravel."

"And the jacket, that accidentally fell into a tub of hot water, on its own?"

"I don't see a jacket. If you had further evidence, why didn't you bring it with you?"

"I dropped it down the wet towel chute. You can find it in the laundry room."

"There's a sign above that chute. All wet washable clothes are to be put into the smaller chute."

"Mrs. Mallory, it was a plaid jacket! It could stain someone's clothing."

"Exactly what I mean. It could also stain white towels and washcloths."

My lips began to tremble. "I had to put it somewhere so the girls who did it couldn't hide the evidence and say it never happened."

She fingered the pretty blue sweater, looking thoughtful. "Why don't you take these sweaters and try to mend them with needle and thread? I have to confess, I really don't want to find your wet jacket. If I do, that means I will have to take action and question all the girls. Things like this have happened before. If we side with you, will that help you to be accepted here? I'm sure your guardian will buy you new sweaters."

"You mean I should let them go unpunished?"

"No, not exactly. Just handle this yourself, without our aid." She smiled at me in a tight way. "You must remember, Miss Casteel, though they want you to think you are scorned and beneath their contempt, there isn't a girl here who is more envied. You are very lovely and have a touching freshness that is rare. You seem like someone from a hundred years ago, shy and proud and much too sensitive and vulnerable. Those girls see what I see, what everyone here sees, and you frighten them. You make them uncertain about what they are, and what their values are. And, you are also the ward of Tony Tatterton, a very admired and successful man. You live in one of the finest old homes in America. I realize you have a past that has scarred you, but don't let it wound you permanently. You have the potential to become anything you set your mind to be. Don't let silly schoolgirl pranks ruin what can be the best learning years of your life. Now, I can tell from your expression that you are outraged and want some sort of revenge or recompense for the clothes you have lost. But aren't clothes relatively unimportant to you? Won't they be replaced? Did those girls ruin something of real value you might have hidden in your room?"

Oh, oh! I hadn't thought of that! In the bottom of my hamper I had hidden a heavy box containing the silver-framed portraits of Keith and Our Jane! I had to check the moment I was back there to see if they had been taken or destroyed!

I started to leave, then I turned and met the stern but sympathetic eyes of Mrs. Mallory. "I think you owe me something, Mrs. Mallory, for keeping my silence—and peace in this school.''

Her eyes went guarded. "Yes, tell me what you think I owe."

"There is going to be a dance this Thursday evening, with the boys from Broadmire Hall. I know I haven't won enough credits in the time I've been here to deserve an invitation to that dance, but I want to go."

For the longest time she stared at me, her eyelids half-lowered, and then she smiled, her eyes amused. "Why, that's a small thing to ask. Just see that you don't embarrass the school."

The portraits of my two little ones were safe. I put them back until Friday when I would take them to Troy, so he could turn them over to the detectives he'd promised he'd hire to find my younger sister and brother.

I thought of Tom, who had always been my champion. I knew what he'd want me to do now that I had things going my way: "Don't rock the boat," he'd say.

Maybe it was having Farthinggale Manor for my home, with Tony as my guardian, with Jillian for a grandmother, even a reluctant one, and Troy for my friend that gave me more audacity than common sense should have allowed. For I was going to rock the boat. Come hell or high water, I wasn't going to let those girls get the best of me! I glanced in the nearest mirror and saw very little of the old Heaven Leigh Casteel in the image of a girl with shoulder-length, smartly styled dark hair that gleamed. But what to do? Already I knew Mrs. Mallory wasn't likely to do anything to risk her cash donations.

I fell prone upon the bed, hanging my head over the side, and began to brush my hair up and over, so it fell like a dark shawl around my face, closing out the brightness of the three lamps. I heard the chimes in the bell tower beginning the evening melodies of patriotic songs flavored with faith in God. And my brushstrokes caught the timing as I stroked, stroked, stroked, as I plotted and planned how to get even with those six girls who had obviously waited in the bathroom, knowing just what I'd do with a dripping wet jacket that would ruin new green carpeting and earn for me several demerits.

Back in Winnerrow I'd cringed and cowered in my shabby, ill-fitting clothes and scuffed, worn-out, secondhand shoes, feeling too weak from perpetual hunger to fight back effectively. I felt too humiliated and ashamed of who I was, a scumbag Casteel, to find the right methods of proving my individuality and merits. But now, things were different. I had storebought courage, despite my ruined sweaters and jacket. I was still too well outfitted to cringe and cower like a Casteel.

And as I brushed and brushed, forgetting to count, an idea was born. The perfect way to have my own revenge . . . and we'd see who won this game in the end. Boston boys were basically the same as boys all over the world. They drifted like bees to the prettiest, sweetest-smelling flower. And I knew I could be that.

## ~ Eight ~
## The Dance

THAT VERY TUESDAY EVENING, WHEN ALL THE OTHER
girls in my wing were obviously trying not to whoop it
up too noisily, I heard my name mentioned several
times, and always laughter followed. It made me
uneasy to know I was the brunt of so many jokes.
Still, I had a friend that I could call. Locking my door
first, I put in a call to Troy. His telephone in the
cottage rang and rang, giving me nagging fears that he
wasn't there, and I didn't know where else to reach
him. Then he answered, sounding very busy. And if
his voice hadn't warmed when he knew who it was, I
would never have requested what I did. "You want
me to go into your closets and choose the party dress
that will best make a sensation? Heaven, do you have
several?"

"Oh, yes, Troy. Tony had me try on at least ten,
and though he'd intended to buy me only two, he
ended up with four. I didn't bring any with me,
thinking it would be a long time before I earned

enough merits to be invited to one of their dances—
but here I am, invited."

He kind of groaned. "Sure, I'll do what you ask,
but I don't know much about what a fifteen-year-old
girl should wear to one of those school functions."

True to his word, late that very evening, while I hid
in shadows of the front parlor and waited, and all the
other girls slept, Troy eased his car into the drive of
Winterhaven, and I slipped out the front door to meet
him. Behind me the front door was kept from closing
tight and locking by a thin book I had inserted.

"I am so sorry to cause you this trouble, Troy," I
whispered, slipping into the front seat beside him. I
couldn't help moving close enough to put my cold lips
on his cheek. "Thank you! I'm ever so grateful to
have a good friend like you. I realize you must think
me a terrible pest and nuisance, calling you up so late.
I know you have a thousand better things to do, but I
need this dress, I really do!"

"Hey," he objected, seemingly embarrassed with
my overdone apologies, "don't be too grateful. I
really had nothing better to do." He moved a bit
farther from me, and this put him very close to the
driver's door—causing me to move back toward the
passenger door, and not crowd him. "I found the four
dresses you spoke of and tried to decide between
them. However, all of them were so pretty, I couldn't
decide. So I brought all four, and you can make the
choice."

"You had no preference?" I asked, very disappointed, for I'd depended on his being male and wise
about what men liked best. "Troy, surely you must
like one better than the others."

"You'll look beautiful no matter what you wear," he said in a shy way. And for a few moments we sat there, his car motor idling, with the wind blowing the last of the dead fall leaves into the shrubbery.

It was twelve o'clock. Very seldom did any of the "after hours" school parties last past eleven. It almost seemed the girls of Winterhaven feared midnight and the "witching hour" as they called it. "I have to go now," I said, opening the door and putting one leg outside. "Would it be all right if I called you once in a while?"

His hesitation lasted so long, I hurriedly left his car. "Forgive me for presuming again."

"I'll see you Friday," he said, without committing himself to anything more. "Have fun at the dance."

His low, dark car sped away, leaving me standing in the wind that pressed my long, heavy blue robe close to my body, and I had a huge garment bag to handle this time when I stole as quietly as possible inside the main building of Winterhaven. The wind behind me took the heavy door and blew it inward. All the little crystal prisms on the wall sconces tinkled, and down the front hall a heavy fern toppled over and made a terrible crash! On the first floor the faculty had their private rooms, and I saw a yellow line appear beneath one closed door. Quickly I picked up my little book, grabbed my garment bags with a more secure grip, and then I ran silently up the stairs, with only my huge bags making scraping noises on the railings. How eerie the dim halls were at night, with only small sconces burning. How quiet and hushed the atmosphere, making me glance often over my shoulder as I crept on tiptoes to the safety of my own room. But as I closed and locked the door behind me, I had the uneasy feeling that my little nighttime adventure had been witnessed by someone.

There were a hundred things I had to do to make that dance work out as I wanted it to, with me as the belle of the ball! And to do that I had to find out what the other girls were going to wear. During the day all the dorm rooms had to be left unlocked so they could be inspected to see if the beds were made and clothes were hung up, and each blind at the windows was pulled to the standard level so that Winterhaven would look symmetrical from the outside.

Long before the wake-up bells in their high towers began their loud morning tolling, I was up and in the huge bathroom, enjoying a shower before any other girls entered. So far, my early-to-bed-and-early-to-rise habit had given me the privacy I wanted. However, this day, I was only partially dressed when three or four sleepy-eyed girls drifted in, all in various styles of sleep attire. If their daytime outfits were dowdy and sloppy, what they wore at night must have come straight from Frederick's of Hollywood. They saw me in my brief bikinis and they froze, as if stunned to have caught me, at last.

"She doesn't wear long johns," whispered Pru Carraway to her best friend, Faith Morgantile.

"I was sure she'd wear red ones," Faith whispered back.

They were giggling now, struck by something vulnerable they saw on my face, or hidden in my eyes, for once upon a time in the Willies I'd wanted white or red long johns just as much as I wanted a new coat, or new shoes, or anything that would keep me warm. And as other girls swarmed into the bathroom, each with at least one friend, I stood like an island with the sea eddying around me, so miserable and unhappy, the Willies didn't seem such a terrible place to be after all. At least there I'd been with my own kind. And then, almost crying, I pulled on the remainder of my clothes and left that lavatory full of steam and odors of toothpaste and soap. Behind me their laughter continued on, on, on.

Midway back to my room, I hesitated. Was I going to let them get the best of me? What about my plan? They were all bathing, showering, fiddling with hair and makeup. Now was the best time to dash into three rooms, each shared by two girls. It wasn't something I exactly liked to do, but I was driven to do it, and without any difficulty at all, I found my two stolen jackets, and I also found out just what kind of party dresses the girls of Winterhaven wore to their hospitality dances.

Wearing a skirt, blouse, and one of the jackets I'd just recovered, under a heavy coat, with high boots, I strolled through the softly falling snow toward Beecham Hall. The school campus gave the impression of being a tiny village, charming and quaint, and for me it would have been paradise realized if only I could fit in, and begin to enjoy myself.

In class the girls saw the jacket I'd taken from Pru Carraway's closet, and from the way they eyed me up and down, they considered me more than brazen to confront them. "I could have you dismissed for sneaking uninvited into my room—" began Pru Carraway.

"And stealing my own jacket?" I asked. "Don't threaten me, Prudence, just use prudence before you plan your next destructive trick. Now that I know the way into your closets, and know where you hide your

141

goodies, just make sure you hide them very well in a new place." Lazily I pulled from my coat pocket a candy bar. Her eyes bulged as I bit into the chocolate. Perhaps she was remembering her box of expensive candy bars had been hidden under her stacks of books with titles such as: *Fraught with Passion, The Priest and His Undoing, The Virgin and the Sinner*.

That Thursday night I dressed with more care than ever before. Behind me in my closet hung the four dresses that Troy had brought, still sealed in a long garment bag that was impossible to open without a key. It could have been cut open, but apparently the girls of Winterhaven were not prepared with a knife strong enough to cut through such heavy material. From what I'd seen in the closets of three rooms, the Winterhaven girls were very fond of strapless gowns that fitted tightly, and the more glitter and sparkle the better. My own four dresses, which Tony had chosen, were cocktail length; one was bright blue (the one I'd worn to the Farthinggale Manor dinner), the second was bright crimson, the third white, and the fourth, an odd kind of floral print dress that made me wonder why Tony had chosen it. It had seemed to me when I was growing up that all the housewives in the hills and in the valley had worn print dresses to church. A passion for print dresses, as if they feared solid colors revealed what food had been carelessly dropped. And because of this I had developed a distaste for any print, even beautiful watercolor ones such as the dress Tony had chosen. Blue, green, violet, and rose were intermingled on that long, fluttering gown with its full bell sleeves bound with green velvet ribbons. But the more I looked at it hanging there, the more like springtime it seemed—and it wasn't spring. It was now November.

Downstairs the decorating committee had removed most of the tables from the large dining room. The rugs had been rolled and put aside. Colorful streamers and festive paper decorations had been hung from the ceiling, and spinning where a more sedate chandelier had once hung was a large, mirrored ball. I had never guessed that this room, which was sunny and bright by day, since it faced east and south, could be converted into a very passable ballroom.

Amy Luckett saw me as I headed for the dance, and she stopped to stare, her small hands rising to cover her short cry of admiration. "Oh, oh," she gasped, "I didn't know you could look like that . . . Heaven."

"Thank you," I said, recognizing an obscure compliment from the look in her eyes. "I thought you were on the guest list."

Again her hands covered her mouth. Her eyes grew huge. "I wouldn't go if I were you . . ." she mumbled from behind those hands.

But I went.

Nothing was going to stop me from going, not now, not when I had on that crimson dress that hung like a clinging sheath from a wide, sparkling cuff that crossed over my bust and went around to the back, and the entire dress was held up by two glittering red shoestring straps. Upstairs was a small crimson jacket meant to cover the skin the dress revealed, but I was out to prove something to the boys, to the girls, to myself, and that modest jacket was left behind. It was a slender dress, revealing to advantage my figure. The saleslady in the shop had been surprised when Tony had wanted me to try it on. "A bit too old, Mr. Tatterton, don't you think?"

"Yes, indeed, much too mature. But dresses like this aren't easy to find, and I love this shade of red. This will never go out of style. My ward can wear it ten years from now. When the right woman wears this, she'll seem to be made of liquid fire."

That's what I felt like too as I approached the improvised ballroom where music blared forth. I was a bit late on purpose, wanting to make my impression by coming in last . . . and oh, I did make an impression.

The girls of Winterhaven stood in a line to the left of the door, and the boys were across the room, also lined up. Every single face turned to stare at me when I appeared in the archway. And only then did I see what Amy Luckett had meant. Not one single girl had on a fancy dress, not one!

They were wearing, more or less, what I wore every day, skirts with blouses or sweaters. Nice skirts, new blouses, and expensive sweaters, with nylons and small-heeled pumps. I wanted to go through the floor, I felt so wrong in my long, slinky red dress that suddenly made me feel like a tramp—oh why had Tony chosen something like this for me, why?

And all the boys were staring at me, beginning to show toothy, knowing grins. For a flashing moment I considered spinning about and running and leaving Winterhaven for good. Then, as if unable to turn, or run, I braced myself and tried to saunter nonchalantly into the room as if all my life I'd known how to overdress, and how to carry it off with panache. And they came at me, fast, those boys who suddenly changed their minds about other dance partners. For the first time in my entire life, it was I and not Fanny who had boys crowded around her—all pleading for the first dance, and if not that, the second or third. Before I knew what was happening I was swept off in the arms of some gangling, red-haired fellow who kind of reminded me of Tom.

"Wow! Wow!" he breathed, trying to pull me embarrassingly close. "We all hate these sissy exchange dances, but when you showed up, honey, it wasn't boring anymore."

It was the red dress, of course, not me. This was exactly the kind of dress that Fanny would scream and fight for. Red, the color medieval aristocracy had assigned to the street harlots. Red, still the color associated most with women of loose virtue. Red, the color of passion and lust and violence and blood. And here I was having to fight off strong, male bodies seeking cheap thrills from rubbing against me. Whirled around as I was, pulled from the arms of one boy by another, I caught but brief glimpses of the other girls. My hair, which I'd piled high on my head, was caught by sparkling barrettes; soon I felt it beginning to slip. My hair fell and the curls bounced on my shoulders. I grew tired, angry that my partners wouldn't let me sit between dances and take a breather.

"Let me go!" I finally yelled above the loud music. I saw the teachers and others in the room hazily as I pulled away and tried to seat myself on one of the pretty settees taken from one of the formal parlors and put in here for dance night. Dainty cups of punch were shoved at me, plates with tiny sandwiches and pretty canapés, and male fingers several times successfully managed to feed me. The tea and fruit punch had been spiked. Two cups to slake my thirst had me feeling giddy. Two tiny sandwiches I nibbled before my treats were taken from my hands, and I was pulled back onto the dance floor. The twenty girls of Winterhaven with enough merits to attend this dance watched my every movement with peculiar intensity. Why did their eyes glow so expectantly?

I was having a good time, or so I had to believe when all the boys were lavishing on me such flattering attention. A good time at the expense of all the other girls who were neglected. Why were they watching me without envy? Even when other couples danced, it was I who drew all eyes. It made me uneasy the way everyone watched only me. What was I doing wrong, or doing right? Even the members of the faculty stood off to one side with dainty cups in their hands and kept their eyes riveted on me. Their curious interest added to my nervousness, when before I'd been terrified I'd have none.

"You sure are beautiful," said the boy whirling me around. "And I love your dress. Are you trying to tell us something by wearing red?"

"I don't understand why the other girls aren't wearing their party dresses," I whispered to this boy, who seemed less bold and insensitive than the others. "I thought we were supposed to dress up."

He said something about wild and crazy Winterhaven girls who were never predictable, but I only half heard him. A cramp, sharp and dreadful, shot across my abdomen! It wasn't my time of the month, and even then my cramps were never really severe. The dance ended, and before I could recover my breath, my next partner was heading my way, a devilish grin on his face. "I would like to sit the next one out," I said, heading for a settee.

"You can't! You are the belle of this ball, and you are going to dance every dance."

Again one of those hideous pains in my belly almost doubled me over. My eyes went unfocused. The faces of the girls watching me smeared into distorted images such as seen in fun-house mirrors. A short, plump, nice-looking boy was tugging on my hands. "Please, you haven't danced with me. Nobody ever dances with me." And before I could protest again he'd tugged me to my feet and I was out on the dance floor, this time moving to a different kind of music. Today's kind of music that had a strong beat. All my life I'd dreamed of being so popular every dance was taken, and I'd never have to sit as a wallflower.

Now all I wanted to do was escape. Something dreadful was going on in my abdomen. The bathroom! I needed the bathroom!

Even as I broke away from one boy, another seized me and began his grinding motions, but this was hands-off music, and I turned to run. Suddenly, the music stopped, a new record was put on—a slow waltz, the cheek-to-cheek kind, the kind I needed least of all at this particular moment, and yet someone had me, trying to hold me too close, and the pains, the horrible pains were coming faster, closer together!

Violently I shoved him away and took off on the run. I thought I heard laughter behind me—vicious, spiteful laughter.

The first floor lavatory had been assigned to our guests, so it was the stairs I raced toward, running as fast as I could for the bathroom. The door was locked!

Oh, my God! I raced for another in a distant wing, feeling panic that it was so far away. I'd never make it in time! And when I reached there, it too was locked!

I was sobbing by this time, unable to understand what was happening to me, but happening it was.

Back to my rooms I sped, doubled over and groaning, gasping, my breath coming hard and fast. When I reached there I slammed and locked the door behind me. There was no commode in my room, but I hadn't lived fourteen years in the Willies and dreaded going to that distant outhouse without learning how to improvise. And when it was over, I still sat on, feeling any second another attack would begin.

For a solid hour my bowels rampaged, until I was quivering and weak, and a film of moisture clung to my skin, and by this time the dance downstairs had ended and the girls were returning to their rooms, laughing, whispering, quite excited about something.

Rap-rap-rap on my bedroom door. No one ever knocked on my door! "Heaven, are you in there? You certainly were the queen of the night! Why did you disappear so quickly, like Cinderella?"

"Yes, Heaven," called another voice. "We just loved your dress. It was so *right!*"

Very carefully I removed a frail plastic garment bag from my wastebasket. When I had it out, I quickly put it into a second bag, then tightly twisted the thin, plastic-covered wire. I had solved my dilemma, and saved my clothes in the nick of time, but now I was left with a bag full of filth I didn't know how to dispose of. The dirty linen chutes in the bathroom were one solution; nothing in the soiled linen baskets below would be ruined unless the plastic broke.

With the bag hidden beneath a robe I carried over

my arms, I headed for the bath. I entered quietly, though I needn't have. All twenty of the girls who had attended the dance were in the lounge section, where several hair dryers were set up, and there were small vanities with lights for putting on makeup. In there they were laughing almost hysterically.

"Did you see her face? She went dead white! I almost felt sorry for her. Pru, how much of that stuff did you drop in her punch?"

"Enough to give her a blast—a real blast!"

"And weren't the boys wonderful, how they cooperated?" asked another girl whose voice I didn't recognize. "I wonder if she made it to a bathroom in time?"

"How could she, when we had all the bathroom doors locked?"

Their hilarity could have generated enough electricity to light up New York. And I was feeling sick enough without adding to it. Even in the Willies people hadn't been so cruel. Even the worst village boys in Winnerrow had respected *some* things. I dropped my plastic bag into the largest towel shoot, thinking it wouldn't break open when all those wet and damp towels down there would cushion its fall. And then I set about taking my shower and shampooing my hair. I used the one stall with a door that could be locked from the inside. After ten minutes of lathering and sudsing and using conditioner, I toweled dry, pulled on my white terry-cloth robe, and stepped out. All the girls who'd been in the lounge had gathered to watch what happened next. Forbidden cigarettes dangled from slack lips and fingers.

"You look *so clean*, Heaven," merrily chirped Pru Carraway, out of her college-girl clothes and into her transparent baby dolls. "Did you feel a special need for staying so long in the shower?"

"Just the same old need I have every night since I came to Winterhaven—to wash the atmosphere from my skin and hair."

"The atmosphere is dirty here? Dirtier than where you came from?"

"There are coal mines and cotton gins where I come from, and the coal soot is carried on the wind to dirty clean clothes on the line, and curtains have to be washed once a week. And the airborne cotton lint invades the lungs of the millworkers, and even the lungs of people who live downwind. But since I came to Winterhaven I have experienced nothing but clean, wholesome, American fun. I cannot wait to write my thesis about my experiences at Winterhaven. It should be very enlightening to those who don't know what goes on in private schools like this."

Suddenly Pru Carraway was smiling, smiling broadly. "Oh, come now, Heaven, are you any the worse for wear? We always play that joke on a new girl. It's fun to mislead them and let them dress incorrectly. It's all part of our initiation. Now, if you complete the last ritual, you can become one of us, and pull the same tricks on the next new girl."

"No thanks," I said coldly, the memory of those awful cramps that had left me weak still very much with me. "I don't care to become a member of your club."

"Of course you do! Everyone always does! We have oodles of fun, and food and drinks stashed away that you wouldn't believe. And the next step will complete our requirements; we don't like girls who chicken out." She smiled at me winningly, with more charm than I had previously suspected she possessed. "All you have to do is slide down the dirty linen chute, then find your way out of the cellar, which is always kept locked. There is a way out, but you'll have to find it."

The pregnant pause stretched and stretched as I thought this over. "But how do I know the chute isn't dangerous?"

"Why we've all done it, Heaven, every last one of us, and none of us were harmed!" Pru smiled at me again. "C'mon, be a good sport . . . besides we want to visit you this Christmas."

An anger difficult to describe was building within me. There were all kinds of petty tricks they could have played that wouldn't have been so physically violent. And down there on top of all the dirty linen was a double bag of filth just waiting . . .

"If someone would prove to me that the chute is safe, and there truly is a way out of the locked basement, maybe . . ." I said. "I wouldn't want to be caught down there in the morning by one of the washwomen, who would immediately report me for being off limits—then maybe . . ."

"We've all done it!" flared Pru, as if she considered my caution utterly overdone. "It's only a swift down-hill ride and you end up on damp towels. No big deal."

"But I want to make sure I can find my way out of the basement," I insisted.

"All right!" shouted Pru. "I'll do it first myself to prove it can be done! And when you see me again, you'll realize I'm the only truly brave person here, for someone other than the president of the club *should have* volunteered."

Destiny was at hand. Whatever happened next was none of my doing, I thought, as I watched Pru Carraway preen and praise herself, then prance toward the very largest of the clothes chutes where I'd dropped my plastic bag. With a great show of bravery, and a flourish of her hand, waving farewell as she called "See you later," she crawled through the round opening while the strong, heavy door was held open by one of her friends.

With Pru out of sight, the door was released, and with a loud bang it slammed shut. Beyond and out of sight Pru was telling the world in a loud, shrilling yell that the ride down was fun, fun, fun!

I held my breath. Maybe the double plastic bags would hold, maybe.

Then, quicker than I anticipated, came a different kind of scream. Horrified! Disgusted! Anguished!

"Doesn't she always overdo it?" said some girl I didn't turn to identify.

Amy Luckett leaned to whisper. "Forgive us, Heaven, for what we did. But all of us have to endure some ordeal, and I overheard your guardian tell Mrs. Mallory not to give you any help or protection from what the other girls did. It seems he wants to 'test your mettle' and see what you're made of."

I didn't know what to think. Far away Pru was still screaming and sobbing. Her wails began to drift away, becoming fainter and fainter. And with each passing second the nineteen girls who surrounded me became louder and louder with their comments, wondering why it was taking Pru so long to return.

Finally Pru Carraway showed up. She was pale, shaken, and so darn clean. Even her hair had been freshly shampooed. Her skin had been scrubbed with such force it looked shiny and raw. Her pale and stony gaze riveted on me. The girls around me grew very quiet. "Okay, I've proven it can be done. It's your turn now."

"I don't really care to belong to your club," I pronounced in a cold and haughty manner that rivaled her own. "Fun is fun, but anything that is dangerous and insulting and embarrassing physically goes beyond good taste, and good sense. I will go my way, and the rest of you can go yours."

Every one of those girls stared at me with absolute shock in her eyes, but in the glittery eyes of Pru Carraway glowed something else—relief that I hadn't exposed her shame, and resentment and hostility because, while she was gone, I had somehow managed to make a few friends.

## ～ Nine ～
### Logan

I NEVER BECAME ONE OF THE *SELECT* IN WINTERHAVEN, but at least the majority of the girls accepted me for what I was, different and independent in a shy and uncertain way. Subconsciously I had found the same old shield that I had used in the Willies and Winnerrow; indifferent, that's what I'd pretend to be. Let them throw slings and arrows, what did I care? I was here, where I wanted to be, and that was enough.

When Troy called the day after the dance to see how it had gone, I told him someone had played a terrible trick on me, but I was much too embarrassed to tell him what the trick had been. "You weren't harmed were you?" he asked, seemingly very worried. "I've heard those Winterhaven girls can be quite nasty to new girls, especially those they haven't grown up with."

"Oh," I answered in a new, nonchalant way, "I think this time the trick was also on them."

The very next Friday evening, sooner than expected, Jillian and Tony came back from California, full of holiday spirits. They gave me gifts of clothes and jewelry, and Troy in his small cottage was a constant, dependable comfort, just knowing he was there, every weekend, my secret friend. I more than suspected he didn't really want me there, distracting him from his chores, and if he hadn't been so polite and sensitive to my needs he would have sent me away.

"How do you entertain yourselves on Saturdays?" Tony asked one day, when he saw me scurrying from the library with an armful of books.

"Studying, that's how," I said with a little laugh. "There's so much I thought I knew but I don't. So if Jillian and you don't mind, I'm going to lock myself up in my bedroom and cram."

I heard his heavy sigh. "Jillian usually has her hair done on Saturdays, then she goes to a movie afterward with a few of her friends. I was hoping you and I could make a day of it in the city, doing some Christmas shopping."

"Oh, ask me again, Tony, please do, for there's nothing in this world that I would rather do than visit the main store of Tatterton Toys."

For a moment he appeared startled. Then a slow grin spread on his handsome face. "You mean you really want to go there? How wonderful. Jillian has never shown any interest in it whatsoever! And your mother, knowing we quarreled about that often, took her mother's side and said she was too old to be bothered with silly toys that didn't make the world go around, and didn't improve social or political conditions—so what good were they?"

"My mother said that?" I asked, totally astonished.

"She was echoing your grandmother, who wants a

playmate, not a businessman. For a short time, when she made exquisite doll clothes, I had hopes one day she'd really become a part of Tatterton Toys."

Soon I'd slipped away to Troy's stone cottage, where I wanted to be more than anyplace else. Just to be with him gave me excitement. Why had Logan never made my pulse beat so hard?

While I lay on the thick carpeting in front of Troy's hot fire, I wrote to Tom, pleading for him to give me some advice on how to approach Logan again in a way that wouldn't seem too aggressive.

Finally, just when I believed Tom was never going to answer my last letter, one showed up in my post office box.

*I don't understand all your fears. I'm sure Logan will be thrilled if you give him a call, and arrange to meet some place. By the way, in my last letter, did I forget to tell you that Pa's new wife is expecting a baby? I have not heard from Fanny directly, but I still have some old friends in Winnerrow who keep in touch. It seems the good reverend's wife has gone home to stay with her parents until her first child is born. What about you, have you heard from Fanny, or from the people who have Our Jane and Keith?*

No, I hadn't heard one word. And here was Pa, blithely making more babies, when he should never want to see another! Not after what he'd done! It hurt to feel that Pa could do evil and never be punished, at least not enough! That little brother and sister I used to feel so necessary in my life were growing fainter and fainter in my memory, and that scared me. My heart was no longer feeling the sharp anguish of losing them, and I couldn't allow that to happen. Troy told me he had contacted his law firm in Chicago and they would begin their investigation soon. I had to keep my flame of anger alive, keep it new and raw, and never allow the passing of time to salve the wounds Pa had delivered. Together again, all five Casteel children all under one roof. That was my goal.

Just as I'd feared, when finally I had the nerve to dial Logan's number, his voice didn't show the warmth and approval that had been there when he loved me. "I'm glad you called, Heaven," he said in a chilly, detached way. "I'd be happy to meet with you this Saturday, but our meeting will have to be short. I have a big paper due next week."

Oh, damn him! Double damn him! I was stung by the cold tone in his voice, the same that his mother had used whenever she was so unfortunate as to find me with her one and only beloved son. Loretta Stonewall hated me and had made little pretense to hide her disapproval of her son's devotion to hillbilly trash. And her husband had followed her lead, though he had looked embarrassed a few times by his wife's obvious hostility. But I was going to go and meet Logan this afternoon, no matter how cold he sounded. I spent two hours getting ready—I was determined to look my very best.

"Well, what a pretty picture you make, Heaven," Tony sang out when he saw me. "I love that color dress you're wearing. It is very becoming, though I don't remember selecting that one." He frowned a little as he reflected, while my breath caught and held, for it was a dress that Jillian had given me, one Tony

157

had given her, and she had never worn it because she didn't like the style, the color, or the fact that her husband considered his taste better than hers. "On a day like this, dear girl, you need more than just an ordinary coat," he said, reaching into a closet and pulling out a heavy, dark sable coat. He held the fur for my arms to slide into the sleeves. "This fur is three years old, and Jillian has many others, so keep it if you want. Now, where are you going? You know you have to tell me in advance of your plans, and have my approval."

How could I tell him I was planning to meet a boy from my past? He wouldn't know that Logan was different, out of place in Winnerrow. He'd presume he was just any young man in a mountain valley village he'd never seen: uncouth, uncultured, and uncivilized.

"Some of the friendlier girls at Winterhaven have asked me to one of their luncheons in town. And Miles doesn't have to drive me. Nor do you. I've already called a cab."

My heart beat faster, louder, as I told my lie that should have been the truth. Something Tony detected in my expression or tone made his eyes narrow as he weighed my words. Shrewd, sophisticated eyes that seemed to know all the wicked and tricky ways of the world. Long seconds passed as those observant eyes took in my forced calmness, my feigned assurance that struggled to show only innocence, and perhaps I convinced him, for he smiled. "I'm very pleased you have made friends at Winterhaven," he said with pleasure. "I've heard all kinds of tales about what those Winterhaven girls do to newcomers, and perhaps I should have warned you. But I wanted you to learn from experience how to handle every kind of difficult circumstance."

He smiled at me in such an approving way, somehow I just knew, absolutely knew, he'd heard every embarrassing detail of what happened to me the night of the dance. He chucked me under the chin. "I'm glad you have spirit and fire, and know how to handle things yourself. You have their approval now, even if you think you don't need it. Now that you've been accepted, you can go your own way, with my approval. Be tough. Refuse to be bullied. And be confident with the girls—but when it comes to boys, you come to me first. Before you date I'll have your escort and his family checked out. I can't have you running around with trash."

What he said made me shiver a bit, for it seemed I could have no secrets from him. And yet as he stood there looking me over with a great deal of approval, something proud sprang into my spine and made me stand taller. And something warm and sweet between us made me step forward to kiss his cheek. He seemed very surprised and just as pleased. "Why, thank you for doing that. Keep it up, and I may become just another soft touch."

My taxi arrived. Tony stood at the front door and waved, and I headed for one of the haunts of the B.U. boys, The Boar's Head Café.

I anticipated all kinds of difficulties in finding Logan. I even thought he'd pretend not to notice me again, or pretend he didn't know me, for I had not done one thing to make myself look like that shabby mountain girl who was my shame. And then, sitting in the window of the café, I spotted Logan. He was laughing and talking expressively to a pretty girl seated across from him. This contingency had never brushed my mind, at least not seriously, that he could be seeing someone else. So there I stood in the lightly falling snow, not knowing what to do now. October had come and gone. We were now midway into November. How nice it would have been to invite Logan to Farthinggale Manor, and before a cozy fire, Logan and Tony would have the chance to get to know each other. I sighed wistfully for all my wishes that seemed never to come true. And then, then, while I disbelieved what my eyes saw, Logan leaned across the table and teased that girl's face with his lips, ending up in a real kiss, the kind that lasted and lasted—kissing her in a way he'd never kissed me!

I hated him! I hated her! Be damned to you, Logan Stonewall! You're no different from any other guy on the make!

I spun on my heel, not realizing the fresh snow would be so slippery. And down I went, flat on my back. Ungainly sprawled, I stared up at the sky, totally stunned that I could have done something so stupid. I wasn't hurt. I refused everyone who tried to assist me up . . . and then Logan ran out of the café. His first words proved that this time he knew me. "My God, Heaven, what are you doing flat on your back?"

Without asking permission to help, he put his hands under my armpits and lifted me up. I struggled to keep my footing, and that forced me to cling to him, amusement sparkling in his eyes. "The next time you buy boots, I would try some with lower heels."

The girl in the café was staring out, her eyes angry.

"Hi, stranger," I greeted in a husky low voice, trying to hide my embarrassment. I released my grip on him, having found my footing, then brushed snow from my coat. I threw him an angry look that would have stung if looks could stab. "I saw you in the coffee shop kissing that girl who is staring out at us, looking furious. Does she own you now?"

He had the decency to blush. "She means nothing to me, just a way to spend Saturday afternoon."

"Really," I replied, with as much ice in my voice as I could manage. "I'm sure you wouldn't be so understanding if you caught me in the same situation."

His color deepened. "Why do you have to bring up that? Besides, it was more than a few kisses between you and that Cal Dennison!" he almost shouted.

"Yes, it was," I admitted. "But you would never understand how it came about, even if you were generous enough to give me the chance to explain."

As he stood in the snow that was falling harder now, he seemed very strong, with his jawline set in a firm, determined way, so his cheek dimple no longer played hide-and-seek. His clean-cut good looks caused many a female passerby to pause and look at him twice . . . and he was staring at me with a stranger's uninterest.

The cold wind hissed around the corners of buildings and whistled to the ground with buffeting force, causing his hair to fan wild in the wind. My own hair was lifted and blown forward. I found myself breathing fast and hard, wanting so much to win his approval again. Just to be so near his strength and goodness made me realize how very much I needed him. I craved with a terrible yearning to have his love again, his warmth and his caring, for he had loved me well when I was a nobody, a nothing, and with him I didn't have to pretend to be more than what I was. "Heaven, it was sweet of you to call me. I've been wanting to do that every time I thought of you. I drove by your Farthinggale Manor once, just the gates, and they so impressed me I lost my nerve and turned around."

Then he was seeing me, really seeing me. Incredulity flashed through his eyes, lighting them briefly with pleasure. "You look so different," he said, moving his arms as if to embrace me, before his arms dropped to his sides and his hands found their way into his pockets, as if they'd found a safe, confining harbor.

"I hope it's for the better."

He looked me over with so much disapproval, I began to tremble slightly. What had I done wrong?

"You look so rich, too rich," he answered slowly. "You've changed your hairstyle and you're wearing makeup."

What was wrong with him? None of my "improvements" seemed to make him happy. "You look like one of those models on magazine covers."

And that was bad? I tried to smile. "Oh, Logan, I have so much to tell you! You look terrific!" The snow began to freeze my face. Specks of fluffy white caught in his hair and in mine, and touched the tip of my nose with cold. "Isn't there somewhere we can sit and talk, where it's comfortable and warm, and maybe then you won't glare at me like you are doing now." I kept making small talk as he led me inside to a table where we ordered hot chocolate. I noticed the girl he had been with continued to glare at us. But I ignored her, and so did Logan.

He was moving his eyes over my fur coat, noticing the gold chains I wore at my throat, seeing the rings on my fingers as I pulled off my fine leather gloves.

I tried to smile. "Logan," I began with my eyes lowered, determined to keep my expectations high, "can't we let bygones be bygones and start again, fresh?"

It took him a long time to reply, as if he were struggling to free himself from some past resolution he'd made, and every second I spent with him brought back flooding memories of how sweet our youth had been because we had had each other. Oh, if only I'd never allowed Cal Dennison to touch me! If only I'd been stronger, wiser, more knowledgeable about men and their physical desires! Maybe then I could have held off an older man who was basically weak, and wrong to have taken advantage of a stupid young hillbilly.

"I don't know," he finally said in a slow, hesitant way. "I can't stop thinking of how easily you forgot me and our vows to one another once you were out of sight."

"Please try harder!" I implored. "I didn't know at the time what I was getting into, and I felt trapped by circumstances that I couldn't control—"

His stubborn jaw set in a hard line. "Somehow, seeing you as you are today, wearing expensive jewelry and that fur coat, you don't seem the same girl I used to know. I don't know how to relate to you now, Heaven. You don't seem vulnerable anymore, you seem like you don't really need anyone, or anything."

My heart contracted. What he saw was only surface confidence given to me by expensive clothes and jewelry. Scratch the surface and the hill-scum Casteel girl would still be there. And then it hit me what he was really getting at.

He had liked me better when I was pitiful! He had been drawn to my vulnerability, my poverty, my ugly, faded dresses and shabby shoes! The strengths I'd believed he admired most about me weren't even important to him now!

I fixed my eyes on his deep maroon sweater, for some reason wondering if he still had that awful red knit cap I'd made for him once. I felt that again circumstances were beyond my control, and yet I couldn't give up so easily.

"Logan," I began again, "I'm living with my real mother's mother now. She is as different from Granny as night is from day. I never knew grandmothers in their middle years could look so young and not only pretty, but glamorous."

"This grandmother lives in a different world than the one you knew in the Willies." How quickly he formed his opinion, as if never in doubt about anyone or anything. Then, finally, he picked up his mug and sipped. "And how do you like your grandfather?" he asked. "Is he young and fabulously handsome as well?"

I tried to ignore his sarcasm. "Tony Tatterton isn't really my grandfather, Logan, but my grandmother's second husband. My mother's father died two years ago. I'm sorry I never had a chance to know him."

His deep blue eyes took on an abstracted look, his gaze still lingering somewhere behind my head. "I saw you one day in mid-September, out shopping with an older man who held your elbow and guided you where he wanted you to go. I wanted to call out and tell you I was there, but I couldn't. I stupidly followed the two of you for a while, and watched through the shop windows as you endlessly tried on different outfits and modeled them for that man. It stunned me how what you wore changed your appearance. And not only that, I was stunned by the changes it made in you! Everything new he bought for you brought on laughter, smiles, and the kind of happiness I'd never seen on your face before. Heaven, I had no idea that young-looking man could be your grandfather. Jealously was all I could feel. When I loved you and planned for our future together, I wanted to be the one to put joy in your eyes and the glow on your face."

"But I needed the warm coats he bought me, the boots, the shoes. And the fur coats I have are second hand, given to me by Jillian, who grows quickly bored with clothes and everything else. I don't have as much as you think I do. And it's not so wonderful at Farthy. My grandmother hardly even talks to me!"

Logan leaned closer, riveting me with his hard glare. "But the step-grandfather is delighted to have you around, isn't he? I could tell that by his manner that day I saw the two of you shopping. He got as much kick out of those new clothes as you did!"

It alarmed me the way he looked, so fiercely jealous. "You watch out for him, Heaven. Remember what happened when you lived in Candlewick with Kitty Dennison and her husband; it could happen again."

I felt my eyes go huge and round with the pain of his surprise attack. How could he think that? Tony wasn't the least like Cal! Tony didn't need me for a companion while his wife worked late hours. Tony had a full, rich life, busy with vacations and business and hundreds of friends delighted to entertain him and Jillian. Yet I could tell that Logan would refuse to believe me if I pointed out these facts. My head moved from side to side, rejecting his suspicions, angry that he had them. Disappointed that he couldn't forgive and forget, and not trust me as he used to.

"Do you still hear from him?" he shot out, his eyes narrowed.

"Who?" I asked, bewildered by the quick turn of his suspicions.

"Cal Dennison!"

"No!" I cried out again. "I have not heard from him since the day I left Winnerrow! He doesn't know where I am! I never want to see him again."

"I'm sure he'll find out where you are." Logan's voice had gone flat. He picked up his mug and drained it to the bottom, then set it down hard so it clunked loudly on the table. "It's been nice seeing you again, Heaven, and knowing you now have everything you wanted. I'm sorry your real grandfather died before you knew him, and happy you like your step-grandfather so much. I have to admit you look very beautiful in your fine clothes and fur coat, but you're not the same girl I fell in love with. That girl was destroyed in Candlewick."

Stunned and deeply hurt, so much so I felt mortally wounded, I was speechless. My lips gaped, and I wanted to plead for him to give me another chance. Hot, blinding tears stung my eyes. I struggled to find the right words to say, but already he'd turned away and was heading for the girl who still waited for him at the table by the window. Without once looking back, he joined her.

And all the care I had used in getting ready for this meeting, hoping to impress him, had been totally wasted. I should have come wearing my rags, with my long hair disheveled, with hollows from hunger shadowing beneath my eyes—then maybe he'd have shown more compassion.

Then it hit me, hard, the truth I'd never suspected until today.

Logan had never truly loved me! Logan had only pitied a waif from the hills and had wanted to shower me protectively with the largess of his generosity! He had considered me a charity case!

It all came flooding back, his small gifts of toothbrushes and toothpaste, soaps and shampoos, all taken from the shelves of his father's pharmacy. Oh, the embarrassment of his condescending pity filled me with shame! The regrets for having allowed myself to believe he saw in me something admirable! I brushed impatiently at the hot well of tears that flooded onto my face and down over my cheeks; then, jumping to my feet, I seized my purse and fur coat and fled toward the door, moving faster than he did. In another second I was outside, pulling on my coat as I ran. Ran from the very one I'd always run to!

The snow was coming down slantwise in streaks, wild and wind-driven. It was freezing cold as I struggled to put on that full-length fur coat. My breath puffed out in billows of vapor as I choked and sobbed and wanted to die. Right behind me I heard the sound of Logan's steps. Whipping around, my coat fanning wide in the wind, I glared with hatred straight into his look of concern that came too late.

"You don't have to pity me anymore, Logan Grant Stonewall!" I shouted into the wind, heedless of who overheard my words. "No wonder I betrayed you unconsciously with Cal Dennison! Perhaps my instinct knew exactly what your true feeling for me was! Not love, not admiration, and not genuine friendship—or anything I really need and want for myself. So you were right to suggest that we call it quits! It is all over between us! I never want to see you again as long as I live! Go back to Winnerrow and find some other hillbilly poverty case from the Willies!—and give her the blessings of your detestable pity!"

I whirled around and ran for the nearest corner, where I quickly waved down a taxi.

Goodbye, Logan, I sobbed to myself as the taxi pulled away from the curb. It was tender and sweet when I thought you loved me for myself, but from this day forward, I'll not think of you again!

You have even managed to make me feel guilty about Troy, and you don't even know about him. Dear, wonderful, talented, handsome Troy, who was not at all like Cal Dennison, who never excited me at all.

# ~ Ten ~
## Promises

SCALDING TEARS WERE STILL FLOWING WHEN MY CAB passed under the impressive black gates of Farthinggale Manor—tears that choked my voice so I had difficulty telling the driver where he had to turn off in order to reach the small cottage where I hoped Troy would be.

I was running to the only remaining friend I had, almost blinded by my tears, grieving inside as if everyone I'd ever lost had been taken away anew, and the grief was compounded over and over. Always a small but confident part of me had believed that Logan was eternally and rightfully mine, and because of that I could somehow win him back.

Nothing was eternal! Nothing was right! my disappointment screamed. Nothing!

"Twelve dollars and fifty cents," said the taxi driver, waiting impatiently as I dabbed at my eyes and tried to count out the exact amount. However, I had only a twenty, and I thrust that into his hands and quickly left the warmth of the back seat.

"Keep the change," I croaked hoarsely.

Snow, sharp as tiny ice swords, slashed at my face. The wind was wild and tore at my hair as I ran blindly for the cottage. Without regard for Troy's privacy I tugged to open the blue door, but the wind was behind me, making opening it difficult. When finally I had it open and was able to step inside, the wind slammed the door behind me with a loud, crashing bang. Startled into reality by the noise, I leaned back against the door and tried to gain some control of my emotions.

"Who's there?" called Troy from another room, and then he appeared in the frame of his bedroom doorway, his naked body wrapped by a towel swathed about his hips, and water stood in droplets on his skin. His dark hair was wet and matted. "Heaven!" he exclaimed, his eyes startled by my sudden and dramatic appearance. He raised the towel in his hands to dry his hair vigorously. "Come in, sit down, make yourself at home, and give me a minute to put on some clothes."

Not a word to say he didn't need me, or to reprimand me for coming without an invitation. Just his troubled smile, before he turned and disappeared.

Despair heavied my legs, making them feel nailed to the floor. I was making too much of this, I knew I was, and still I couldn't catch my breath enough to control the gasps that sounded as if they came from someone other than myself. I was still leaning against the door, my arms pressed backward as my fingers clutched at the wood for stability, when Troy came striding from his room, fully clothed in his white silk blouse and his tight black trousers. His hair, still slightly damp, lay in shiny waves to frame his face.

Compared to Logan's ruddy color and deep tan, Troy seemed extraordinarily pale.

He advanced my way without speaking, and gently caught hold of my hands, pulling me away from the door, taking my purse from my shoulder before he eased off my heavy, wet fur coat. "Now, now," he soothed, "nothing can be that bad, can it? On a beautiful snowy day like this, with the wind howling and telling you to stay indoors, there's nothing as cozy as a crackling fire, and good food to eat, and a pleasant companion to be with." He put me in a chair he drew close to his fire, then knelt to take off my boots, and with his hands he rubbed my cold, nyloned feet into warmth again.

I felt tired enough to sag in the chair, my eyes wide and stark as the tears eventually stopped coming. My chest lost some of the heavy weight that gave it terrible pain. Only then could I look around. No lamps were lit, just the cheery glow of the fire to throw patterns of dancing lights and shadows on the walls. And as I looked around, Troy stayed on his knees, staring up at me as he pulled a hassock closer. Lifting my legs, he put my feet on that before he covered me to my waist with a bright wool afghan. "Now it's time for the food," he said with a small smile of approval, watching me dab at the last tear with my frivolous small handkerchief. Every tissue in my purse had already been used. "Coffee, tea, wine, hot chocolate?"

The mention of hot chocolate immediately brought fresh tears to my eyes. Alarmed, he quickly suggested, "A bit of brandy to warm you up first. Then hot tea, how about that?"

Without waiting for my consent, he stood and

moved toward the kitchen, pausing to switch on the stereo so it could flood his dim, firelit room with soft classical music. For a brief second I heard behind my eyes the loud country twang of Kitty's kind of music, and I shivered.

But this was another world, Troy's world, where reality lay far beyond the iron gates, and here, safe, snug, and warm, there was only beauty and kindness, and the faint aroma of freshly baked bread. I closed my eyes, and thoughts of Tony drifted vaguely to mind. It was almost dark outside. He'd be pacing the floor and glancing often at his watch, anticipating my return, no doubt angry because I was not keeping my word. And sleep, like a blessing, chased away Tony and all despair.

Minutes must have passed before I heard Troy's voice saying: "Come, wake up and sip the brandy." Obediently, even as my eyes stayed closed, my lips parted and the stinging, warm liquid burned its way to my stomach, and then I was coughing, bolting upright, startled by the taste of liquor I'd never tried before. "Now, that's enough," he said, withdrawing the small snifter. He smiled as if amused by my reaction to just one swallow. "It can't compare with mountain dew, is that what you're telling me?"

"I've never tasted mountain dew," I whispered hoarsely, "and I never want to." Pa's strong, brutal, and handsome face flashed before my eyes. Someday, someday, he and I would meet again, someday when I could be as cruel as he knew how to be.

"You just sit there and doze and let me make you dinner. Then you can tell me what brought you here with tears in your eyes."

My lips parted, but he hushed what I would say with the signal of his forefinger over his own lips. "Later."

I watched him slice the fresh bread and put the sandwiches together with the quick dexterity that made all his chores seem effortless and enjoyable.

Over my lap he placed a tray, and then his silver, napkin-covered tray of sandwiches and tea. On the floor before the fire he sat cross-legged to eat his meal. We had fallen into silence by this time, comfortable with each other as from time to time his eyes met with mine, ever watchful to see that I ate, and drank, and didn't lapse into the sleepy stupor that struggled to invade my body again.

Snow slashed at the windows so they iced over. The whistling wind competed with the music. Still, compared to the wind in the Willies screaming through the cracks of that mountain cabin this was tame and muffled. This cottage, six times larger, was snug and well built, with sturdy walls and insulation. Through the walls of our cabin we had been able to see the sky.

I began to nibble on his sandwich and before I knew it I'd consumed it all and polished off his steaming cup of tea. And he was smiling at me in a pleased way, having eaten three sandwiches to my one. "Another?" he asked, preparing to get up and enter the kitchen again.

I leaned back, shaking my head. "Enough. I never knew sandwiches could be so satisfying until I tasted yours."

"An art form when you care enough. How about dessert, say a slice of homemade fudge cake."

"Yours?"

"No, I don't ever bake cakes or pies, but Rye Whiskey always sends me a huge chunk of cake when he bakes. There's plenty for both of us.

But I was full. I shook my head, rejecting the cake, though he polished off a slice that made me sort of regret my decision. Already I'd learned that Troy never offered anything twice. He gave you one chance to accept, or forget it.

"I'm sorry to burst in on you as I did," I murmured, gone sleepy again. "I should hurry back to Farthy before Tony gets angry with me."

"He won't expect you to travel in a blizzard like this. He'll figure that you've holed up in some hotel lobby, and will come home the first chance you have. But you could give him a call and put his worries to rest."

But the dial tone was gone when I lifted the receiver. Lines were down.

"It's all right, Heaven. My brother is not a fool. He'll understand."

Slowly he scanned my face, perhaps seeing the emotional weariness. "Do you want to talk about it?"

No, I didn't want to talk about Logan's rejection, it hurt too much. Still, despite my will and my need to keep my pain from him, my tongue babbled out the entire story of how once I'd failed Logan in an important way, and now he couldn't forgive me. ". . . and what's just as bad, he's angry that now I'm not poor and pitiful!"

He got up to put the dishes we'd used into his washer. Then, falling again on the floor, which obviously he preferred to his comfortable sofa and chairs, he spread his long length on the thick comfort of his carpet to lie on his back with his hands tucked beneath his head, before he said thoughtfully: "I'm sure one day very soon Logan will regret what he said today, and you'll hear from him again. You are both very young."

"I never want to hear from him again." I choked and tried to keep from crying. "I've finished with Logan Stonewall, now and forever!"

Again a small smile played about his beautifully shaped lips. Only when that smile faded did he turn his face away from me. "It's nice that you dropped in to share the blizzard with me, whatever the reason. I won't tell Tony."

"Why doesn't he want me to come here?" I asked, not for the first time.

For a flashing second shadows seemed to darken his expression. "In the beginning when first I met you, I didn't want to become involved with your life. Now that I know you better I feel obligated to help. When I lie down to sleep at night your eyes come to haunt me. How can a sixteen-year-old girl have such depth in her eyes?"

"I'm not sixteen!" I cried out in a hoarse choked voice. "I am already seventeen years old—but don't you dare tell Tony that." The moment the words were out of my mouth I regretted them. He owed Tony loyalty, not me.

"Why in the world would you lie about something so inconsequential as one year? Sixteen, seventeen, what's the difference?"

"I will be eighteen this February twenty-second," I said with some defensiveness. "In the hills girls of eighteen are usually married and have children."

That made his face turn my way. "I am very glad you no longer live in the hills. Now tell me why you told Tony you were sixteen instead of seventeen?"

"I don't know why I did it. I wanted to protect my mother from appearing foolish and impulsive when she married my father, whom she knew only a few hours before she said yes to his marriage proposal. Granny always said it was love at first sight. I didn't understand what she meant, and I still can't understand how she, a girl from a rich and prominent family, with such a cultured background, could have fallen for a man like my father."

His dark eyes had the kind of deep forest pools have; in them I could drown.

His grandfather clock began to strike the hour of eight o'clock, and still the blizzard raged on. A music box that must have also been a clock began to play a sweet and haunting melody, while tiny figures emerged from a small door one by one. "I never saw a clock like that," I said irrelevantly.

"I have a collection of antique clocks," Troy murmured absently, rolling on his side to study me with soft understanding. "When you are as rich as a Tatterton, you don't know how to spend your money . . . and to think, all the time you were in the Willies, needing what I could have given so easily. It seems an obscenity now to know I have so much while others have so little. It shocks me too to know I never gave poverty a thought before, perhaps because I've always lived in my own world, and the people I knew had as much as I did."

I bowed my head even lower, realizing now how different Troy's life had been from mine. And even as I continued to sit, Troy gazed at me until I grew uneasy from his long survey, squirming before I stood and stretched. "I've taken too much of your time already. Now I have to go home so Tony won't ask too many questions."

Truthfully, I expected him to object, to tell me again leaving was impossible, but this time he rose to his feet and smiled at me. "All right. There is a way that I didn't want you to know about. It's a cold climate here, and when Farthy went up, with the surrounding barns and stables, my practical ancestors anticipated the deep snows. They had tunnels dug to the barns and stables, so the horses and other animals could be taken care of and fed. A long time ago where this cottage stands now, there was a barn with a deep cellar. And that, of course, makes this cottage very accessible to the main house during the worst of weather. I could have told you this before, but I wanted you to stay and keep me company." His eyes moved from my face and turned slightly glassy. "It's very strange how comfortable I feel with you, a mere child." Again his penetrating eyes fixed on me. "If you enter the cellar of Farthy and use the west door that is painted green, the tunnel will bring you to the cellar beneath this cottage. The other doors of blue, red, and yellow will take you nowhere, for Tony had those tunnels sealed. He thought too many passages, no matter how secret, made Farthy vulnerable to thieves."

He brought my coat and boots from his guest closet and held the coat while I slipped my arms in, and when he had the fur coat snugly on my shoulders, his hands lingered. He was behind me, so I couldn't see his expression. When I turned around, he smiled before he reached for my hand and led me to a door in his kitchen that took us both down steep, wooden stairs into his cellar, which was damp and cold and very large. And then Troy was showing me the green door with its arched top. "I'll go with you to the house," he said, leading the way and still holding my hand. "When I was a boy these underground tunnels always scared me. Every time the tunnel made a bend, I expected monsters to appear, or ghosts, something I didn't want to see."

Even with him leading the way, and giving me security with the warmth of his hand covering mine, I knew exactly what he meant. I was reminded of a coal mine tunnel that Tom and I had entered once despite signs that had read "Danger! Keep Out!"

Troy released my hand only when we'd reached the end of the freezing tunnel, having arrived at the bottom of steps that were steep and narrow and going up. "You will come out in the back kitchen hall," he whispered. "Listen carefully before you open the door you see at the top. Rye Whiskey often works late." He touched my cheek then and asked, "How are you going to explain to Tony?"

"Never mind. I'm a good liar, remember?" And with those words I threw my arms about his neck, but I didn't kiss him. I only pressed my cold cheek against his. "Without you I don't know what I'd do."

He held me fast against him for a brief, exciting moment. "You just remember all the time that it is Logan you love and need, not me."

I ran up the stairs, hurting all the way because he thought it so necessary to warn me to keep my distance. What was wrong with me? I needed someone like Troy. Desperately needed his sensitivity and understanding. There were times when I looked at

Tony, then quickly I'd make myself forget his charm and good looks. He was too dominating, like Pa.

Beginning to sniffle now, I entered the narrow hallway in back of Farthinggale Manor's huge kitchen. Even at this hour of the night, Rye Whiskey was in there, preparing the food to be served the next day. He was singing to keep rhythm with each roll of his pastry pin, and beyond him the young black boy he was teaching used spoons to keep the beat. On tiptoes I slipped past the kitchen door, and only then did I quicken my steps.

An hour later I lay on my bed, staring out the windows, hearing the wind and thumping of my heart. I had great difficulty falling asleep, though I was deep in dreams when my bedroom door was thrown open, and Tony's voice roared loud enough to bolt me wide awake.

"When did you slip into the house without my seeing you?"

Disoriented and frightened by his voice, I bolted upright, clutching the topsheet and blankets to my bosom. Untruths, which could sometimes come readily to my tongue, failed me this time, so I could only tremble. And I suspected even Troy could not protect me from Tony's anger once I'd earned it.

Tony strode into my bedroom and lit the lamp beside my bed. Towering above me he stared long and hard at my face. "Where were you, and how did you manage to return from Boston? There hasn't been a road open north of the city since three o'clock!"

As I floundered, trying not to let him see how terrified I was of his anger and disapproval, thoughts of what was likely to happen choked in my throat. Falling back on my pillows, I gazed at Tony with wide eyes of terror. How intimidating and how cold he seemed as he glared down at me.

His voice came low and hard. "Don't you lie to me, girl, and expect to get away with it. We have made a bargain, you and I, and I expect you to live up to your side of it."

"I . . . I . . . I never left," I faltered, feeling for the lying words. "When the taxi passed under the gates I suddenly lost my nerve. I felt ashamed to let you know I don't really like those Winterhaven girls, and I was too insecure to pretend I do. So I slipped in the side door and stole back to my bedroom, and then . . ."

"Then what?" he asked coldly, his blue eyes narrowing suspiciously.

"I was afraid you'd check my room, so I hid myself away in one of the unused rooms."

"You lost your nerve?" he asked scornfully. "You hid? Now that is interesting. In which room did you hide?"

Oh, God! How easily he could trap me! "It was the second room in that northern wing, you know, the room Jillian wants to redecorate. The room full of pale peach. The room she considers passé."

His frown deepened. "And at what time did you decide to leave that room and return to this one?"

Now he was baiting his trap. All through the evening he could have checked this bedroom . . . two hours ago he could have seen the bed empty. "I don't remember, Tony, really I don't. I fell asleep in the peach room, and when I stumbled back here, I didn't look at the time. I just undressed and went to bed."

"And not a thought of me, and how worried I might be?"

"I'm sorry," I whispered, "but I'd trapped myself, and I didn't know how to tell you the truth without losing face."

"You have already lost face," he said harshly, glaring down at me. "I don't know whether or not to believe your story. Jillian and I had a terrible argument this afternoon. She is terrified that her friends will suspect you are her granddaughter, and they will ask questions about Leigh."

Nervously I fingered the narrow ribbon beading the neckline of my pink nightgown.

At the open doorway his figure almost blocked out the light in the hall. "Heaven," he said with his back turned. "I don't admire cowards. I hope you will never again do what you did today."

He closed the door.

## ~ Eleven ~
### Holidays, Lonely Days

WONDERFUL PREPARATIONS FOR THANKSGIVING DAY began a week ahead of time. From Friday to Monday I had a whole week's vacation. Upstairs where Jillian and Tony reigned supreme all seemed as usual, but downstairs in the kitchen such an array of produce began to arrive that my breath caught in my throat and seemed to stay. Fresh pumpkins, three of them, and only six guests had been invited to dinner. But with Jillian and Tony, and Troy and me, that made ten. Oh, at last, at last, Troy was going to be included as a genuine member of this family!

"Tell me about the others who are coming," I eagerly asked Rye, perched beside him on a high stool, and busily chopping vegetables and anything else he thought I could handle. And he was a hard master to please. Just from his smiling or frowning expression I knew when I wasn't putting enough "slant" on my vegetable chopping, or I knew when I was doing it right.

"Friends," he said, "of the mistress and her husband. Important friends who fly in just to eat in Farthinggale Manor. I flatter myself that I help draw them here with all the fine dishes I'll prepare. But that's not the only reason they come. Mr. Tatterton has a winning way with people, they all adore him. And they also come to see Mrs. Tatterton, so they can see how much she has aged since they saw her last. And now they also come to see Mr. Troy, who only shows up at very important functions. He is a mystery to them, just as he is to the rest of us. Don't expect to see anyone younger than twenty. Mrs. Tatterton hates children at her parties."

Thanksgiving Day dawned bright and sunny and very cold. I was so thrilled that Troy was coming, every once in a while I caught myself singing. I was wearing a very special wine-red velvet dress that Tony had chosen, and it was so flattering I was glancing in a mirror to admire myself every few minutes.

Troy was the first guest to arrive, and because I'd been watching the maze, it was I who ran to open the door instead of Curtis. "Good afternoon, Mr. Tatterton. What a pleasure and delight to have you favor our dining table, at long, long last."

He was staring at me as if he'd never seen me before. Did a dress do that much? "I have never seen you look so lovely as you do this very minute," he said, as I reached to help him off with his topcoat. And Curtis, way back in the broad hall, stared our way with a certain kind of sarcasm. But what did I care, he was just a presence, very seldom a voice.

I hung his coat carefully in a closet, making sure his shoulder seams were right, and then I spun around to catch both of his hands in mine. "I'm so glad you're here I'm nearly bursting. Now I won't have to sit at a table with six guests I've never met."

"They won't all be strangers. Some you have met before at other parties . . . and there is one special guest who flew all the way from Texas just to meet you."

"Who?" I asked, my eyes growing huge.

"Jillian's mother, who is eighty-six years old. It seems Jillian wanted to cover the tales she'd told about you, and your great-grandmother became so intrigued she telephoned to say she was coming, despite the fact that she has a hip fracture."

He smiled and pulled me to a sofa in the grandest salon of all. "Don't look so concerned. She's a tough old bird, and she's the only one who doesn't tell lies one after the other."

She overwhelmed me right from the beginning when she came through the front door with two men supporting her weight on both sides. She was hardly five feet tall, a thin wisp of an old woman whose hair still held most of that silvery gold. On her scrawny fingers she wore four huge rings, ruby, emerald, sapphire, and diamond. Her colored jewels were all ringed with diamonds. Her bright blue dress hung loosely from her shoulders, and a heavy choker of sapphires decorated her neckline. "I hate tight clothes," she said as she glanced at me, and cringed a little closer to Troy.

She also hated crutches, which couldn't be trusted. Wheelchairs were an abomination. Pillows, shawls, and afghans were brought in from the car outside. In thirty minutes she was made comfortable, and only then did she turn those sharp, small eyes on me.

"Hello, Troy, it's nice to see you for a change," she said without even looking his way. "But I didn't fly all this way just to talk to family I already know." Her eyes scanned me again from head to toe. "Yes, Jillian is right. This is Leigh's daughter. There is no mistaking the color of her eyes—just the way mine used to be until the years stole the best of my features. And that figure, it's Leigh's all over again, when she wasn't hiding it behind some shapeless garment. I never could understand how she could wear such clothes in such miserable winter weather as this." Her small eyes, lined with wrinkles, narrowed as she briskly asked: "Why did my granddaughter die at such an early age?"

Down the stairs Jillian drifted, looking stunningly beautiful in a wine-red dress, very much like mine, except hers had a broad insert of jewels around the neck. "Oh, dear, dear Mother, how wonderful to see you again. Do you realize it's been five years since you came last?"

"I never intended to come again," answered Jana Jankins, whose name had been kindly provided to me by Troy as Jana was being arranged in her seat. And even as I watched Jillian with her mother, I could almost smell the smoke of animosity between them.

"Mother, when we knew you were coming, despite your leg cast, Tony very thoughtfully went out and provided you with a wonderfully handsome chair that used to belong to the president of Sidney Forestry."

"Do you think I'd sit in a chair used by a killer of trees? Now don't mention the subject again. I want to hear about this girl here." And almost faster than I could answer she was plying me with questions, how had my mother met my father, and where had we lived, and did my father have money? And were there other family members she could meet.

I was saved from making up more lies by the chiming of the door bells. Tony stepped out of his office looking like a fashion plate, and Thanksgiving began despite Jana Jankins, who just couldn't manage to out-shout everyone.

Then, to my dismay, Jillian finally noticed me sitting as quietly and demurely—and as close to Troy—as I could manage. Jillian's eyes grew large. "Heaven, the least you could do is check with me about what color I'm wearing when we are entertaining."

"I'll go and change mine right now!" I offered, about to jump up to change as quickly as possible, though I truly loved this dress.

"Sit down, Heaven," commanded Tony. "Jillian is being ridiculous. Your dress is not bejeweled, or nearly as lavish as my wife's. I liked the dress when I saw it on you, and I want you to wear it."

It was a strange kind of Thanksgiving dinner. First Jillian's mother had to be carried in and put at the end of the table (the hostess end, because Tony's chair was too near the wall), and once Jana assumed the role of hostess, she ruled, no one else. This great-grandmother of mine was rude, abrasive, and totally honest. It amazed me that Tony and Troy seemed so fond of her.

Still, it was a tiring meal, an exhausting evening, during which I was plied with a thousand questions I didn't know how to answer unless I lied. When Jana asked me how long I'd be staying at Farthinggale Manor, I didn't know what to answer. I looked hopefully at Tony and saw next to him a steely-faced

Jillian, who held her fork midway to her mouth and turned to Tony and glared as he began to rescue me. "Heaven has come to stay for as long as she likes," he announced, smiling first at me, then turning to Jillian and giving her a shut-up-or-else rictus. "She's already begun school at Winterhaven. In fact, she did so well on her entrance exams that she entered as a senior—a year ahead of her age group. And we've already applied to Radcliffe and Williams so she won't have to go too far away for a first-rate college. We're both so happy to have Heaven here. It's a bit as if Leigh had at last returned to us, isn't it Jill?"

All during this little speech Jillian had been shoveling food into her mouth, as if to cram it too full for any betraying words to slip out. She said nothing, merely glared at me. Oh, how I wished she could learn to love me. I needed so badly to have a real mother, someone I could really talk to, someone who could teach me how to be the right kind of woman. But I was beginning to realize that Jillian would never be that. Perhaps if she were more like Jana—rude and overbearing, but at least interested in getting to know me.

Thankfully, Jana had little chance to do that. I spent the meal in agitation, afraid she would begin asking about my past again, afraid some truth would slip out and contradict what I'd told Tony. But the meal was finished amidst a din of small talk and soon after dinner Jana left for her elegant hotel in Boston.

"I'm sorry I can't stay and get to know you better Heaven, but I've never been comfortable staying here at Farthy"—here she cast an accusing glare at Jillian —"and I must get back to Texas tomorrow. Perhaps you'll come and visit me sometime." And before she left she gave me a kiss on each cheek, making me feel that at least one female in the family had accepted me.

Early the next morning, Tony tucked me into his most impressive limo, covered my legs snugly with a heavy fur rug, and we were off to Tatterton Toy Company for the official starting day of the Christmas season.

I was stunned at the size of the store. Six floors of nothing but toys! It wasn't yet ten o'clock, and hordes of warmly dressed people crowded outside, staring into the display windows. Tony had a commanding way of pushing through the crowds until he and I were next to the steamy glass, our noses cold from staring in. Every window had a different theme, and I could have cried for the one with Tiny Tim without a goose, until the door popped open and Scrooge was there.

The display windows impressed me so much I was breathless, like a child caught in a dream of riches. The salespeople were dressed in red, black, and white uniforms with lots of gold embellishments. To my surprise, even those who didn't look wealthy did their share of buying as well. "You can't tell a person's worth by their clothes anymore," said Tony. "Besides, everyone is collectible-conscious today."

It wasn't until we reached the sixth floor that I spied the special glass and gold case containing the Tatterton Toy Portrait Dolls.

I gave each young girl there extremely critical attention, before I asked Tony: "Who makes the portrait doll?"

"Oh," he answered casually, "aren't they beautiful? We look the world over for young girls with special qualities, and then our best artisans make a portrait doll of them. It takes many months."

"Was my mother of the type original dolls are modeled from?"

Tony smiled before he turned his head my way. "She was the most beautiful girl I've ever seen— except for you. But she was a modest, shy girl, who didn't want to pose, so I lost my chance to immortalize Leigh . . ."

"You mean there never was a portrait doll of my mother?" Deep in my heart I felt waves of dread. Why wasn't he telling me the truth?

"Not that I know of," he answered blandly, then directed me to the other toy attractions he wanted me to see.

He tugged me off to show me historical dolls in authentic costumes. "Are you sure a portrait doll was not made of my mother, without your authorization?"

"Nobody does anything without my authorization. Now, please, Heaven, drop the subject. It's a sore one with me."

Why was he looking like that? Why, as if what happened or didn't happen yesterday had nothing at all to do with today—when it did, it did!

In my mind, the most important events had happened long before I was born, to create my life, to shape my world, to give me endless questions to ask that no one wanted to answer.

After Tony finished showing me the store, he went to his office, and I stayed on in Boston to do my own Christmas shopping. What a thrill to do Christmas shopping, to have money to buy whatever presents I wanted to give those I loved. How exciting to walk in the crowds past gaily decorated shops and know that I could enter them without shame. I no longer had to look longingly in windows, dreaming of possessions I could never afford; now I could afford so many things.

Week by week I was growing richer. Tony was depositing money in a checking account that he'd opened for me. And he gave me a very generous allowance. I lived thriftily and put away what I could in a savings account that drew interest. On rare occasions Jillian would hand me twenty-dollar bills as if they were pennies. "Oh, don't be so damned grateful!" she yelled when I thanked her perhaps too enthusiastically, "It's only money!"

The savings account was meant for that wonderful day when I had my family back together again; I spent very little on myself. When I shopped that year, I shopped for all of us, as if we were back together. A beautiful white cableknit sweater for Tom, along with a fine camera and dozens of rolls of film so he could have a friend take pictures of him that he could mail to me. It was easy to find the kind of heavy wool jacket he'd so longed for when we lived in the Willies, and trudging back and forth to school had been a real struggle when neither your feet or any other part of your body was warm. A coat just like the one Logan used to wear, genuine leather and fleece-lined. I wanted to give him everything he'd ever wanted. I shopped for Fanny, though I didn't know where to send my gifts. I put them in the bottom dresser drawer along with all that I'd bought for Keith and Our Jane, promising myself I'd have the joy of seeing them open my gifts someday . . . someday.

Troy and I met early Christmas morning in his cottage, long before Jillian and Tony were up. He had his breakfast all ready, the tree we had trimmed together, and the gifts we had for each other stacked beneath. "Come in, Merry Christmas! Don't you look lovely with roses in your cheeks. I was so afraid you'd be late. I've made us the most delicious Swedish Christmas bread."

Later, we opened our gifts like two young children. Troy gave me a blue cashmere sweater that matched my eyes perfectly. I gave him a rich brown leather diary, tooled with gold. "What in the world is this? A diary for me to record my most ridiculous or remarkable words?"

He was joking, I was dead serious. "I want you to write in it, beginning the first time you heard about Jillian from Tony. Everything they told you about my mother before they were married. How she felt about her father, about the divorce. Write about the first time you saw her, what she said to you, and what you said to her. Recall what she wore, your first impressions."

His expression seemed strange as he nodded and accepted the book from me. "All right, I'll do my best. However, you have to keep remembering I was only three—are you listening, Heaven, only three. She was twelve."

"Tony told me you were always older than your age when it came to intelligence, and younger than your age when it came to being left alone."

I had other gifts for him that pleased him more. What he gave to me I cherished more than anything Jillian and Tony put under one of the huge Christmas trees placed before every front window in Farthinggale Manor.

Jillian, Tony, and I went out to a fancy Christmas

party at one of their friends' houses. It was the first time they'd ever taken me anywhere with them, but somehow that wasn't enough to keep me from feeling miserably lonely that day, and the rest of the week until New Year's and the week after when I returned to school again. Tony went off to work every day, and almost every night he and Jillian went out together. Jillian was scarcely to be seen during the day; and when, on occasion, I'd see her in the music room playing solitaire, she no longer invited me to share a card game with her. Ever since Tony had publicly announced on Thanksgiving that I was to be a permanent resident at Farthy, Jillian had retreated from me totally. To her I was a resident, not a member of the family.

Jillian seemed pleased that I kept so busy I had little time to share her lifestyle, which included one social or charity affair after another. And all the togetherness I had believed once she and I would share faded with the realization we would never be close. She was not going to love me, or let herself grow attached so she might miss me later on. Oh, I knew her now, only too well.

I sneaked over to visit Troy as often as I could—which wasn't that often, since I had the feeling that even though I didn't see her, Jillian was quite aware of exactly where I was. I also went into Boston frequently to go to the library and to the museums. A few times I went by The Red Feather and B.U. hoping to "accidentally" run into Logan, but I didn't once see him. Perhaps he'd returned to Winnerrow for the holidays. And that's when the tears would start to come. For Logan hadn't even sent me a Christmas card, neither had anyone in my family. Sometimes I felt that Farthinggale Manor was as impoverished as the Willies—only in a different way. For here there was a dearth of love, and caring, and sharing, and joy. Even in our rickety cabin we'd known those things. Here all that was given was money, and, much as I longed for it, I was beginning to crave love and affection even more.

February arrived with my eighteenth birthday, which Tony and Jillian still believed was my seventeenth. Tony arranged everything for that birthday party given in my honor. "Invite all those snobby Winterhaven girls and we'll knock their eyes out." And, finally, all the Winterhaven girls had their chance to gawk at the splendors of Farthinggale Manor. The lavish food spread on a table took my breath away. The gifts given to me that year left me even more breathless, and feeling strangely guilty. For how was the rest of my family faring?

The success of that party impressed those silly girls so much, I was finally accepted as good enough to be treated decently.

In early March such a terrible storm blew in I was trapped at home the Monday I was due to be driven back to Winterhaven. Tony and Jillian were out of town, giving me the perfect opportunity to use the underground tunnel that connected Farthinggale Manor to Troy's cottage. Breathlessly I arrived, having run all the scary, dim way, making a great bit of noise as I climbed his cellar stairs, just to tell him I was coming up. Busy, as always, still he seemed to be expecting my visit, lifting his head from his work to smile my way, "Glad you're here. You can keep an eye on the bread in the oven until I finish what I've started."

Later, he and I settled down before a log fire, and I handed him one of his own books of poems. "Please read them to me." He didn't want to, and tried to put the book away, but I kept insisting. Relenting, he read. I heard the emotions in his voice, heard the sadness, and I wanted to cry. I didn't know much about poetry, but he did string words together in unique and beautiful ways. I told him this.

"That's the trouble with all my poems," he responded with unfamiliar impatience. He tossed the slender volume away. "Everything I write is too sweet and too pretty . . ."

"Not sweet," I objected, jumping up to retrieve the book. "But I don't understand what you're trying to say. I feel an undercurrent of something morbid and dark in all your words, though you put them together beautifully. If you won't tell me what your poems mean, let me have this book to read over and over again until I understand your meaning."

"It would be smarter if you didn't try to understand." His dark eyes for a second seemed tormented. Then they brightened. "It's wonderful to have you here, Heaven. I admit I hide my loneliness in work. Now I can hardly wait for you to show up." And because we were sitting side by side, very close, on impulse my head rested against his shoulder, even as my face turned, my lips more than ready for his first kiss. His pupils enlarged as I waited and waited, growing tense when he took so long. Then, sharply, he drew away, leaving me bewildered.

Feeling rejected, soon I made some flimsy excuse

about having to do my homework. Here I was losing again! I could do nothing right to please any man enough! Angry with him, even angrier with myself, I returned to Farthy to swim in the warm water of the indoor pool. Back and forth across the long pool twenty times, and still I couldn't swim my anger away. I dressed, and while my hair was still wet I read before a huge hearth with a blazing fire made just for me. Prone on the floor I stared at the open, leather-bound volume, filled with random unhappiness that wouldn't allow me to concentrate on the written words.

All about me dead ancestors of the Tattertons fixed watchful eyes on my every movement. I thought I heard their painted lips whispering that I didn't belong here, and why didn't I leave and not sully their reputations with my Casteel heritage! It was silly, I knew that, and yet the library, with its rich leather chairs, seemed hostile. And the first thing I knew, I was getting up from the floor and heading toward the stairs and the cozy familiarity of my own rooms.

Halfway down the hall in my wing I faintly heard my phone ringing. My heartbeats quickened. No one ever called me. Maybe it was Troy! Logan! Maybe . . .

Slamming the door behind me, I ran to answer before the rings stopped.

"Heaven, is it ya? Really ya?" asked a twangy country voice I knew only too well. Relief and happiness like warm wine flooded through me. "It's me, Heaven, yer sista Fanny! An ya know what, I'm a motha! Had my baby jus' two hours ago! It came early, bout three weeks, an I neva thought anythin' so normal could hurt so blessed much! I yelled an screamed an t'nurses tried t'hold me down, an Mrs.

Wise ordered me t'be quiet or t'whole world would
hear me yellin . . . but that were an easy thin' fer her
t'say when it was me who was havin her baby . . ."

"Oh, Fanny, thank God you called! I've been so
worried about you! Why didn't you call before?"

"Why I done called ya a hundred times, I have, an
nobody there understands what I say. Or who I want
t'talk ta. What's wrong with 'em? They talk funny,
like ya do now. Did ya hear me say I had a baby girl?"

What was that catch I heard in her voice? Regrets?
Sorry now she'd schemed with the Reverend and his
wife to have a baby for ten thousand dollars? "Fanny,
tell me, are you all right? Where are you?"

"Sure I'm fine, jus' fine. Weren't nothin t'it once it
were ova. An she's so t'prettiest lil ole girl with black
hair that's curly an everythin'. Got two of what she
should have, an none of what she shouldn't. An
t'Reverend is sure gonna be so happy when he sees
her . . ."

"Fanny, where are you? Please tell me! It's not too
late to change your mind. You can refuse to accept the
money and then you can keep your baby, and when
you're older you'll never have regrets for selling your
own child. Now please listen to me! I can send you the
money you need to fly to Boston. My grandfather
won't take you in, but I could put you up in a nice
rooming house, and do what I can to support you and
your baby." I was endangering my own precarious
situation, but I did it on pure instinct, alarmingly
homesick to see Fanny again.

For a moment or so her deep silence on the other
end made me think she was giving my alternative
serious thought, and then came her decision. "Tom
done tole me bout where ya'll live. An iffen yer gonna

invite me an my baby t'come an t'stay, ya gotta invite me t'where ya live in a house big as a palace! Wid more bathrooms than ya kin count! Don't ya go insultin' me an my baby with no roomin' house, or motel room! Not when I'm jus' as good as ya are . . ."

"Fanny, be reasonable. I wrote and told Tom that my grandparents have eccentric ideas. Why, Jillian doesn't even want anyone to know that I am her granddaughter!"

"She mus' be crazy!" came Fanny's loud and instant decision. "Nobody so ole kin look so young as ya tole Tom . . . now ya go on an invite me, Heaven! Crazy people like her won't know no difference! Iffen ya don't, I'm sellin' my baby an takin' off fer Nashville or New York City!"

At that moment I heard the deep, sonorous rumble of the Reverend Wayland Wise's voice as he came into the hospital room and greeted Fanny. And so help me God, Fanny slammed the receiver down and didn't even say goodbye!

I was left with the dial tone, realizing she hadn't given me her address. Still she had mine, and my phone number.

Fanny, oh Fanny. She was doing the same thing Pa had done—selling her own child. Oh, how could she do it! Even though Fanny was capable of being a selfish and heartless girl, I knew she'd regret selling her little baby. I just knew it. And I also knew that I could help her. I had money now, and I could find a way to support her and the baby, to buy it back from the Wises. But I couldn't invite Fanny here to live. If I did, I'd be tossed out myself, and I would lose all I had gained. For I'd learned that I had been accepted at Radcliffe, and Tony had already promised that I could count on him to put me through school, and I could stay at Farthinggale Manor or live on campus, whichever I prefered. Could I give all that up for Fanny? No, I couldn't. For Fanny was a confused girl, I rationalized, and it would take her a while to realize what she was doing was wrong. When she did, she would come to me for help. I knew that as surely as I knew it was snowing. And with a certain amount of relief to know that Fanny had come through her first delivery safely, and that someday she would come to me and I would help her to get her child back, I read until it was time to go to bed.

Sleep was a hard-won prize this night. I was an aunt! I wished I dared to call Tom this second, and tell him Fanny's news. But Pa might be the one to pick up the telephone.

The very next day I telephoned Tom, risking the chance my father would answer. "Hi," said my brother's voice, making me sigh with relief. "Oh, good golly gosh-jeebers!" he cried when he heard my news. "It's great news to know Fanny is all right, and terrible to think she's really going to sell her very own baby! It's like history repeating itself. But you can't risk your future for her, Heavenly, you just can't! You keep your mouth shut about Fanny and the rest of us. We'll see you again, all of us, even Keith and Our Jane, now that you have set those lawyers on their trail."

In late March the blustery cold winter began to abate. The snow melted and hints of spring made me nostalgic for the Willies.

Tom wrote to tell me to forget the hills, and the way it used to be. "Forgive Pa, Heavenly, please do. He's different now, like another man. And his wife has given him the look-alike, dark-haired son that Ma wanted, and didn't get."

In April, for the first time, I could open a window and listen to the sound of the pounding surf without feeling nervous.

Logan had not even made an effort to contact me, and day by day he was turning into only a memory, and it hurt, really hurt when I stopped to give his indifference more than a skipping thought. I had no desire to find a new boyfriend, and I declined most of the dates offered me. Once in a while I'd go out to the movies or out to dinner with a boy, but inevitably, as soon as he learned that he couldn't get past "first base," he gave up on me. I just didn't want to set myself up to be hurt again. Later, later, I would worry about love and romance; now I was content to concentrate on my educational goals.

The one man I did see a lot of, and the one man who was replacing Logan in my heart, was the one man I was supposed to stay away from—Troy Tatterton. At least once a week, when Tony and Jillian were out, I'd sneak over and spend hours talking to him. It was such a joy to have someone to talk to, someone who really cared about me and knew the truth of who I was.

I wanted in the worst way to talk to Tony about Troy, but it was a dangerous topic that brought immediate suspicion to Tony's eyes.

"I hope to God you are heeding my warning and staying away from my brother. He'll never make any woman happy."

"Why do you say that? Don't you love him?"

"Love him? Troy has always been my biggest

responsibility, and the most important person in my
life. But he isn't easy to understand. He has a
touching vulnerability that draws women to him, as if
they realize his kind of sensitivity is rare in such a
handsome and talented young man. But he's not like
other men, Heaven, you remember that. All his life
he's been restless, searching for something that is
always out of reach."

"What is it he's searching for?"

Tony gave up trying to read his morning newspaper
and frowned. "Let's be done with this conversation
that goes nowhere. When the time is ripe, I'll see to it
that you find the right young man."

I resented his saying that. I'd find my own right
young man! I resented anything he said that was
critical of his brother, when I found Troy so admirable. And what woman wouldn't be delighted to have a
man with so many homemaking abilities? Lucky,
lucky would be the girl who married Troy Tatterton.
The wonder of it all was he didn't even have a
girlfriend.

One day in May, while I was dressing after gym
class, and all about me girls were showering, or
changing clothes as I was, and talking incessantly, a
red-haired girl named Clancey poked her head into
my dressing cubicle.

"Hey, Heaven, wasn't your mother really Jillian
Tatterton's daughter by her first husband? Everybody's talking about how you go around telling people
she's your aunt, when all of Boston knows you can't
be. It makes us wonder if the whispered rumors can't
be true."

"What whispered rumors?" I asked nervously.

"Why, my mother heard Leigh VanVoreen married a Mexican bandit . . ." Mockingly she jabbed at the girl who was her best friend, who had come to join her.

The entire dressing area hushed as all the girls turned off shower water and waited for my answer. I knew then that this attack had been planned to take me by surprise. I felt cornered and trapped by their hostile silence. And they had been so friendly after my birthday party.

However, by this time I had learned a few tricks from my encounters with Tony; the best defense was to be on the offense, or to be completely and indifferently flippant.

"Yes, your mother heard right," I admitted, adjusting the bow on my white blouse before I gave everyone what I hoped was a charming and confident smile. "I was born in the middle of the Rio Grande. Just beyond the American line by a foot or so." I raised my voice deliberately, as if to buck them off my back all at the same time. "And at the age of five my father taught me to shoot grapes from his lips, and the seeds from his fingertips," and there I'd gone and used one of Tom's favorite hill-bragging boasts.

No one said a word, not a word. And in the silence, I slipped my feet into my shoes and walked out, slamming the door behind me.

Soon preparations for graduation took precedence over all other Winterhaven activities. At last, at last, I was well on my way toward college and self-respect. In the worst way I wanted Tony and Jillian to come to my graduation, to hear my name called as an honor-roll student.

Jillian frowned when she read the thick, white invitation. "Oh, you should have told me sooner, Heaven. I promised Tony I'd go with him to London that week."

Disappointment almost put tears in my eyes. Not once had she made the least effort to share my life. I turned my head to plead mutely with Tony. "I'm sorry, dear," he said with softness, "but my wife is right. You should have prepared us well in advance of the date of your graduation. I thought it was in the middle of June, not the first week of June."

"They moved the date forward," I whispered in a choked voice. "Can't you postpone your trip?"

"This is a business trip, and an important one. But trust me to make up for our negligence in more ways than just gifts."

Naturally, as I'd already found out, making money came before obligations to family. "You'll be all right," said Tony with confidence. "You are a survivor just like me, and I'll see that you have whatever you need."

I needed family, someone in the auditorium to see me accept that certificate! But I refused to plead more.

At my first opportunity after learning that Jillian and Tony would be away on one of the most important days of my life, I slipped over to the cottage beyond the maze. Troy was my consolation, my solace, and without reservations I blurted out my pain. "Most of the Winterhaven grads are expecting not only their parents, but their entire families— aunts, uncles, cousins, and friends."

By this time we were outside his cottage, both on

our knees weeding his flower beds. Already we'd taken care of his small vegetable plot. The work we did together reminded me of a long time ago when Granny and I had knelt side by side on the ground just like this. Only Troy had all the gardening equipment to make what we did easier, more pleasant. Our knees had soft, stain-proof pads, our hands wore gloves, and on my head Troy had put a huge straw hat so I wouldn't ruin my complexion with "too much tan."

We had grown so familiar and comfortable with each other, sometimes we hardly needed to speak, and mere thought communication made the work go twice as fast. When we were done with weeding and planting I said, "It doesn't mean I'm not terribly grateful for everything that Tony and Jillian have done for me, for I am grateful. But whenever something special happens, I feel so alone."

Troy threw me a sympathetic glance without responding.

And he could have said he'd be happy to fill at least one seat in the auditorium, but he didn't volunteer! He didn't like public places and ceremonies.

Miles drove me to Winterhaven the Friday of my graduation, and the girls flocked to stare at the new Rolls-Royce that Tony had given to Jillian for her sixty-first birthday. A beautiful white one with a cream-colored top, and a cream interior. "Yours?" asked Pru Carraway, her pale eyes wide and impressed.

"Mine to use until my aunt Jillian is home again."

Frenzy ruled that early morning when I entered Winterhaven. Girls ran about in various stages of undress, some with their hair still in curlers; not many of them lived within driving distance of home as I did. I felt resentful and slightly bitter as I watched other graduates introducing their family. Was this the way it was always going to be, my hill family thousands of miles away, present to me only in my thoughts, and my Boston family finding any excuse not to be present at my small victories? It was Jillian, of course, that I blamed.

Easily my grandmother could inundate me with her generosity, but when it came to giving me a little of herself, and her time, I could have starved. And Troy could sometimes be so absentminded after he started on a new project that dominated his thoughts. Oh, I was self-pitying that day as I put on my lovely white silk dress with wide bands of Cluny lace rimming the full skirt and puffed sleeves. The very kind of frock that Miss Marianne Deale had once told me she'd worn on her high school graduation day, and at the time she'd described it, I had mentally recovered every detail, thinking that Logan would be there to admire me.

As we forty girls lined up in an antechamber, donning our black robes and mortarboards, through the broad door that opened and closed constantly, I glimpsed the crowded auditorium flooded with bright June sunlight. It was like a dream coming true for me, after having feared so long this day would never happen, and tears wanted to flood my eyes and streak my face. *Oh, I hoped Tom had told Pa about this day!* If only I weren't alone . . .

Some of the graduating girls had ten and more relatives in the audience, the youngest ready to stomp their feet, applaud wildly, and whistle (considered in bad taste even in Winnerrow), and there would be no one to clap for me. Lunch was going to be served on the lawn under bright yellow- and white-striped umbrellas. Who would sit at my table? If I had to eat at my reserved table all by myself, I'd die again of humiliation . . . but I'd slip away unseen, and cry alone.

The coordinating director of this event gave her signal, and I, like the others, squared my shoulders, lifted my head, and with my eyes straight ahead, began the slow and measured step that would take us to our seats. In single file we paraded. I was eighth from the front girl, since we were arranged alphabetically. I saw only a blur of faces turning, none familiar, all looking for their graduate. And if he hadn't half stood, perhaps my glazed eyes would have moved right over Troy. As it was, my heart jumped in the overwhelming appreciation of his *not* forgetting, for caring enough.

I knew he hated social affairs like this. He wanted the Boston world in general to think he was off in some remote area of the world, and yet, he'd come. When finally my name was called, and I stood to make my way to the podium, it was not just Troy who rose to his feet, but an entire row of men, women, and children stood to applaud!

Later, when all the graduates were seated under bright awnings with the sun and shade making it both warm and cool, and utterly beautiful, I felt a rush of happiness such as I'd seldom known before, because Troy had come and had asked several of Tatterton Toy Company officers and their families to show up as my family. They wore such "right" clothes that the girls stared at my "hillbilly" relatives, mouths agape, eyes disbelieving.

"Please don't thank me again," said Troy when he was driving us both home late that night, after the school dance was over, and all the girls had envied me with my handsome "older man," who was also very admired and considered a real catch. "Did you really think I wouldn't come?" he admonished. "It was little enough I could do." He chuckled before he added, "I never knew a girl who needed a family more than you, so I wanted to give you a huge one. And by the way, they are all family in a way, aren't they? Some of them have grown old working for the Tattertons. They were delighted to come, couldn't you tell?"

Yes, they had been delighted to meet me. Suddenly shy, I sat silently, very happy and yet deeply disturbed by what I was feeling. I had to admit to myself that I was falling in love with Troy. Was it right that dancing with Troy seemed ten times more exciting than it had when Logan had taught me to dance? I stole a glance at his profile, and wondered what he was thinking.

"By the way," he said still alert and watching traffic, "the detective agency my attorneys hired to find your younger brother and sister think they have a clue. They've been searching to find a Washington lawyer with the first name of Lester. There are at least ten Lesters, and forty L initials within the confines of D. C., and twenty or more in Baltimore. They are also checking out the R his wife uses . . . so perhaps it won't be too long before we can find your brother and sister."

My breath came faster. Oh, to hold Our Jane again! To hug and kiss Keith! To see them before they forgot all about their sister "Hev-lee." But were they the real reason I was tingling all over? Despite myself, I moved closer to Troy so my thigh pressed against his, and his shoulder brushed mine. He seemed to stiffen before he grew silent, and then we turned off the expressway onto the road I'd first traveled with Jillian and Tony. A silver ribbon road, twisting and winding toward the high, arched black gates. Home to me now, this road and the huge house that was hidden from view until you were almost upon it.

I heard the roar of the sea, the pounding of the surf, smelled the salty brine, and with each minute, the richness of this night deepened.

"Oh, let's not say good night just because it is after one," I said, catching hold of Troy's hand when we were out of his car. "Let's walk in the gardens and talk."

Perhaps the warm, velvety night held some charm for him as well, for agreeably enough he linked my hand through the crook of his elbow. The stars seemed close enough to touch. Intoxicating perfume filled my nostrils and made me giddy. "What is it that smells so sweet?"

"The lilacs. It's summer, Heavenly, or almost."

Heavenly, he'd called me that again, just as Tom did. No one had called me that since I'd first come here almost a year ago now.

"Did you know today, after lunch, the girls were friendlier to me than ever before? Of course they wanted me to introduce you to them . . . and I wouldn't do it. But I would like to know how you've managed to stay so uninvolved with the opposite sex."

He chuckled and ducked his head shyly. "I am not gay, if that's what you want to know."

I flushed with embarrassment. "I never thought you were! But most men your age date as often as they can, if they are not already engaged or married."

Again he laughed. "I won't be twenty-four for another few months," he said lightly, "and Tony has always advised me not to rush into any commitment before I'm thirty. And, Heavenly, I've had some experience in dodging girls with matrimony in mind."

"What do you have against marriage?"

"Nothing. It's an old and honorable institution, meant for other men, not for me." And the cold, abstract way he said that forced my hand from his arm. Was he warning me to stay only a friend, become nothing more? Was it possible that no man ever was going to give me the kind of love and warmth I longed for?

And all the magic of this perfect summer night evaporated; the stars seemed to shrink away, and dark clouds slid from behind silvery ones and chased away the moon.

"It feels like rain now," said Troy, looking upward. "I used to feel when I was a child that all my expectations for happiness ahead were drowned before they even had a chance to bloom. It's very difficult to feel stepped on time after time, until finally you have to accept what can't be changed."

What did he mean? He had been born with a silver spoon in his mouth! What did he know about the kind of despair that had been mine?

He turned on his heel, crunching beneath his shoes loose gravel on the flagstone walkway, and with some effort to tactfully get away from me, from the specialness of this night, he gave me his congratulations again from ten feet away, then wished me a good night. He strode very fast toward the maze and the cottage beyond.

"Troy," I called, half running after him, "why are

you going inside? It's still early, and I'm not the least bit tired."

"Because you're young and healthy and full of dreams that I can't possibly share. Good night again, Heaven."

"Thank you for coming to my graduation," I called, deeply hurt and trembling, because it seemed I'd done something wrong and I didn't know what it was.

"The least I could do." And with those words he disappeared into the darkness. Now clouds obscured the moon, and quickly the stars disappeared, and a drop of rain fell on the tip of my nose. And here I was, long past midnight, sitting on a cold stony bench in a deserted rose garden, allowing the softly falling rain to drench my hair and ruin the prettiest dress in my closets. *It didn't matter, it didn't. I didn't need Troy, any more than I needed Logan. By myself I'd come out on top . . . by myself.*

I was eighteen years old, believing Logan was gone forever. And the need for romance was filling all my thoughts; love had to blossom for me soon, or I'd never be able to survive. *Why not me, Troy? Why not?*

Alone in the garden, quivering all over, my heart hurting, my graduation day didn't seem such a great achievement after all. It was just a step in the right direction. I had yet to prove myself in college. I had yet to manage to keep a man in love with me. I gazed down at the ruins of my white clothes that no woman in Winnerrow could ever hope to own.

Pity, that's all any man could feel for me, just pity! Cal had taken pity on me!—and ruined my chances with Logan. Logan wanted only the pleasure of bringing into my blighted and deprived existence his material blessings! Now that I wasn't deprived or blighted, his philanthropic urges were thwarted. And Troy—I understood him least of all! I had thought many times lately that I had glimpsed something more than friendship burning in his dark eyes.

What flaws stood out on me that overcame all the beauty that I saw reflected in my mirrors?

More and more I was resembling my dead mother —and Jillian—but for my hair, my betraying dark, Indian Casteel hair.

# ～ Twelve ～
## Sin and Sinners

EARLY ONE JUNE EVENING, BEFORE JILLIAN AND Tony returned from London, I heard from the music room the lilting notes of Chopin on the piano. The kind of music I'd heard only in Miss Deale's Friday music appreciation class, the kind of romantic melody that could charm and thrill me, and fill me with such longing that I was pulled to the stairs and drifted down to see Troy seated at the concert grand piano. His long, slender fingers rippled over the keyboard with such mastery I marveled that he could keep so much talent hidden from the world.

Just the sight of him touched me. The set of his shoulders, the way his head bowed over the keys, the passion and longing he put into his music, seemed to tell so much. He was here, where he had to know I'd hear. He needed me, he just didn't know it. I needed him. As I stood trembling in the archway, leaning against the frame in my nightgown and robe, I allowed the music to persuade me of so many things. He wasn't happy, nor was I. We had so much in common. From the very beginning I had liked him; he was like some fantasy man I'd created long ago, even before Logan appeared in my life. A man so sensitive he could never hurt me. Bigger than life I made Troy. Better than life, too good to be true. But he was true.

He seemed in some vague way younger than Logan, ten times more sensitive and vulnerable, like a young boy who expected to be loved on sight—so he struck out so as *not* to be loved for his looks or his wealth or his talents. And even as I thought this, Troy sensed my presence, and instantly he stopped playing and turned to shyly smile my way. "I hope I didn't waken you."

"Don't stop, please."

"I'm rusty now that I don't play every day."

"Why did you stop?"

"I don't have a piano in my cottage, as you know."

"But Tony told me this was your piano."

His smile was slight and twisted. "My brother wants to keep me away from you. Since you came I've not used this piano."

"Why does he forbid our friendship, Troy? Why?"

"Oh, let's not talk about that. Let me finish what I started, and then we'll talk."

On and on he played until I grew so weak I had to sit, and only then did I stop trembling. As he played on, I fell into a romantic reverie, pretending we were together, dancing as we had on my graduation night.

"You're sleeping!" he cried when the music ended. "Was it that bad?"

Instantly my eyelids parted. I gazed at him softly, dreamily. "I have never heard music like yours before. It scares me. Why is it you didn't play professionally?"

He shrugged indifferently. His skin through the silk of his thin white shirt glowed with heightened color. The collar was open so that I could see the faint sprinkling of dark hair on his chest. I closed my eyes again, disturbed by all the sensations I was feeling.

"I've missed your visits." His voice came to me soft and hesitating. "I know I hurt your feelings the night of your graduation, and I'm sorry, but I'm only trying to protect you."

"And yourself," I whispered bitterly. "You know I'm nothing but hillbilly trash and sooner or later I'll embarrass you and your family. I've been thinking I'd go away. I have enough money saved up now to put me through my first year of college. And if I find a job, I can work through the remaining years."

Alarmed, he said something that I couldn't quite make out, though I parted my lids enough to see his concern and alarm.

"You can't do that! Tony, Jillian, and I owe you a great deal."

"You don't owe me anything!" I stormed, jumping up. "Just leave me alone from now on, and I'll not impose on your privacy again!"

He flinched, then raked his long fingers through his mass of waving hair. His disarming, boyish smile flashed. "My music was my way of saying I'm sorry for leaving you alone in the garden. My way of confessing I've grown too fond of you not to make an effort to bring you back again. When you're not in the cottage, I seem to sense you there, and often I turn abruptly, hoping to find you, and feel such disappointment because I'm alone. So please, start coming again."

So I went back to Troy's cottage with him, and ate dinner with him there. But I was tired of always being cooped up in that cottage with him. I felt the wind of my emotions pushing out so strongly that I needed to be outside, lest I make a fool of myself. But before I left, I was determined to make sure I saw him the next day. For he was softening toward me, I could feel it. And he couldn't fight his feelings for me if we spent entire days together. I could bring sunshine and life into his melancholy life, and I was determined now to force him to accept my love.

"Troy, can't we do something outside in the fresh air for a change? In the stables are beautiful Arabian horses that only the grooms exercise when Jillian and Tony are away. Teach me how to ride a horse. Or swim with me in the pool. Share a picnic in the woods with me, but let's not stay shut up in your cottage when the weather is so beautiful. Jillian and Tony will come home soon, and we'll be forbidden each other. Let's do now what we can't do then."

Our eyes met and held. A flush of color rose from his chest to flood his face, forcing him to half turn and break the bind of our eyes. "If that's what you'd rather do. Tomorrow at ten we'll meet at the stables. You can learn on the most gentle mare there."

Almost as if I'd swallowed a powerful drug, I fell under the spell of something beyond my control. The next morning shortly before ten, I met Troy at the stables. Troy was waiting for me, wearing casual riding clothes. The wind had tousled his hair, and already the sun had put healthy color in his cheeks, and that sad little something that lingered always in the depths of his eyes wasn't there. I ran to him, delighted with the response of his immediate smile. "We are going to have the most wonderful day!" I said, giving him a quick hug before I looked eagerly toward the stables. "I just hope the grooms won't tell Tony."

"They know better than to carry tales," he answered lightly, seeming charmed by my happy excitement. "You look great, Heavenly, absolutely great."

I spun around to give him a full view, spreading my arms, and tossing my hair. "Tony gave me these riding clothes for Christmas. First time I've worn them."

For a week Troy gave me riding lessons each morning and taught me the difference between the English and Western styles. It was more fun than I'd ever expected (though I hurt each night when I sat), learning how to race with the wind, and duck the low branches, and heel into the flanks of my mount when I wanted to stop. In short order I lost my fear of the horse and its impressive height.

After my lessons each morning, we'd go back to his cottage to have lunch, and then he'd send me back to the big house, saying he had to work. I could feel him resisting spending too much time with me, yet I could tell that he really wanted to. So I avoided seeing him in the evening, hoping that he'd miss me, and long for me, and indeed, each morning he seemed so happy to see me that I was certain that someday very, very soon, he would realize he loved me.

It was a full eight days after my riding lessons began that Troy felt I was ready for a really long ride into the woods surrounding Farthinggale Manor. Time and again he kept glancing at the sky. "The early morning news predicted violent electrical storms, so we shouldn't go too far."

With us we had a picnic hamper full of what Troy had put together himself, and some special treats that

Rye Whiskey had sent over from the big house for us to enjoy.

Troy was the one who selected a sun-dappled little mound under one of the most beautiful beech trees I'd ever seen. Not so far away was a gurgling stream of water, and birds darted between the gently swaying branches above. The wonderful feel of the summer day put songs in my heart and joy in my every movement, as Troy knelt to spread the red-and-white checkered tablecloth on the grass. Our two horses were tethered not far away and contentedly munched on whatever they could eat. I heard the hum of honey bees, smelled the scent of clover, brushed tiny gnats from my face as I busied myself emptying the picnic basket. The sweetness of the day, the prettiness of the setting, lit up my eyes whenever I glanced at Troy, who couldn't move his fascinated gaze from whatever trivial move I made. I felt self-conscious as I shifted plates and plastic flatware around, and three times I moved the potato salad, the fried chicken, the sandwiches.

When finally I had everything prettily arranged, I sat back on my heels and smiled his way. "There, doesn't it look pretty? But don't dig in until I say grace, just like my granny used to say whenever Pa wasn't at home." I felt so happy today that I just had to thank someone.

He seemed bewitched. Dazed-looking, he nodded, then inclined his head slightly while I said the familiar words.

"Dear Lord, we thank you for the food before us. We thank you for the caring hands that prepared our bounty. We thank you for our many blessings and all the joys this day and all our tomorrows will bring us. Amen."

I lowered my hands, raised my bowed head, looked up, and found Troy staring at me in the most quizzical way. "Your granny's grace?"

"Yes, we didn't have blessings or bounties, but Granny never seemed to know that. She was always expecting the best would show up one day. I guess when you're not used to anything, you don't expect too much. When she said grace, I used to silently pray that God would take away her aches and pains."

He fell into silence after that, appearing thoughtful as we both ate our sumptuous picnic lunch. And I myself had made the yellow cake with thick fudge frosting in Troy's own kitchen.

"This is the best cake I've ever eaten!" He licked the chocolate from his fingers. "Another slice, please."

"Wouldn't it be nice if we could always be together like this? You and me. I could go to college, while we live in your cottage."

His dark eyes shadowed with so much pain, suddenly the sunny day went dark.

He didn't love me! He didn't need me! I was seducing him, or trying to, just as Cal Dennison had seduced me with his own needs and desires, disregarding mine. I handed him his second slice of cake, now too embarrassed even to look at him. With my head lowered so he couldn't see my suffering, I quickly cleared the tablecloth, and without washing the used plates and flatware in the stream as I'd intended doing when first I saw the water, I threw everything back into the picnic hamper in a grand heap that wouldn't allow me to close the top. Fiercely angry I shoved the basket his way.

"Here's your basket!" I choked.

His stunned expression forced me to scramble to my feet, then I ran toward my horse. "I'm going home!" I cried out childishly. "I realize you don't need anybody like me stuck permanently in your life! All you need is work, and more work! Thank you for the last ten days, and forgive me for being impulsive. I promise not to waste your time again!"

"Heavenly!" he called, "Stop! Wait . . ."

I didn't wait. Somehow I reached the saddle, not caring if I did it right or wrong. My heels dug into my mount's flanks, and she leaped forward while I was blinded by silly tears, more angry with myself than with him. I did everything wrong. My mare was made confused and uncertain. To correct my mistakes I yanked hard on the reins. Rearing upward almost vertically, the mare snorted, pawed at the air, then bolted forward, running wild and fast through the woods. Low branches came at me one after another, branches that could sweep me out of the saddle, break my neck, back, legs. With more luck than skill I managed to duck each branch. And the more I moved in the saddle, the more erratic my horse ran! My screams were like long, thin scarfs blowing behind me. Almost too late I remembered Troy's advice on how to cling to a runaway horse. I fell forward and clung to my mare's thick, brown mane. Over ravines and ditches, jumping dead trees felled by storms, my uncontrolled horse raced. Squeezing my eyes shut, I began to say her name over and over, trying to calm her.

The next thing I knew she stumbled; I was thrown

from her back straight into a shallow ditch half-full of slimy green rainwater. Scrambling to her feet, my mare whinnied, shook herself, threw me a disgusted look, and wheeled about to head for home, leaving me stunned and shaken and hurting. I was also missing my left boot. I felt a total fool as I lay sprawled on my back in the fetid water, staring up through the canopy of leaves to find the sun full in my face.

God's punishment, I sourly thought, for presuming too much! I should have known better than to fall for the first man who made my blood run fast and hot, especially after Cal, and Logan's rejection. No Casteel had ever won any prize! Why should I think I was any better!

Other stupid thoughts filled my head before I had sense enough to sit up and shake the filthy water from my hair, then used the sleeve of my shirt to clean my face of mud. Wild honey bees were attracted, perhaps by my perfume, or by the bright yellow of a once pretty blouse.

"Heaven, where are you?" I heard Troy calling from a distance.

*You're too late, Troy Tatterton! I don't want you now!* Still I began to tremble from the effort it took not to respond. I didn't want him to find me, not now. Somehow I'd make my way back to that huge, lonely house, and never again would I disobey Tony and steal over to his cottage.

So, sitting in the water, I stayed very quiet, slapping at the insects who idiotically found me attractive. Endless time passed before he stopped calling and thrashing about in the woods. The wind picked up and began to rustle the leaves above. Dark, stringy clouds converged as they always seemed to do whenever I was on the verge of finding something valuable. My rotten luck!

Oh, you bet, I felt so damned sorry for myself, even before the drizzle of rain began, I couldn't stifle my sobs.

Then a small noise came from behind me, and an amused voice. "I always wanted to save a maiden in distress."

My head swiveled around to see Troy about ten feet away. How long he'd been watching me I couldn't guess. His riding clothes were snagged in several places, and a long tear had ripped one sleeve from shoulder seam to elbow. "Why do you keep sitting there? Are you hurt?"

"Go away!" I yelled, flipping my head so he couldn't see my mud-smeared face. "No, I am not hurt! I don't need to be rescued! I don't need *you!* I don't need *anybody!*"

Without replying he stepped into the wet ditch and tried to feel my legs for broken bones. I tried to slap him away, and yet he managed to pick me up after three attempts. "Now, be serious, Heaven. Tell me if you hurt anywhere."

"No! Just put me down!"

"You're lucky you are still alive. If it had been hard ground instead of water and a soft muddy stream bottom, you might very well be seriously injured."

"I can walk. Please put me on my feet."

"All right, if that's what you want," and obeying my command, he tentatively stood me up. I cried out from the hot pain that shot through my left ankle. Instantly he seized me up in his arms again. "We've got to hurry. No time to play games. I had to dismount to follow the trail you made. No doubt from the looks of that swelling ankle, you have sprained it."

"That doesn't make me crippled! I can still walk. Many a time I've walked seven miles to Winnerrow with something hurting more than that ankle!"

Another amused grin quirked his lips. "Sure you have, a hurting stomach, not a sprained ankle."

"What do *you* know about it?"

"Only what you've told me. Now stop struggling and behave yourself. If I don't find my horse in short order, both of us are going to be caught in the storm that's coming."

Patiently his tethered mount waited while Troy lifted me up and sat me before him on the saddle. I felt mean and spiteful as he swung up to sit behind me, guiding his mount skillfully, even as he put his free arm about my waist protectively.

"It's already raining."

"I know that."

"We'll never make it back to the house before the storm strikes in full force."

"I suspect we won't. That's why I'm heading for an old abandoned barn that used to store the grains earlier Tattertons grew."

"You mean your ancestors knew how to do something besides make toys?"

"I suspect everyone's ancestors had more than one skill."

"Yours, I'm sure, had servants to do all the farming."

"You are probably right. However, it takes some talent to make the money to pay tenant farmers."

"It takes more than talent to survive in the wilderness."

"*Touché*. Now keep quiet and let me get my bearings." He brushed his wet hair from his forehead, looked around, then turned his horse eastward.

Black thunderclouds blew in from the southwest, soon followed by sizzling bolts of lightning, and despite my will to escape him, it felt good to have his arm about me, holding me secure as the barn came finally into sight.

It smelled old and sour in the dilapidated building half-full of rotting hay. In the dimness rain leaked through in a hundred places to splatter down on the dirt floor and create puddles. The roof holes allowed me to see the darkened sky now full of terrifying lightning bolts that seemed to converge directly overhead. I sank down to my knees as Troy took care of the horse, unsaddling him, rubbing him dry with the saddle blanket; then he came my way to rake with his hands at the hay until he found some that was dry and not so smelly, and on that we both sat in the damp and miserable barn.

As if there hadn't been any interruption at all, I continued in my angry way: "It's a wonder rich people like the Tattertons didn't have this barn torn down long ago."

He ignored my remark, leaned back on the mound of hay he'd created, and spoke softly. "I used to play in this barn when I was a boy. I had a make-believe friend I called Stu Johnson, and with him I'd jump from that loft over there." He pointed to show me where. "I would jump down to this haystack we are sitting on."

"What a silly and dangerous thing to do!" I stared with disbelief at the attic loft, and its great height. "You could have been killed."

"Oh, I didn't think about that. I was five at the time, and very needing of a friend, even my imaginary one. Your mother had run away and left me lonely. Jillian was crying and calling Tony long distance all the time, begging him to come home, and when he did, they fought day after day."

Breathless now that he was remembering a little about my mother, I turned toward him. "Why did my mother run away?"

Instead of replying, he sat up, took a handkerchief from his pocket, dipped it in a nearby puddle of rainwater, then began to wipe smeared mud from my face. "I don't know," he said, leaning to touch the tip of my nose with his lips. "I was too young to realize what was going on." He kissed my right cheek, then my left one, his breath warm and exciting on my face and neck as he kissed and talked. "I only knew that when your mother left, she promised to write me. She said she'd come back one day when I was grown up."

"She told you that?"

His soft kiss found my lips. A number of times Logan had kissed me, and not once had I felt as aroused by his clumsy, boyish approaches as I did by a man who obviously knew exactly what to do to make my skin tingle. When I should have known better, I responded much too quickly, then jerked away. "You don't have to take pity on me and make up lies."

"I would never lie to you about something so important." Both his hands cupped my head so he could tip it at an angle that suited him, and his next kiss on my lips was more intense. I could hardly breathe. "The more I think back, the more I remember how much I loved your mother."

Gently he eased me back on the hill of hay, holding me close to his chest, as my arms rose automatically to encircle him. "Go on. Tell me more."

"Not now, Heaven, not now. Just let me hold you until the storm is over. Let me think more about what's happening between us. I have held back from loving you. I don't want to be just another man who hurts you."

"I'm not afraid."

"You're only eighteen. I'm twenty-three."

I couldn't believe what I said next. "Jessie Shackleton was seventy-five when he married Lettie Joyner who lived ten miles outside the Willies, and she gave him three sons and two daughters before he died at age ninety."

He groaned and buried his face in my wet hair. "Don't tell me anything more. We both need to think before it's too late to stop what's already begun."

Wonder filled me. He did love me! It was in his voice, in the way he held me and tried to warn me.

With the pounding of the rain overhead, with streams of water slipping through the holes in the roof, while the thunder crashed and the lightning crackled, we lay wrapped in each other's arms without speaking, our hands caressing, our lips meeting from time to time, and it was sweeter than anything I'd known before.

He could have claimed me then and there, and I wouldn't have resisted, but he held back, making my love for him grow even more.

The rain lasted for an hour. Then he put me on his

horse, and slowly we rode toward that huge house whose chimneys and towers we could see over the treetops. On the steps before the side door, he drew me into his arms again. "Isn't it odd, Heavenly, how you came into my life when I didn't need or want you, and now I can't imagine life without you."

"Then don't. I love you, Troy. Don't try to put me out of your life just because you think I'm too young. I'm not too young. Nobody my age in the hills is considered young."

"Those hills of yours are awe-inspiring, but I can't marry, not you, not anyone."

What he said made my heart hurt.

"Then you don't love me?"

"I didn't say that."

"You don't have to marry me if you don't want to. Just love me long enough to make me feel good about myself." Quickly I rose on my toes to press my lips on his, as my fingers curled into his damp hair.

His arms tightened about me while I thought of all the women who must have filled his arms before. Rich, wild, beautiful, sophisticated women! Women of charm, brains, culture. Bejeweled, fashionable, witty, self-assured—what chance did a hillbilly Casteel have of capturing such a man as Troy, when they had failed?

"I'll see you tomorrow," he said, breaking away, and backing off down the steps. "That is, if Jillian and Tony don't return. I don't know what's keeping them away for so long."

I didn't know either, but it was good not to have to be so furtive about meeting Troy. And the more I thought about that, after I was in bed, the more restless I became. I wanted to be with Troy now. I didn't want to wait any longer. Silently I willed him to come to me, come to me now.

For endless hours I dwelled fitfully on the rim of sleep, never finding the peaceful oblivion I desperately sought. From one side to another I flipped, trying my back, my stomach. Then, suddenly I heard my name called. I bolted wide awake to stare at the electric clock on my nightstand. Two o'clock—that's all the time that had passed? I got up to pull on a frail, green peignoir that matched my nightgown, then went down the upstairs hall to the stairs, and without design, I found myself in the maze, barefooted. The grass was damp and cool. What I was doing here I didn't want to analyze.

The electrical storm had washed the atmosphere to such clarity moonlight lit up the darkness. The tall hedges with their millions of leaves snagged tiny bits of starlight so they sparkled. Then I was there, hesitating before his closed blue door, wishing I had the nerve to knock, or to open the door and go in. Or the will to turn around and go back where I belonged. I bowed my head until my forehead pressed against the wood, then closed my eyes, beginning to softly cry as all the strength went out of my body and I sagged limply. At that moment the door opened, causing me to fall forward. Directly into Troy's arms.

He didn't say a word as he caught me, then swung me up into his arms and carried me into his bedroom.

Light from the moon fell across his face as he lowered his head to mine, and this time his lips were more demanding. His kisses, his hands put me on fire, so it happened between us so naturally and beautifully, I didn't feel any of the guilt and shame that Cal Dennison's lovemaking had caused. We came together as if we had to, or die, and when it was over, I lay in the circle of his arms quivering with the fading spasms of the first orgasm of my life.

When we wakened it was dawn, and through his open windows the morning wind blew damp and cold. The sweet morning chirpings of the sleepy birds brought tears to my eyes, before I sat up to reach for the blanket folded on the foot of the bed. Quickly Troy's arms pulled me back. Tenderly he plied small kisses over my face as his free hand stroked my hair before he cradled me against him. "Last night I lay here on my bed thinking about you."

"I had a hard time falling asleep . . ."

"So did I."

"Just when I was about to sleep, I bolted wide awake and I thought I heard you calling me."

He made a noise deep in his throat, holding me tighter against his warm body. "I was on my way to you when you fell through the door, just like a prayer answered, and yet, I shouldn't have allowed this to happen. I'm so afraid you're going to be sorry. I never want to hurt you."

"You could never hurt me, not ever! I have never met a man so gentle and kind."

His chuckle was low. "How many men have you known at the tender age of eighteen?"

"Only the one I told you about," I whispered, hiding my face when he wanted to gaze into my eyes.

"Will you tell me more about him?"

He listened without asking questions, his slender hands caressing me all the while, and when my words died, he kissed my lips, each one of my fingertips. "Have you heard from this Cal Dennison since you came to live in Farthy?"

"I never want to hear from him, not ever!"
How vehemently I cried that!

We were silly during our first meal of the day, acting like two adolescent kids just finding each other. I had never eaten a fried egg and bacon sandwich before, or known that strawberry jam enhanced the flavor of both egg and bacon. "It was pure serendipity how I discovered this gourmet treat," he went on to explain. "I was about seven years old and recovering from another of those childhood diseases that used to plague me, and Jillian was scolding me for being messy at the table, when I dropped my toast with strawberry jam face down into my plate. 'You eat it anyway!' she yelled, and when I did, I found out for the first time that I liked eggs and bacon . . ."

"Jillian used to yell at you?" Astonishment filled me. I had believed a great deal of her grouchiness with me was because she was resentful of having a younger female around.

"Jillian has never liked me . . . listen . . . it's thundering again. The weatherman predicted a week of storms, remember?"

I heard the faint pitter-patter of rain on the roof. Soon Troy was building a fire to chase away the morning chill and damp, and I was sprawled on the floor watching him. It amused me the way he even stacked kindling with such precision. However, it delighted me to watch him when he was relaxed. How wonderful that the weather would enclose us in his cottage.

The fire burned hot, bright. The stretch of silence between us began to palpitate with sensuality. The play of the orange firelight on the hard planes of his face sent tingles through my body. I saw him watching me as I watched him, studying my face when I was staring at his hands . . . and then he moved to prop himself up on his elbow, and his face was very close. He was going to make love to me again. My pulse quickened.

Instead of kisses he gave me words.

Instead of his arms wrapping about me, he fell back to tuck his hands behind his head again, his favorite position. "Do you know what I think about when it's summer? I think soon it will be autumn, and all the brightest, prettiest summer birds will fly away, leaving the darkest and drabbest ones to stay. I hate the days when they grow short. I don't sleep well during the long winter nights; somehow the cold seems to creep through the walls and into my bones and I toss and turn and flit in and out of bad dreams. I dream too much in the winter. Summer is the time for sweet dreams. Even with you here beside me, I feel you are a dream."

"Troy . . ." I protested, turning toward him.

"No, please allow me to talk. I seldom have anyone who listens as attentively as you do, and I want you to know more about me. Will you listen?"

I nodded, somehow scared by his serious tone of voice.

"Winter nights for me are too long. Giving time for too many dreams to be born. I try and hold back sleep until just before dawn, sometimes I succeed. If I don't, I grow so restless I have to get up and dress. Then I walk outside and let the fresh cold air wash my dreary thoughts away. I walk the trails between the pines, and when my brain is cleared, only then do I come back here. And in work I can forget the coming night and the nightmares that haunt me."

I could only stare at him. "No wonder you kept shadows beneath your eyes last winter," I said, distressed that he could now be so melancholy. *He had me now.* "I used to think you were a workaholic."

Troy rolled on his side, facing the fire, reaching a long arm for a bottle of champagne he'd put in a silver bucket to chill. He poured the bubbling vintage into two crystal goblets. "The last bottle of the best of the wine," he said, turning again toward me, and lifting his glass so it brushed lightly against mine.

I had grown used to champagne during the past winter, since it appeared so often on Jillian's party tables, but I was still child enough to feel giddy after one glass. Uneasily I sipped my champagne, wondering why his eyes kept avoiding mine. "What do you mean, the last of the wine? You've got a wine cellar beneath this house with enough champagne for the next half-century."

"So literal," he said. "I spoke poetically. Trying to tell you that winter and cold bring out the morbid side I try to hide most of the time. I care too much about you to let you become too entangled in our relationship, without understanding just who and what I am."

"I know who and what you are!"

"No you don't. You know only what I've permitted you to see." His dark eyes swung my way, commanding me not to question. "Listen, Heaven, I'm trying to warn you while you can still pull away."

My lips parted to speak and object, but he reached to hush me with his fingers put over my lips.

"Why do you think Tony ordered you to stay away

from me? I find it very difficult to hang on to the cheerful, optimistic side of me that blossoms only when the days grow long, and the warmth returns."

"We can always move south!" I cried, hating his seriousness, the shadowed look in his eyes.

"I've tried that. I've spent winters in Florida, in Naples, Italy, all over the world I've traveled trying to find what others find so easily, but I take my winter thoughts with me." He smiled, but I wasn't comforted. He wasn't joking, though his tone tried to be light. There was a darkness deep as a bottomless pit behind each of his pupils.

"But the spring always returns, followed by the summer," I said quickly, "that's what I used to keep telling myself when we were cold and hungry and the snow was six feet high and it was seven miles to Winnerrow."

His soft, dark eyes caressed me and flooded warmth into my face. He poured more champagne into my glass. "I wish I could have known you then, and Tom, and the others. You could have given me so much of the kind of strength you have."

"Troy! Stop talking like that!" I flared, frightened because I didn't understand his mood and angry because he should be kissing me now, taking off my clothes, not talking. "What are you trying to tell me? That you don't love me? That you're regretting you've made me love you? Well, I'm not sorry about anything. I'll never be sorry you gave me at least one night with you! And if you think you can scare me off, you are quite wrong. I'm in your life, Troy, deep into your life. And if the winter makes you sad and morbid, then together we'll follow the sun, and all during those nights my arms will hold you so fast you'll never have another nightmare!"

But even as I passionately reached for him, my heart teetered on the edge of a precipice, ready to plunge and die if he rejected me!

"I don't want to hear anymore!" I cried before my lips pressed down on his. "Not now, please not now!"

# PART TWO

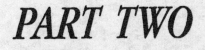

## ~ Thirteen ~
### *January in July*

SEVERAL TIMES TROY TRIED TO TELL ME HIS CHEER-less tale of winter and weakness and death. But I was protective of our joy and passion and I kissed him into silence, again and again. For three nights and two days we were ardent lovers who could not bear to be parted for more than a few minutes at a time. We didn't go beyond the gardens that surrounded Farthy, didn't even risk riding through the woods anymore. We chose the safe paths for our horses, never going too far, eager to return to the cottage and the security of each other's arms. And then one early evening when the rain had moved off to sea and the sun finally showed again on the horizon, Troy again held me on the floor in front of his fire. This time he was very insistent.

"You have to listen. Don't try to put me off again. I don't want to ruin your life just because there's a shadow over mine."

"Will your story ruin what we have now?"

V.C. ANDREWS

"I don't know. That will be your decision."

"And you are willing to risk losing me?"

"No, I hope never to lose you, but if I have to, I will."

"No!" I cried, jumping up and racing for his doorway. "Let me have all of this summer without thought of winter!"

Out of his cottage, and into the maze I walked, through the chill evening mists that were gathering in the tight lanes of the hedges. To my great consternation, I almost dashed headlong and heedless into the small group that was before the front steps of Farthinggale Manor, unloading Tony's long black limousine.

Jillian and Tony were back! Quickly I ducked again into the maze. I didn't want them to see me now, coming back from Troy's cottage.

As the chauffeur carried in the luggage, I heard Tony rebuke Jillian for not having notified me. "You mean you didn't call Heaven yesterday as you promised?"

"Really, Tony, I thought about it several times, but there were interruptions, and she'll be more surprised and thrilled if we return unexpectedly. I know at her age, I'd have been delighted to receive all the nice things we've brought her from London."

As soon as they disappeared into the house, I ran to the side door and up the back stairs to my rooms, and once there, I hurled myself down on the bed and broke into a torrent of tears, tears that I quickly dried when Tony knocked on my door and called my name.

"We're home, Heaven. May I come in?"

In a way I was very glad to see him again, he was so

236

smiling and animated as he plied me with questions as
to what I'd been doing, and how I had managed to
keep myself happy, occupied, and entertained.

Oh, the lies I told should make Granny flip over in
her grave. Behind my back I kept my fingers crossed.
He asked about my graduation ceremony, said again
he was very sorry he had had to miss it. He quizzed
me about the parties I'd attended, whom I'd seen, and
had I met any young men? And not once did he look
suspicious as the lies rolled from my tongue. Why
didn't he suspect it was Troy I'd find most convenient?
Had he forgotten all the rules he'd laid out for me to
obey?

"Good," he said, "I'm glad you enjoyed summer
television fare. I find TV a bore, but then, I didn't
grow up in the Willies." He gave me a broad smile of
great charm, even if it did appear mocking. "I hope
you found time to read a few good books."

"I always find time to read."

His blue eyes narrowed as he leaned to hug me
briefly before he turned again toward the door. "Before dinner Jillian and I want to give you all the gifts
we very carefully selected for you. Now, how about
washing the tear stains from your face before you
change your clothes for the evening."

I hadn't fooled him, only deluded myself into
believing he wasn't as discerning as before.

Still, when I was in the library, and Jillian was
wearing a long hostess gown, smiling at me as I
opened my gifts from London, he didn't ask what had
made me cry. "Do you like everything?" asked Jillian, who had given me clothes, clothes, and more
clothes. "The sweaters will fit, won't they?"

"Everything is beautiful, and yes, the sweaters will fit."

"And what about my gifts?" questioned Tony. He had given me extravagant costume jewelry, and a heavy box that was lined with blue velvet. "They don't make toilet items today like they did in the Victorian era. That dresser set you have is antique and very valuable."

On my lap I carefully held the tapestry box with a heavy silver hand mirror, a hair brush, a comb, two crystal powder boxes with ornate silver tops, and two perfume bottles that matched the set. Staring down at them I was taken back in time to when I'd first opened my mother's suitcase at the age of ten. Upstairs, hidden deep in one of my closets was the old suitcase that my mother had carried with her into the Willies, and inside it, another silver dressing set, though not as complete as the silver set I held.

I felt suddenly helpless, snared in a time warp. Surely Tony had noticed the dresser set that Jillian had already given me. I didn't need another. The most peculiar thought came to my mind, for at that very moment I realized how very unfair it was of me not to listen to what Troy had to say. Unfair to him, and to myself.

Late that very night, long after dinner was over and Jillian and Tony had retired, I stole back through the maze to the cottage, to find Troy moodily pacing his living room floor. His welcoming smile shone bright and immediate, lifting my heart. "They're back," I informed breathlessly, closing the door and leaning against it. "You should see all the things they brought me. I have enough clothes for a dozen college girls."

He didn't appear to listen to what I said, only appeared to hear what I left unsaid. "Why do you look so disturbed?" he asked, holding out his arms so I could run into them.

"Troy, I'm ready to listen to what you have to say, no matter what it is."

"What did Tony say to you?"

"Nothing. He asked a few questions about how I'd spent my time while he and Jillian were gone, but he didn't mention you. I found it strange that he didn't ask where you were, and if we had met. It was almost as if you didn't exist, and it scared me."

He pressed his forehead to mine briefly, then pulled away, his expression totally unrevealing, and now that I was more than ready to hear him out, he seemed reluctant to begin. With gentleness rather than passion he kissed me and touched my hair. He traced his forefinger over my cheek, and then, holding me close he turned toward his huge picture window that overlooked the sea. His arm slipped around my waist so he could draw my back tight against his front. "Don't ask questions until I've had my say. Listen with an open mind, for I'm serious."

As he began to talk I sensed every molecule of his being was striving to reach out and force me to understand even what he himself must have found inexplicable.

"It's not that I don't love you, Heavenly, that I kept persisting in saying what I have to. I love you very much. It's not that I'm trying to find an excuse not to marry you, it's only my frail attempt to help you find a way to save yourself."

I didn't understand, and yet by this time I knew I

had to be patient and give him his chance to do what he considered "the right thing."

"You have the kind of character and strength that I both admire and envy. You are a survivor, and everything that has ever happened to me tells me I am not. Now don't tremble. Lifestyles shape and mold us when we're youthful, and I know for a fact that you and your brother Tom will prove to be made of much hardier stuff than I." Turning me toward him, he gazed down at me with his eyes deep, dark, and desperate.

I bit down on my tongue to keep from asking questions. It was still summer; autumn hadn't even tinged the trees with deep green. Winter seemed a lifetime away. *I'm here, You'll never have a lonely night again if you don't want it*—but I said none of this.

"Let me tell you about my boyhood," he continued. "My mother died shortly before my first birthday. Before I was two years old my father died, so the only parent I can remember in my life was my brother Tony. He was my world, my everything. I adored him. For me, the sun set when Tony went out the door, and rose when he came in again. I thought of him as a golden god, able to deliver anything I wanted, if I wanted it badly enough. He was seventeen years older, and even before my father died, he'd assumed the responsibility of seeing to it that I stayed happy. I was a sickly child from the very beginning. Tony has told me my mother had a very difficult labor giving birth to me. Always I was on the verge of expiring from one thing or another, giving Tony so many anxious moments he'd come into my room at night just to check and see if I was still breathing. When I was in the hospital he visited three or four times a day, bringing me treats to eat and toys and games and books, and by the time I was three, I thought I owned every second of his life. He was mine. We didn't need anyone else. And then came that horrible day when he found Jillian VanVoreen. At the time I knew nothing about her. He kept her a big secret from me. When finally he told me he was going to marry Jillian, he made it seem he was doing it only so I'd have a new and loving mother. And also a sister. I was both thrilled and angry. A child of three can feel very possessive of the only caring person in his life. I was jealous. He's told me since, laughingly, that I threw temper tantrums. For I didn't want Tony to marry Jillian, especially after she met me. I was sick and in bed, and he thought she'd be touched by such a frail and handsome little boy who would really need her. He didn't see what I saw. Children seem to have some special insight into adult minds. I knew she was appalled by the idea of taking care of me . . . and yet, she went through with her divorce and married Tony, and she moved into Farthy with her twelve-year-old daughter. Very vaguely I can remember the wedding, no details, just impressions.

"I was unhappy, and so was your mother. I have other impressions of Leigh trying to be a sister to me, and spending a great deal of her free time at my bedside trying to keep me entertained. However, what embedded itself deepest in my brain was Jillian's obvious resentment of every moment that Tony dedicated to me, and not to her."

For an hour he talked, making me see it all; the loneliness of a small boy and a young girl, thrown together by circumstances beyond their control, so they grew to need each other, and then one day something dreadful happened that he never understood, and the new sister he'd grown to love ran away.

"Tony was in Europe when Leigh ran from here. He came flying back in response to Jillian's desperate calls. I know they hired detective agencies to try and find her, but Leigh disappeared as if from the face of the earth. They both expected her to show up in Texas where her grandmother and aunts lived. She never showed up. Jillian cried all the time, and I know now that Tony blamed her for your mother's disappearance. I knew Leigh had died long before you came here with your news. I knew it the very day it happened, for I dreamed it, and you have only confirmed that my dream was true. My dreams always come true.

"After Leigh left, I fell ill with rheumatic fever and was confined to bed for almost two years. Tony ordered Jillian to give up her social activities and devote all her time to taking care of me, even though I had a British nanny named Bertie that I adored, and I'd ten times rather have been left alone with Bertie than with Jillian. Jillian frightened me with her long fingernails and quick, careless movements; I sensed her impatience with a little boy who just didn't know how to stay well.

" 'I've never been sick a day of my life,' she used to say to me. I began to get the idea that I was, indeed, a flawed and inadequate child, who was spoiling the lives of others—and that's when the dreams began. Sometimes they were wonderful, but more often they were terrifying nightmares that led me to believe I'd never really be happy, never really be healthy, never really have anything that others find easy to obtain—ordinary things that everyone expects to come about in their lives, such as having friends, dating and falling in love, and living long enough to see my own children grown. I began dreaming of my own death—my own death as a young man. And as I grew older and began school, I pulled away from those who made attempts to befriend me, afraid in the end I'd be hurt if ever I made myself too vulnerable. Alone and different I heard my own drummer, made up my own music, dedicated to my lonely course through life until it was all over. I knew it would be over in not so many years. I wasn't going to involve anyone in my misery so they could be hurt as I was hurt by knowing fate was against me."

Unable to hold back, I flared, "Troy, certainly a man of your intelligence doesn't believe fate rules everything!"

"I believe what I've been forced to believe. Nothing that was foretold in my nightmares has failed to come true."

Summer winds from the ocean blew cold and damp through his open windows. Sea gulls and gannets shrilled plaintively as the waves of the sea crashed on the shores. My head lay on his chest and through his thin pajama jacket I could feel the thump of his heart. "They were only the dreams of a sick little boy," I murmured, knowing even as I spoke that he'd held his beliefs far too long for me to change them now.

He didn't seem to hear me. "No one could have had a more devoted brother than I did, but still there was Jillian, who used her grief for the loss of her daughter to pull Tony from me more and more. She had to travel to forget her grief. She had to shop in Paris, London, Rome, and escape the memories of Leigh. Tony would mail me postcards and small gifts from all over the world, instilling in me the determination that I, too, once I was an adult, would see the Sahara, climb the pyramids, and so forth. School was no real challenge for me. High grades came much too easily, so the friends I might have made were turned off by what the teachers considered a child prodigy. I sailed through college without ever being accepted by anyone. I was years younger, and an embarrassment to older boys. The girls teased me for being just a kid. I was always on the outside looking in, and then at age eighteen, I graduated from Harvard with honors and straight from my graduation I went to Tony and told him I was going to see the world as he had seen it.

"He didn't want me to go. He pleaded for me to wait until he could accompany me . . . but he had business to attend to, and time was pushing at me, telling me to hurry, hurry, for soon it would be too late. So in the end I rode, perhaps, the same camels over the same sands of the Sahara as Tony and Jillian had, and climbed the same rugged steps of the pyramids, and I discovered, much to my chagrin, that the exotic trips I made in my imagination, while I lay on my bed picturing how it would be, were by far the best voyages."

By this time his voice held me in a tight bind of fear. When he stopped talking, I came back to myself with a startling jolt. I was disturbed by all that he'd left unsaid. He had everything at his fingertips, a huge fortune to share, intelligence, good looks, and he was letting childish dreams rob him of hope for a long and happy future! It was that house, I told myself, that huge house with its many rambling halls and unused spooky rooms. It was a lonely little boy with too much time on his hands. Yet, how could that be, when the sibling Casteels, who had so little, had always clung tenaciously to the belief that the future held everything?

I lifted my head and tried to say with kisses everything I didn't know how to put into words. "Oh, Troy, there is so much we both haven't experienced. All you needed was a companion with you when you traveled, and you would have found every place just as exciting as you imagined, I'm sure that's true. I'm just not going to believe that all the dreams Tom and I had when we were growing up about exploring the world will be disappointing when realized."

His eyes turned into dark forest pools, holding the infinity of the ages. "You and Tom are not doomed as I am. You have the world ahead of you; my world will always be shadowed by the dreams I've had that have already come true, and by my knowledge of the others that are about to come true. For I have dreamed of my death many times. I've seen my own gravestone, though I can never read more than my full name etched on it. You see, Heavenly, I was never really made for this world. I've always been sickly and melancholy. Your mother was like me—that's why we became so important to one another. And when she disappeared, when I dreamed of her death and knew my dream told the truth, I couldn't understand why I went on living. For I, like Leigh, long for things that can never be found in this world. Like her, I shall die young. Truly, Heaven, I have no future. How can I take someone as young, bright, and loving as you down the dark path that is mine? How can I marry you only to make you a widow? How can I father a child who I will soon leave fatherless, just as I was left fatherless? Do you really want to love a man who is doomed, Heaven?"

Doomed? I shivered and clung to him, suddenly washed over with the stunning realization of just what his poetry was all about. Mortality! Insecurity! Wishing for an early death because life was disappointing!

But I was here now!

Never again would he feel needing, or lonely, or disappointed, and with desperate passion I began to unbutton his jacket, as my lips pressed down on his, until both of us were naked and wet, and sensuality ruled, and even if it had been snow falling outside rather than merely a light drizzle of rain, surely our burning need to possess one another time and time again would lead him onward into the future, until we were both so old death would be welcomed.

That night, even though Tony and Jillian were back, I stayed with Troy. I was not going to let him sink into his morbid fantasies. Tony or no Tony, I would stay with Troy and convince him to marry me, and Tony would have to accept it. I awoke late the next morning, knowing that Troy had at last decided to trust me, to marry me. I could hear him rattling around in the kitchen. The aroma of fresh, homemade bread wafted to my quivering nostrils. I had never felt so alive before, so beautiful and feminine and perfect. I lay with my arms crossed over my breasts, listening to the sound of the kitchen cabinets opening and closing as if

I were hearing Schubert's *Serenade*. The slam of the refrigerator was a cymbal crashing at exactly the right time. Music that wasn't there moved the hairs on my head and on my skin. All my life I'd been searching for what I felt now, and then I was crying from the relief of knowing the search was over.

He was going to marry me! He was giving me the chance to color all the rest of his life with rainbows instead of gray. Languid and sleepy-eyed, full of almost delirious happiness, I drifted toward the kitchen. Troy turned from the stove to smile at me. "We'll have to tell Tony we plan to marry, and soon."

A flutter of panic made my heart skip, but I didn't need Tony's support now. Once Troy and I were husband and wife, everything would work out fine—for him, and for me.

That very afternoon, we went hands clasped, through the maze toward Farthinggale Manor, and into the library where Tony was seated behind his desk. The late afternoon sun beamed through his windows and fell in bright patches on his colorful rug. Troy had called to tell him we were on our way, and perhaps it was wary cunning I saw on his face, and not a genuine smile of pleasure. "Well," he said on seeing our hand-holding, "you have both disregarded me, and now you come to me looking like two people very much in love."

Tony took the wind from my sails, if not Troy's, and nervously I tugged my hand free from Troy's. "It just happened," I whispered weakly.

"We're going to be married on my birthday," said Troy defiantly. "September ninth."

"Now wait a minute!" roared Tony, rising to his

feet and putting both palms flat on his desk. "You have told me all your adult life, Troy, that you would never marry! And never wanted children!"

Troy reached for my hand and pulled me close to his side. "I didn't anticipate meeting anyone like Heaven. She's given me hope and inspiration to go on, despite what I believe."

As I pressed against Troy's side, Tony smiled in the oddest kind of way. "I suppose I'll just be wasting my breath if I object and say Heaven is too young, and her background too different to make you a suitable wife."

"That's correct," said Troy staunchly. "Before the leaves of autumn fall to the ground, Heavenly and I will be on our way to Greece."

Again my heart skipped. Troy and I had only talked vaguely about a honeymoon. I had thought of some local resort where we could spend a few days, and then on to Radcliffe, where I would study English. And soon, much to my amazement, all three of us were seated on a long leather couch, making plans for the wedding. Not for one minute did I believe he was going to let that marriage occur, especially when he smiled at me time and again.

"By the way, my dear," Tony said to me pleasantly, "Winterhaven has forwarded to you a few letters without return addresses."

The only person who wrote me was Tom.

"Now we must send for Jillian and give her your good news." Was that sarcasm behind his smile? I couldn't tell, for Tony was not someone I could read.

"Thank you for accepting this so well, Tony. Especially after your reports of how I behaved when you told me about your upcoming marriage to Jillian."

At that moment Jillian sauntered into the room and fell gracefully into a chair. "What's this I hear . . . someone getting married?"

"Troy and Heaven," explained Tony, turning hard eyes on his wife, as if ordering her to say nothing to alarm either one of us. "Isn't this wonderful news to hear at the end of a perfect summer day?"

She said nothing, nothing at all. She turned those cornflower blue eyes on me, and they were blank, totally, alarmingly blank.

The wedding plans and guest lists were made that very evening, leaving me speechless with the swiftness of Tony's and Jillian's acceptance of a situation I had believed neither would allow to happen. By the time Troy and I kissed good night in the front foyer, we were both overwhelmed by the pace of Tony's plans. "Isn't Tony wonderful?" he asked. "I truly believed he'd have all sorts of objections, and he had none. All my life he's tried to give me everything I wanted."

I undressed in a daze before I remembered the two letters that Tony had put on my small desk. Both letters were from Tom, who had heard from Fanny.

"She's living in some cheap rooming house in Nashville, and wants me to write to you for money. You can bet she'd call you herself, but it seems she lost her address book, and she's never had the kind of memory to retain numbers, you know that. Besides, she keeps in touch with Pa, begging him to send money. I didn't want to give Fanny your address again without your permission. She could ruin everything for you, Heavenly, I know she could. She wants part of what you've got, and will do anything to get it, for it seems she went through that ten thousand the Wises gave her in short order." It was just what I'd feared most; Fanny didn't know one thing about handling money.

His next letter gave even more disturbing news. "I don't think I'll be going on to college, Heavenly. Without you beside me urging me on, I just don't have the will or the desire to keep on studying. Pa's doing pretty good financially, and he never even finished grade school, so I've been thinking I'd go into his business and get married one day when I meet the right girl. It was just a joke to please you, that talk of being president of our country. Nobody would ever vote for a guy like me, with a hillbilly accent." And not one word to even hint at just what business Pa was involved in!

Three times I read over Tom's two letters. Everything wonderful was happening to me, and Tom was stuck down there in some hick town in south Georgia, giving up his dreams of becoming someone important . . . it wasn't right or fair. I couldn't believe Pa could ever be successful in any really important way. Why, I'd heard Pa say he'd never read a book through to the end, and adding a string of figures had taken him hours. What kind of work could he do that would pay well? Tom was sacrificing himself in order to help Pa! That's the conclusion I reached.

Again I raced through the moonlit, crooked paths of the maze, startling Troy out of sleep when I called his name.

He came out of dreams looking boyishly confused before he smiled. "How nice that you've come," he said sleepily.

"I'm sorry to wake you up, but I couldn't wait for morning." Switching on his bedside lamp, I handed him Tom's two letters. "Please read these, then tell me what you think."

In seconds he finished both letters. "I see nothing alarming enough to put that desperate look on your face. All we have to do is send your sister the money she needs, and we can help Tom in that way, too."

"Tom won't take money from you, or from me. Fanny will, of course. But it's Tom I am most worried about. I don't want Tom stuck down there doing whatever Pa is, giving up his life in order to help Pa support his new family.

"Troy," I said, daring to disappoint him with my plan. "I must go visit my family before our wedding." I grabbed his hands and kissed them over and over again. "Do you understand, darling? I'm so happy, my life is so good, I must do something to help them before I begin my wonderful new life with you. I know I can help both of them, just by visiting them, showing them I still care, showing them they can always count on me. And they can, can't they, Troy? You won't mind if my family comes to visit us after we're married, will you? You'll welcome them into our home, won't you?" With pleading eyes I waited for him to reply.

Troy pulled my hands that grasped his, and brought me down on top of him on the bed. "I've been waiting to tell you my news, Heaven, for several days. I hope you'll forgive me for postponing it, but I couldn't bear for our idyll to come to an end and I knew as soon as I told you that you'd rush off." He kissed me again and again before he smiled and continued: "I've heard from the attorneys. Darling, I have such good news for you. Now you'll be able to visit your entire family, for we have found Lester Rawlings! He lives in Chevy Chase, Maryland, and is the father of two adopted children named Keith and Jane!"

It was difficult to breathe, not to be drowned by everything that was happening so fast.

"It's all right, all right," Troy soothed as I began to cry. "There's plenty of time before our wedding for you to set everything straight. I'll be happy to go with you to visit the Rawlingses and to see your younger brother and younger sister; we can then decide just what action you want to take, if any."

"They're mine!" I cried out unreasonably. "I have to have them under my roof again!"

Again he kissed me. "Decide later what to do. And after we've seen Keith and Our Jane we will travel on to visit your brother and father, and finish our trip by visiting Fanny, and in the meanwhile, let's telegraph Fanny a few thousand dollars to see her over until we arrive."

Unfortunately, it wasn't to be that way.

While I slept safe and secure in my Farthinggale Manor bed, thinking now that Troy and I should deny our passion until we were married, Troy fell into deep sleep with all of his bedroom windows open. And a terrible northeaster swept in to blast us with rain, hail, and blustery winds. The worst of the wind and rain didn't waken me until six in the morning. I looked out of my bedroom windows to see the devastation of the perfect lawns, now littered with uprooted trees, broken branches, and other debris. And when I ran to Troy's cottage, I found him feverish and congested, barely able to breathe.

I was truly terrified as I called Tony and an ambulance came to rush Troy to the hospital. Just when he was supposed to be the most happy, he had fallen deathly ill with pneumonia. Had he somehow brought it on purposely, unable to accept the love and happiness he deserved? I would not let this happen again. When we were married, I would be there always to protect him from his worst fears, which now seemed to have a way of making themselves come true.

"It's what I want," whispered Troy from his hospital bed, days later. "The worst of my pneumonia is over, and I know you are anxious to see Keith and Our Jane again. There's no need for you to hang around while I recover my strength. By the time you are back, I'll be totally well."

I didn't want to leave him, even though he had the best of care, with private-duty nurses around the clock, and time and again I protested. Still, he kept insisting I should have what I'd wanted for so long, my chance to see Keith and Our Jane again. And as he urged me, and assured me he'd be fine, something kept insisting that I hurry, hurry, before it was too late.

"You're leaving him?" Tony shouted, when I told him I was planning a short trip. I didn't want to tell Tony the truth about where I was going, fearing he'd try to stop me. "Now, when he needs you, you are shopping in New York for a trousseau? What kind of idiocy is that? Heaven, I thought you loved my brother! You promised me you would be his salvation!"

"I do love him, I do, but Troy is insisting I go ahead with our wedding preparations. And he's out of danger now, isn't he?"

"Out of danger?" Tony repeated dully, "No, he will

never be out of danger until the day his first son is born, and maybe then he can give up his belief that he will not live long enough to reproduce himself."

"You love him," I whispered, awed by the pain I saw in his blue eyes, "really love him."

"Yes, I love him. He's been my responsibility and my burden to carry since I was seventeen years old. I have done everything I can to give my brother the best life possible. I married Jillian, who was twenty years older, though she lied to me about her age and said she was thirty, not forty. I believed with boyish naivete that she was what she pretended to be at that time—the sweetest, kindest, most wonderful woman in the world. Only later did I find out that she disliked Troy on first sight. But by that time it was far too late to change my mind, for I had fallen in love, stupidly, madly, insanely in love."

His head bowed down into the cradle of his hands. "Go on, Heaven, do what you feel you have to, for in the end you will anyway. But remember this, if you hope to marry Troy, you hurry back and don't bring with you even one member of your hillbilly family." His face lifted to show me the knowing look in his eyes. "Yes, silly girl, I know everything, and no, Troy did not tell me. I am not gullible or stupid." He smiled at me again, devilishly mocking. "And what is more, dear child, I was aware all the time that you were slipping through the maze to visit my brother."

"But . . . but," I stammered, gone confused, awkward, and embarrassed, "why didn't you put a stop to it?"

A cynical smile quirked his lips. "Forbidden fruit is the most compelling. I had a wild hope that in you, someone totally different from any girl or woman he'd met before, someone sweet, fresh, and exceptionally beautiful, Troy would find, at last, a good reason for living."

"You planned for us to fall in love?" I asked, astonished.

"I had hopes, that's all," he said simply, appearing for the first time totally honest and sincere. "Troy is like the son I can never have. He is my heir, the one who will inherit the Tatterton fortune and carry on the family tradition. Through him and his children I hope to have the family Jillian couldn't give me."

"But you are not too old!" I cried.

He winced. "Are you suggesting I divorce your grandmother and marry a younger woman? I would if I could, believe me, I would. But you can sometimes trap yourself so deeply there is no way out. I am the keeper of a woman obsessed by her desire to stay young, and I have feeling enough for her not to shove her out into the world where she wouldn't survive two weeks without my support." Heavily he sighed. "So go on, girl. Just make sure you come back, for if you don't, what happens to Troy will give you such terrible guilt to carry for the rest of your life, you may never be happy again."

## ~ Fourteen ~
### Winners and Losers

THE SECOND FLIGHT OF MY LIFE TOOK ME FROM
Boston's Logan Airport to New York City, and there I
changed planes and headed straight to Washington,
D.C. My veneer of sophistication was pitifully thin. I
wanted to appear cool and controlled while underneath I was ridden by anxiety, terrified of doing
everything wrong. The bustling activity of LaGuardia
confused me. I had hardly reached my gate when
passengers began to board. I wanted a window seat
and was grateful when a young businessman eagerly
stood up and offered me his. Soon I found out there
was a price to pay for the seat, for he plied me with
too many questions, wanting me to meet him later,
and share a drink, and keep him from being lonely.
"I'm on my way to meet my husband," I said in a
cool, forbidding voice, "and I don't drink." Shortly
after that, he abandoned his seat and found another
unaccompanied young woman to sit beside. I felt
much older than I had when I flew away from West
Virginia last September.

From September to August, not quite a year, and I had graduated high school, been accepted to college, and found a man to love, a man who really needed me, who didn't pity me as Logan had. I looked around at the other passengers, most of whom were dressed far more casually than I was in my pale blue summer pants suit that had cost more than the Casteels used to spend on a year's supply of food.

High above the ground, with only the billowing white clouds to see, I felt the strangest sensation of waking from an enchanted sleep that had begun the day I arrived at Farthinggale Manor. This was the real world, where sixty-one-year-old women didn't appear to be thirty. No one looked fastidious and impeccably elegant, even those seated with me in the first class section. Babies were crying back in the tourist section. And for the very first time I realized that not once since I entered Farthinggale Manor had I really left its influence. Even at Winterhaven its tentacles had reached out to let me know who was in full control of my life. I closed my eyes and thought of Troy, silently praying for his swift recovery. Had Troy spent too much of his life in that huge house, where the invention and selling of make-believe dominated? For now that I was away from the influence of Farthy, his cottage beyond the maze seemed but an extension of what could seem to some a make-believe castle.

When I arrived in Baltimore, I felt grateful to Tony, who had called to make hotel reservations for me.

So this was not truly an unmapped quest. Not when a limousine with a driver waited for me. Even on this journey to find my long lost brother and sister, the control and influence of Farthinggale Manor still pulled the strings of Heaven Leigh Casteel.

"You will have to make your own arrangements for visiting the Rawlingses," Tony had warned early this morning, "and I anticipate you are going to meet with a great deal of resentment from two parents who won't want you bringing back the past to children who may have adjusted to their new lifestyle very well. And you must keep remembering that you are one of us now, no longer a Casteel."

I would always be a Casteel; I knew this even as I pulled in my breath, rose from my luncheon table, and made my way to a telephone booth. In my mind I had pictures of just how it would be. Keith and Our Jane would be thrilled to see me again.

Hev-lee, Hev-lee, Our Jane would shriek, her pretty, small face lit up with happiness. She'd then race into my welcoming arms and cry from the relief of knowing I still cared and wanted her.

Behind her would come Keith, much slower and shyer, but he'd know me. He'd be thrilled and happy, too.

Beyond that I couldn't plan. The legal fight to take Keith and Our Jane from those substitute parents would take years perhaps, according to what the Tatterton attorneys had said, and Tony didn't want me to win. "It won't be fair to Troy to saddle him with two children who may resent him, and you know how sensitive he is. When you are his wife, devote yourself to him, and the children *he* will father."

Holding the receiver tight to my ear, I grew nervous and apprehensive as the telephone rang and rang. What if they had gone on vacation? Breathlessly I let their phone ring and ring, waiting for someone to respond. I waited for the sweet voice of Our Jane. I didn't expect Keith to respond to a telephone, not, that is, if he was still the reticent little boy I used to know so well.

Three times I called the number Troy had given me, and no one was home. I ordered another slice of blueberry pie to remind me of the pies that Granny used to make on rare occasions, and sipped my third cup of coffee.

At three o'clock I left the restaurant. An elevator took me to the fifteenth floor of the magnificent hotel, the very kind of posh hotel that Tom and I used to dream about when we lay on mountain slopes and planned our exceptional futures. I was planning to stay in Baltimore only over the weekend, and yet Tony had thought it absolutely necessary that I have a suite of rooms instead of only one. There was a pretty sitting room, and adjoining that, a fully equipped small kitchen where everything was black and white and very shiny.

Hours passed. It was ten o'clock when I gave up on the Rawlingses, and put in a call to Troy.

"Now, now," he soothed, "perhaps they took the children on a special outing that lasts all day, and tomorrow they will be home. Of course I'm all right. In fact, for the first time I'm really excited by the future, and all it holds for both of us. I have been a fool, darling, haven't I? Believing that fate planned, even before I was born, to kill me before I reached the age of twenty-five. Thank God you came into my life when you did, just in time to save me from myself."

Dreams of Troy filled my sleep with restlessness. Time and again he shrank to child size, and drifted away from me, calling out as Keith used to do, "Hev-lee, Hev-lee!"

I was up early the next day, impatiently waiting for

eight o'clock. And this time when I called, a woman's voice answered. "Mrs. Lester Rawlings, please."

"Who is calling?"

I gave her my name, saying I wanted to visit my brother and sister, Keith and Jane Casteel. Her sharp intake of breath communicated her shock. "Oh, no!" she whispered, then I heard the click of her phone. I was left with the dial tone. Immediately I called her back.

On and on the phone rang, until Rita Rawlings finally answered. "Please," she begged with tears in her voice, "don't disturb the peace of two wonderfully happy children who have adapted successfully to a new family and new lives."

"They are blood-related to me, Mrs. Rawlings! They were mine long before they were yours!"

"Please, please," she begged. "I know you love them. I remember very well how you looked that day when we took them away, and I do understand how you must feel. When first they came to live with us, it was you they were always crying for. But they haven't cried for you in more than two years. They call me Mother or Mommy now, and they call my husband Daddy. They are fine, mentally and physically . . . I'll send you photographs, health and school reports, but please, I beg of you, don't come to remind them of all the hardships they had to endure when they lived in that pitiful shack in the Willies."

Now it was my turn to plead. "But you don't understand, Mrs. Rawlings! I have to see them again! I have to make sure they are happy and healthy, or else I can't find happiness myself. Each day of my life I vow to find Keith and Our Jane. I hate my father for what he did, it eats at me night and day. You have to allow me to see them, even if they don't see me."

The reluctance expressed in her delayed reply could have turned aside someone less relentless than I was.

"All right, if you must do this thing. But you have to promise to keep yourself hidden from my children. And if after you see them they don't appear to you to be healthy, happy, and secure, then my husband and I will do everything within our power to see that we remedy that situation."

I knew at that moment that this was a strong-willed woman, determined to keep her family intact, and through hell she'd fight to keep them hers and not mine.

All that Saturday I prowled small shops, looking for just the right gifts to give Fanny, Tom, and Grandpa. I even bought several things for Keith and Our Jane to add to the others I was saving for that day when we would be a family again.

Sunday morning I awakened with high hopes and great excitement. At ten the limousine and driver put at my disposal drew to a slow, careful stop before an Episcopalian church that was almost medieval in design. I knew just where the two children I longed to see would be, in their Sunday School class. Rita Rawlings had given me detailed instructions on how to find their classroom, and what to do once I was there. "And if you love them, Heaven, keep your promise. Think of their needs and not your own, and stay out of sight."

The church was cool and dim inside, the many halls long and twisting. Well-dressed people smiled at me.

Somewhere in a back hall I grew confused, not knowing which way to turn . . . and then I heard children singing. And it seemed, above all the other voices, I could hear the sweet, high-pitched voice of Our Jane, as she tried earnestly to duplicate the soprano tones of Miss Marianne Deale, when she had sung hymns with us in Winnerrow's one and only Protestant church.

Their sweet singing voices led me to them.

I paused in the doorway that I cracked open to listen to the song of worship sung so joyfully by many children, with only a piano for accompaniment. Soon I stepped inside the large room, where at least fifteen children, aged approximately ten to twelve, were standing, holding hymn books, and singing loudly.

The children of Winnerrow would have been shamed by this assembly in their pretty pastel summer clothes.

The two I sought were standing side by side, Keith and Our Jane, both supporting the same hymn book, both singing with rapt expressions, more for the pure delight of expressing themselves than from holy fervor, I thought, as I stood and silently cried, even as I delighted in their obvious good health and prosperity. Oh, thank God I had lived long enough to see them again.

Once skinny little legs and arms were now strong and tanned. Pale, small faces had developed into radiant, glowing faces, with rosy lips that knew now how to smile rather than pout and droop, and eyes that weren't haunted by hunger and cold. Oh, to see them as they were now sent light through all the shadows I had deliberately kept in my mind.

The song ended. Quietly, I moved to the thick

square post beside which I was to sit and shield myself from their view.

The children sat and put their hymn books in the back pocket of the chairs in front of them—front chairs where no one sat. My tears were chased by a smile when I saw Our Jane fuss with her pretty white and pink dress. Each accordion pleat had to be arranged carefully so it wouldn't later on be crinkled and fall out of place. She took great pains to see that her short skirt covered her tanned knees, which she kept together in proper, ladylike fashion. Her bright hair was artfully styled so it fell to barely brush her shoulders before it flipped upward in charming casual curls. And when she turned her head to profile, I could see the feathery fringe of bangs across her forehead. Her hair knew the kind of professional care that mine and Fanny's had never known at the age of ten. Oh, how lovely she was! How flushed with good health and vitality, so much that she appeared to glow.

Seated beside her, Keith stared solemnly ahead at the woman teacher who began to tell the story of the boy David, who had slain a giant with a stone hurled from a slingshot. Straight and true that stone had flown to find its mark, because the power of the Lord was with David, and not Goliath. It had always been one of my favorite Bible stories. But I forgot to listen as my eyes scanned over Keith, who wore a bright blue summer jacket with long white summer trousers. His dress shirt was white, and his small tie was blue. Several times I had to get up and move just so I could see them both better. He radiated the same kind of good health and vitality that Our Jane did.

The years since I'd seen them last had added inches

to their heights and given both their faces more maturity and character, and yet I would have known them anywhere, for time had not changed some things. Repeatedly Keith glanced at his younger sister, checking on her comfort, on her happiness, showing a remarkable amount of manly concern for her welfare, while Our Jane habitually held on to her babyish mannerisms that had won her so much attention in the past. It was not likely she would abandon them.

Oh, Granny would be so happy to know her beauty hadn't been permanently sacrificed in the hills, for Annie Brandywine lived again in Our Jane! And beside her Keith had to resemble Grandpa more than he did any of Sarah's large, rawboned family. Once I had thought the shadowed hollows beneath both sets of their eyes would never go away, and such small, pale faces would never look as they did now, happy to be alive.

Several children just in front of me turned to stare quizzically my way. I held my breath until their stares were satisfied, and once again they pivoted to listen to their teacher. If either my younger sister or brother turned to look back in my direction, I intended to hide quickly. I prayed that no one would come to question why I was there.

The story of David ended. I listened to the question-and-answer period that followed and heard the sweet, small voice of Keith as he hesitatingly responded only after he had been directly prompted. However, Our Jane was constantly waving her small, shapely hand, eager to pipe her question or answer. "How could a tiny stone kill a huge giant?" she asked. I didn't listen to the teacher's answer.

Soon the children were standing, and prissy little girls adjusted their clothes. Our Jane clutched her small white purse more securely.

The excited chatter of the departing children might have hidden what Our Jane said next, but my ears were keened for her voice.

"Hurry, Keith!" she urged, "We're going to Susan's party this afternoon, and we don't want to be late."

I followed at a distance behind the two little ones that I dreamed of, and jealously I watched Our Jane fling herself into Rita Rawlings's waiting arms. Slightly behind his wife, Lester Rawlings stood, as fat and bald as ever. He laid a possessive hand on Keith's shoulder before he turned his head and looked directly at me. More than three years had passed since he had seen me, backed up to the wall in that mountain shack, my dress dirty and ragged, my feet bare. And yet it seemed he recognized me. I had changed a great deal from that waif, but still he knew me. It could have been the tears streaming down my face that betrayed me. He said something to his wife, who hustled the two children into a Cadillac, and then he smiled at me with genuine sympathy.

"Thank you," he said simply.

For the second time in my life I watched that lawyer and his wife drive off in a Cadillac, taking with them two parts of myself. I stood staring after them until the drizzle of rain evaporated into steam, and the sun came out hot and brilliant, and a rainbow arched in the sky, and only then did I stroll toward my own waiting car. Not yet, not yet, some small voice in me warned. Later on you can claim them.

Still, I instructed my driver to follow the dark blue

Cadillac ahead, for I wanted to see the house where the Rawlingses lived. After a ten-minute drive, the Cadillac ahead turned onto a quiet, tree-lined street, then pulled into a long, curving drive. "Stop across the street," I ordered my driver, thinking that the heavy shade and many thick tree trunks would shield the limo if the Rawlingses just happened to check and see if they were followed. Apparently they didn't check.

Theirs was a nice, colonial-style house, large, but not huge like Farthinggale Manor. The red bricks were old and partially covered with ivy, and the lawns were wide and well tended, with flowers and shrubs in full summer bloom. Oh, indeed, this was a palace in comparison to that listing shack perched high on a mountainside. There was no reason for my heart to hurt. They were better off here, they were, they were. They didn't need me. Not now. A long time ago they'd stopped speaking my name, stopped having bad dreams. Oh, the cries of hunger in the night that I used to hear coming from the floor pallet of the two small children that once I'd considered mine!

"Hev-lee, Hev-lee, are ya goin somewhere?" they had asked, after their own mother abandoned them, their shadowed eyes pleading with me never to leave them.

"Will you be driving back to the hotel now, miss?" asked my driver after half an hour had passed. I couldn't tear myself away.

On impulse I opened the door and stepped out on the shady sidewalk. "Wait for me here. I'll be back in a few minutes."

I couldn't just drive off without seeing and knowing

more, not after all the heartache I'd suffered since that horrible day when Pa sold his two youngest.

Furtively I slipped into the side yard where a colorful, heavy-duty gym set seemed to wait for the children who used it. I stole quietly onto a broad, flagstone patio where chairs and a table with a pretty striped umbrella jostled each other for closest position to the kidney-shaped swimming pool. Keeping so close to the house I was beneath the level of the many back windows, and I was soon rewarded with the sound of children's voices coming through the open windows of one room.

Soon I was crouched low behind huge masonry pots holding living shrubs, staring through the glass of French doors that opened into what had to be an enclosed sun porch.

The beautiful room was full of sunlight, and chairs and a sofa sported soft, fat cushions covered with pretty flowered chintz. Houseplants in macramé holders hung from the ceiling in healthy array, and the floor was covered with rich, sea blue rugs. On the largest blue rug Keith and Our Jane were seated, playing with glass marbles that they had arranged inside the main center oval of the rug. Both children had changed from their church outfits into dressier clothes. From the meticulous way they moved, they were obviously trying to keep themselves clean and neat for the upcoming party.

I couldn't stop staring.

The tiered and ruffled skirt of Our Jane's white organza dress fell from a high, smocked bodice, and fastened to the right of where the tiers met the bodice were pale green satin ribbons that fell to the hem of her skirt. Tiny, pink silk rosettes formed a bouquet from which the ribbons streamed. She had taken great pains to arrange the skirt around her so it formed a flattering circle. Her red gold hair had been brushed back from her face and was held high on the crown of her head with another green satin ribbon tied into a bow, and the ribbon streamers were finished off with the same tiny, silk rosettes. I had never seen a child's dress that was more beautiful or becoming to its wearer than the one Our Jane now wore.

Directly across from Our Jane, sitting cross-legged, his feet in shiny new white shoes, Keith's fresh suit was white linen, and his bow tie matched exactly the pale jade green of the ribbons decorating Our Jane's dress and hair. It was very apparent that a great deal of thought had been given to their clothes.

When finally I could skip my eyes away from them long enough to see the appointments of the room, I saw a long table that held a small computer. Nearby was another table with a printer. A radio was playing. In a corner was an artist's easel, and a table and taboret. I knew who the easel was meant for—it was for Keith, who had inherited his grandfather's artistic talent! Any paint that Keith might drop or spill would fall on tile that could easily be wiped up. And everywhere there were dolls, as if Our Jane wasn't reaching maturity as swiftly as other girls ten years old.

Then, to my dismay, low on the bottom door panel in front of me appeared two small paws and the friendly face of a small puppy. His tail wagged furiously as he saw me down on my hands and knees, my nose almost pressing on the glass. He whined, opened his mouth to yip several times—and the children, whom I had not expected to turn their heads my way, fixed their wide, surprised eyes directly on me!

I didn't know what to do!

The wiggling puppy began to yip louder, and afraid now that the Rawlingses would be alarmed, I quickly rose to my feet and stepped through the unlocked door.

Neither Keith nor Our Jane spoke.

They seemed frozen as they sat on the floor before their colorful ring of marbles.

It was too late now to slip away unseen. I tried to smile reassuringly. "It's all right," I said softly, standing just inside the doorway. "I'm not going to do anything to disturb your lives. I just wanted to see you both again."

Still they stared, their rosy lips parted, their eyes huge and growing darker, as shadows came into the clarity of Our Jane's turquoise eyes and deepened the amber in Keith's. The puppy frolicked about my feet, sniffed at my ankles, then stood on hind legs to paw at my skirt. My brother and sister seemed terrified. It pained me to see their expressions.

Softly, softly, lest I frighten them more: "Keith, Our Jane, look at me. Surely you haven't forgotten who I am?"

I smiled, still anticipating their cries of delight when they recognized me, as many a time in my dreams I'd heard them say, "Hev-lee! You've come! You've saved us!"

But neither one said that. With some awkwardness Keith slowly rose to his feet. The pupils of his amber eyes enlarging with each beat of his pulse. He glanced with concern at Our Jane, tugged at his green bow tie, tightened his parted lips, looked again at me, then wiped a hand across his face. All his life he'd done that when he was confused or disturbed.

Our Jane had no such reticence. She jumped to her feet in one lithe movement, scattering the marbles everywhere. "Go away!" she cried, throwing her arms about Keith and hugging close. "We don't want you!" Her mouth opened to scream.

I couldn't believe the fear they both showed. Couldn't believe either one knew who I was. They thought I was a stranger, perhaps a door-to-door salesperson, and they had been warned not to let anyone in.

Stunned, I started to speak and tell them my name. The thickness in my throat almost caused my voice to fail so that my name came out hoarse, strange, unintelligible.

Our Jane's lovely face turned alarmingly white. Her pale, frightened face took on an expression of hysteria. For a dreadful moment I thought she was going to throw up, as she used to do so often in the past. Keith, glancing at her face, turned several shades lighter. He glared at me with small, angry lights flickering on and off in his eyes. Did he know me? Was he trying to remember?

"Mommy!" Our Jane wailed in a high, thin voice, cringing against Keith. "Daddy . . . !"

"Shhh!" I warned, putting my forefinger before my lips. "You don't have to be afraid. I'm not a stranger, and I won't hurt you. You used to know me very well when you lived in the mountains. Do you remember the mountains called the Willies?"

I swear to God Our Jane paled even more. She seemed on the verge of passing out.

My emotions were in turmoil. I reeled with indecision. This was not the way I had anticipated they would react. They were supposed to be delighted to see me! "A long time ago you both had a mountain family, and every weekday we trudged to school and home again through the woods. We went to church on Sundays. We had chickens, ducks, geese, and sometimes a cow. And always lots of dogs and cats. It's me, your sister you used to call Hev-Lee! I just want to see you and hear you say you're happy."

Our Jane's wail was loud, full of even greater panic!

Before he stepped forward, Keith protectively shoved his sister behind him. "We don't know you," he said in a gruff boy's voice that trembled.

Now it was my face that went pale. I felt his words as slaps, one two three four.

"Make her go away!" loudly cried Our Jane.

It was the worst moment of my life.

To have yearned for them for years and years, and dreamed of finding and saving them, and now they didn't want me. "I'm going," I quickly said, backing toward the open door. "I have made a terrible mistake, and I'm sorry. I have never seen either one of you before!"

I ran then, ran as fast as my high heels would allow, heading for the limo that waited, and once I had thrown myself on the back seat, I burst into tears. Our Jane and Keith had not lost the day Pa sold them. They had been winners in that game of chance.

## ∽ Fifteen ∽
### Family Support

I COULDN'T BEAR TO SPEND ANOTHER HOUR IN THAT CITY, so I collected my things from the hotel, and the limo took me to the airport, where I boarded the next plane to Atlanta. I felt desperate to cling to the past I'd always been in such a hurry to escape—for I didn't want to begin my new life with Troy only to find I'd lost my family. To Tom I would go and there find the welcome I longed for and the loving brother who'd promised always to be my true-blue brother.

The telephone rang three, four, five times before a deep and familiar voice answered, and for one agonizing moment I felt Pa could see me through the telephone lines. I stood petrified in the phone booth.

"I'd like to speak to Tom Casteel," I finally managed to whisper hoarsely, and it was such a strange voice, it gave me confidence that the man I hated would not recognize his firstborn, just as he'd never acknowledged my presence in his life with any warmth. I could almost see his Indian face as he hesitated, and for a heartbreaking moment I thought he might ask, "Is that you, Heaven?"

But he didn't. "May I tell Tom who is calling?"

Well, listen to that! Someone was teaching Pa good grammar and proper manners. I swallowed and almost gagged. "A friend."

"Hold on, please," he said, as if he did this a hundred times a day for Tom. I heard him lay down the receiver, heard his steps on a hard surface, and then his voice roared in characteristic hillbilly fashion: "Tom, you've got another of those anonymous girlfriends of yours on the phone. I wish you'd tell them to stop calling. Now don't talk longer than five minutes. We've got to get the show on the road."

The thud of Tom's running feet came clearly across the many miles that separated us. "Hi!" he breathlessly greeted.

I was taken aback at how much his voice had changed; he sounded very much like Pa. I found it difficult to speak, and while I hesitated, Tom must have grown impatient. "Whoever you are, speak up, for I don't have but a minute to spare."

"It's me, Heaven . . . please don't speak my name and let Pa know who it is."

Surprised, he sucked his breath in. "Hey, this is great! Terrific! Gosh, I'm so glad to hear from you. Pa's gone out in the yard to be with Stacie and the baby, so I don't have to whisper."

I didn't know what to say.

Tom filled the awkward space: "Heavenly, he's the cutest lil ole kid. He's got black hair, dark brown eyes, you know, just the kind of son Mom wanted to give Pa . . ." He stopped talking abruptly, and I just knew he'd started to add, "He's the spitting image of Pa." Instead he said, "Why aren't you saying anything?"

"How nice that Pa always gets what he wants," I commented bitterly. "Some people are lucky that way."

"C'mon, Heavenly, stop that! Be fair. The kid isn't guilty of any crime. He's damned cute, and even you would have to admit that."

"What did Pa name his third son?" I asked out of pure, spiteful vindictiveness.

"Hey! I hate your cold tone of voice. Why can't you let the past die in peace, like I have? Pa and Stacie let me name the baby. Remember a long time ago who used to be our favorite explorers? Walter Raleigh and Frances Drake? Well, we got us Walter Drake. We call him Drake."

"I remember," I said, ice in my voice.

"I think it's a terrific name. Drake Casteel?"

More merchandise for Pa to sell was my mean thought before I abruptly changed the subject. "Tom, I'm in Atlanta. I'm planning on renting a car and driving to your place, and I don't want to run into Pa."

"That's wonderful, Heavenly, just wonderful!" he enthusiastically cried.

"I don't want to see Pa when I come. Can you arrange to have him out of the house?"

Pain came into Tom's voice as he promised to do what he could to keep Pa and me from meeting. Then he gave me detailed directions on how to reach the small town where he lived, about twenty miles from where a commuter plane would let me off in south Georgia.

"Tom," roared Pa from a distance. "I said five minutes, not ten!"

"I've gotta go now," Tom said urgently. "I'm mighty happy yer comin, but I'm gonna say this right now, ya made a big mistake when ya shoved Logan out of yer life, an let that Troy guy in! He's not yer kind. That Troy Tatterton ya've written to me about will never understand ya like Logan does, or love ya even half as much."

His country dialect had come back, as it always did when he grew passionate. Quickly I corrected him. It hadn't been I who shoved Logan away, it had been Logan who had changed his mind.

"Goodbye, Heavenly . . . see you tomorrow morning about eleven." He hung up without further ado.

I stayed that night in Atlanta and early the next morning rented a car and drove south, rethinking all of Tom's letters that should have warned me. "I thought nothing would ever come between you and Logan. It's living in that rich house, I know it is. It's changing you, Heavenly! Why you don't even write or talk like yourself!"

"You're not Fanny," he'd written once. "Girls like you fall in love just once, and don't ever change their minds."

What did he think I was, anyway? An angel? A saint without flaws? I wasn't an angel or a saint; I had the wrong shade of hair. I was a dark angel, through and through a no-good, scumbag Casteel! Pa's daughter! He'd made me what I was. Whatever I was.

I had talked to Troy only last night, and he'd told me to settle all my family affairs quickly, and hurry back to him.

"And if you can persuade Tom to come to our wedding, despite what Tony said, you won't feel that all the guests are on my side. And perhaps Fanny will come as well."

Oh, Troy didn't know what he was asking for when he invited my sister Fanny! I had all kinds of weird thoughts as I drove in the early morning toward a small town I'd marked with a red circle on a local map. I stared at the red dirt along the roadside, allowing it to take me back to my time spent with Kitty and Cal Dennison. For the first time since I'd flown from West Virginia, my thoughts lingered on memories of Cal, and what had happened to him. Was he still living in Candlewick? Had he sold the home that had belonged to Kitty? Was he married again? Surely he'd done the right thing when he put me on the plane for Boston, allowing me to think that Kitty would live despite her massive tumor.

I shook my head, not wanting to think of Cal when I had to concentrate on my meeting with Tom. Somehow I had to persuade him to leave Pa and continue his education. Troy would pay his tuition fees, buy his clothes, and whatever else he needed. And even as I thought this, I had to block out Tom's stubborn pride, the same kind that I had.

Then suddenly I was lost on back country roads. I pulled into a run-down station with two gas tanks and asked the red-faced, skinny little man there for directions. He stared at me as if he thought me crazy to be so dressed up on a sizzling hot day like this. I wore a lightweight summer suit, and I was hot, you bet, but I wasn't going to show up in just an ordinary summer dress. My hands wore too many rings, and my neck was heavy from too many necklaces. I was going to impress somebody, even if they thought me foolish. My car was the most expensive one I could rent.

I had to back up and turn around to find the right road that would take me to Tom and the house where Pa lived with his new family. A bit of Florida had stolen into Georgia and given the landscape a semitropical look. As I drew closer to my destination, I pulled my car to the side of the road to freshen my makeup, and ten minutes later my long, dark blue Lincoln slowed to a halt in front of a low and sprawling contemporary ranch house.

A numb kind of sensation in my chest made me feel unreal, to have come all these miles and put myself within the reach of Pa's cruelty again. What kind of fool was I, anyway? I shook my head, glanced again in the rearview mirror to check my appearance, and then I looked again at the modern house. It was constructed of red cedar shingles. The shallow roof overhung the many wide windows to create shade. Many trees shaded the roof, and well-trimmed shrubs outlined the house, while flower beds curved outward from the shrubs to create colorful areas where not a weed grew. Oh, surely Pa was proving something to the world with this house that had to have four to five bedrooms. And not one time had Tom even hinted at just what Pa did to earn enough money to pay for such a house.

Where was Tom? Why wasn't he coming out of the door to greet me? Finally, growing impatient, I left the car and stepped along the walkway leading to the recessed door. I feared that Pa himself might be the very one who responded to my knock, despite Tom's pledge to keep us apart. But I was all right. My designer suit that had cost more than a thousand dollars was as good as a suit of armor. My costly rings and necklaces and earrings were my shield and my sword. I could slay dragons dressed as I was. Or so I thought.

Impatiently I jabbed at the door bell. Inside I heard chimes play a few notes. My heart thudded nervously. Butterflies beat small wings of panic in my stomach. Then I heard footfalls approaching. I had Tom's name on my lips when the door opened.

However, it was not Tom, as I'd hoped and prayed it would be; nor was it the dreaded appearance of Pa. Instead, a very pretty young woman with blond hair and bright blue eyes swung open the door and smiled at me as if she'd never known fear of strangers or dislike of anyone.

She took my breath away with her air of fresh innocence as she stood behind the screen door, the cool rooms dim and shadowy and clean-smelling in the background, smiling and waiting for me to identify myself. She wore white shorts with a blue knit top, and carried easily in one arm was a young child who appeared sleepy. Oh, that had to be Drake, Pa's look-alike son . . . his third son.

"Yes . . . ?" she prompted when I failed to speak.

I stood there nonplused, staring at a woman and little boy whose lives I could easily destroy if I wanted.

And now that I was here, I knew from my very shock, that in a way I had not come just to save Tom; I had an ulterior motive, to ruin what happiness Pa had found. All that I could have shouted out to make her hate Pa stuck like a lump in my throat so I had difficulty even murmuring my name.

"Heaven?" she asked, looking delighted. *You* are Heaven?" Her welcoming smile broadened. "You are *the* Heavenly that Tom is always talking about? Oh, how wonderful to finally meet you. Come in, come in!" She pulled open the screen door, then put the little boy down on the couch and self-consciously tugged down her blue top. Her eyes darted to the nearest wall mirror to check her appearance, making me realize that perhaps Tom had not told her I was due at eleven o'clock. I had not thought of this woman at all when I made my plans.

"Unfortunately an emergency arose, so Tom had to leave with his father," she explained breathlessly, now checking to see that her house was in order. She led the way from the front foyer into a large, handsome living room. "I noticed this morning that several times Tom seemed on the verge of confiding something to me, and yet his father kept urging him to hurry, so he didn't have the time. I'm sure your visit must have been his secret."

While she talked, she tidied a stack of decorating magazines, and quickly folded the morning newspaper that she must have been reading. "Please sit down and make yourself at home, Heaven. Is there anything I can get you? I'll be preparing lunch soon for Drake and myself, and of course you must stay. But can I get you something cold now? It's such a hot day."

"A cola drink would be very nice," I admitted, my throat parched from anxiety as much as from thirst. I couldn't believe Tom hadn't waited for me. Wasn't I important to him anymore either? It seemed none of my family wanted to see me as much as I wanted to see them. Soon she was back from the kitchen with two glasses. The shy little boy, about a year old, stared at me with huge brown eyes fringed by long black lashes. Oh, yes, he was the look-alike son that Sarah had prayed to have when her fifth child had been deformed and stillborn.

Poor Sarah. Not for the first time I wondered just where Sarah was now, and what she was doing.

I slipped out of my too-warm jacket, feeling ridiculous now as I wished I'd had better sense than to be so ostentatious.

Stacie Casteel gave me one of the sweetest smiles I'd ever seen. "You are so beautiful, Heaven, exactly as Tom described you many, many times. You are lucky to have a brother who admires you so much. I always wanted brothers and sisters myself, but my parents thought one child was enough. They live about two blocks from here, so I see them often, and they make wonderful baby-sitters. In fact your grandfather is out now with my father, fishing in a nearby lake."

Grandpa. I had forgotten all about Grandpa.

She went on, as if starved for someone to talk to about her family. "Luke would like for us to move to Florida, so he could be closer to where he works, but I can't bring myself to move that far from my parents. I know they won't make any changes in their lifestyles now that they're so old and contented. They are so devoted to Drake."

She was seated now across from me, allowing her small, very handsome son a sip or two of her cold drink. He could hardly manage to swallow he was so intimidated by my silent presence. Gently she shoved him forward a bit. "Drake dear, this is your half-sister named Heaven. Isn't that an appropriate name for such a lovely young lady?"

The huge dark eyes of Pa's youngest son batted as he tried to decide if I was friendly or not, before he ducked his head and turned to try and hide himself. When he felt safe, he peeked at me from his close position near his mother's legs with his thumb stuck in his mouth. And oh, it did hurt to be reminded so much of how Keith used to act, only in the old days it had been my legs Keith had hidden behind, or beside, never Sarah's. Sarah had always been too busy and too tired to "mess with" shy children who needed special attention—until Our Jane came along.

Despite the decision I'd made not to love this particular child, I found myself kneeling so I could be on eye level with him. I found a smile. "Hi Drake. Your uncle Tom told me about you. He told me you like trains and boats and airplanes. And someday very soon I am going to send you a whole huge carton of trains, boats, and airplanes." I glanced at Stacie with some embarrassment. "The Tattertons have been toy makers for centuries. They make toys such as can't be found in ordinary toy stores, and when I go back, I'll ship Drake all he can play with."

"That would be very nice of you," she said with another of her devastating, sweet smiles that stabbed right into my heart, for I could have sent Drake many a plaything a long time ago, and not once had I thought of doing so.

As the minutes passed and she chatted on while preparing lunch, I soon found out that she loved the man I hated, loved him very much. "He is the kindest, most wonderful husband," she enthused, "always trying his very best to see that his family has everything we need." She threw me an appealing glance. "I realize, Heaven, that you might not see him that way, but your father has had a very difficult life, and to find himself, he had to get away from those hills and the Casteel heritage. He is not a slothful, lazy man. He was just a resentful one for finding himself trapped in what seemed a relentless circle of poverty."

Nothing she said indicated that she knew how much Pa had hated me, and probably still did. She didn't mention my mother or Sarah, and because she didn't I began to think of her as just another guileless and gullible Leigh Tatterton, so then it flashed through my mind that my father had a predilection for loving the same type of delicate female. Just as he favored redheads, like Sarah and Kitty, for occasional rough romps in the sack.

And if he had from time to time taken brunettes to bed, I'd yet to hear about them.

We returned to the living room after our lunch of tuna salad on a crisp bed of lettuce, with cubes of cheese, and hot rolls served with iced tea. Our dessert was chocolate pudding that Drake managed to smear all over his beautiful face.

No biscuits and gravy, I thought bitterly.

My bitterness soured more when we returned to the bright cheerful living room. I looked at the wide windows that looked onto a back garden full of flowers in full bloom, and I tried my best to picture Luke Casteel living in this kind of nice, modern house, sitting on that long, pretty sofa behind a coffee table free of dust and fingerprints. Green plants relieved the monotony of all the browns, tans, and creamy colors accented with touches of turquoise. A very masculine room, with only the sewing basket to hint that someone besides a man and a child lived here.

"This is your father's favorite room," she said, as if she noticed how preoccupied I was with my thoughts. Pride was in her voice. "Luke told me I could decorate it as I wanted, but I wanted a room where he would feel free to put his feet up, and a sofa where he could lie and not worry about rumpled cushions. Tom and your grandfather enjoy this room as well." It seemed she would say something else, for she flushed and looked guiltily confused for a second or so before she lightly touched my arm and smiled warmly. "It is truly wonderful to have you under our roof at last, Heaven. Luke doesn't talk much about his 'mountain home family,' for he says it hurts too much."

Oh, yes, I could imagine just how much it hurt! "Did he tell you about my mother, who was only fourteen when he married her?"

"Yes, he told me how they met in Atlanta, and he said he loved her very much. But no," she elaborated with wistfulness, "he never really talks about her so I can picture their life together in that mountain shack. I know that her premature death scarred him in a way he will never recover from. I also know he married me because I remind him of her, and when I kneel to say my prayers at night I pray that someday he will stop thinking of her. I know he loves me, and I've made him happier than he was when first we met, but until you can forgive him, and he learns to accept your mother's untimely death, he can't fully enjoy his life, and the moderate success he's found for himself."

"Did he tell you what he did?" I almost shouted. "Do you think he was right to sell his five children for five hundred dollars apiece?"

"No, of course I don't think it was right," she answered calmly, taking the winds from the sail of my attack. "He told me about what he did. It was a terrible decision he had to make. You five could have starved while he recovered his health. I can only justify his actions by saying he did what he thought best at the time, and none of you have suffered permanent damage, have you, have you?"

Her question hung in the air as she sat with her head bowed, quietly waiting for me to say I forgave Pa. Did she believe that the worst he'd done to us had been his Christmas betrayal? No, that had been only the climax! And I could not speak up and say anything to redeem his cruelty. The hope that had flared briefly on her face faded. Her eyes dropped to her son, and deeper sadness came over her face. "It's all right if you can't forgive him today. I just hope you will be able to one day in the near future. Think about it, Heaven. Life doesn't give us many chances to forgive. The opportunity comes, flits by, time passes, and it's too late."

I jumped to my feet. "I thought Tom would be here to meet me. Where can I find him?"

"Tom pleaded with me to hold you here until he returns about four-thirty. Your father won't be home until much later."

"I don't have time to wait until four-thirty." I was afraid to stay. Afraid she'd win me over to forgiving a man I hated. "When I leave here I'm flying to Nashville to see my sister Fanny. So please, tell me where to find Tom."

Reluctantly she gave me an address, her blue eyes still pleading with me to be kind and understanding, even if I couldn't be forgiving. And I said my polite goodbyes, kissed Drake on the cheek, then hurried away from the young wife who wore blinders.

I felt pity for such a naive woman who should have looked beneath the surface of a handsome, almost illiterate man who used women and eventually destroyed them. A list of discarded women behind him that I knew about, Leigh Tatterton, Kitty Dennison, and Lord knows what had happened to Sarah after she walked out on her four children and me. Only when I was in the rented car and speeding toward the border of Florida did I remember I should have gone out of my way to say hello to Grandpa.

An hour later I reached the small country town where every day Tom worked during his summer vacation, according to what Stacie had told me. I gazed around with disapproval at the small houses, the inadequate shopping center with its parking lot showing a sprinkling of late-model cars. What kind of place was this for Tom and his high ambitions? And like an avenging angel, determined to do what I could to upset Luke Casteel's plans for his eldest son, I guided my luxurious car to the outskirts of this nothing town and found the high wall Stacie had told me about.

Some things she hadn't prepared me for, such as the long line of colorful banners snapping in the hot wind. The banners kept on such a move I couldn't read the message they imparted. Insects hummed and badgered my head as I headed for a gate that was open. No one tried to prevent me from entering a huge, grass-covered arena with many worn dirt paths crisscrossing the lawns. What kind of place was this, I thought, my heart racing, so disappointed to think that my brother

Tom would settle for . . . for . . . and then I knew just what future Tom had set for himself in order to please Pa!

Tears seeped into my eyes. Circus grounds! A small, cheap, crass, unimportant circus struggling to survive. Tears began to streak down my cheeks. Tom, poor Tom!

As I stood beyond the gate in the hot afternoon sun and listened to the sounds of many people at work, some hammering, some singing and whistling, some shouting orders, others answering back in irritable voices, I also heard laughter, and saw children running, chasing one another. They threw me curious glances, and I guess I must have looked very strange in my early fall Boston attire that was totally wrong for Florida. Strange-looking people in bizarre clothing idled about. Women in shorts washed their hair over basins. Other women acted as hairdressers. Laundry was hung up to dry in the hot sunlight. A few palm trees offered some shade, and if I had been less prejudiced, I might have found this scene picturesque and charming. However, I wasn't about to be charmed. Strong animal odors wafted to my nostrils. An assortment of men in scant attire, with deeply tanned skins and bulging muscles, moved with purpose from here to there, setting up stands and booths with signs that read "Hot Dogs" "Hamburgers" and so forth. They repaired colorful posters that advertised a half-man and half-woman, dancing girls, the world's fattest woman, the world's tallest man, the world's smallest husband and wife, and a snake that was half-alligator and half–boa constrictor. Not one man failed to stare my way.

Many a time Tom had hinted in his letters that Pa

was doing something glamorous that he'd dreamed about all his life. Working for a circus? A small, second-rate circus?

Almost numb with despair I moved forward, staring into cages where lions, leopards, tigers, and other large wild cats were caged, seemingly awaiting transportation to another area. I stopped before one of the antique animal wagons, staring at the tiger poster adhered to its side where red paint was peeling off.

A time warp ricocheted me back to the cabin. It could have been the original of the tiger poster that Granny had described to me so many times, the one her youngest son Luke had stolen from a wall in Atlanta that time when he went there at the age of twelve, and his Atlanta uncle forgot to keep his promise of taking his hillbilly nephew to the circus.

And Luke Casteel, at age twelve, had walked fifteen miles to the circus grounds outside the city limits and had slipped into the circus tent without paying.

Almost blind now with tears, I ducked my head and used one of my linen handkerchiefs to blot my face. When I looked up, the first thing I saw was a tall young man coming my way, carrying with him something that looked like a pitchfork and, cradled under his left arm, a huge tray of raw meat. It was feeding time for the big cats, and as if they knew, lions and tigers began to toss huge shaggy heads, showing long, sharp, yellowish teeth, sniffing, gnawing, crunching bones, ripping into the bloody raw flesh the youth poked through the cage bars with the fork. They made deep rumbling noises in their throats that I had to take for pleasure.

Oh, my God! My God! It was my own brother Tom

who gingerly thrust the meat forward for savage paws to rake closer before teeth began to work.

"Tom" I cried, running forward. "It's me! Heavenly!" And for a moment I was a child of the hills again. The designer clothes I wore faded into a shabby, worn-out, shapeless dress gone gray from repeated washings in lye soap on a metal scrubbing board. I was barefooted and hungry as Tom turned slowly toward me, his deep-set, emerald eyes widening before they filled with delight.

"Heavenly! It's ya, really ya? Ya came t'see me, after all, drove all this way!"

As always when he was excited, Tom forgot his good diction and reverted to country dialect. "Oh good glory day! It's done happened! What I prayed fer!" He dropped the large tray that was now empty of meat, let go of the pitchfork, and opened his arms.

"Thomas Luke Casteel," I called, "you know better than to slur your contractions. Did Miss Deale and I waste our time teaching you good grammar?" And into his welcoming embrace I ran, throwing my arms about his neck, clinging fast to this brother who was four months younger, and all the time gone by since I'd seen him last vanished.

"Oh holy Jesus on the cross," he whispered emotionally, his voice hoarse, "still scolding and correcting me just like old times." He held me an arm's length away and stared at me with awed admiration. "I never thought you could grow prettier, but you're more than pretty now!" He swept his gaze over my rich clothes, pausing to take in the gold watch, the polished fingernails, the two-hundred-dollar shoes, the twelve-hundred-dollar handbag, and then he was staring at my face again. He exhaled in a long, whistling breath. "Wow! You look like one of those unreal girls on magazine covers."

"I told you I was coming. Why do you seem so surprised that I'm here?"

"I guess I thought it was just too good to be true," he answered rather lamely, "an' I guess in another way I didn't want you to come and spoil what Pa is trying to accomplish. He's just an uneducated man, Heavenly, trying his best to make a living for his family, and I know what he does is not much to someone like you are now, but being part of circus life has always been Pa's goal."

I didn't want to talk about Pa. I couldn't believe Tom had taken Pa's side. Why, it seemed Tom cared more for Pa than he did for me. But I didn't want to let go of Tom, didn't want him to become a stranger to me.

"You look . . . look, well, taller, stronger," I said, trying not to say he looked even more like Pa, when he knew I hated Pa's handsome face. The lean gauntness had gone from Tom's bony structure. The hollowed-out, dark shadows had vanished from his eyes. He appeared well fed, happy, satisfied. I could tell without asking.

"Tom, I just came from visiting Pa's new wife and child. She gave me directions to this place. Why didn't *you* tell me?" I glanced again around the arena where tents were mingled with permanent buildings. "Just exactly what does Pa do?"

His smile spread all over his face. His eyes lit with pride. "He's the barker, Heavenly. And a great one! He does a terrific job at rolling out the spiel that pulls in the customers. You see how dull it looks around here today, well, you just hang on till this evening, and from five hundred miles around customers will show up and shell out their money to see the animal acts, and the show girls, and the freaks who make up the carnival show. And we got rides, too," he said proudly, pointing to a Ferris wheel that I hadn't noticed until now. "We're hoping this year to add a carousel; you know, the kind we always wanted to ride?

"Heavenly," he gushed as he caught my arm and led me off in a new direction, "the circus is Pa's world now. You didn't know, any more than I knew, that the circus was always his dream when he was a boy. A thousand times he ran from the hills to sneak into the circus. I guess it was his way of escaping the ugliness and poverty of that mountain shack where he grew up. You remember how he hated the coal mines, and so he took to running moonshine. He ran, too, from the scorn everyone had for the Casteels, who seemed to know nothing better to do than wind up in jail, caught for petty crimes. When the Casteel sons would have been admired if imprisoned for more daring and major ones, short of murder, that is."

"But Tom, this is not your dream! It's his! You can't give up your college education just to help him out!"

"Eventually he wants to buy out the owner, Heavenly, and then this circus will be his. When I found out what Pa was up to I'm sure I looked just as amazed as you do right now. I wanted to tell you, really I did, and yet I was reluctant to tell you, pretty sure you'd feel and show nothing but scorn for his ambitions. I understand him more than I used to, and I want him to succeed for once in his life. I don't hate him like you do. I don't know how to hate him like you do. He's looking for his self-respect, Heavenly, and if what he's doing now seems trashy and nothing to you, it's the biggest thing he's ever attempted in his life. When you see him, don't make him feel small."

Again I looked around. Some women had recently showered in their tiny trailer shower stalls, and wrapped in towels, they stood in groups staring at where Tom and I stood. I had never felt so conspicuous. Other women were working on torn costumes. Everyone chatted in an animated fashion, and pretty girls born into the circus life threw Tom and me many a curious smile. Strong-looking acrobats practiced on dirty canvas mats, and at least a dozen dwarfs ran about doing odd jobs. I guess to some like Pa this might be the very kind of place he could hide himself away in, for no one here would care where he came from, or how lowly his background. However I knew exactly what Tony would feel if he could see what I was seeing, or perhaps he even knew, and that's why he had forbidden me to bring back even one Casteel.

"Oh, Tom, this is all right for Pa. Much safer and better than running moonshine. But it's not right for you!" I pulled him to a small bench put under the shade of a tropical-looking clump of trees. Bits of food were on the ground where birds fed, daring to pause and dine even at our feet. The heat and the odors had me feeling faint. The jewelry I wore seemed a heavy, sticky burden. "Troy has given me more than enough money to see you through four years of college," I began breathlessly. "You don't have to give up your dreams just so Pa can achieve his."

Tom's lean face flushed deeply red before he bowed his head. "You don't understand. I have already taken college boards and failed. I always knew my dreams

291

would never be realized. I just wanted to please you. You go on and get your college degrees and forget about me. I like my life. I'll like it even more when Pa and I earn enough to buy out the present owner of this circus. Why, one day we might even take the show out on the road farther than Georgia and Florida."

I could only stare at him, completely stunned that he would cave in so easily. And the longer I stared the deeper shade of red he turned. "Please, Heavenly, don't embarrass me. I never had your kind of brains, you just convinced yourself that I did. I haven't got any special talents, and I'm as happy here as I ever expect to be."

"Wait," I cried out. "Take the money . . . do what you want to with it, anything to get yourself out of this kind of trap! Leave Pa and let him take care of himself!"

"Please stop," he whispered. "Pa might overhear you. He's standing right over there by the galley tent."

My eyes had passed several times over a tall, powerful-looking man with his black hair stylishly trimmed and shaped, though his jeans were faded and tight, and the white shirt he wore was more or less the same kind of loose smock shirt that Troy so favored. It was Pa!

Pa, cleaner and fresher and healthier-looking than I'd ever seen him, and if he'd aged even one day, I couldn't tell it from the fifty feet that separated us. He was talking to a stout, jocular-looking, white-headed man wearing a red shirt, and was, apparently, giving him orders. He even glanced at Tom as if to check why his son wasn't busy feeding the animals. His dark intense eyes skimmed over me without coming back to gawk the way most men did when first I filled their vision. That alone told me that Pa wasn't interested in picking up young girls. His casualness also told me he hadn't recognized me at all. He smiled at Tom in a fatherly, congratulatory way, then turned to talk again to the man in the red shirt.

"That's Mr. Windenbarron," whispered Tom. "The current owner. He used to be a clown with Ringling Brothers. Everyone says there's not room in this country for two major circuses, but Guy Windenbarron thinks with Pa's help, the two of them can really grow. He's old, you know, and can't live much longer, and he needs ten thousand dollars to leave to his wife. We've already saved up seven. So it shouldn't be too long now, and Mr. Windenbarron will stay on to help us out as long as he can. He's been a real friend to Pa, and to me."

Tom's enthusiasm made me feel a bit sick. Only then did I realize that his life had gone on, just as mine had, and he'd found new friends and new aspirations.

"Come back in the evening," Tom invited, as if to hurry me out of reach from Pa, "and listen to Pa's spiel, and see the circus, and when the lights are turned on, and the music plays, maybe you will catch some of the circus fever that a great many people feel."

Pity for him was what I felt. Sorrow for someone determined to destroy himself.

I spent the remaining afternoon hours in a motel room, trying to rest and put my doubts at ease. There didn't seem anything I could do to change Tom's mind, and yet I had to give it another try.

That evening, about seven, I dressed in a casual summer dress and set out again for the fenced-in circus grounds. A startling metamorphosis had taken place. The Ferris wheel spun slowly, dazzling the eyes with its triple rows of colored lights. In fact every building, tent, and caravan trailer was brightly lit. The lights, the music, the hordes of people, created a certain kind of magic I'd never expected. Shoddy, ill-painted buildings appeared pristine and beautiful. The day's shabby circus wagons with their scratches and missing chips of red paint and gold appeared brand new. Music from a dozen sources was playing, and to my utmost surprise, those hundreds of casually dressed country people streaming through the open gates created great excitement with their happy anticipations of having a wonderful time. I followed, just another in the stream. I stared at girls my age hugged up close to boyfriends, wearing the briefest kind of costumes that would have brought scowls to Tony's face. Flushed parents held fast to the hands of children who wanted to run wild and explore; moving stiff and slow far to the rear of family groups staggered grandparents obviously more accustomed to spending their evenings in porch rockers.

In my entire eighteen years I had not been to even one circus performance. My experience with the circus had been as an observer watching a TV set, and that had not assaulted my senses with the sound, sight, and smells of animals, humans, hay, manure, sweat, and over all, from dozens of sources, the overwhelming fragrance of hot dogs and hamburgers, ice cream and buttery popcorn.

As I wandered over the circus grounds to stare at sideshow tents, where near-naked girls wearing heavy makeup undulated their hips provocatively, and freaks displayed their misfortunes with amazing indifference, for the first time I began to understand what had appealed to a twelve-year-old hillbilly boy straight from the Willies—appealed to him so much he'd returned to the hills to hypnotize himself into believing this was the best of all possible worlds: Better than the dark and dim coal mines, the spinning colored lights. Better than making and running moonshine and daring the Feds. Better in a thousand ways, all this, than that grim mountain shack and all the others like it, where reputations never died and your past mistakes lived on to haunt you forever. I could almost feel sorry for that ignorant boy.

Fine for Pa, all of this, now that he was too old to aim higher. Not fine for Tom, any of this, once he'd had enough of the tastes and flavors that would one day grow boring. I hadn't come to be seduced.

First I needed a ticket, and to buy that ticket I had to advance in single file toward where a man stood on a high pedestal and touted the virtues of the circus performance held inside. I knew who he was even before I heard his voice. Snared in the line, I stared up at him, at his feet clad in black patent-leather boots that almost reached his knees. Then came his strong, long legs clad in the tightest possible white pants. His masculinity was very obvious, taking me back to grade school days when the kids had snickered at pictures of dukes, generals, and other notables who so blatantly displayed themselves in pants fitted like those Pa wore. His long-tailed scarlet coat was emblazoned with gold stripes on the sleeves, epaulets on the shoulders, and double-breasted with gold buttons. Above the crisp clean white of his cravat was the same handsome face that I remembered, remarkably the same. His sins were not written on his face, nor had time taken from him what it had taken from Grandpa. No, Pa stood strong and powerful, in full prime, healthier-appearing than I'd ever seen him, better groomed, his face so closely shaven there wasn't even a shadow of whiskers. His black eyes sparkled, giving him a charismatic, magnetic quality. I saw women staring up at him as if at a god.

From time to time he whipped off his black top hat and used it for grand flourishes. "Five dollars, ladies, gentlemen, that's all it costs to enter another world, a world such as you may never have the chance to encounter again . . . a world where man and beast challenge one another, where beautiful ladies and daring men risk their lives high in the air for your entertainment. Two dollars and fifty cents per child under twelve. Babes in arms are free! Come see Lady Godiva ride her horse and spring into the air from the back of that horse, to land fifty feet above . . . and that hair moves, gentlemen, it moves!" On and on he cajoled as the cash register four feet to his right rang its bells and chimed its cash flow. I heard about the dangers of the kings of the jungle soon to waltz to the snap of the bull whip, as inch by inch I was moving closer and closer to Pa. So far he hadn't seen me. I didn't plan on allowing him to see me. I wore on my head a wide-brimmed straw hat that was held in place by a blue silk scarf that tied under my chin. And I had sunglasses with me to put on. But it was night, and somehow I forgot to slip the shades on.

Then I was there, at the head of the line, and Pa was looking down at me. "Why, a young thing like you doesn't need to hide her light under a bushel," he cried, and swooping to lean over, he tugged at the blue silk scarf, and my hat came off. Our faces were only inches apart.

I heard his sharp intake of breath.

I saw his shock. For a moment he seemed speechless, paralyzed. And then he smiled. He handed me my hat with its attached dangling blue silk. "Now," he boomed for all to hear, "that's the kind of beautiful face that should never be put in the shade . . ." and with that I was dismissed.

How quickly he could cover surprise! Why couldn't I? My knees went weak, my legs shaky; I wanted to scream and berate him and let these trusting people know just what kind of evil monster he was! Instead I was shoved along, ordered to hurry, and before I knew what was happening, I was seated on a bleacher bench, and my own brother Tom was grinning at me. "Wow, that was something, the way Pa took off your hat. Without a hat you wouldn't have pulled his attention nearly as much . . . please, Heavenly, stop looking like that! There's no need to tremble. He can't hurt you, he wouldn't hurt you." Briefly he hugged me against his chest, just as he used to do when I panicked. "There's somebody behind you who's dying to say hello," he whispered.

My hands, heavy with all the rings I'd worn to impress Pa, rose to my throat, as slowly I turned to meet the faded blue eyes of a wizened old man. Grandpa!

Grandpa dressed as I'd never seen him before, in summer sports clothes, with hard, white, summer shoes on his feet. His watery, bewildered eyes swam with tears. Obviously, from the way he kept staring at me, he was trying to place me in his thoughts, and while he did that, I saw that he'd gained weight. Healthy color flushed his cheeks.

"Oh," he cried finally, having pushed the right buttons, "it's chile Heaven! She's done come back to us! Just like she said she would! Annie," he whispered, giving the air next to him an elbow nudge, "don't she look good, don't she, Annie?" His arm went out as if to embrace the Annie who'd been at his right arm for so many years, and it hurt, really hurt to think that he couldn't live without his fantasy that she was still alive. I threw my arms about his neck, and pressed my lips on his cheek.

"Oh, Grandpa, it's so good to see you again, so good!"

"Ya should hug yer granny first, chile, ya should," he admonished.

Dutifully I gave the shade of my dead granny a hug, and I kissed the air where her cheek might have been, and I sobbed for all that had been lost, and sobbed some more for all that had to be gained. How did I grab at air and convince stubbornness and pride such as all Casteels had, and bring Tom to his senses?

The rinky-dink circus life was no place for Tom, especially when I had more than enough money at my disposal to see him through college. As I stared at my grandfather, I thought I saw a weak spot in Tom's armor of hillbilly pride.

"Are you still lonesome for the hills, Grandpa?"

I shouldn't have asked.

His pathetic old face lost all its glow. Wistful grief smeared his good health and he seemed to shrink.

"Ain't no betta place t'be, than there, where we belong. Annie says that all t'time . . . take me back t'my place. Back t'where we belong."

# ～ Sixteen ～
## Dream Chasers

I DROVE AWAY FROM TOM AND GRANDPA FEELING frustrated, angry, and determined now to save Fanny from the worst in herself, since I couldn't save anyone else. Loosely contained in Grandpa's pants pocket was a wad of bills he hadn't even bothered to count. "You give this to Tom after I'm gone," I'd instructed. "You make him take it, and use it for his future." But the Lord above was the only one who would know exactly what a senile old man would do with so much money.

And once more I flew, westward to Nashville where Fanny had moved the day after she sold her baby to Reverend Wayland Wise and his wife. Once in the city, I gave a cab driver Fanny's address, then leaned back and closed my eyes. Defeat seemed all around me, and there was nothing I could do right. Troy was the only safe harbor in sight, and achingly I longed for his strength beside me; yet this was something I had to do alone. I could never allow Fanny into my private life, never.

It was sultry and hot in Nashville, which appeared quaint and very pretty. Storm clouds hovered overhead as my cab cruised down pretty, tree-lined streets, past old-fashioned, gingerbread Victorian houses, and some modern mansions that were breathtakingly beautiful. However, when the cab parked before the address I'd given, the four-storied house that might once have been genteel was run-down, with peeling paint and sagging blinds, as was every house in what had to be one of the worst areas of this famous city.

My heels clicked on the sagging steps, causing several young people sprawled on porch chairs and swings to lazily turn their heads and stare my way. "Great balls of fire," breathed one good-looking young man wearing jeans and nothing on his sweaty chest. He jumped to his feet and bowed my way mockingly. "Look at what's come to call! High society!"

"I am Heaven Casteel," I began, trying not to feel intimidated by seven sets of eyes staring at me with what seemed hostility. "Fanny Louisa is my sister."

"Yeah," said the same young man who had jumped up, "I recognize you from the pictures she's always showing of her rich sister who never sends her any money."

I blanched. Fanny had never written to me! If she had photographs they had to be ones that I'd mailed first to Tom. And for the first time I thought that maybe Tony had deliberately kept from me any correspondence he thought unnecessary. "Is Fanny here?"

"Naw," drawled a pretty blond girl in shorts and a halter top, a cigarette dangling from her full, red lips, "Fanny thinks she's got a hot lead that should have been mine—but she won't make it. She can't sing or act or dance worth a hoot. I'm not worried at all that tomorrow they'll audition me."

It was like Fanny to try and beat someone out of a job, but I didn't say that. I had called Fanny in advance to tell her what time I would be arriving, and still she wasn't polite enough to wait. My expression must have shown my disappointment.

"She was so excited I guess she just forgot you were coming," explained another nice-looking young man who had already stated I didn't talk like Fanny's sister.

By this time a crowd of young people had formed around me on the porch to gape and stare, and it was with relief that I finally escaped, driven inside by a sudden roll of thunder. "Room 404," a girl named Rosemary shouted.

The rain that had threatened began to slice down as I entered Fanny's unlocked door. It was a small but fairly nice room. Or it could have been nice if Fanny had bothered to pick up her clothes, and dust and run the vacuum once in a while. Quickly I set about making her bed with the clean sheets I found in a drawer. When I had the room in fairly good order, I sat in the one chair near the window, staring blindly out at the storm, and thought about Troy, about Tom, about Keith and Our Jane, and that was enough to put rain on my face. How young and stupid I was to live and feed on emotions of the past, allowing the richness and beauty of life to pass me by because I couldn't control fate and the lives of others. I'd take from now on what was offered and forget the past. No one was suffering more than I was, not even Fanny.

My hands rose to press against my throbbing forehead. The lull of the rain and the thunder and lightning through the open window sent me into light sleep. Troy and I were running side by side in the clouds, fighting mists of steam and five old men who were chasing us. "You run on," ordered Troy, shoving me forward, "and I'll divert them by running in another direction."

No! No! I screamed in my mute dream voice. And those five old men weren't diverted. They followed where he ran, not where I did!

I bolted awake.

The rain had freshened and cooled the room that had been unbearably stuffy. The dusty shadows of late afternoon enhanced the view, turning the old houses with their fancy porches and verandas softly romantic. I felt disoriented as I stared around the small room with its cheap furnishings. Where was I?

Before I could decide, the door burst open. Dripping wet and complaining loudly to herself about the weather and the loss of her last pocket change, my sister Fanny, age sixteen, hurtled across the narrow space that separated us and threw herself into my arms.

"Heaven, it's ya! Ya really did come! Ya do kerr 'bout me!" One swift embrace, one peck on my cheek, and she shoved away, to stare down at herself. "Damn rain done gone an messed up my best outfit!" Fanny turned to yank off her sodden red dress before she fell into a chair and tugged off her black, midcalf plastic boots that were beaded with water. "Damned if my feet don't hurt clear up t'my waist."

I froze. Kitty flashed before my eyes. Often she'd used those words, but then, all hill and valley people in the Willies used more or less the same expressions.

"Damned agent hurries me out of here when I planned t'stay an wait fer ya t'show up, and when I get there all they want me t'do is 'read.' I already told 'em I kin't read good yet. I want a dancin' part or a singin' role! But they don't give me nothin' but bit parts without lines . . . an' I been poundin' these sidewalks fer almost half a year or more!"

Fanny had always been able to discard her frustration like a garment easy to rip off, and she did that now. Flashing my way her brilliant smile that revealed small, white, even teeth, she turned on her charm. Oh, the lucky Casteel children born with their healthy teeth!

"Ya bring me somethin? Did ya? Tom done wrote an said ya got tons of money t'waste, and ya sent him lots of Christmas gifts, an gifts t'Grandpa. Why Grandpa don't need no money! no gifts! I'm t'one who needs all ya kin spare!"

She had grown thinner and prettier since the last time I saw her, seemingly taller, or perhaps her height was only exaggerated by the tight, black slip she wore, so she resembled a shapely pencil. Her black hair lay in long wet strands on her head, but even wet and disheveled she was still striking enough to turn many a man's eye.

I was confused in my feelings about her—loving her because she was blood kin, feeling I had to love her and take care of her.

The eager greed in her dark eyes repelled me as one by one I took from the large leather shopping bag the gifts I'd brought her. Even before I had the last box from the bag she was ripping open the first gift that she'd seized, heedless of the beautiful and expensive wrappings and ribbons, heedless of anything but what was inside. Fanny squealed when she saw the scarlet dress.

"Oh, oh! Ya brought me jus' what I need fer t'party I'm goin ta next week! A red dancin' dress!"

Tossing the dress aside she ripped into her second present, her squeals rising and falling in the excitement of discovering the scarlet evening bag decorated with wide bands of rhinestones. The red satin slippers were a bit too small, but somehow she managed to jam her feet inside, and her beautiful, exotic face wore a rapt expression when finally she pulled out the white fox stole. "All this ya bought fer me? My own new fur? Oh, Heaven, I neva thought ya liked me, an ya do! Ya'd have t'love me t'give me so much."

Then, I guess for the first time, she really saw me. Her black eyes narrowed until the whites were only glimmers between her heavily lashed lids. I had changed a great deal, my mirrors told me that. The beauty that had been but slight when I lived in the hills had intensified, and a clever hairstylist had worked miracles that flattered my face. My expensive dress clung to ripe curves fitted neatly onto a slender body, and I knew as she looked me over that I had dressed with particular care for this meeting with my sister.

Her dark eyes skimmed down over my body to my shoes, back to my face. She drew in her breath, making a whistling sound. "Well, looky here, my ole-maid sister done gone an made herself sexy lookin'."

Hot, embarrassed blood flooded my face. "We don't live in the hills anymore. Girls in Boston don't marry at twelve, thirteen, or fourteen. You could hardly call me an old maid."

"Ya talk funny," she stated, open hostility in her eyes now. "All ya brought me is *thins!* When ya sent Grandpa money, an he's got no place t'spend it!"

"Look in your purse, Fanny."

Again squealing with delight, she yanked open the delicate small purse that had cost two hundred dollars, and she stared at the ten one-hundred-dollar bills as if she expected more. "Oh, Jesus Christ on t'cross," she breathed, busily counting, "look what ya done gone an' did . . . saved my life. Was broke . . . had me only enough left to finish out this week." She looked up, her dark eyes sparked with red highlights from the dress. "Thank ya, Heaven."

She smiled, and when Fanny smiled her white teeth flashed brilliantly in contrast to her Indian coloring. "Go on now, ya tell me what ya been doin' in ole bean town, where I hear all t'ladies wear blue stockins an t'men are hotter fer politics than they are fer screwin'!"

I was a fool that day—careless, forgetful of just what kind of girl Fanny was.

Maybe it was because for the first time in her life Fanny really listened attentively to me. And only when it was too late did I falter and curse myself for revealing much that I should have kept secret, especially from Fanny.

By the time I came to my senses, she was curled up on the bed wearing nothing but her black panties and her front-hook bra that she kept unfastening, then automatically fastening. "Now let me get this queer thin' straight—yer grandma Jillian is sixty-one years ole an looks young? What kind of air they got up there anyway?"

The sharpness in her eyes gave me sanity again, and put me on guard. "Tell me what you've been doing," I hastily said. "What do you hear about your baby?"

Apparently I'd chosen the right topic of diversion. She lit into the subject with a vengeance. "Ole lady Wise sends me snapshots of my baby all t'time. They call her Darcy. Ain't that some pretty name though? She's got black hair . . . oh, gosh, she's some pretty thin'," and then she was jumping up and pawing through a drawer scrambled with clothes, and from a large brown envelope she pulled out twenty or more snapshots showing a baby girl in various stages of development. "Ya sure kin tell who her ma is, kin't ya?" Fanny asked proudly. "Of course she's got some of Waysie, too. Not much, but some."

Waysie? I smiled to think of the good Reverend called "Waysie." But Fanny didn't exaggerate. The little girl I gazed at was a beautiful child. It stunned me that a baby born from such an unholy union would turn out so well. "She's beautiful, Fanny, truly beautiful, and as you said, she has inherited the best of your features, and her father's."

Dramatically Fanny's face distorted. She threw herself on the bed she'd rumpled, crushing her new red dress and shoes and purse that she'd left there, and she began to wail and cry, beating at the cheap pillows with both fists.

"It ain't no good here, Heaven! Ain't at all like I thought it'd be when I were a youngun in t'hills! Those directors an' producers at t'Opry like my looks an' hate my voice! They tell me t'go an take voice lessons, an go back t'school, an learn how t'talk, or betta yet, they tell me t'study dancin' so I don't have ta say *nothin'*! I went one day an took a lesson t'learn grace like they said I had t'have, an it hurt so bad stretching my muscles I neva went back! I thought all ya had t'know how t'do was kick high, an ya know I've been kicking high all my life! An my singin' voice makes 'em screw up their faces like it hurts their ears. They say I got too much *twang!* I thought country singers couldn't have too much of anythin'! Heaven, they say I've got a great face an body, but I'm only a mediocre talent—what do they mean by that? If I'm medium bad, that means I'm medium good an' I could get betta!

"But I don't want it no more! It hurts t'hear 'em laugh at me. An' now all my money is gone. It went so fast once I got used t'spendin it. I used t'sleep on top of it. Fraid somebody'd take it. Iffen ya hadn't come I'd have me only fifteen dollars t'finish out t'week, an then I were plannin' on hittin' t'streets an' peddlin' my wares."

Her eyes flicked my way to notice my reaction, and when she saw none, she flipped over and used her fists to grind away her tears. And like a switch had been pushed, her tears fled, and her look of frustrated depression disappeared. She smiled again. A wicked, hateful smile.

"Ya smell *rich* now, Heaven. Ya truly do. Bet that perfume yer wearin' cost plenty. An' I neva saw such soft-lookin' leather as that yer purse an' shoes are made of. Bet ya got ten fur coats! Bet ya got hundreds of dresses, thousands of shoes, millions of dollars t'waste! An' ya come bearing gifts that cost real dough. An' ya don't really like me, not like ya do Tom. Yer sittin' there feelin' sorry fer me cause I kin't

cut t'mustard when *ya* done snatched t'whole jar!
Look at my room, an' think of where ya jus came
from. Oh, I done heard from Tom all t'stuff yer not
tellin' me. Ya got everythin' up there in that mansion
that's got fifty rooms an eighteen bathrooms, an Lord
knows what ya do with all of 'em! Ya got three rooms
all yer own, wid four closets full of clothes an'
handbags an' shoes, jewels an' furs, an' college comin'
up, too. Me, I got nothin' but sore feet an' resentments fer this whole damned city that don't know how
t'be kind!"

Again her fists rubbed ruthlessly at her eyes until
the flesh around them turned red and bruised-
looking. "An ya got goody-two-shoes Logan Stonewall fer good measure! I guess it neva crossed yer
stupid brain I might have wanted Logan fer myself. Ya
went an took him away from me, an' I hate ya fer that!
Every time I think of what ya did t'me, I hate ya!
Even when I miss ya, I hate ya! An' it's time ya did
somethin' fer me 'sides givin' me a handful of measly
bills that don't mean anythin' to ya anyway! It's all
ova ya now, ya kin give ten one-hundred-dollar bills
cause ya got plenty more where they come from!"

Before I could blink she was up on her feet, striking
out at me!

I slapped back at her for the first time in my life.
The surprise of the sting my hand made on her face
made her draw away and whimper.

"Ya neva hit me before," she sobbed. "Ya done
turned mean, Heaven Casteel, mean!"

"Put on your clothes," I said sharply. "I'm hungry
and want to eat." I watched her scramble into a short
red skirt that resembled leather, and over this she
pulled a white cotton sweater that was much too

small. Gold hoop earrings swung from her pierced ears. The scuffed and thin-soled red plastic shoes she put her feet into had black heels five inches high, and the contents of her small, red plastic purse had spilled on the floor when she dropped it on seeing me. A crumpled pack of cigarettes lay beside five little square boxes of condoms. I looked away. "I'm sorry I came, Fanny. After dinner we'll say goodbye."

She was silent all during our meal in an Italian restaurant down the street from where she lived. Fanny devoured everything on her plate, then polished off what I left, though I would have paid for another entree. From time to time she'd gaze at me furtively in a calculating way, and I knew without guessing that she was plotting her next move. Eager to part from her and return to Troy, still I allowed her to talk me into returning to her small room. "Please, Heaven, please, for ole times' sake, 'cause yer my sista an' ya jus' can't up an' leave me t'fend fer myself."

Once we were back in her room, she whirled to confront me. "Now ya wait a minute!" she screamed, putting her fists on her hips and spreading her legs. "Who ya think ya are, anyway? Ya kin't jus come an' go without doin' somethin' more than givin' me a free meal, cheap clothes, an' a lil scrap of money!"

She angered me. Fanny had never given me a kind word in her life, much less anything material. "Why don't you ask me about Tom, or Keith and Our Jane?"

"I kin't worry 'bout nobody but myself!" she yelled, moving to block my way so I couldn't reach the door without shoving her aside. "Ya owe me, Heaven, owe me! When Ma went away ya were supposed t'do yer best fer me—an ya didn't! Ya let Pa sell me t'that Reverend an his wife, an' now they got my baby! An' when ya knew I shouldn't have sold her! Ya could have stopped me, but ya didn't try hard enough!"

My lips gaped open! I had done my very best to bring reality into Fanny's decision to give up her baby for ten thousand dollars. "I tried, Fanny, I tried," I said with weary impatience. "Now it's too late."

"It's neva too late! An' ya didn't try hard enough! Ya shoulda found t'right words t'say an' I woulda known betta! Now I got nothin'! No money an' no baby! An I want my baby! I want my baby so much it hurts! I kin't sleep fer thinkin' they got her, an' I'll neva have her . . . an' I love her, need her, want her. Neva held my own baby but once, for they took her away an' give her t'ole lady Wise."

Dumbfounded by Fanny and her irrational swings of temperament, I tried to express sympathy, but she wanted none of that.

"Don' ya try an' tell me I should have known betta. I didn't know betta, an' now I'm sorry. So here's what ya kin do with all that moola ya got stashed somewheres . . . ya go back t'Winnerrow an' ya give t'Reverend an his wife that ten thousand they paid me fer her! Or pay 'em twice that much, but ya buy back my baby!"

I couldn't speak. What she asked was impossible.

Her dark eyes burned into mine. "Ya hear me? Ya've got t'buy back my baby!"

"You can't mean what you say! There's no way I can buy back your baby! You told me when you entered that hospital you signed release papers of adoption—"

"No, I didn't! I jus' signed papers that said Mrs.

Wise could keep my baby till I was old enough t'take kerr of her."

I couldn't tell whether or not she was lying; I'd never been able to read Fanny as I had Tom. Still, I tried to rationalize. "I can't go back there and take a baby away from parents who adore her and take good care of her. You showed me the photographs, Fanny. I can see they love her enough to give her everything, and what can you give her? I can't turn a helpless baby over to you and your kind of life." I flung my arms wide, indicating the hopeless room where a baby crib wouldn't fit. "What would you do with a child so young and demanding? Where would you keep her while you go out to earn a living? Can you tell me that?"

"I don't have t'tell ya nothin'!" she cried, her eyes flashing before they watered. "Ya jus' do as I say or I'll use this thousand bucks t'fly up t'Boston! An' when I'm wid yer grandmother Jillian, who looks like some freaky kid, I'll tell her all about her lil angel gal who ran away from Boston. I'll spill it all out, that mountain shack wid no inside plumbing, an' Pa an' his moonshining, and his five brothers all in jail, an' when Jillian hears everythin' about how her lil angel girl lived 'fore she died, she won't look so young no more. I'll tell her about Pa an' how he visited Shirley's Place even when he were married t'her. An' I'll tell her about t'revenue men, an t'outhouse an t'stinks, an t'hunger her rich lil girl suffered through. An' I'll polish her little girl off jus' as it happened, givin' birth with no doctor, jus Granny t'help. An' when I'm done tellin her all kinds of rotten thins about *ya*, she'll end up hatin' ya!—if she don't lose what mind she's got left first!"

Again stunned, I could only stare at Fanny, overwhelmed that she could hate me so much, when all my life I'd done the best I could for her. I didn't know how to confront someone as obsessed as she appeared to be. Nervously I ran my hands over my hair, then I headed for the door.

"Don't ya go yet, *Heaven Leigh Casteel!*" Her twangy sarcasm rang familiar bells of shame in my ears. Oh she knew all the ways to hurt me most, reminding me of who I was and where I'd come from.

I felt colder than I'd ever felt, and it was midsummer, and the summer storm had only freshened the hot day, not chilled it.

"I'll do anythin' I kin think of t'hurt ya—unless ya go an' get my baby an' bring her back t'me!"

"You know I can't do that," I said again, so tired of Fanny and her shrill voice I wished I'd never come.

"Then what kin ya do fer me? Huh? Can ya give me everythin' ya've got fer yer own? Give me a room in that huge house, so I kin enjoy what ya have? If ya loved me, like yer always sayin', ya'd want me where ya kin see me every day."

Colder and colder I was growing. The last person I needed to see every day of my life was Fanny. "I'm sorry, Fanny," I began in icy tones, "I don't want you in my life. I'll send you money once a month, enough to see you through comfortably, but you'll never be invited to live where I do. You see, my grandmother's husband made me promise I'd never allow any Casteel relative of mine to mar the perfection of his days, and if you're plotting now on blackmailing me by threatening to tell him I've seen you, and Tom, then forget it. For he would cut me out of his life without a cent, as easily as you can bat your eyes—and then there would be no money for you—and no money left with which to buy your baby back."

Her slitlike dark eyes narrowed even more. "How much ya gonna send me each month?"

"Enough!" I bit back.

"Then send twice as much, fer when I have my baby girl, I'll need every cent ya kin spare. An if ya disappoint me, Heaven Casteel, I'll find my way inta yer life, an I won't give a damn if ya lose everythin'! Ya don't deserve it anyway!"

The wind from the Willies reached out and chilled me even more. I thought I heard the distant wolves howling; I thought I saw the snow banking high around the mountain shack, closing me in. With difficulty I tried to focus on what to do and what to say, as long seconds ticked slowly toward eternity and the dirty, tattered curtains billowed out into the room like wraiths of God.

Not for a moment did I doubt that Fanny would do exactly what she said she'd do, just to strike back at me for being born first, and having what she considered some sort of invisible advantage, when I'd never had anything advantageous happen to me until Logan chose me instead of her.

And only then did it slap me directly in the face. I hadn't believed her when she said it. Logan was the reason she hated me! All along she'd wanted him and he'd never really looked at her despite all she'd done to draw him her way. I put my hands to my fevered cheeks, wondering just what was wrong with mountain girls who grew up too soon—and determined way before their time just what man was right for them, when none of us could possibly know.

Sarah and her miserable choice. Loving a man like

Luke Casteel. Kitty Setterton and her insane love for
a man who had only used her to scratch his itch. But
Fanny standing there with her dark, hating eyes,
trying to glare me into extinction, when Logan wasn't
mine anymore—but damned if I'd turn him over to
her to ruin!

"All right, Fanny, calm down," I said with as much
authority as possible. "I'll go to Winnerrow. I'll talk
to the Wises about buying back your baby that you
sold. But while I'm gone, you sit down and you think
long and hard about just what you are going to do to
take care of that little girl, and see to it that she has a
healthy and good life. It takes more than money to
make a good mother. It takes devotion and caring
more for your daughter than for yourself. You'll have
to give up your stage aspirations and stay home to
take care of Darcy."

"Ain't got what it takes t'hit it big at t'Opry, like I
always thought I could," she wailed pitifully, and for a
moment I felt pity. "So I might as well give up.
There's a guy here who's asked me t'marry up wid
him, an I might as well go on an do it. He's fifty-two
years ole, an I don't really love him, but he has a good
job an kin support me an my kid—wid yer help, that
is. I'll wait here fer ya t'come back, an by t'time ya do,
him an' me will be hitched fer life. An I won't spend
no more of this here money ya gave me than I have
ta."

Maybe I said something smart, or something dumb
then, but I said it out of desperation. "Don't be so
stupid as to marry a man so much older. Find a young
man, near your own age, then get married, and keep
quiet, and when I'm back with your baby I'll see you
through until you no longer need me."

Her brilliant and pleased smile shone. "Sure, I'll stay. I won't say a word. Not even t'Mallory. He's t'guy who loves me. Ya jus' go on an' do what ya kin . . . an' you'll win . . . don't ya always win, Heaven, don't ya?"

And once more she swept her greedy eyes over my clothes and the jewelry I'd grown so accustomed to wearing I had forgotten I had it on.

But it wasn't Winnerrow I headed for when I left Fanny lying on her bed in Nashville. It was Tom I called. "Fanny wants me to buy her baby back, Tom. Use some of the money I left with Grandpa and fly to Winnerrow and come with me when I confront the Wises."

"Heavenly, you know I can't do that! You were a dope to give Grandpa all that money, for now he can't even find it! You know he's never had more than a buck in his pocket—whatever possessed you to give him cash?"

"Because you wouldn't take it!" I cried, near tears from his stubbornness.

"I want to earn my way, not have it bought for me," Tom said stubbornly. "And if you're smart you'll forget about keeping that promise to Fanny, and let the Wises have the little girl everyone thinks is their own. Fanny won't make a fit mother, even if you feed her a million a month—and you know it."

"Goodbye, Tom," I whispered with a certain feeling of finality. Time and circumstances had robbed me of the brother who had once been my champion. Now I had only Troy, and he wasn't feeling exceptionally well when I called.

"I wish you'd hurry back, Heaven," he said in an

odd voice. "Sometimes when I wake up at night I think you are only a dream and I'll never see you again."

"I love you, Troy! I'm not a dream! After I've seen the Wises I'm flying back to be your wife."

"But you sound distant and different."

"It's the wind on the telephone lines. I always hear it. I'm glad someone else does, too."

"Heaven . . ." He paused, then said, "Never mind, I don't want to beg."

I waited on stand-by for a flight to take me to West Virginia, to Winnerrow, to Main Street where Logan lived in the apartment over Stonewall's Pharmacy.

Oh, I was tempting fate to do its worst, but I didn't know that at the time. I only knew I wanted to win at one game of chance I played . . . and maybe money could buy back one little girl who might be grateful in the future . . .

## ~ Seventeen ~
### *Against All Odds*

THEY WERE SINGING IN THE CHURCH WHEN I ENTERED, singing with pious faces upraised, the glorious, spiritual songs that reminded me of my youth when Sarah had been my mother, when home had been the cabin in the Willies, and the sweetest things in my life had been my love for Logan Stonewall, and the hours we both spent on Sundays in this church.

And their voices, so uplifted in celebration of the best part of their lives that came on Sundays, were incredibly clear on this sizzling hot summer's evening. Electric heat bolts lit up the sky every so often. Following the last of the stragglers into the church, where hand-held fans fluttered the air, as if the central air conditioning was off, I was again transported back in time to when I was just a scumbag Casteel.

Oh, those sweet and wholesome angel voices were the same ones that could rant and rave and curse, but who could believe that now? Not any stranger who didn't know them intimately, as all residents of the

317

valley and hills knew each other. I quietly sat in the last side pew of the last row and was surprised to see that quite a number of hill folks were in church, when customarily they didn't attend evening services in overwhelming numbers, especially on a scorching night like this one. The town folks wore their newest and best, and didn't bother to turn their heads, only their eyes to stare my way. Look down their noses over my clothes, in their combined hypocrisy they united to form mindless judgments seldom based on facts, only on suspicions and herd instinct.

They knew me despite my fine raiment.

Despite my clothes, they didn't want me in their midst. They didn't even have to speak a word; their animosity was sharp and needling, and if I hadn't been in such a determined mood, I might have been driven away, knowing that, no matter how rich or famous I might become, I'd never win their respect, or their admiration, or what I wanted more than anything else, their envy. Nothing had changed in the order of what they considered right and wrong and suitable—for such as me.

The hill folk still took the back benches, the valley folk still reigned supreme in the middle, and those deemed worthiest sat closest to God in the first rows, center aisle, those on the front pews were also those who contributed most to whatever charity or building fund that was currently popular. There, prim and proper, was Rosalynn Wise, staring up at her husband with blank eyes as he stepped up to his podium. His slick, black, custom-made suit fitted him so beautifully he appeared as slim as he had when first I saw him when I was ten. And everybody knew Reverend

Wayland Wise had such a gluttonous appetite he gained at least ten pounds each year.

It had been my intention when I entered to stay, as always, in my place, but that was also where it was warmest from the hot blasts of air coming in the door that opened and closed every few minutes. To my own surprise I didn't stay seated. Soon I found myself standing, and in the third row, center aisle, while all eyes riveted on my audacity, I found an empty pew and there I plucked a hymn book from the pocket of the seat ahead, and automatically turned to page 216 and began to sing. Really sing—loud, clear, high. For all the Casteels could sing, even when they had nothing to sing about.

I had gained their attention now, shockingly gained it. They stared at me, open-mouthed, wide-eyed, stunned and alarmed, that I, a Casteel, would dare so much! And I didn't try to ignore them. I met each pair of accusing eyes and never faltered as I sang the old familiar hymn that Our Jane had loved so very much. "Bringing in the sheaves, bringing in the sheaves, we shall come rejoicing, bringing in the sheaves."

As I sang I could almost snatch their thoughts from the air. *Another crummy Casteel had come again into their sanctified midst!* Their hostile eyes swept again over my face, over my clothes, sneered at the jewelry I wore in ostentatious excess just to show them what I had now—everything!

A murmur of disapproval rippled through the crowd, but I didn't care. I had given them all a good chance to look me over in my jewels and my expensive suit.

But those eyes still weren't impressed, or if they

were, they didn't widen with admiration or narrow with surprise. To them a porkbelly had more of a chance of transforming into ten billion bats of gold than I had of becoming respectable.

As abruptly as the heads had swiveled to see me advance to the front, now each and every one of those heads turned away, almost like a fan of faces folding. The hillbillies to the sides of me and behind me did as the valley folk did, and that was to turn slightly from me. I squared my shoulders, sat down, and waited. Waited for whatever cue would come along from whatever sermon the good and holy Reverend chose this particular Sunday night. There was suspense in the air, a silence pregnant with ill will. Perched uneasily in the pew, I thought of Logan and his parents, wondering if they had chosen tonight to come to church. I slipped my eyes around as best I could without turning my head, hoping and fearing to see the Stonewalls.

Then, suddenly, heads were again turning to stare at an old man who was hobbling with a stiff-kneed gait down the center aisle. I kept my eyes straight ahead, but I saw him nevertheless in my peripheral vision— coming to sit beside me!

It was Grandpa!

My own grandpa, whom I had seen only two days ago! Grandpa, who had pocketed the hundred-dollar bills, promising vacantly to give the money to Tom. And here he was, far from Florida and Georgia, grinning at me shyly, showing the sad state of his toothless mouth. Then he whispered, "Good t'see ya, Heaven girl."

"Grandpa," I whispered. "What are you doing

back here?" I slipped my arm about his waist and hugged him as best I could. "Did you give the money I gave you to Tom?"

"Don't like flat places," he mumbled in way of explanation, casting down his pale eyes that seemed to shed tears, though I knew they often watered.

"What about the money?"

"Tom don't want it."

I frowned, not knowing how to pursue something in the brain of an old man who didn't know how to separate reality from fantasy. "Did Pa ask you to leave?"

"Luke's a good boy. He wouldn't do that."

It made me feel good to have him at my side, lending support just with his presence. He hadn't turned away as had Keith and Our Jane. Tom must have told him I was coming to Winnerrow and he had managed to get here to give me moral support; and no doubt, Pa had the money I'd meant for Tom.

Church members turned in their pews to glare hard at us, putting cautionary fingers before pursed lips, causing Grandpa to slump down in the pew so he ended up on the end of his spine in his efforts to obediently disappear. "Sit upright," I hissed, elbowing him sharply. "Don't let them intimidate you." But Grandpa stayed where he was, clutching his worn-out old straw hat as if it were a shield.

Reverend Wise stood silent and tall and impressive behind the podium, looking directly at me. The distance from him to me was about twenty feet, still I thought I saw in his eyes something like a warning.

Obviously he'd opened the service earlier, for he didn't begin with one of his long-winded prayers that went on forever. He began in a smooth, conversational voice that was rich and compelling:

"The winter has ended. Springtime has come and gone. We are well into another summer, and soon autumn will brighten our trees, and then the snow will fall again—and what have we accomplished? Have we gained ground, or lost it? I know we have suffered and we have sinned since the day we were born, and yet our Lord in his infinite mercy has seen fit to keep us alive.

"We have laughed and we have cried, and we have fallen ill and we have recovered. There are some of us who have given birth, and some of us who have lost loved ones, for that is the way of our Lord, to give, to take, to exchange losses with gifts, to restore only to destroy with the whims of nature.

"And always, no matter how great our travail, the stream of His love carries us through, so we can gather together in places of worship like this, and celebrate life even when death is all around us, and tragedy is tomorrow's certainty, just as today and this hour and minute is our time of rejoicing. We are all blessed in hidden ways, and cursed in other ways. To hate and to harbor grudges, and to pass judgment without knowledge of circumstances is an evil comparable to murder. And though no one may know our secret hearts, there are no secrets from Him above."

Why, he was like the Bible—ambiguous—and his words could be construed to mean anything. He talked on in a chanting, sing-song tone, never taking his eyes off of me, but I had to shift my gaze or be paralyzed from pure awe, for he had that kind of mesmerizing power.

Then, out of the blend of many furtive stares I encountered the blazing rage of two hard, green eyes beneath the narrow rim of a green straw hat—glaring at me in a contemptuous way was Reva Setterton, the mother of Kitty Dennison!

Icewater trickled down my spine. How could I have come back to Winnerrow without giving a single thought to Kitty's family? Only then did I overtly glance around to see Logan, or his parents. They weren't here, thank God. My hand rose to my forehead, which grew alarmingly hot, aching and throbbing. An onrush of sensations unfamiliar to me was making me feel dizzy, unreal.

Grandpa suddenly sat up, then rose shakily to his feet, reaching for my hand so he could tug me to my feet. "Ya don't look so good," he murmured, "an' we don't belong up here." I was weak to allow him to defeat my purpose in this way, and yet for an old man his grip on my hand was strong, so strong the rings on my fingers bit into my flesh. I followed him to the back of the church, and there we again sat. An overwhelming memory of how it used to be swept over me. I was a child again, awed by the fine folks in rich new clothes, impressed by the church with its tall stained-glass windows, made humble by the God who ignored our needs and catered to those who dropped in dollars instead of small change.

The throbbing pain in my head stabbed sharply. What was I doing here? Me, a nobody, a nothing, come to do battle with the man who had to be the champion gladiator in the Winnerrow's Sunday coliseum. I glanced with some dismay around the crowded church, hoping to find one pair of friendly eyes

. . . and what was it the Reverend had said to make all of them turn to glare at me?

Faces smeared into one giant blob with huge, hostile eyes, and all the security Troy's love had bestowed peeled off like new paint applied to wet wood. Trembling and weak with the hate I saw everywhere, I wanted to stand and run and drag Grandpa out of there before the lions were let out of the cages!

Like sleeping beauty waking up in an enemy camp, I lost the enchantment that had begun the day I stepped into Farthinggale Manor. And had deepened the day I found Troy.

Distant and unreal they seemed now, only figments of my overactive imagination. I glanced down at my hands as I began to twist the nine-carat diamond engagement ring Troy had insisted I wear even if we never married. Then I was playing thoughtlessly with my pearls suspending a diamond and sapphire pendant, a special engagement gift from Troy. Funny how I had to cling to the hardness of those jewels to convince myself that only days ago I'd lived in one of the most fabulous and wealthy homes in the world.

Time lost itself that Sunday night in the church.

I grew old, and I grew younger. Fevered and miserable, my bones ached for bed.

"Let us all bow our heads and pray," instructed the Reverend, at last releasing his riveting gaze, and I could breathe more freely. "Let us humbly pray for forgiveness so we may enter into this new chapter in our lives without carrying into it old sins, and old grievances, and old promises never kept. Let us assign to each new day respect for those who we feel may have harmed us in the past, and pledge to ourselves we will do unto others as we would have done onto us.

"We are mortals put upon this earth to live out our lives with humility, without resentments, harboring no grudges . . ." and on and on he talked, seemingly to me.

Finally the sermon was over, and he'd said nothing I hadn't heard before, so why was it I kept thinking he was cautioning me to keep my peace? Did he know that I knew he had fathered that pretty little girl who was carried in from a backroom nursery, and still sleeping, put in the arms of his wife? I stood up, assisting Grandpa to his feet, and headed for the door, not waiting in place as all hillbilly scum were supposed to do, so they'd be the last to leave and shake the pious, saintly hand of the Reverend.

Hardly were Grandpa and I out on the street steamy with heavy humidity, than a man was fast approaching me and calling out my name. At first I thought it was Logan . . . then my heart sank into my shoes. It was Cal Dennison, stretching forth his hand and beaming a happy smile into my face. "Heaven, dear Heaven," he breathed, "how wonderful to see you again! You look beautiful, absolutely wonderful. . . now tell me all about yourself, what you've been doing, and how you like Boston."

When streets were hot in Winnerrow, and inside it was even hotter, the residents of the village were not prone to enter bedrooms when porches were so inviting. I heard the clink and clank of ice in pitchers of lemonade, as I stood and floundered and wondered how to talk to Cal Dennison, who had once been my friend, and my seducer.

"I like Boston very much," I said, as I caught hold of Grandpa's arm and headed for the hotel where I had registered. Strolling Main Street was like walking a gauntlet of enemies, everyone stared at us, and I didn't need or want to be seen with Cal Dennison!

"Heaven, are you trying to brush me off?" asked Cal, his good-looking face glistening with a layer of sweat. "Please, can't we go somewhere and sit down and share a drink and talk?"

"I have a terrible headache, and I'm looking forward to a long, cool bath before bed," I said honestly.

His entire countenance seemed to collapse on hearing my excuse. "You sound like Kitty," he mumbled, bowing his head, and instantly I was stricken with guilt.

I remembered then that Grandpa was still at my side. "Where are you staying, Grandpa?" I asked, when we were outside the one and only hotel in Winnerrow.

"Luke done fixed up t'cabin fer Annie an me. I'm stayin' there, of course."

"Grandpa, stay with me in the hotel. I can rent you another room, one with a color TV."

"Gotta git me back t'Annie . . . she's waitin."

I resigned myself. "But Grandpa, how will you get there?"

His bewilderment made him sway even as he stood and waited for me. "I'll ketch me a ride with Skeeter Burl. He likes me now."

Skeeter Burl? He was the worst enemy Pa had ever made in the hills—and he liked Grandpa now? That was like believing July sunbathers liked January snow. And like the damned fool I could sometimes be, totally out of my head, I gently took Grandpa by the arm, and together we turned toward the hotel. "Grandpa, it looks as if you're going to have to spend the night in the hotel after all."

Instant alarm was his. He'd never slept in a "rented" bed. He didn't want to. Annie needed him! He had animals at home who would suffer if he didn't return. His pale and leaking eyes pleaded pitifully. "Ya go on t'yer hotel, Heaven girl. Don't ya worry none about me."

Desperation gave him needed strength. He tore loose from my restraining grip, and moving more swiftly than I could believe, Grandpa began hobbling off down Main Street. "Ya go on an tend t'yer business. Don't like beds not my own!"

"I'm glad he's gone," said Cal, catching hold of my arm and guiding me into the hotel lobby and toward a small coffee shop. "This is where I'm staying, too. I've come to Winnerrow to settle some estate legalities with Kitty's parents, who have fought me tooth and nail, claiming I contributed nothing to their daughter's estate, therefore I don't deserve to have even the part she left me."

"Can they break her will?" I asked wearily, wishing to God I'd not had the misfortune to run into him.

We settled down behind a small round table, and soon Cal was placing an order for a late-evening snack. He acted toward me just as if nothing had altered our relationship, and very well he might expect to end up with me in his bed. I sat stiff and uncomfortable, knowing I was going to disillusion him the moment he made even one small advance.

Nibbling on my bacon-lettuce-and-tomato sandwich, I half listened to Cal as he spilled out all the difficulties he was having with his Setterton in-laws. "And I'm lonely, Heaven, so lonely. Life just doesn't seem right without a woman nearby. I am legally entitled to everything Kitty left me, but when her family contests, it forces me to hire lawyers, and that holds up all the settlements. I will lose half of Kitty's estate in court and attorney costs—but they don't care. They are having their revenge."

My eyes had grown very heavy by this time. "But they don't hate you, Cal, so why are they doing this?"

He sighed and bowed his head into his cradling hands. "It's Kitty they hate for not leaving them more than her good wishes." He glanced upward, tears shining in his eyes. "Is there a chance a beautiful young girl will turn my way again? We could get married this time, Heaven. We could have a family. I could finish my education, as you finish yours, and we could both be teachers."

I was numb with fatigue, unable to resist when Cal picked up my hand and held it to his lips, then pressed my palm against his cheek. And just at this point, Logan Stonewall, with a pretty girl at his side, sauntered into the coffee shop and pulled a chair for the girl, whom I recognized as Kitty's own sister, Maisie!

Oh, my God! I had hoped not to see Logan. He looked wonderfully healthy but somehow older than when I'd seen him last. A certain youthful quality had been replaced by cynicism, which twisted his smile crookedly. Had I done that to him? His dark sapphire eyes met mine briefly before he lifted his hand and saluted, and then his eyes moved to stare with surprise and disgust at Cal. From that point on he made a studied effort not to look our way. However, Maisie was not as discreet. "Logan honey, ain't that yer ole girlfriend, Heaven Casteel?"

He didn't bother to dignify her question with an answer. Quickly I was on my feet. "I'm not feeling well, Cal. Please excuse me. I'm going straight to my hotel room and to bed."

Disappointment flooded Cal Dennison's face. "I'm very sorry to hear that," he said, standing and reaching for the check. "Please allow me to see you to your room."

It wasn't necessary, and I didn't want him to come, but pain was behind my eyes, and fatigue was deep in my bone marrow. What was wrong with me? Despite all my objections, which were many, Cal followed me into the hotel lobby, stepped into the elevator, which took us to the sixth floor, and then insisted on opening my door. Quickly I stepped into the room and tried to close the door behind me, but he was quicker. Before I knew what was happening, Cal was in my room and holding me in his arms, raining on my face hot and passionate kisses.

I struggled to free myself. "Stop! No! This isn't what I want! Leave me alone, Cal! I don't love you! I don't think I ever did! Now let me go!" I struck out at his face with a balled fist and just missed giving him a black eye.

The surprise and fury of my attack caught him off guard. His arms fell away, and he stepped backward, seemingly on the verge of tears. "I never thought you'd forget all the good things I did for you, Heaven," he said with sadness. "Ever since I came back to Winnerrow three days ago, I've hoped and prayed and dreamed of seeing you again. People here have heard about your good fortune, but they don't want to believe it. And I know Logan Stonewall is seeing half a dozen girls, including Maisie."

"I don't care who he sees!" I sobbed, shoving at Cal and trying to push him out of my room. "All I want to do is take a bath and go to bed—now get out and leave me alone!"

He went then. He stood in the hotel hall beyond my open door and stared in at me with the saddest expression. "My room number is 310 in case you change your mind. I need someone like you. Give yourself a chance to love me again."

Images of Cal and Kitty together flashed through my mind. Kitty saying no to his nightly advances; his pleading voice coming through the walls and into my room—oh, yes, he had needed me! Needed someone young and gullible and stupid enough to think he was a genuine friend . . . and still, as he stood there with those tears in his eyes, I pitied him. "Good night and goodbye, Cal," I said softly, stepping to where I could slowly close the door in his face. "It's all over between us. Find someone else."

The click of the closing door almost smothered his sob. I turned the key, put on a dead bolt, and ran for the bathroom. My thoughts were in turmoil—why had I come back to Winnerrow? To buy back Fanny's baby? What a ridiculous idea! My hand went to my head. When the tub was full, I stepped into the water and carefully sat down. The water was a bit too hot. Kitty had liked very hot bath water. Where had Grandpa gone? Could it be he would return to that miserable cabin?

After I finished my bath, I couldn't get Grandpa out of my thoughts. What had he done with all the money I'd given him? I had to find Grandpa. I wouldn't be able to sleep until I knew he was safe at the cabin. My head was throbbing as I left the hotel.

Main Street was steamy with humidity. Hardly a breeze blew. Up in the Willies the wind would sing through the tree leaves, having chased over the mountains, so it could sometimes cool even the tiny, cluttered rooms of that miserable shack.

I got in my rented car and drove through town. It was ten-thirty at night. All business but the pharmacy counter in Stonewall's closed after ten in the evening.

No sooner had I hit the outskirts of Winnerrow and begun to climb the spiraling highway, than my car began coughing and sputtering and then died. Undecided as to what to do now, I got out and opened the hood. Who was I fooling? I knew nothing about cars. I stared around at familiar territory that had taken on nightmarish proportions. I should walk back to the hotel and go to bed, I told myself, and forget about Grandpa and the money. Tom would never accept help from me. Grandpa didn't need me, not really. All over I was trembling.

I tried to start the car again and again, to no avail. The wind picked up and brought with it the scent of rain soon to fall. And this was going to be no ordinary summer storm. This storm had wild fierce winds, the kind that brought hail, then a sluice of water. Stronger and stronger the wind blew into my face. I had no choice but to sit in my car and hope that someone would drive by and stop to help me. My body ached all over, and I began to wonder if I hadn't caught a bit of Troy's illness.

I must have sat there for a half hour before a car appeared, unexpectedly slowed, and the driver pulled over to the side and got out of his car. As I rolled down the window, I was shocked to recognize the familiar figure. "What are you doing out here alone at midnight?" Logan Stonewall asked.

I tried to explain what had happened as he regarded me suspiciously. "C'mon, I'll drive you up there," he finally said, his eyes hard and commanding as he led me to his car. Feeling an absolute fool, I sat on the front seat beside him, and didn't know what to say.

"I was just going to check on your grandpa myself," he said in way of explanation the minute he gunned his motor and shot forward.

"He's not your responsibility!" I cried out like a child, my voice gone strange and thick.

"I'd do the same thing for anyone all alone up there at his age."

Silence thicker than fog came between Logan and me. The trees along the roadside were lashed unmercifully by the winds, before the hail pelted down and Logan was forced to the side of the highway to wait until the worst was over. That took about ten minutes, and during that time neither of us spoke.

Once more Logan drove his car toward a familiar dirt road that would branch out any second. Fastening my eyes on the road ahead, I tried to control my trembling.

Long ago I had considered Winnerrow's one and only hotel superbly grand; now I knew it was seedy. But still it was far better than the shack he was driving me to! I felt like crying. I wanted a comfortable bed, clean sheets and nice blankets, and heat to drive this sudden chill from my bones. And now I'd have only the cabin with its outhouse, and the inadequate heat of Ole Smokey. I felt a tragic sense of loss as civilization was left behind in Winnerrow.

Instead of crying, I lit into Logan.

"And so you play the good Samaritan to my grandfather, do you? I suppose you just need someone in your life you can pity and demonstrate your generosity to."

He flicked me another of his scornful glances, and I looked at him long enough to see there wasn't a spark of the love that was once in his eyes. It hurt to know that my best friend had turned into a worst enemy, the kind of enemy who would kill me with hard glances and cruel words; the knives he'd save for others to throw.

I pressed back hard against the seat and slid as far from him as possible, vowing to myself not to look at him again, though in the dark, I couldn't see him very well anyway. Something was going wrong with my vision. Unreality had me squeezed in a tight fist. That ache in my bones had spread to my chest, behind my eyes, and my face burned as well as hurt. Moving became more difficult.

"I drive your grandfather to Winnerrow when he wants to go," Logan said stiffly, flicking me a glance. "He comes up often from Georgia and Florida to check on his cabin."

"He said Skeeter Burl would drive him home . . ."

"Skeeter Burl did drive him a few times to and from church, but he was killed in a hunting accident about two months ago."

Why would Grandpa tell me a lie? Unless he'd lost touch with reality and had forgotten. And of course, Grandpa had forgotten reality the day his Annie died . . .

Logan fell into another prolonged silence, as did I. The world had lost a mean man when Skeeter Burl departed, even if he had favored Grandpa with a ride or two.

Using all the shortcuts it was seven miles from Winnerrow to our cabin. This road made it three times that distance. My fuzzy mind tried to sort out clues. "Why aren't you in Boston? Doesn't your school start in late August?"

"Why aren't you?"

"I'm planning to fly back to Boston tomorrow afternoon . . ." I said vaguely.

"If the rain stops," he said flatly.

The rain came down in torrents. I'd never seen such rain except in early spring. This was the kind of strong driving rain that turned small creeks and springs into tiger rivers that tore down bridges and uprooted trees, and flooded the banks. Sometimes in the Willies it had rained for a week, and more, and when it was over, lakes of water had kept us from going anywhere, even to school.

And Troy was expecting me to return late tomorrow. I'd have to call him as soon as I got back to Winnerrow. Another few miles passed. "How are your parents?" I asked.

"Fine," he answered shortly, discouraging me from asking more.

"I'm glad to hear that."

At this point he turned off the main highway, and now the road turned into hardly more than a dirt path full of deep ruts flooded with water. The rain still sluiced down, slashing at the windshield, at the windows on my side. Logan switched off the wipers, and leaned forward to peer ahead. I'd never seen Logan look so hard before, so unaccommodating. Then he moved suddenly, seizing hold of my left hand, and for seconds he stared at the huge diamond on my ring finger. "I see," he said, dropping my hand as if he never wanted to touch me again.

I clamped my lips together, sealed my mind, and tried to think of something but the way Our Jane and Keith had rejected me. That horrible sense of loss clung to me like old rotting moss.

Paying strict attention to the road, Logan said nothing more, and it was with relief that he turned into the space that represented the yard of the mountain cabin I'd not expected to see again.

This time I came to the cabin where I'd been born, with Boston perspective, my sensibilities trained now to appreciate beauty and fine construction; my taste cultivated with an eye for the best that life had to offer. So I sat, ready to feel appalled and disgusted; ready to wonder how anyone could want to go back . . . back to *that!* I could see it all in my mind's eye, the listing, ramshackled shack with the sagging front porch, the old wood gone silvery and streaked with stains from the tin roof. The dirt yard grown over with weeds and brambles, though the puddles of rainwater would conceal the worst, and I wouldn't look toward the outhouse and worry about how Grandpa managed to shuffle himself back and forth. I had to see the Reverend in the morning. Then I had to return to Troy.

Logan was parking the car, and I had to look, had to face up to the horror of Grandpa out here, alone in the rain, half-protected by a leaky roof, with the ghost of his wife on a night when the wind was blowing, and that always made the cabin so drafty.

I sat staring, barely giving credence to what I saw.
The listing cabin was gone!

In its place was a strong-looking, well-made log cabin, the kind city men called "hunting lodges."

Surprise almost had me paralyzed. "How?" I asked. "Who?"

Logan gripped the wheel hard, as if to keep from shaking sense into me. Nor did he look my way as we sat on in the parked car. And inside the cabin lights shone. Electricity! I was trapped in disbelief, feeling this was a dream.

"From the way I've heard it, your grandpa was unhappy living in Georgia where it is flat and stifling hot," explained Logan, "and he didn't know anyone there. He missed the hills. He missed Winnerrow. And from what Tom wrote me, you sent him hundreds of dollars last October to pay for a few of his 'critters' and that got him going. He wanted to go back to where he could see his Annie. And he had that money you mailed him, so he came back. Tom has contributed his share of money, too, he works night and day. The old cabin was torn down, and this one was put up. It didn't take but twelve weeks, and still it is a very nice cabin inside. Don't you want to go in and see? Or are you planning to leave the old man alone with the ghost who shares his home?"

How could I tell Logan it wouldn't make any difference if I stayed or went, Grandpa would still live with his beloved ghost, no matter what. But I couldn't say it. Instead I stared at the two-story cabin. Even from the outside I could tell it was nice inside. There were two sets of triple windows across the front that had to allow lots of sunshine to flood inside. I remembered the two small rooms that had always been dim and smoky, with never enough light or fresh air. What a difference six windows could make!

And I did want to see the inside, of course I did. But I was feeling peculiar, quivering one second from chills, flushed and hot the next. My joints began to ache more severely; even my stomach felt rebellious.

I opened the passenger door of the car and said, "I can walk back to town, Logan, tomorrow morning. You don't have to wait for me."

I slammed the door, uncomfortable with old times now that I'd adjusted to new times, and running against the cold rain, I entered the log cabin. To my astonishment the cabin, which had seemed small on the outside, had a large living room where Grandpa was on his hands and knees, busy fiddling with the logs he hoped to burn in the stone fireplace that reached the ceiling and spread across one entire side of the room. There were fine, heavy brass andirons, a handsome firescreen, and a heavy grate, and even before a match was lit, the house was already warm. Pulled close to the hearth, situated on a large braided rug such as Granny had once made from old nylon stockings given to her by the church bazaar ladies, were the two old rockers that Granny and Grandpa had used on the porch of the old cabin. And in the winter they had been brought inside. They were the only articles of furniture left from the original cabin.

Two chairs that looked old, faded, worn, and yet they touched me as none of the new furniture did.

"Annie . . . didn't I tell ya she were here?" said Grandpa excitedly, reaching to lay his gnarled hand on the arm of the best rocker where his wife used to sit. "She's come t'stay, Annie. Our Heaven girl, come t'take kerr of us in our time of need."

Oh, dear God, I couldn't stay!

Troy was waiting for me!

Logan had followed me into the house and watched me from the door. I tried to pull myself together and fight whatever it was that was making me feel ill. I rambled around the four downstairs rooms that were paneled with wood. In the kitchen I gazed with wonder on the bright modern electric appliances. There was a double stainless steel sink, and beside it a dishwasher! Folding doors revealed a laundry room with a washer and dryer! A large double-door refrigerator! More cabinets than even Kitty'd had in her kitchen. Country curtains at the windows, blue gingham with a row of yellow daisies to trim the hem, and white cotton balls fringed the edges. A round table was spread with a matching gingham tablecloth. The tile on the floor was bright blue, the cushions tied to the chairs, sunny yellow. I'd never seen such a pretty and homey-looking kitchen.

Why, it was the kind of kitchen I used to dream about when I was a child. Tears stung my eyes as I reached to caress the smooth wood of the cabinets, when once we'd had only one open shelf on which to stack our pitifully few dishes. And nails had supported our few pots and pans. I was sobbing openly now, seeing all the conveniences that Sarah and Granny would have enjoyed, to say nothing of the rest of us. And like the hillbilly kid I used to be, I turned on the hot and cold water spigots and held my hand under . . . instant water here in the mountains? I flipped on electric switches. I shook my head. A dream, that was all. Another dream.

Wandering onward, awed, I found a small dinette with a wide bay window that would overlook in daytime a spectacular view of the valley but for the trees. My dream to cut down some of the trees so the

city lights of Winnerrow would sparkle the night like
fireflies in the summers. I could see nothing but rain
on this night.

A small hallway beyond the dinette led to a downstairs bath and an adjoining bedroom that had to be
Grandpa's. I saw his "critters" placed neatly on open
shelves with mirrors behind them, and small hidden
lights dramatized the array of tiny animals and freak-
ish but clever mountain folk.

On Grandpa's big brass bed (not the old one) was
one of Granny's best handmade quilts. There was a
night table with a lamp, two lounge chairs, a bureau, a
chest. I turned in circles, wandered back to the
kitchen, and in the center of the floor I began to really
wail.

"Why are you crying?" asked Logan from behind
me, his voice soft and strange, "I thought you might
like it now. Or have you grown so used to huge
mansions that a cozy cabin in the mountains seems too
poor?"

"It's pretty, and I do like it," I said, trying to hold
back my tears.

"Please stop crying," he said in a hoarse voice.
"You haven't seen it all. There are rooms upstairs.
Save a few tears for those." And catching hold of my
elbow, he drew me forward even as I searched in my
handbag for tissues. I dabbed at my tears, then blew
my nose. "Your grandfather has some trouble with
steps . . . not that he can't climb them, he just thinks
there shouldn't be any stairs in his home."

Someone had thought of everything. But I was
tired, sick feeling, needing to lie down, and I tried to
pull away. Logan grew forceful, almost shoving me up
the stairs. "Isn't this the kind of cabin you always

wished for when you were a kid growing up and feeling cheated of everything nice? Well, here it is, so look! And if it comes too late for you to appreciate all the trouble it took to make it this way, I'm sorry . . . but you look around and you see it and appreciate it *now,* if you never see it again!"

Two medium-sized bedrooms were up there, and a large double bath.

Logan leaned against the closet door. "From what Tom has written me, your father has put money in this place, too. Perhaps one day your pa is planning on bringing his family here."

Something deep in his voice made me turn to meet his eyes, and this time I really saw him. He wore casual clothes as if he didn't go to church anymore on Sundays. Apparently he hadn't shaved today, and the stubble there made him seem different, older, less handsome and perfect.

"I'm ready to go now." I headed for the stairs. "It's a very nice house, and I'm glad Grandpa has a nice place to stay, with plenty of food in the pantry."

He didn't reply this time, only followed me downstairs where I said goodbye to Grandpa and kissed his gaunt, pale cheek.

"Good night, Grandpa, good night, Granny. I'll be coming back to see you again tomorrow. After I've taken care of a few things."

Grandpa nodded absently as his eyes went stark and his fingers began to work nervously at the fringe of the shawl he'd thrown about his shoulders. Granny's shawl!

"Been good t'see ya, chile Heaven, real good t'see ya."

He wasn't going to plead. "You take care, Grandpa, you hear?" I said in the country way that came readily back. "Is there anything you need, or anything I can bring you from town?"

"Got everythin' now," Grandpa mumbled, looking around with his rheumy eyes. "Lady comes from town an' fixes our meals. Every day she does that. Annie says that's nice of her, but Annie could cook fer us if she could see betta."

I touched the arm of Granny's chair, worn slick and shiny from the clutch of her hands. Leaning, I pretended to kiss her cheek, and that made Grandpa's eyes shine.

On the porch I stumbled twice. The wind and rain seemed an animal, wild to destroy. The cold was so stunning it stole my breath, and the rain blinded me. Logan grabbed quickly to keep me from falling down the stairs.

He shouted something in my ears. The wind howled louder than his voice. On the steps I sagged, my knees giving way. Then Logan had me in his arms, carrying me back to the cabin.

## ❤ **Eighteen** ❤
## *Deliver unto Me*

TIME PLAYED TRICKS ON ME. I SAW AN OLD WOMAN who reminded me of Granny. She bathed me, and fed me, and all the time she talked about how lucky it was that her home was only a skip and a jump away, now that the bridges were down and a doctor couldn't come from the village. I saw Logan time and time again, when I woke up in the daylight, when I woke up in the darkness, always he was there. In my delirium I saw Troy's face as he repeatedly called my name. "Come back, come back," he kept saying. "Save me, save me, save me."

And the torrential rains kept pouring down, down, making me think even when my eyes were open and I was more or less rational, that I was caught somewhere in purgatory, not heaven, but almost hell. Then came that stark day when my mind wasn't smeared with fever, and the room around me came into focus, and I was stunned to be where I was. I lay on a big bed in the upstairs bedroom of that rebuilt mountain shack, weak and wan, realizing I had just pulled through the worst illness of my life. I had been luckier health-wise than Our Jane; seldom had anything forced me to spend even one day in bed.

To lie helpless and too weak even to lift my hand or turn my head was a totally unnerving experience. So unnerving I closed my eyes and fell into sleep again. The next time I awakened in the night, hazily to see Logan hovering above me. He needed a shave; he looked tired and worried, and more than a little harassed. Later on when the sun was up, I awakened to find him washing my face, and humiliated, I tried to shove his ministering hands away.

"No," I tried to whisper, but I broke out into paroxysms of coughs that stole even my whispers.

"I'm sorry; but Shellie Burl slipped and sprained her ankle and can't come today. You'll have to make do with me," Logan said in a deep, gruff voice, his expression solemn.

Appalled, I could only stare at him. "But I need to go to the bathroom," I whispered, embarrassment flushing my face. "Please get Grandpa so I can lean on him."

"Your grandfather can't climb the stairs without wheezing, and he has all he can do to stay upright himself." And without further ado, Logan tenderly helped me from the bed. My head reeled so I would have fallen without his arms about me, and step by slow step, supporting me as if I were a small child, he assisted me into the bathroom. I clung to a towel bar until he closed the door, and then I fell upon the commode almost in a dead faint.

I learned all about humility during the next few days when Logan had to assist me to and from the bathroom. I learned how to swallow my pride and tolerate the way he had to give me a sponge bath as modestly as possible, keeping all but the skin he was cleansing under a flannel sheet. Sometimes I childishly whimpered and cried and tried to fight him off again, but the effort of doing that would cause me such fatigue I could only submit. Then I realized the fruitlessness of my resistance. I needed his caring and nursing. And from that time on, I lay without moaning and complaining.

In my fevered delirium I knew I'd called for Troy. I pleaded time and again with Logan to telephone him and explain why I hadn't returned to keep our wedding plans. I'd see Logan nod, hear him say something to assure me he was trying to contact Troy. But I didn't believe him. I never believed him. When I could find the strength I slapped at his hands when he tried to spoon medicine into my mouth. Twice I crawled out of the bed in frail, failing efforts to telephone Troy myself—only to stand and find myself so weak I crumpled almost immediately to the floor, forcing Logan to spring up from his pallet near the foot of my bed so he could pick me up and carry me back to my bed.

"Why can't you trust me?" he asked when he thought me asleep, his voice tender, his hands gentle as he smoothed back the damp fringe of hair from my forehead. "I saw you with that Cal Dennison and wanted to shove him through the wall. I saw you once with that Troy you keep calling for, and I hated him. I've been a fool, Heaven, a damned fool, and now I've lost you. But why is it you always have to go elsewhere to find what I was so willing to give? You never gave me the chance to be more than a friend.

You held me off, resisted my kisses, and my efforts to be your lover."

My lids parted to see him sitting on the side of my bed, his head bowed wearily. "I know now I was a fool to have been so considerate—for you love me. I know you love me!"

"Troy," I moaned softly, seeing Logan hazily, with Troy standing in the shadows behind him, his face in darkness. "I have to save Troy . . ."

He turned from me then, his head lifting before he murmured, "Go back to sleep and stop fretting over that man. He'll be all right. You've talked a lot about him, and I know this, people in real life don't die from love."

"But . . . but you don't know Troy . . . don't know him . . . not as I do."

Logan whipped around, his patience on a leash. "Heaven, please! You can't recover if you don't stop resisting what I try to do for you. I'm not a doctor, but I do know a considerable amount about medications. I am trying to do my best for you. A few weeks ago I brought your grandpa a good supply of cold medicine, never suspecting it would be you who'd be the one most needing. All the roads to town are flooded. It's been raining for five solid days. I can't drive out of the yard because the dirt roads are so rutted and flooded. Three times I've had to dig my car out of mud up to the hubcaps."

I submitted to his ministrations, not knowing what else to do. Nightmarish dreams took me to Troy. He was always riding on a horse away from me, and when I called, he rode even faster. Into the night, into the dark, I chased after him.

Into my hazy vision Grandpa drifted several times, his breath coming in short gasps and wheezes, his wizened old face hovering anxiously over me, his hands reaching to brush back my long damp hair with weak fingers. "Yer lookin peaked, Heaven chile. Real peaked. Annie's gonna fix ya up somethin' healin' . . . her herbal tea. An she's made ya some soup. Ya eat it now . . ."

Finally the day came when my fever stopped. My thoughts cleared. For the first time I fully realized the horror of my situation. I was in the Willies again, back where the cabin used to stand. Far from Troy who had to be frantic with worry.

I stared weakly at Logan as he took clean sheets from the small linen closet in the dressing area, and striding my way, he smiled. His beard made him seem older, and he looked exceedingly tired.

As a young child I'd often hoped to be sick just to test Pa and find out if he'd care for me as lovingly as once I'd seen him care for Fanny. But of course he wouldn't have bothered himself even to hand me a glass of water.

"Go away!" I sobbed, when Logan handed me another capsule, another glass of water. "It's embarrassing what you've done!" I cringed from the touch of his hands. "Why didn't you telephone for a nurse after Mrs. Burl hurt her ankle? You had no right to do what you did!"

Like a deaf and mute man he was heedless of what I said. He rolled me over, draped the mattress under me with a flannel sheet before he disappeared to come back with a basin of warm water, and several towels, plus a washcloth and a dish with soap. I clutched the covers, bringing them high under my chin. "No!"

He dipped the washcloth into the water, soaped it, then handed it to me. "Wash your own face then. The phone lines were the first thing to go. That was the evening we arrived. I just heard the weather report on a battery radio. The rain is due to let up tonight. It will take a few days for the roads to drain of water, and by that time you should be well enough to travel."

I seized the washcloth from his hands, then glared at him until he left the room. He slammed the door shut behind him, and with ruthless determination, I scrubbed at my skin. I put on a fresh sleep shirt, one of the many that I had mailed to Grandpa, this time without Logan's help.

On this day I made myself eat when Logan carried in a tray with soup and sandwiches. He would not meet my eyes, nor would I meet his.

"The roads . . . ?" I managed to ask, just as he was carrying the tray out of the door.

"Clearing. The sun is out. The linemen will soon be restoring electricity and telephone service. Once I can bring in a nurse for you, I'll leave. I'm sure that will make you very happy. You'll never have to see me again."

"You're pitying me now, aren't you?" I shouted with what frail strength I had. "You can like me now that I'm sick and needing, but you can't like me at all when I'm not needing. I don't need your kind of compassion and pity, Logan Stonewall! I'm engaged to one of the most wonderful men in the world. I'll never be poor again! And I love him, love him so much I'm hurting inside because I'm not with him instead of you!"

There, I'd said it, in the cruelest way possible. He stood, caught in a random beam of weak sunlight, his face gone very pale before he whirled around to stalk out of the door.

I cried when he was gone. Cried for the longest time. Cried for all that used to be, and all the dreams left unfulfilled. But it was all right. I had Troy. He didn't pity me. He loved me, needed me, would die without me.

That afternoon I forced myself to walk to the bathroom alone. I took a bath in the tub. I shampooed my hair. In a day or two I'd leave this place and never return.

My strength took longer to return than I'd expected. Just as it took the roads longer to clear of flood water than Logan predicted, and he didn't leave the minute the mud began to dry. He patiently waited downstairs, until one day the mailman appeared and told him that all the roads down to Winnerrow were passable now, if he didn't mind digging in the mud now and then. Around four that day, while Logan sprawled on the living room sofa and dozed, I was able to negotiate the stairs alone, and in the kitchen I helped prepare a simple meal. Grandpa seemed very contented. Logan said nothing at all when I called him to the kitchen table, though I felt his eyes following my every movement.

I was still weak, pale, and trembling when Logan let me out in front of Winnerrow's only hotel, and in another rented room I changed into fresh clothes before I made my long-distance call to Troy. Troy didn't answer the telephone in his cottage. I grew nervous and faint waiting for him to respond. I hung up and dialed another number. This time one of the servants at Farthinggale Manor answered.

"Yes, Miss Casteel, I'll tell Mr. Troy that you called. He's out for the day."

Unsettled and disconcerted to think Troy wasn't where he should be, I used the elevator again, to find Logan waiting in the hotel lobby for me. He rose politely when I advanced, but didn't smile. "What can I do for you now?"

My hands rose to my forehead. I had four hours before my flight left for Boston.

"Reverend Wise, I have to see him. But I can make it there on my own." My eyes lowered to study his hands while I began my apology. "I'm sorry I was ugly acting. I thank you for helping me, Logan. I wish you all sorts of happiness. You don't need to do anything else for me. From now on I'll take care of myself."

For the longest time I felt his eyes on my face, as if trying to read my mind. Then, not responding with words, he took my arm and led me to his parked car, and while we were on our slow way, he tried to answer my questions.

"Does Pa come often to visit Grandpa?"

"I think he comes when he can."

Logan didn't say another word until he let me out on Main Street, directly in front of the parsonage, where the Reverend Wayland Wise lived with his wife, and infant daughter.

"Thank you again," I said stiffly. "But you don't have to wait."

"Who is going to carry your bags and put them in your rented car . . . if you still have a rented car?" he asked with irony.

So he waited, insisting on doing that, and I tried not to stumble or wobble as I made my way up the walkway recently swept free of all storm debris. Once

I had reached the high porch, I turned to see Logan waiting patiently, his head slightly bowed, as if he'd fallen asleep behind the wheel from the fatigue of waiting on me night and day.

And as I stood there and waited for someone to respond to my knock, a terrible anger washed over me, erasing my weakness and giving me sudden strength.

The Reverend and his wife had no right to steal Fanny's baby! He had seduced Fanny when she was just a child, a minor! Fourteen years old. Statutory rape!

Yes, I was here to bring into the family fold at least one child to replace the two I'd lost. Though I doubted very much that Fanny should be the one to raise the child.

It was Rosalynn Wise herself who came to respond to my sharp raps on her door. She scowled to see me, though surprise didn't show in her eyes. It was as if she knew from my visit to the church eight days ago that sooner or later I'd show up. As usual, she wore a dark, unflattering dress that succeeded admirably in making her look like a stick wearing clothes.

"We have nothing to say to you," she said in greeting. "Kindly take yourself off our porch and don't come back."

And like Fanny had in the past, she prepared to slam the door in my face, but I was ready this time. Stepping forward I shoved her aside and entered the house. "You have a great deal of explaining to do," I said in my coldest sharpest tone. (I'd learned a great deal in Boston on how to act imperious.) "Take me to your husband."

"He's not here."

She moved to keep me from going farther. "You get out! You and your sister have caused enough trouble." Her long, lean face took on the pious air of those in contact with filth.

"Oh, so now you admit Fanny is my sister. How interesting. Whatever happened to Louisa Wise?"

"Who was that at the front door?" called the Reverend in the kind of ordinary voice he must reserve for at-home use.

His voice led me to his study, where the door was partially open, and I stepped inside, despite all his wife did to prevent this. Now that I was confronting the most influential man in Winnerrow, I longed for stronger health, for all the words I'd had ready to say before fever came and stole them from my memory.

Half-rising from his chair, "Waysie" Wise smiled in a pleasant way, and that left me at a loss. I'd come expecting to catch them both at a disadvantage. It wasn't quite ten o'clock. Yet she was dressed, and so was he. The only concession he gave to at-home comfort were black velvet house slippers lined with red satin. For some odd reason those exotic, elegant slippers threw me.

"Aha!" he said, rubbing his dry palms together, his full, handsome face taking on a blank, smooth look. "I do believe it's one of my sheep coming to be embraced, at last, into the fold." He couldn't have found better words to restore my fighting ego. As if I'd been born for this day I felt a rising sense of justification and satisfaction to have a good reason for telling him my opinion of what he was. He seated himself again in his high-backed, comfortable chair before the fireplace where fake flowers took the place of the grate. With care he chose a cigar from a brass

351

box lined with red cedar that was near his chair; he snipped off the end, checked it over with scrutinizing eyes, and only then did he light it. All this time I was left standing.

Obviously they weren't going to invite me to sit down. I strode forward and selected the twin to his chair and sat. I crossed my legs and watched his eyes as they traveled over my legs, which Troy had told me many times were very shapely. My shoes were brand new.

Lazily, the Reverend's dark, sloe eyes looked me over. Smoldering interest thrived deep in those eyes, and gradually it drifted to the forefront and forced him to smile disarmingly. A smile so sweet it was no wonder someone as naive as Fanny had been taken in. Even up close he was a very good-looking man. He had good features, a clear complexion, and robust good health that made his ruddy skin glow. His extra pounds were just beginning to hint at middle age, though later I suspected he'd go from paunchy immediately to obesity.

"Yesss . . . I do believe I've seen you before," he said in a throaty, flattering way, "though forgetting the name of such a lovely girl is simply not my way, absolutely not my way."

When I'd entered this house, I hadn't the foggiest idea of how to approach him, but his very words had given me exactly the impetus I needed. He was afraid. He'd hide behind a guise of innocence.

"You haven't forgotten my name," I said in a pleasant way, swinging my foot and making my high heel a threatening weapon. "No one ever forgets my name. Heaven Leigh has its own distinction, wouldn't you say?"

352

And all that coughing had done something for my throat, something that made it different, slightly hoarse, and my time in Boston had given my voice a certain sophisticated sexiness that surprised even me. "Fanny is very well, thank you for asking, Reverend Wise. Fanny sends her best regards."

I smiled at him, feeling a kind of power growing just because I could tell he was taken with my youth and beauty. I suspected he'd been an easy foil for Fanny's seduction, even though he was a man of the cloth. "Fanny is very appreciative to both you and your wife for taking such good care of her daughter, but now that she has given up a stage career and will soon settle down to married life, she wants her child back."

He didn't blanch or blink an eye, though behind me I heard his wife gasp, then sob.

"Why isn't Louisa here to speak for herself?" he asked in a soft purr.

I tried to find exactly the right words. "Fanny trusts me to say what she cannot say without crying. She regrets her hasty decision to sell her unborn child. She knows now that a woman can never be the same after giving birth. Her arms ache to hold her little girl. And she isn't asking that you take a great loss, for I have come prepared to repay you the ten thousand dollars." His smile stayed pasted on. He even managed to talk while still smiling. "I really don't understand what you mean. What ten thousand? What do my wife and I have to do with Fanny's baby? We realize, of course, that dear Louisa was free with her sexual favors, being hill-born and hill-trained, and wild as a bitch in heat, and if she sold her baby and regrets it, indeed we are sorry . . ."

Standing, I strode to his desk and picked up a silver-framed studio portrait of a child about four months old. The baby smiled into the camera lens with Fanny's own dark eyes, true Casteel Indian eyes. The little girl's mop of hair was not straight and coarse like Fanny's, but soft and curly, as the hair of the Reverend must have been when he was an infant. And oh, she was lovely, this baby that Fanny had so heedlessly sold. Plump, dimpled hands, a tiny little ring on one finger. Sweet little white dress with lace and embroidery. A cherished, pampered, beloved daughter.

Suddenly the portrait was snatched from my hands!

"Get out of here!" screamed Rosalynn Wise. "Wayland, why do you sit and talk to her! Throw her out!"

"I came prepared to pay for Fanny's child," I stated coldly. "You can accept twenty thousand dollars. Ten thousand for your care of the child. If you don't I will call in the police, and tell them what you did when you drove to our cabin and paid my father five hundred dollars for Fanny. I will tell the city authorities that you used Fanny as your slave to do housework. I will tell them that their good minister molested and sexually abused a fourteen-year-old girl, and forced her to have his child because his wife was barren . . ."

The Reverend stood up.

He towered above me, his eyes turning into cruel, dark river stones. "You have threat in your voice, girl. I don't like that. A hill-scum Casteel can't threaten me, not with your tone, not with your fierce glare and your silly words. I know all about you and your kind." His confident smile came back as he sought to intimidate me. "Louisa has not called or written to us, after all we did to make her happy and comfortable. Yet it's often that way with our Lord's chosen . . . to try and be the good Samaritan, and in turn be given nothing but malice from those who should be grateful."

He intoned other words, quotes from the Bible that were apt, as if in a million years I could never disturb his equilibrium.

"Stop!" I yelled. "You bought my sister from my father." I named the day and the year. "And my brother Tom and I were there as witnesses to swear this took place in our cabin." I paused, watching him slip his large feet out of the velvet slippers and into loose loafers before he moved to sit ponderously behind his immense desk, kept exceptionally neat. When he settled back in his swivel chair, he tipped it far back, then templed his fingers beneath his chin. He held his hands clasped like that very high so his mouth was hidden. It was only then I found out the lips combined with the eyes made for the best mind-reading abilities. Now I had only his eyes, and they were hooded.

"You can't come to me and make demands, girl. You may wear diamonds, and costly raiment, but you are still a Casteel. And between your word and mine . . . who do you think those in authority will believe?"

I found my own confident smile. "Darcy looks like Fanny."

His smile turned oily and evil. "Let's not debate a proven fact. We have papers to prove my wife gave birth to a baby girl on the third day in February of this year. What legal proof do you have to indicate that Fanny has even had a baby?"

My smile wavered, then grew strong. "Stretch marks. Does your wife have those? Fingerprints. Footprints. We Casteels are not quite as dumb as you think. Fanny stole a copy of her daughter's birth certificate. On that certificate she is named as the mother, not your wife. You had a forgery made—how will that sit with those in authority?"

Behind me Rosalynn Wise groaned.

The Reverend blinked his eyes once or twice. And I knew I had them! And I had lied! As far as I knew Fanny didn't have any proof. None whatsoever.

"No man would ever need go to the trouble of seducing your promiscuous sister!" yelled Rosalynn Wise, her face gone paper white as she backed toward the door.

My head jerked higher. "That is beside the point. The point being, Reverend Wise took advantage of a fourteen-year-old girl. He, a man sworn to the cloth, fathered Fanny's baby when she was a minor! A baby that this honorable minister now tells everyone was conceived in his wife's own womb! It can easily be proven by a physical examination that your wife has never given birth. Fanny wants her little girl. I want her to have her daughter. I have come to take Darcy home to her mother."

Rosalynn Wise whimpered like a beaten dog.

But the Reverend hadn't finished his battle.

The Reverend's eyes turned harder, colder. "I know who you are. Your maternal grandmother married into the Tatterton Toy clan. And so you have millions behind you, and you think that gives you power to wield over me. Darcy is my daughter, and I will fight you tooth and nail to see she stays here in my house and not in the home of a tramp. So get out, and stay out!"

"I will go to the police!" I cried with my own anger growing.

"Go on. Do everything you say. See if anyone
believes you. There isn't one soul in this city that
doesn't know what Fanny Casteel is, and was, and will
always be. My congregation will sympathize with me.
Knowing that in my own home that wicked, sinful girl
did steal into my bed and with her lewd, naked body
that she pressed against me, she seduced me, for I am
only a man, and human . . . pitifully, shamefully
human."

It was his scornful winning smirk that made me say
without hesitation, despite his clever plea, "You either give me Darcy so I can take her to Fanny, or I will
enter your church tonight and stand in front of your
congregation and tell them exactly what transpired on
the day you bought Fanny for your own sexual gratifi-
cation! And I believe they will be shocked and outraged. You could have left her alone! You have just
admitted that you knew what Fanny was before you
brought her into your home—and still you did it! You
deliberately put temptation in your home, and you
failed to resist that temptation! In the case of the
Devil versus Reverend Wayland Wise, the Devil won.
And I know your congregation. They will not forgive
you!"

The Reverend thoughtfully eyed me as if I were still
only a white pawn on his chessboard, and if he could
but move his black queen he'd find a way yet to thwart
me.

"I hear you've been sick," he said in a soft,
conversational voice. "You don't look well, girl, not
well at all. And by the way, what do you think of that
nice house your grandfather is living in? Do you
believe your paltry gifts could build such a fine log
cabin? Out of the kindness of my heart I took from

my own pocket the extra money needed to see that
cabin was finished after the foundation was laid, so
the great-grandfather of my daughter would have
enough cash to see it through. For I am human . . .
pitifully, shamefully human."

Minutes passed, many minutes, and the Reverend
never moved his eyes from my face.

I heard the baby wailing upstairs, as if suddenly
awakened from a nap. I turned to see Rosalynn Wise
carrying Fanny's child. And when I saw her tearful
eyes, her red pouting lips, dark curling hair, and very
fair skin, I was more than touched by her beauty. I
was also touched by her small hand that clung tightly
to the fingers of the only mother she knew. And then
my storm of rage began to break, and I realized that
Fanny was only using Darcy as an instrument of
revenge. What was I doing here upsetting this baby
and her mother? And all the time the Reverend
droned on and on, filling my ears with just what I
didn't want to think about.

"I had a feeling one day you would come after me,
Heaven Casteel. You used to sit on a back pew and
stare at me with those clear blue eyes of yours, and
you questioned every word that left my lips. I could
tell by your face that you wanted to believe, needed to
believe, and were trying hard to believe, and yet I
could never put the words in the right order to
convince you that there is a God, a loving, caring
God. So I began to judge all my sermons by your
reaction to them . . . and once in a great while it
seemed I did manage to reach you. Then that day
came when your granny died, and I said the words
over her grave, and over the tiny grave of that

stillborn child of your stepmother; I felt a complete failure. I knew I would never reach you, for you don't want to be reached. You seek to control your own destiny, when that is not totally possible. You want no help from man, and none from God."

"I didn't come for a lecture on what you think I am," I said stiffly. "You don't know me."

He jumped to put himself always in front of me. His eyelids parted to mere slots so his eyes glittered in the shade of his lids. "You are wrong, Heaven Leigh Casteel. I do know you very well. You are the most dangerous kind of female the world can ever know. You carry the seeds for your own destruction, and the destruction of everyone who loves you. And a great many will love you for your beautiful face, for your seductive body; but you will fail them all, because you will believe they all fail you first. You are an idealist of the most devastatingly tragic kind—the *romantic* idealist. Born to destroy and self-destruct!"

His solemn, hateful, pitying eyes gazed at me, seemingly staring through me and reading my mind.

"Now it's time for me to discuss my daughter, Darcy. I did not, as you said, bring your sister into my home with anything but good intentions, hoping to help by taking one more mouth to feed from your father at the time of his great distress. You refuse to believe that, I can tell by your expression. Rose and I have done what we think God wanted us to do. We legally adopted (and we have papers signed by your sister) the child your sister gave birth to. And now to tell you the real truth, if your father had not shoved his second daughter at us so forcefully, I would have chosen *you!* Do you hear that? You! Now ask me why." When I only stared at him with shock, he answered himself. "I wanted to explore at close hand your resistance to God . . ."

Contemplating me with serious eyes, with compassionate eyes, with eyes expert at concealing duplicity, I realized I was no match for anyone as clever as Reverend Wayland Wise, and it was no wonder he had managed to become the richest man in our area of the state. Even knowing all the games he played to gain respect from those too ignorant to know better, I was feeling snared in the same web as any stupid fly.

"Stop talking, please stop!"

Flooded with guilt, I knew I had lost everything. Tom was already headed for his goal, and he didn't need me. Keith and Our Jane were wise enough even when they were young to turn away from a destructive sister. Grandpa, living where he most wanted to be, close to his Annie, in a mountain cabin ten times better than he had any right to expect, would lose his home. I was crashing the world down on everyone's head.

My fever seemed to come back. I slumped in the chair. A hot flush of nerves rose up from my waist and tingled behind my ears. Fanny didn't need this baby. Fanny had refused to do one thing for Keith and Our Jane, so why had I thought she'd be a good mother for her own? My head throbbed with sharper pain. Who was I to try and take this baby from the only mother she had ever known? It was clear that the child belonged here, with the Wises, who loved her and were in a position to give her the best of everything. What could a Casteel offer this child in comparison to this happy home? I wanted to get away from there as quickly as I could. Shakily I stood up and looked at

Rosalynn Wise. "I'm not going to help Fanny take the baby away from you, ma'am," I said. "I'm sorry I came here. I won't bother you again." And as my tears began to flow, I turned and hurried to the door, even as I heard the Reverend calling after me, "God will bless you for this."

## Nineteen

## Rising Winds

## ∽ Nineteen ∽
### *Rising Winds*

LOGAN DROVE ME TO THE NEAREST AIRPORT AND SAT WITH me in the terminal until my flight was announced. He gazed solemnly into my eyes and told me again that I had done the right thing when I left Fanny's baby in the arms of Rosalynn Wise.

"You did the right thing," said Logan for the third time, when I voiced my doubt to him about the logic of my rationalizations. "Fanny isn't the mother type, you know it and I know it."

Far back in my mind maybe I'd harbored the thought of taking the baby back with me to Farthinggale Manor, praying against hope that her sweet innocence and beauty would win Troy over, and he'd want to raise her as his daughter. Foolish, idiotic thought. What an idiot I'd been even to make an attempt. Fanny didn't deserve a child like Darcy. Maybe I didn't either.

"Goodbye," said Logan, standing and gazing over my head. "I wish you all kinds of good luck and

362

happiness," and whirling on his heel, he strode off before I could thank him again for taking care of me.

He looked back and smiled in a tight way. Across fifty feet we stared at one another before I turned and hurried onto the plane.

Hours later I arrived in Boston. Exhausted, half-sick, and ready to collapse into bed, I slipped into a taxi and hoarsely whispered the address. Then slumping to the side, I felt dizzy and faint. I closed my eyes and thought of Logan and the way he'd smiled at me when I told him how I'd left things with the Wises. "I understand why you did what you did. And you keep remembering if Fanny had really wanted that little girl she could have found a way to keep her. *You* would have found a way."

It was all so unreal, so terribly unreal. The smile the butler Curtis wore when he opened the door because I couldn't find my key, not like him at all. Nor were his welcoming words. "It is good to have you back, Miss Heaven."

Startled that he would speak to me and address me by my Christian name, I watched him disappear with my suitcases before I turned to stare into the huge room that had been formed by throwing open the wide doors to the major salon and the one beyond that. A party. And I wondered absently what occasion was about to be celebrated? But then Tony was home, every day was a reason to celebrate.

From room to room I wandered, staring at the huge bouquets of fresh flowers everywhere. Crystal, silver, gold, and brass gleaming. And in the main kitchen, where the entrees were prepared, Rye Whiskey smiled as if he hadn't even noticed my absence. I left the kitchen, the sight of all that food making my stomach queasy, and headed for the stairs.

"So, you are back!" called a strong, authoritative voice. Tony strode from his office, his good-looking face grim. "How dare you do what you did? You didn't keep your word. Do you know what you have done to Troy, do you know?"

I felt myself go pale. My knees began to quiver. "He's all right, isn't he? I was sick. I wanted to come back."

Tony strode closer, his full lips set in a long thin line. "You have disappointed me, girl. You have disappointed Troy, and that's more important. He's over there in his cottage in such a deep depression he refuses to answer his telephone. He doesn't leave his bed, not even to finish work that he's started."

My legs gave way and I sagged to sit on a step. "I had the flu," I said weakly. "My fever rose to a hundred and two. The doctor couldn't come because it rained every day and the bridges went down, and the roads flooded." He heard me out, patiently heard me out. He stood with his hand on the newel post, looking up at where I crouched on the steps, and in his eyes I saw something that I'd never seen before. Something that scared me. My excuses took too long. He waved his hand, dismissing what else I had to say. "Go to your rooms and do what you have to, then come to my office. Jillian is giving a shower this evening for one of her friends who plans to marry soon. You and I are going to settle a few things."

"I have to see Troy!" I cried, as I wearily rose to my feet. "He'll understand even if you don't."

"Troy has waited this long. He can wait another hour or so."

I ran up the remaining stairs. I felt his eyes following me until I disappeared into my rooms. The maid Percy was in my bedroom unpacking my bags. She gave me a small smile. "I'm glad you are home again, Miss Heaven."

The look I gave her was distraught. Home? Would I ever feel at home in this huge house?

Quickly I washed my face and changed my clothes and did what I could for my hair, which had not been set after my shampoo in the rebuilt cabin. My dressing room mirror showed shadows under my eyes, and a weakness in my expression, and yet there was strength in the set of my lips.

As I descended the stairs, my makeup only a light dusting of face powder, the door chimes began to sound. Curtis hurried to answer the door, admitting several women carrying beautifully wrapped gifts. They were so taken with the party appointments they didn't seem to notice me, thank God. I didn't want to be seen by any of Jillian's friends, who always had too many questions.

Lightly I tapped on the door to Tony's office. "Come in, Heaven," he called. He was seated behind his desk. Through the row of windows behind him, shades of night were chasing away the soft violet colors of twilight. Because the first floor of Farthy was at least fifteen feet above the ground, his windows gave a perfect view of the maze that seemed so private when you were within it. The maze represented to me the mystery and the romance of Troy, and the love that we had found. I couldn't pull my eyes away from the ten-foot hedges.

"Sit down," he ordered, his face shadowed and hidden in the deepening gloom. "Tell me now about your shopping spree in New York. Tell me again about the days of deluging rain, and the bridges going down, and the flooded roads, and the doctor that couldn't come."

Thank God Logan had talked to me a great deal about the weather when he washed my face and brushed my hair, so easily I could speak of the terrible rainstorm that had brought disaster to the entire East Coast, even as far north as Maine. And Tony listened without asking one question until I had thoroughly hung myself.

"I despise people who lie," he said when my voice faded away, and I could only sit with folded hands that tried not to twist, just as my feet tried not to shuffle nervously. "A great many things have happened since you went away. I know that you did not go to New York to shop for a trousseau. I know that you flew to Georgia to visit your half-brother Tom. You drove to Florida to see your father. You later flew to Nashville to visit your sister Fanny, whose stage name is Fanny Louisa."

I couldn't see his expression. By this time the room was in deep shadows, and he made no effort to turn on even one of his many lamps. Through the walls I could very faintly hear the voices of many women gathering. Nothing they said was distinguishable. I wished like crazy to be out there with them, instead of in here, with him. Heavily I sighed and started to stand.

"Sit down." His voice was cold, commanding. "I have not finished. There are a few questions you have to answer, and answer honestly. First of all, you must tell me your truthful age."

"I am eighteen," I said without hesitation. "I don't

know why I lied to you about my age when I came and said I was sixteen, except it has always made me a bit embarrassed the way my mother rushed into marriage with my father, when she had never seen him before that day they met in Atlanta."

His silence was so viable it quivered the air. I wished desperately for light.

"And what difference does one year make?" I asked, gone breathless from the scary way he just sat there in the dark and didn't speak. "I told Troy right from the beginning that I was seventeen, and not sixteen, for he didn't seem as critical as you are. Please, Tony, let me go to him now. He needs me. I can pull him out of his depression. Truthfully, I was very sick. I would have crawled back to Troy if I could have."

He moved in his chair, to put his elbows on his desk, and he cradled his head in his hands. The window light behind him made a dark-purplish frame, and the quarter moon slipped in and out of dark, stringy clouds. Tiny stars twinkled on and off. Time was slipping by. Time that could be better spent with Troy. "Let me go now to Troy, please Tony."

"No, not yet," he said, his voice hoarse, gritty. "Sit there now and tell me what you know about how your mother met your father—the month, the day, and the year. Tell me the date of their marriage. Tell me all that your grandparents said about your mother, and when you have answered every question I ask, then you may go to Troy."

I lost track of time as I sat in the dark and talked to a man that I saw only in silhouette, on and on telling the story of the Casteels and their poverty; Leigh VanVoreen and what I knew of her, which was pitifully little, and when I'd finished, Tony had a thousand questions to ask. "Jailed brothers, five of them . . ." he repeated. "And she loved him enough to marry him. And your father hated you right from the beginning? Did you ever have a clue as to why he hated you?"

"My birth caused my mother's death," I answered simply. All the security my new clothes gave me had vanished. In the gloom and chill of that early evening, with the party guests so far away now even their loudest laughter couldn't be heard, the hills came again and surrounded me, and I was again a hillbilly scumbag Casteel, no good, no good, no good. Oh, God, why did he stare at me like that? Little bits of all my doubts congealed to form a mountain in front of me. I wasn't good enough for the Stonewalls; I couldn't possibly be suitable for a Tatterton. So I perched, uneasily, waiting, waiting.

It seemed thirty minutes passed after I answered his last question, and he just sat with his back to the window, while the moonlight fell upon my face, and turned the rose of my summer dress to ash. When he spoke his voice was calm, perhaps too calm. "When you first came I thought you were an answer to my prayers, come to save Troy from himself. I thought you were good for him. He's a withdrawn young man, difficult for most girls to know, I suspect for fear he will be hurt. He's very vulnerable . . . and he has those strange ideas about dying young."

I nodded, feeling blind in a world that only he could clearly see. Why was he talking so cautiously? Hadn't he encouraged us to marry by not saying anything to prevent us from making plans? And why, for the first time since I'd known him, was he devoid of humor, of all lightheartedness?

"He's explained to you about his dreams?" he asked.

"Yes, he's told me."

"Do you believe as he believes?"

"I don't know. I want to believe because he believes that dreams often foretell the truth. But I don't want to believe his dream about dying young."

"Has he told you . . . about how long he thinks he will live?" His voice sounded troubled, as if a little boy who had cried in the night had partially convinced him—when he should know better.

"When Troy and I are married and there are no more lonely, shadowed nights in his life, he'll forget all about dying. I'll study him. I'll learn what gives him pleasure. I'll make him the core and essence of my life, so he can be set free from worries that no one will ever care enough to stay. For that is the seat of his anxieties, fear of losing again."

At last he turned on his desk lamp. I had never seen his eyes burn so blue, so deeply blue. "Do you think I didn't do my best for Troy, do you? I was only twenty when I hastened into marriage just to give Troy a mother, a real mother and not just some teenage girl who wouldn't want to be bothered with a needing little boy who was frail and often seriously ill. And there was Leigh to be his sister. I was trying my best."

"Perhaps when you explained his mother's death you made paradise seem better than what he could find in life."

"You may have something there," he said with sadness in his voice, shrugging and leaning back, looking around as if for an ashtray, and finding none he put his sparkling cigarette case back in his pocket. (I'd never seen him pull out a cigarette before.) "I've thought the same thing myself—but what was I to do with a child who cherished grief and never let it go? After I married Jillian, Troy attached himself to Leigh, so when she ran from this house he cried every night, blaming himself as the cause for her leaving. For three months after she went he was confined to bed. I used to go to him when he cried out in the night and I'd tell him one day she'd come back, and he fastened on that like a leech. I suspect he began daydreaming about the time when she did come home again, and she'd be just nine years older, not so old he couldn't love her as he wanted to love her . . . and so all these years, until your father called, Troy has been biding his time, waiting for your mother to return, and be the woman he couldn't seem to find anywhere. And you showed up, not Leigh."

Thunderstruck, I felt my head swim. Now I was the one to wince and blanch! "Are you trying to tell me I am just a substitute for my own mother?" I cried out in rising hysteria. "Troy loves me for what I am! I know he does! A little boy of three, four and five can't possibly fall in love and stay in love over a period of seventeen years! That's too ridiculous to even suggest!"

"I guess you're right." His eyes narrowed before he sighed, and again he reached inside his jacket for that same cigarette case. Again he absentmindedly looked around for an ashtray. "It just occurred to me that Troy put Leigh on a pedestal and compared all other women to her, and it seems only you can measure up."

Heat flushed my face. My hands rose to my throat. "You're talking nonsense. Troy loved my mother, yes, he's told me that. But not as a man loves a woman. He loved as a lonely, needing little boy who had to have someone for his very own. And I'm glad to be that someone. I'll make Troy a good wife." And as much as I'd tried to keep the pleading from my voice, I was pleading. "He needs someone like me who has not lived inside a cultured pearl, who has everything and still can't enjoy. I have been deprived, starved, beaten, burned, humiliated, and shamed, and still I find life rewarding, and under no circumstances would I give up my life. I'll teach him the same thing."

"Yesssss," he said slowly, "I suspect you would be good for him, and *have* been good for him. Until you went away and left him, I've never seen him look better, or more contented. I thank you for that. However, you can't marry him, Heaven. I can't allow it."

There it was, what I'd feared!

"You said you liked me!" I cried, again stunned. "What have you found out? If you are thinking of the Casteel part of me, you must remember I also have VanVoreen genes!"

His eyes filled with pity, and it seemed he aged a little as he sat and stared at me with so much regret. "How lovely you are in your tragic wrath, how very beautiful and appealing. I can understand why Troy loves you and wants you. The two of you have so much in common, although you don't know the connection. I don't want to tell you the connection. Just tell me you will go to him, and as gently as possible, with sensitivity for his feelings, break your engagement. Of course you can't keep on living here, so accessible, but I'll see to your financial welfare. You'll never want for anything, I promise."

"You want me to break my engagement to Troy?" I repeated with incredulity. "You and your great concern for his welfare! Don't you know the last thing in the world he needs is for me to disappoint him? He feels he's found the one woman in the world who can understand him! The only one who will stay and love him until the day he dies!"

He stood up, looking around, refusing to meet my eyes. "I am trying to do what I think is best." His calm underlined the passion I had displayed. "Troy is the only heir I have. The Tatterton Toy Company will pass into his hands when I die, or into the control of *his* son. It has been this way for three hundred and fifty years, from father to son, or brother to brother . . . that's the way it has to be. Troy has to marry and produce a son—for I have a wife too old to bear children."

"There is nothing physically wrong with me! I can have children! Troy and I have already discussed that and have decided on two."

His look of abstraction became more profound. He stood, leaning heavily on his desk. "I was hoping to save myself some embarrassment. I prayed you would withdraw politely. I see now that it isn't possible. But I'm going to try one more time. Just believe it when I say you cannot marry Troy. Why don't you just leave it like that?"

"How can I? Give me one good reason why I can't marry him? I'm eighteen, I'm of legal age. No one can stop me from marrying him."

He sat down again, *heavily* sat down. He shoved his chair from his desk, crossed his legs, and moved his foot back and forth. And for the life of me I couldn't understand how I could still admire his polished shoes and the kind of dark socks he wore. His voice sounded different when he spoke again. "It's your age that has brought this all about. You see, I thought you were younger than you are. I didn't know your true age until one day while you were gone Troy casually mentioned it. Not once did any suspicions cross my mind until then. I'd look at you and you'd be all Leigh, but for your hair. Your mannerisms are very like hers when you are happy and when you feel at ease in your surroundings, but there are other times when you remind me of someone else." He stared again at my hair, which during the summer had taken on streaks of brighter brown, with reddish highlights. "Have you ever worn your hair short?" he asked, quite out of context.

"What has that got to do with anything?" I almost shouted.

"I suspect the weight of your hair pulls out the natural curl, and that's why your hair 'frizzes' as you say, when it rains."

"What has that got to do with anything?" I again shouted. "I'm sorry my hair isn't platinum like my mother's hair and like Jillian's! But Troy likes my hair. He's told me so many times. He loves me, Tony, and it took him so long to tell me that. He had given up on life until I came along, he told me that, too. I've convinced him that his precognition of his own death doesn't have to happen."

For the second time he rose, like a cat undulating and stretching until he leaned to crease his trousers between thumb and index fingers. "I confess I'm not partial to dramatic confessions such as this. I would prefer all dramas to be confined to the stage or to movie screens. I am an even-tempered person, and I have to admire someone like you who can ignite and explode so easily. Perhaps you don't know this, but Troy has the same kind of temper, only he is a slow burn, and when he explodes it turns inward on himself. That's why I'm trying to be careful. If I never speak another true word the rest of my life, I say again I love my brother more than I love myself. He is like my son, and because of him I honestly confess I've never truly wanted my own son, who would disinherit Troy. You see, or I guess you've already seen, Troy is the genius behind Tatterton Toys. He is the one who creates, designs, and invents, while I fly about the world as a glorified sales rep. I am a figurehead ruler. If given ten years I couldn't come up with one original idea to create a new toy or board-game, yet Troy originates without effort; he suggests themes for games, indoor and out, like he invents those eternal sandwiches he loves."

I could only stare at him. Why was he telling me all of this now? Why now?

"It's Troy who deserves to be president, not any son I might have. So please, ease out of his life with little to-do. I'll stay to see him through. You can go to your boyfriend Logan what's-his-name, and I'll put in your bank account *two . . . million . . . dollars*. Think about it. Two million. People kill for that much money."

He smiled at me charmingly, winningly, pleadingly. "Do it for Troy. Do it for yourself and the career you want. Do it for me. Do it for your mother. Your beautiful, dead mother."

I hated what he was doing to me! "What has she got

to do with this?" I screamed, terribly angry that he would have the bad taste to bring her up at a time like this.

"Everything . . ." and his voice was growing louder, angrier, as if my passion were consuming the air and putting fire under his feet.

# ∿ **Twenty** ∿

## *My Mother, My Father*

"WHATEVER IT IS, I WANT TO KNOW!" I CRIED, TWISTING in my chair and leaning forward.

Tony's tone of voice turned hard. "This isn't easy for me, girl, not easy at all. I am trying to do you a favor, and in so doing I am not serving myself well at all. Now keep your silence until I've finished . . . and then you may hate me just as I deserve."

Those cold blue eyes glued my tongue. I sat without moving.

"From the very beginning of my marriage to Jill, Leigh seemed to hate me. She could never forgive me for taking her mother away from her father. She adored her father. I tried to win her affections. She wanted none of that. I didn't do a thing to harm her, and eventually I stopped trying to win her over. I knew she blamed me for her father's desperate unhappiness.

"I came home from my long honeymoon with Jill disillusioned. Horribly disillusioned. I tried not to let anyone see it. Jill isn't capable of loving anyone more

376

than she loves herself and her everlasting youthful image. My God, how that woman loves to look in mirrors!

"I grew disgusted seeing the way she had to have every hair in place all the time, always glancing to check on the shine on her nose, checking for lipstick smudges."

His smile was crooked, bitter. "And so I came to realize too late that despite all the beauty Jill possessed, no man could love Jill for anything other than her facade. Jill has no depths. She's just a shell of a woman. Everything sweet, and thoughtful and kind went into her daughter. I began to be more aware of Leigh in a room than I was of her mother. Soon I was noticing a lovely adolescent girl who seldom glanced in any mirror. A girl who loved to wear simple, loose garments that fluttered when she moved, and her hair was long and loose and straight. Leigh waited on Troy, with pleasure and joy she waited on Troy. I loved and admired her for doing that.

"Leigh was sensual without knowing she was. She radiated health that exuded sex. She moved with undulating hips, her small breasts jiggling unfettered beneath those fluttery garments. And Leigh was always angry with her mother, resenting me, until finally she discovered one day that her mother was very jealous. And that's when Leigh began to play up to me. I don't think it was malicious, it was just her revenge against a mother she thought had ruined her father's life."

I knew what was coming!

I just knew it! I pulled back and raised my hands to ward off his words, wanting to cry out and say no, no!

"Leigh began to flirt with me. She dared to mock

and tease me. Often she danced around me tugging at my hands, taunting me with words that often stung, for they hit the mark so often. 'You married a paper doll,' she'd chant to me time and again. 'Let Mother go back to my father,' she pleaded, 'and if you do, Tony, and if you do, I'll stay! I'm not in love with myself like she is.' And God help me, I wanted her. She was only thirteen years old and she had more sexuality in one small, white finger than her mother had in her entire body."

"Stop!" I screamed. "I don't want to hear any more!"

He went on relentlessly, like a river of melted snow that had to flood and destroy. "And one day when Leigh had taunted and teased me ruthlessly, for it was her game to punish me as much as she punished her mother, I grabbed her by her arm and pulled her into my study and locked the door behind me. I planned only to frighten her a little bit and make her realize she couldn't play a girl's game with a man. I was still just twenty years old, thwarted and angry, disgusted with myself for falling so witlessly into the trap Jill had set. Before we married, Jill had her lawyer draw up papers that would put half my gross worth into her hands if ever I sued her for divorce. And that would mean I could never divorce her and hope to salvage anything for Troy. And so when I slammed and locked that door, I was punishing Jill for cheating me, and punishing Leigh for making me so aware of my stupid mistakes."

"You raped my mother . . . my thirteen-year-old mother?" I asked in a low, hoarse whisper. "You, with your background and your education, acted like some scumbag hillbilly?"

"You don't understand," he said in a desperate kind of voice. "I had thought only to tease her, frighten her, believing she'd be more sophisticated and laugh and call me a fool, and then I wouldn't have been able to perform. But she excited me with her fright, with her panic, with her innocence that was so appalled by the thought of what I planned to do. I told myself she was pulling an act, for the girls of Winterhaven are notoriously open about sex. Yes, I raped your mother. Your thirteen-year-old mother."

"You beast! You horrible man!" I yelled, jumping up and throwing myself at him and striking his chest. I tried to scratch his face, but he was quick. "No wonder she ran away, no wonder! And you drove her into my father's arms so the hills and the cold and the hunger could kill her!"

I kicked at his shins, so he released my hands to back off, and then I ran back at him, to strike again at his face. "I hate you! You killed her! You drove her from here into another kind of hell!"

He easily seized my fists and held me off, his cynical smile growing more ironic. "She didn't run after the first time. Nor did she run after the second or the third. You see, your mother found out she enjoyed our forbidden lovemaking. It was exciting, thrilling. For her, and for me. She'd come to me, stand in the doorway, and wait. And when I advanced, she'd begin to shiver and quake. Sometimes tears would streak her face. When I touched her she'd fight and scream, but she knew no one could hear her screams, and in the end she'd succumb to my lovemaking like the promiscuous child she was beneath all that angelic sweetness."

The flat of my palm found his face this time!

The sting of my slap left a red stain there. I curled my fingers and tried to scratch his eyes from his face!

"Stop it!" he commanded, thrusting me away so I staggered backward. "I won't have it! I meant never to tell you."

Again I threw myself at him, striking at his face. He held me firmly by my shoulders and shook me until my hair flew wild. "Until I heard your birth date I didn't count the months. Now I have. Leigh ran from this house on the eighteenth day of June. And you were born on the twenty-second of February. That's eight months. She had lain with me at least two months off and on, and so, I have to presume there is a strong possibility that you are *my* daughter."

I stopped flailing my arms in useless efforts to inflict some further harm to him. My blood drained from my face. A tingling started behind my ears, and my knees went weak. "I don't believe you," I said brokenly. I felt bruised, beaten. "It can't be true. I'm not Troy's niece, I can't be!"

"I'm sorry, Heaven, so sorry. For you would have been perfect, the very one to save him from himself. But I have sat here this evening and heard your story of how Leigh met Luke Casteel, and heard the day of their marriage, and there is no way you can be Luke Casteel's daughter, unless you were born prematurely. Did your granny ever hint that you came early?"

Backing off from him, I shook my head numbly. I wasn't Pa's daughter. Pa. A scumbag Casteel.

"You said your father hated you, hated you from the day you were born. Heaven, it is entirely possible, Leigh being what she was, that she told your father she was pregnant before she married him. And now I am certain about who you are. It's your hair, Heaven, and your hands. Your hair is the same color and texture as Troy's, and your hands and fingers are shaped like his. Like mine. We both have the Tatterton fingers."

He spread his hands, displaying his long, tapering fingers, before I gazed down at mine. They were the same hands I'd seen all my life, small with long fingers and long oval nails—and half the women in the world had hair my color. Nothing exceptional. And I'd always believed Granny's hands would have looked like mine if she hadn't kept them working slavishly most of her life.

Stunned and aching, sickened almost into vomiting, I turned and left his office. Stumbling up the stairs and into my room, I threw myself on my bed and cried.

Not a Casteel? Not a no-good, rotten, scumbag Casteel with five uncles imprisoned for life?

Tony strolled into my bedroom without knocking, to perch lightly on the foot of my bed, and this time his voice was soft and kind: "Don't make it so difficult, darling. I'm so sorry to ruin your romance with my brother. Though I am delighted to have you for my daughter. Everything will work out, you'll see. I know I have shocked and hurt you, and despite all that I've told you, I did love your mother. She was only a kid, and still I can't forget her. And in my own way I love you. I admire you and what you have done for my brother. I will be more than generous, so keep that in mind when next you see Troy. Tell him anything that will sound plausible. Don't give him pain that would drive him to end his life, For don't you know that's what his dreams are all about? He was born self-destructive! He is disappointed in the world, in everyone who died or went away and failed him, and so he seeks to escape."

He moved to lay his heavy hand briefly on my shoulder before he got up and half turned toward the door. "Be good to him, for he's fragile, not like you or me or Jillian," he said in a choked voice. "He is an innocent in a world of vultures. He doesn't know how to hate. He only knows how to love, so he can later suffer and feel inadequate. So give to him the best you have in you, Heavenly, the very best you have to give. Please."

"I already have!" I screamed, sitting up to hurl a pillow at the door where he stood. "Does he know? Have you told him that you could be my father?"

I saw the shiver that ran down Tony's body. "I could not bring myself to tell him. He respects me, admires me, loves me. He has always been the best thing in my life, despite all the trouble he was. I am begging you, on my knees, to find some other reason for breaking your engagement. He will hate me if he knows the truth. And will I be able to blame him? You could have saved him . . . and I am responsible for taking you from him. I only hope and pray you can find the right words, for I cannot."

An hour passed during which my tears evaporated. An hour in which I bathed my face and eyes with ice water, and very carefully I applied makeup. Then, with no real words stashed in my brain to help him survive without me, I slipped through the maze. I knocked on Troy's blue door. There was no response, just as Tony had warned me there would be none.

It was late now, about ten. There had never been a more glorious evening. Birds snuggling down for the night chirped and cheeped sleepily. Hundreds of rose bushes wafted sweet perfume to tickle my nostrils. Primroses and pansies glimmered beside his blue door. Gardenia bushes waxed brightly in the moonlight, their blossoms huge and almost blue. The air was as soft as a lover's kiss, and he was inside, shut away.

"Troy," I called as I opened his door and hesitated on the threshold. "It's Heaven. I'm back. I'm so sorry I fell ill and couldn't return on the day I promised . . ."

There was no response. There was no scent of bread baking in the oven, or bread that had recently been baked. The cottage was too still, too orderly, frightening.

I ran to his bedroom, throwing open the door. He lay on the bed, with his head turned toward the open window. Soft breezes fanned out his curtains, almost brushing a vase full of roses from a table.

"Troy," I said again, moving closer to the bed. "Please look my way. Please say you forgive me for not keeping my word; I wanted to, desperately wanted to."

Still he didn't look my way. I drew closer, then moved onto the bed, and gently turned his head my way. The moonlight through the windows showed me his glassy eyes, his blank stare. He was a million miles away, snared in some horrible dream. I knew that, just knew that!

My lips pressed down softly on his. I murmured his name over and over. "Come back to me, Troy, please, please. You are not alone. I love you. I will always love you."

Over and over I called him back, until at last the glassiness in his eyes departed, and slowly they came into focus. Delirious and happy delight took away the stare, even as his fingers reached to trail over my face. "You did come back . . . oh, Heaven, I was so terrified you wouldn't. I had a weird feeling you went to that Logan Stonewall again, and discovered you love him, and not me."

"You, only you!" I cried passionately, raining kisses all over his chilled, pale face. "I had the flu, darling. I ran a high fever for days and days. The telephones were down, the bridges were out, and the roads were flooded. I returned to you as soon as I could."

His smile was thin and weak. "I knew I was being silly to allow myself to become so depressed. I knew you would come back, subconsciously I knew that . . ."

I snuggled into his embrace and felt his hands slip into my hair. My face pressed down against his chest. I heard his heart beating slowly, so slowly—how fast was a normal heart supposed to beat? "I don't want a big wedding, Troy. I've changed my mind about that. We'll slip away from Farthinggale Manor and have a small private ceremony."

He held me tightly against him, stroking my hair, putting small kisses on the top of my head. "I'm so tired, Heaven, so tired. I thought you wanted a large wedding."

"No, I want only you."

"Tony has to be at the wedding," he whispered with his lips brushing my forehead. "It wouldn't be real without him. He was like my father . . ."

"Whatever you want," I mumbled, holding his frail body closer. How thin he'd become. "You are totally recovered from your pneumonia, aren't you?"

"As recovered as I ever am from any disease."

"You'll never be sick again! Not when you have me to take care of you!"

All through the night he held me, and I held him. We talked of our dreams, our life together, and for the life of me it all seemed like smoke spiraling out the windows and fading into the night. How could I marry him now? How could I not marry him, no matter what our relationship?

Toward dawn, I brought up the portrait doll of my mother again. Did he know if Tony had made the model? Did at one point in time Tony feel more than a stepfather toward her?

His dark eyes clouded. "No! Not in a million years! Heaven, Tony could have any woman he wanted! He was madly in love with Jillian! There wasn't a woman around who didn't make a play for him . . . why since the time he grew his first beard, he's never had to chase any woman. They chased him."

I knew as I lay in the circle of his arms that he'd never admit to himself that Tony used women, and had used Jillian in his own thoughtless way, to provide his younger brother with a mother and a sister while he went his own merry way chasing every skirt in town, and all over Europe. Tears were in my eyes as I turned to embrace him before I returned to the big house. "I'm sorry to be so suspicious. I love you, love you, love you—and I'll be back as soon as I catch up on some sleep, Don't go away, promise?"

He sat up, clinging to both of my hands. "Have lunch with me, darling, about one."

I thought I could return to my bed and sleep the sleep of the deeply justified, but I tossed and turned, and finally ended up at the dining table downstairs where Tony was already ensconced, eating one slice of honeydew melon after another. He began to ply me with questions immediately. Had I seen Troy? Had I broken our engagement? What had been his reaction? What had been my explanation? I had been kind, considerate, caring, hadn't I?

"I said as little as possible about you." My voice was cold, hostile. I hated him every bit as much as I hated Pa. "Out of consideration for Troy, I covered for you, though if Troy wasn't so sensitive, I would have let him know exactly what kind of man his beloved brother is, and was."

"What reason did you give him?"

"I gave him none. We are still engaged. I don't know how to destroy him, Tony, I just can't do it!"

"I can see you are building a tower of hate for me. Maybe you are right to wait a few weeks before you tell him you've found out you are still in love with that young man of yours. Logan, isn't that his name? Troy will get over you. I'll be here to support him. I'll see to it that he recovers. And the best way to do that is through work. Once Troy accepts the fact that you love someone else and won't be marrying him, he'll make substitutes for your love. I'll do what I can to see he finds another girl he wants to marry."

It hurt so much to hear him say those things that I wanted to bay at the sun like a wolf did at the moon, like Sarah had once done when her last baby died. In my chest was a living pain. And beside me was the man who had started everything. "What a detestable person you are, Tony Tatterton! By God, if I knew it wouldn't hurt Troy, I would tell him exactly what you did to my mother! And he'd hate you! You would lose the one person who is most valuable to you!"

He threw me a pitiful look. "Please . . . remember, you would destroy him. Troy lives on faith and belief. He isn't like you or me, able to survive no matter what the circumstances."

"Don't ever compare me to yourself again!" I yelled.

He didn't respond, only reached for another melon to slice.

"Promise, Heaven, promise to say nothing to Jill about any of this."

I got up and stalked by Tony's chair without promising anything.

"All right!" Tony yelled, abruptly out of patience, jumping up and seizing my arm and whipping me about so I saw his usually pleasant and handsome face turned monstrous with anger. "Go back to Troy! Go on! Destroy him! And when you're done with him, run to Jill and destroy her! And when you've finished off everyone in Farthy, run to your father and ruin his life! Ruin Tom's and Fanny's, and don't leave out Our Jane and Keith! You want revenge, Heaven Leigh Casteel! I see it in your eyes, those incredible blue eyes that speak of a devil inside more than they speak of an angel!"

I slung my balled fist at him blindly, striking nothing as he released me so suddenly I fell off balance to the floor. Quickly I scrambled to my feet, to spurt ahead so fast he wasn't able to say another word before I was running up the stairs to the safety of my bed again. My crying place.

At one o'clock I was again in the cottage, and this time Troy was out of bed, looking a bit stronger as he smiled at me. "Come," he said, beckoning, "I want you to see this train set-up that has just been finished, and then we'll eat."

What he had to show me filled one huge corner of his workshop. It was a tiny stage-set with soft lights glowing, and hidden spots lit up the sets, and miniature trains picked up passengers and let them off, only to pick them up again, repeatedly taking them around mountains steep and dangerous; I thought, as I watched the tiny Orient Express chuggity-chug, chuggity-chug, starting slowly, gaining speed, forever climbing, forever taking risks, daring everything only to reach the heights, only to descend much more quickly than it had ascended, that Troy was trying to tell me something through his tiny trains.

What was it that Troy tried to say with these three little trains that wove such intricate paths through different territory, yet always reached the same destination? Didn't the whole human race ride trains throughout life, reaching highs, sinking to lows, riding the plateau between extremities more often than they soared or fell. I chewed thoughtfully on my lower lip, pressed my forehead with my fingertips . . . and stared at a little girl who had been added to the passengers. A dark-haired little girl wearing a blue coat with matching blue shoes. She was enough like me to cause me to smile. For the trains that apparently led nowhere still gave the passengers thrills. The little girl didn't get off the train at the destination, only an old woman wearing another blue coat with matching blue shoes. And eagerly I went back to the train depot, and saw again the little girl in her blue coat boarding another train . . .

Oh, but he was good at this toy making, giving it meaning, imparting without words his beliefs, and as I turned away from the trains, I felt the familiar fascination gather me into its arms. "Troy, Troy!" I called. "Where are you? We have a thousand plans to make!"

He was seated on one of the window seats again, his long legs pulled up, his skilled and graceful hands loosely locked below his knees—and all the windows were wide open and the cold, damp wind swept through his bedroom!

Alarmed, I ran to pull at his arm, trying to bring him out of the nowhere he had lost himself in. "Troy! Troy!" I yelled, shaking him, and still he gazed straight ahead without blinking. Even as I shook him, the wind gusted in so strong it blew a table lamp to the floor. I had to use all my strength to pull the windows down, and when I had them all closed, I ran to gather up blankets which I swatched about Troy's shoulders and legs; still he had not moved nor spoken.

His face was pale and cold when I touched him, but soft, and that made me cry out in relief. He wasn't dead. Yet his pulse when I felt for it was so faint I hurried to his telephone and dialed Farthy. Over and over again the telephone rang and no one answered! I didn't know what kind of doctor I could call directly. My fingers trembling, I picked up Troy's Yellow Pages and was thumbing through them when I heard him sneeze.

"Troy!" I cried, hurrying to his side. "What are you doing, trying to kill yourself?"

His eyes were unfocused and blurry, his voice weak when he spoke my name. When he could see me, he seized me as a drowning man reaches for anything, and I was pulled hard against him so his face could bury deep into my hair. "You came back. Oh, God, I thought you'd never come back!"

"Of course I came back." Kisses I rained on his face. "Troy, I stayed here with you last night, don't you remember?" More kisses on his face, on his hands. "Didn't I tell you I'd returned so we could marry?" I stroked his arms, his back, smoothed down his wild hair. "I'm sorry I came back late, but I'm here now. We'll marry and build our own traditions, make every day a holiday . . ." And I stopped talking because he wasn't really listening.

The chilly room brought on fresh assaults of sneezes, from both of us, then I was drawing him to the bed, so we could both snuggle under mounds of covers and wait for our shivering to end. Even as we lay there, wrapped tightly in each other's arms, the many clocks began all those subtle grinds and movements that would tell the chimes to toll.

Some errant wind managed to come in and tinkle the crystal prisms of his dinette chandelier.

"It's all right, darling, darling," I crooned, smoothing his dark, rumpled hair. "I came upon you just now during one of your . . . what do I call them? Trances, would that be the right word?"

His arms tightened so much my ribs began to ache dully. "Heaven," he breathed, "thank God you are here. His voice broke and he sobbed, gently pushing me from him. "However much I am grateful, I can't pretend any longer that I can live with you. Or marry you. Your absence gave me the chance to think over what we were doing; your presence deludes me into thinking I'm a normal man, with normal expectations. But I'm not, I am not! I'll never be! I'm warped and unable to change. I didn't think you'd come back, once you got out into the real world and discovered you'd been asleep. This isn't a real house, Heaven.

Not one lived in by real people. We're all fakes, Heaven, Tony, Jillian, me; even the servants learn the rules and play the game."

An ache that had begun when I entered thickened and grew. "What rules, Troy? What game?"

Laughing in a way that chilled my blood, he rolled over, holding me still, rolled again and again until we fell to the floor, and he ripped off my clothes wildly, and his warm kisses soon turned hot. "I hope we both made a baby," he cried when it was over, and he turned away and began to pick up the pieces of my torn garments. "I hope I didn't hurt you. I never want to hurt you. But I'd like to leave behind something real, made of my flesh and blood." Then, crushing me to him, he began to sob—deep, harsh, terrible sobs.

I held him, caressed him, kissed him a thousand times before we both fell onto the bed and covered ourselves from the harsh cold.

As I lay there beside him and heard him choke back his sobs and whatever anguish he suffered, I realized Troy was far too complex for me ever to understand. I'd just love him as he was, and maybe one day when he woke up from a dreamless sleep he'd smile before dawn and throughout the day thoughts of dying young would be forgotten.

And I slept. From time to time I woke up slightly, enough to feel air moving around me. Enough to feel warm arms embracing me.

Then it was another day, and I was in my own room and there was a note on my night table. A short note from Troy.

I didn't like notes. I'd not known one yet that came unposted that hadn't brought sad news.

*My own true love,*

*You found me in the wind last night, just sitting, just trying to figure out what my life is all about.*

*We can't marry. And yet last night I took you and did my best to make you conceive. Forgive me for my selfishness. Go to Jillian. She'll tell you the truth. Make her tell you. She will if you push her hard enough, and call her Grandmother, and force her to abandon her disguise.*

*The love I have for you is the best thing that has ever happened to me. I thank you for loving and giving me so much, even knowing all my weaknesses. And my greatest flaw has been my overwhelming love and devotion to my brother. I have been blind, deliberately blind.*

*Jillian came and told me everything. To save you I have to accept what could have saved your mother. For Jillian had to admit that Tony was wild with his infatuation to possess your mother. I know now, after you have goaded me into thinking backward, that she hated him, and he was the one she ran from. Heaven, you are Tony's daughter, and my own niece!*

*I'm going away until I can learn to live without you. Even if you weren't Tony's daughter, and my niece, I'd ruin your life. I don't know how to live complacently and accept each day as it comes. I have to make every day meaningful and important, for each day I live seems always the last one.*

He signed that note with a huge TLT.

This morning brought back sharply the horrible day I'd bitten into an apple, then wandered into the room where Sarah had left Pa a note saying she was leaving him and never coming back. In leaving Pa, she left all of us to fend for ourselves. Here I was again having to fend for myself in a house that no longer wanted me.

The unbearable pain of my shattered love turned into fury! That fury gave me racing legs. I went to Jillian's rooms and banged on her door, shouting her name, demanding to be let in, when it was only nine o'clock and Jillian always slept until noon or even later.

But Jillian was out of bed, exquisitely dressed, as if ready to go out but for adding the jacket to her dressy, pale suit. Her hair was pulled softly back from her face, and I'd never seen it that way before. She looked older, and at the same time, lovelier, or more correctly, less like a haunted, life-sized doll.

"Troy has gone away," I said accusingly, glaring at Jillian. "What did you say to make him decide to go?"

She didn't reply, only turned to pick up her suit jacket and put it on, then, slowly she turned to stare at me. What she saw on my face made her eyes widen in alarm. Her blue, startled eyes flicked as if to find refuge in Tony's arms. Again came that bewildering, brilliant happiness that lit up her eyes. "Troy's gone! Really gone?" she whispered, her joy so great I felt sickened.

Unexpectedly Tony came into Jillian's rooms without knocking. He ignored her and addressed me. "How is Troy this morning? What did you tell him?"

"Me? I told him nothing! It was your wife who felt he had to know the truth, the ugly truth!"

Jillian's radiance died. Her eyes went blank.

Whirling about, Tony's fire blue eyes lashed at his

wife. "What did you tell him? What could you tell him? Your daughter never confided anything to the mother she despised!"

Jillian stood in her lovely suit in unwrinkled perfection, seeming about to open her mouth and scream.

"Did my mother come to you, Jillian, and tell you why she had to run? Did she, did she?"

"Go away. Leave me alone."

I persisted. "What made my mother run from this house? You've never adequately explained. Was it a five-year-old boy? Or was it your husband? Did my mother come to you with tales of her stepfather's sexual advances? Did you pretend you didn't know what she was talking about?"

Her pale hands pulled at her loosely fitting rings, on and off, on and off. I'd never seen her wear rings before. Mindlessly she dropped three rings into an ashtray. The small clatter of the rings striking crystal caused her eyes to widen. "I don't know what you're talking about."

"Grandmother . . ." and I said this clearly, sharply, causing her to shudder as she went dead white. "Was Tony the reason my mother ran from this house?"

Her cornflower blue eyes, so like my own, went wide, stark, bleak, as if I'd snatched the floor from beneath her feet. Gossamer strands of sanity seemed to shred before they snapped behind her eyes, and her hands fluttered helplessly to her face. Her palms pressed tight on either cheek, so tightly her lips parted and from them came screams, terrible, silent screams that tortured her face—and suddenly Tony was there, yelling at me!

"Don't you say one more word!" He stepped

forward to sweep Jillian into his arms. "Go to your room, Heaven. Stay there until I come and have a chance to talk to you." He carried Jillian to her bedroom, and I watched him lay her carefully on her ivory satin spread, and only then did her mute anguish find its voice.

Over and over she screamed! Hysterical rising and falling screams that buckled her back and flailed her arms, and as I stood there almost paralyzed by what I'd brought about, I watched the youth peel from her face as if all the time she'd worn a mask of onion peelings.

I turned away, appalled by what I'd done, overwhelmed with grief to have destroyed what had been so carefully cultivated.

In my rooms I paced the floor, forgetting everything but Troy and his welfare. On occasion my thoughts flitted to Jillian and what havoc I'd wrought. Then Tony was rapping on the door and coming in without waiting for my response. He saw that I was packing my suitcases and winced. "Jill is asleep now," he informed. "I had to force her to swallow a few sedatives."

"Will she be all right?" I asked worriedly.

He sat with a certain kind of indifference on the frailest of my silk brocaded chairs, elegantly crossing his legs, taking pains to tug up his trouser legs and keep the creases sharp. And only when he'd seen to all the little details only a man of impeccable taste thought important did he smile in a crooked ironic way. "No, Jill will never be 'all right.' She hasn't been *right* since the day your mother ran away. She had always refused to talk about that last day . . . and only now do I have all the pieces together."

Quickly I sat down in the twin chair to his, placed opposite him, and I leaned forward with breathlessness, when already I'd heard the worst—or so I thought. But then, I was still an innocent, not accustomed to the complexities of human nature and all the devious ways it had of maneuvering to salvage its self-respect, when some things could never be salvaged.

He began, lowering his eyes as if ashamed now, now when it was too late. "In the year when your mother ran from this house, I had flown to Germany to confer with a manufacturer there who does some of our small-part mechanical work."

"I don't care about your toys at a time like this." I intervened.

He flicked his eyes upward. "I'm sorry, I'm digressing, but I wanted you to understand why I was away. Anyway, your mother had tried to tell Jillian a number of times that I was making improper advances. And on this day, she screamed at Jillian, who didn't want to listen, that she had missed one of her monthly periods. 'Does that mean I'm pregnant, Mother, does it?' Jill whipped around and tore into her, refusing to believe anything she'd said. 'You filthy-minded little slut,' she shouted. 'Why would a man like Tony want a girl like you, when he has me, me? If that's the way you're thinking, I'll send you away.'"

"'You don't have to bother,' whispered Leigh, her face gone dead white, 'I'll go and you'll never see me again! And if I'm pregnant, I'll be the one to have the Tatterton heir!'"

I was caught unprepared for those words. "How did you find out, how?"

Tony's hands bowed into his hands. His voice came out wretched and torn. "I knew a long time ago Jillian envied Leigh's beauty, which needed no makeup or other enhancements . . . but it was only when she broke a few minutes ago that she screamed the truth at me. Leigh was pregnant when she left here, driven out by her own mother's failure to understand and help. And in loving Leigh, I not only destroyed her, I have destroyed my brother."

I sat on and on, reeling with the full knowledge. I wasn't Pa's daughter. I wasn't a scumbag Casteel, no daughter of the hills. But what good would it do me now, now that Troy was gone?

## ∽ Twenty-one ∽
### Passing Time

TROY WAS GONE. I WAITED EACH DAY FOR A LETTER from him. None ever came. I walked through the maze each day to his cottage, hoping against hope that he'd come back, and we'd be close friends if nothing more. The cottage and its lovely gardens began to look neglected, so that I sent Farthy's gardeners over to bring it back to order. Then, one day at breakfast, with Jillian still upstairs asleep, Tony told me he'd heard from one of his plant managers that Troy was visiting each European factory one by one. "That's a good sign," said Tony brightly, struggling to smile. "As long as he goes out and sees the world it means he's not lying in a bed somewhere, waiting to die."

Tony and I were allies of a kind, united in a common cause, to bring Troy home again, to help him survive. Despite the terrible thing Tony had done to my mother, whether or not she had led him on, each day it lost some of its importance, as I fought the routine of going to college and studying so hard sometimes I fell into bed exhausted. That's when Tony was very helpful to me, assisting me over scholastic hurdles I couldn't seem to climb alone.

As for Jillian, she became a ghost of her former self. Bringing the full truth of her daughter out of the closet and into the light put Jillian in the closet. All the parties and charity affairs she had loved to attend were forgotten in the self-abuse that keep her in bed, so she no longer cared how she looked. She cried constantly for Leigh to come back and forgive her for not listening, for not understanding, for not having cared enough. But of course it was too late for Leigh to come back.

Yet life went on. I shopped again for new clothes. I wrote letters to Tom and to Fanny, and always included a check for both. Striving for the top grades became my main objective in life. Often when Tony and I were forced to join each other just to feel we weren't alone in a huge house, I found his blue eyes riveted on me, as if he wanted to say something that would knock down my wall of hostility, but I was reluctant to let that wall down. Let him suffer, I'd think. But for him my mother wouldn't have run away. She wouldn't have ended up in a mountain shack where poverty killed her. Then, contrarily, I'd remember the sweet days in the Willies when all five of the Casteel children and Logan Stonewall had found a great deal of happiness just in being together.

One cold November day when the sky threatened another snowfall, a letter arrived from Fanny.

*Dear Heaven,*
    *Your selfishness forced me to marry with my*

*rich old man, Mallory. Now I don't need your
stingy ole pin money. Mallory's got a big house,
pretty as one in them fancy house magazines, and
he's got a mean cranky ole ma who'd like to see me
dead. Not that I kerr. Ole fishface is about ready to
kick off any day, so her not liking me don't matter
much no how. Mallory is trying to teach me to act
like a lady, an talk like one. I wouldn't waste my
time with nothing so silly if one day I didn't think
I'd run into Logan Stonewall agin, an if I could
talk and act proper, maybe this time he'd love me.
Love me as I always wanted him to love me. An
you can kiss him off as gone ferever, once he's
mine.*

*Your loving, caring sister Fanny*

Fanny's letter disturbed me. Who would have ever
thought that Fanny, who had played the field far and
wide, and had treated all males more or less like
machines whose buttons she knew only too well how
to push, would have fallen so for Logan, the very one
who scorned her most.

If Fanny wrote just one letter, Tom wrote many.

*I found that roll of bills that you gave to
Grandpa. Really, Heavenly, where was your good
sense? He had it shoved down in his whittling box,
underneath all the wood. He's a pitiful old geezer,
always wanting what he hasn't got, so that when
he's here, he's yearning for the hills, where Annie
wants to be. And then when he's in the hills about
two weeks, he then wants to be with his "chiluns."
I think he gets lonely there with only that old
woman who comes in the morning and fixes*

*enough food to last the day. Gosh, Heavenly, what*
*do you do with someone like that?*

Without Troy, Farthy became just a place to stay on
the weekends. I said as little as I could to Tony, and
yet sometimes I felt sorry for him, prowling alone the
long empty halls of a huge house that no longer
resounded with the laughter and gaiety of many house
guests. Yet I went on about my business, reminding
myself each day that I had come to Boston with a goal
in mind, and on that I concentrated, thinking somehow, at some point in time, I would find the happiness
that was due me.

The years passed swiftly after that tragic day when
Troy decided it was better to put miles and miles
between us. Only once in a great while did he write
home, and then it was always to Tony. Grief and
unhappiness were mine for the longest time, but when
the sun shines, and the wind blows, and the rain
freshens the grass, and you see the flowers you
planted in the fall coming up in the spring, bit by bit
grief and unhappiness slips away. I had my dream
now, my college days. The beautiful campus, the boys
who asked me for dates, all that helped. One very
quiet, unassuming, but nice-looking boy I took home
for Tony to meet. Yes, the son of a state senator was
perfect, even if I did find him more than a bit boring.
Once or twice I saw Logan near the university, and
he'd smile and say a few words, and I'd smile and ask
him if he'd heard from Tom, but Logan never asked
me for a date.

Feeling sorry for Jillian, I made a point of visiting
her as often as my hectic routine allowed. I began to

call her Grandmother. She didn't seem to notice. That alone was enough to tell me some drastic change had taken place within her. I brushed and styled her hair, and did many small things for her that she also didn't notice. And seated always in a far corner, as discreet as possible, was the nurse that Tony had hired to see that Jillian did no harm to herself.

During each of my summer breaks, Tony planned something special for us to do together. London, Paris, and Rome, finally I had my chance to see them. We traveled to Denmark, Iceland, and Finland so he could show me the small Danish town that had been Jillian's mother's birthplace. Not once did we ever make the journey to that Texas ranch where Jillian's mother and two older sisters still lived. Often I had the feeling that Tony was trying to make up for my deprived youth. I think both of us kept up a constant hope of finding Troy during our European vacations.

Many a time I thought about visiting Grandpa, who had made several round trips from Georgia to the Willies, but there was always the threat that Pa would be with him, and I wasn't ready to face Pa. When I thought of Stacie, I thought of that handsome little boy named Drake, and to him I mailed all sorts of wonderful gifts. Each time Stacie wrote back in a few days to thank me for remembering Drake, who thought he was very lucky to receive toys all through the year, and not have to wait for Christmas.

"You could be a huge help to me at Tatterton Toys," said Tony time and time again. "That is, if you've lost your ambition to become another Miss Marianne Deale." He gazed at me steadily. "It would be quite wonderful for me if you had your surname legally changed to Tatterton."

Strange how I took that. I'd never been proud of being a Casteel. And yet it was as a Casteel that I wanted to return to Winnerrow with a college degree, to prove to them that, at last, a scumbag Casteel was not so ignorant and stupid they had always to end up in prison. As I thought over Tony's proposition, I realized I didn't know now exactly what I wanted for myself. I was changing, changing in all sorts of subtle ways.

Tony was trying so hard to make up for the damage he'd done in the past. Doing for me all the things I used to dream that Pa would do. Tony made me the center of his life, gave me all the attention, love, and charm that I used to think Pa owed me. During one cruise to the Caribbean, I relaxed enough to smile and flirt with several good-looking young men, and for a moment or so I didn't worry about Troy. Whatever happened to him, it wasn't my fault, wasn't my fault at all.

But when I dreamed, I dreamed of Troy. Troy somewhere needing me, still loving me, and tears would be on my face in the morning. When I could put worries about Troy behind me, I found a certain kind of acceptance about life, and how much you could do to control it. And then one wonderful day, Tony delivered to me something totally unexpected, and wonderful.

It happened on July the fourth. I had one more year to go in college. "We're going to have a fabulous poolside picnic, with weekend guests I more than suspect you are going to enjoy very much." Tony's smile was very broad. "Jillian seems a bit better, and she'll be there—and other special guests as well."

"Who are the special guests?"

"You'll be pleased," he assured me, smiling his secret smile.

The flags came out, all the red, white, and blue party decorations. Japanese lanterns were strung from tree to tree, from lamppost to lamppost, additional servants were hired as waiters, and Tony, who could not stand rock 'n' roll music, hired several Hawaiian musicians to play in the background.

Twenty or more guests were at the poolside when I came down from my room, wearing a bright blue swimsuit that made me feel a bit embarrassed because it had such high-cut legs. Over this I wore a short white eyelet jacket. Some guests were already in the pool, others sunbathing, and all were laughing, talking, having a wonderful time. A few swimmers had even dared to brave the ocean's rough waves. I went first to Jillian to kiss her cheek, and she smiled at me in a vague, disoriented way. "What are we celebrating, Heaven?" she asked, staring at old friends as if they were strangers.

On another part of the spacious pool terrace, I spied Tony standing and talking to a rather plump little woman, with an even plumper husband. They were more than familiar to me, and my heart began a nervous pounding. Oh, no, no! He couldn't have brought about this kind of reconciliation without warning me in advance.

And yet he had.

Here at Farthinggale Manor, where I could reach out and touch them, if I wanted, were Rita and Lester Rawlings from Chevy Chase. And if they were here

. . . then Keith and Our Jane had to be here as well. My heart flip-flopped. Eagerly I looked around for the two youngest Casteels. I soon spied Our Jane and Keith standing apart from other children, and then, as I watched with utter fascination, Our Jane threw off her beach coat, kicked off her rubber sandals, and ran toward the pool, with Keith close at her heels. They knew how to swim very well, and how to dive, and how to make friends out of strangers.

"Heaven!" called Tony from across the terrace. "Come, we have special guests that I think you already know." I approached Lester Rawlings and his wife Rita with caution, visions of that horrible Christmas Day in the Willies flashing in and out of my mind. Memories of that terrible night after Our Jane and Keith were gone putting tears in my eyes. And I had fresher guilts and memories to make me feel nervous, for I had betrayed my promise that time in Chevy Chase when I gave my word not to speak to Our Jane or Keith, or let them see me. And then there was the way my two youngest had denied me, that pain was still there, aching.

Rita Rawlings immediately opened her arms and drew me into her motherly embrace. "Oh, my dear, my dear, I am so sorry the way things turned out the last time. Lester and I were so afraid that seeing you again would set our darlings back, so they'd have nightmares and crying spells again. And even without seeing you that Sunday, they did subtly change, so they no longer seemed as happy and contented to be with us. If only you had told us how your circumstances had changed. That day when you so unexpectedly showed up, we thought you had come to take our children back to the hills and that awful shack. But

Mr. Tatterton here has made it all very clear. She paused to clasp her plump, beringed fingers together and catch her breath. "Lester and I just didn't understand what happened to our two happy children after that rainy Sunday afternoon. They changed as if by magic. That very night their nightmares came back. They woke up screaming, calling for Hev-lee, come back, come back! We didn't mean it, we didn't! It took weeks and weeks before they would tell us what had happened—that they had denied knowing you— and had ordered you out or they would call the police. Dear Heaven, it was cruel of them, but they were terrified of having to return to that pain, poverty, and hunger that they remembered only too well."

All about me people were having a wonderful time, diving in and out of the pool. Servants carried trays of food and drink from here to there . . . and then I found my eyes meeting with those of the loveliest teenage girl I'd ever seen. Our Jane stood about ten feet away, her turquoise eyes fastened on me in the most pitiful, pleading way. She was thirteen now, her small, hard, burgeoning breasts just beginning to thrust forth her suit top. Her red gold, fiery hair flamed about her small oval face, even as her darkly fringed eyes pleaded with me for forgiveness. Close to her side was Keith, just a year older. He had shot up inches taller, and his amber hair was deep and rich. But he was staring too, and trembling. They were obviously afraid of me now, not in the same way as when I'd approached them in their own home. Now they seemed afraid that I'd hate them for denying me.

I didn't know what to say. I just held out my arms and smiled, and felt my heart pounding like crazy, then watched them hesitate, glance at each other before both came running to hurl themselves into my embrace.

"Oh, Hev-lee, Hev-lee," cried Our Jane. "Please don't hate us for what we did! We're sorry we drove you away. We were sorry the minute we saw your face look so sad and disappointed." She pressed her face against my chest and really began to cry. "It wasn't you we didn't want. It was going back to the cabin, and the hunger and the cold. We thought you would take us back to all that. And we'd no longer have Mommy and Daddy, who love us so much."

"I understand," I crooned, kissing her again and again before I turned to hug Keith close, and that's when *I* really began to bawl. At last, at last, I had my two little ones in my arms again. And they were looking at me with love and adoration, just as they used to do.

The voices of Rita and Lester Rawlings drifted to me from where they were sitting beneath one of our green-and-white-striped umbrellas, both sipping cool drinks and telling Tony about the wonderfully compassionate letter that had come to them one day about two weeks ago. "It was a letter from your brother Troy, Mr. Tatterton. He wanted to mend some bridges, and when we finished reading his letter, we were both in tears. He didn't tell us we had done a terrible thing, he just thanked us for taking such good care of Heaven's younger brother and sister, for she loved them very much. And we had to contact you, just had to, for it was wrong of us to have tried to separate brothers and sisters, we know that now."

"Call me Tony," he said charmingly, "since we are almost family now."

"This letter from your brother made everything so clear, just what Heaven's circumstances were."

Troy had done this for me! Troy was still thinking of me, and doing what he could to give me happiness, and I had to have his letter, just had to have it, even if it were but a photocopy. "Of course, of course," agreed Rita Rawlings. "It was so beautifully written I was going to keep it forever, but my dear, you can have the original, and I'll keep the copy."

In the ten days that the Rawlingses stayed with us that summer, Jane (who didn't want to be called Our Jane anymore) and Keith and I found each other again. They asked questions about Tom and Fanny, and about Pa. They didn't seem to have the resentments against Pa that I did. "And Mommy and Daddy said we could visit you once or twice a year! Oh, Hev-lee, it's going to be so wonderful. Maybe one day we can even see Tom, Fanny, Pa and Grandpa again. But we don't want to leave Mommy and Daddy, not ever."

All that was easily arranged. Farthinggale Manor made its impression, as did Tony—and if Jillian gave them a few weird thoughts they were much too polite to express them. "We'll keep in touch," promised Rita Rawlings, as Lester shook Tony's hand like they were the best of friends. "Christmas would be a nice time to get together for we do want our children to enjoy the pleasures of a large family."

Yes, it was all right for my brother and sister to know me now. I no longer lived in a shack stuck high on a mountain hillside. I was no longer a starving, bedraggled, object of their pity, though they didn't mention Tom, or Fanny, or Pa. Or Grandpa, as Jane and Keith had.

When Rita Rawlings kept her word and mailed me the letter that Troy had written, making such a strong and passionate appeal on my behalf, tears poured from my eyes. He loved me. He still loved me! He still thought about me. Oh, Troy, Troy, come home, come home! Just live somewhere close by and let me see you now and then—that will be enough, enough.

I dated, off and on, some young man that passed Tony's inspection. I never found anyone as unique as Troy, nor anyone as loyal and devoted as Logan. I had to presume Logan had met someone else. Just as I would have to . . . someday. And when I gave Logan long and considered thought, I knew I wanted to see him again, and when I did, I'd have to make all the overtures to patch up our relationship.

Tom wrote often, telling me that the money I was sending had finally worn down his resistance, and he was attending college courses and still helping our Pa during the day. "We're reaching our goals, Heavenly, despite everything, we're going to make it!"

## ～ Twenty-two ～
# *Dreams Come True*

IN THE YEAR THAT I TURNED TWENTY-TWO, ON A BEAU-
tiful day in late June when all the flowers were in
bloom, I received my degree. Both Tony and Jillian
were there to represent me, and though I searched the
audience hoping to see Troy, he was not there. All
along I'd hoped and prayed that he'd be in the
audience, applauding. But I did see Jane and Keith
sitting with their parents not far from Jillian and
Tony . . . but Tom wasn't there, nor was Fanny, and I
had mailed them both invitations.

"Be smart and do all that you can to keep Fanny out
of your life," Tom had warned in his last letter. "I'd
come if I could, really I would, but I'm snowed under
trying to pass my own exams, and I still have to help
out Pa. Forgive me, and know that I am with you in
thoughts."

After the graduation party, we drove back to
Farthinggale Manor. Parked before the front door
was a white Jaguar that Tony had ordered custom-
designed for me. "It's for that day when 'ou drive

back to Winnerrow. If your clothes and jewelry don't impress them, this car certainly should."

It was a fabulous car, all my graduation gifts were fabulous. But oddly, now that I was no longer a student, I had so much time on my hands I didn't know what to do with myself. I had reached my goal. I could become, if I so wished, another Miss Marianne Deale. Now I wasn't sure that was what I wanted. A restlessness grew within me that summer, a terrible itchiness that kept me awake at night, and made me more than a little irritable. "Take a drive off on your own," suggested Tony. "That's what I used to do when I was your age and unable to find peace within myself."

However, even a trip up the coast to Maine, where I stayed ten days in a fishing village, didn't put my itchy feet at rest. There was something I had to do. Something important I had to do.

This time, as I returned from my vacation and drove once again under the ornate gates of Farthinggale Manor, I came again as a stranger, with new eyes, to that long, curving road that led to that huge house of enchantment.

It was just the same. Just as impressive, frightening, and beautiful. And I could have been sixteen again for all the changes I saw. For some intuition was whispering loudly that Troy might be here. Tony had said he couldn't stay away forever.

My heartbeats quickened; my soul seemed to wake up and stretch before it took a deep breath and reached again for the love it had found in this house. I could almost see Troy, feel Troy, sense Troy somewhere near. For long moments I just sat and inhaled the special, flower-scented air of Farthinggale Manor, before I stepped out and approached the high stone portico.

Curtis responded to my impatient jabbing at the doorbell, smiling warmly when he saw who it was. "It's so good to see you again, Miss Heaven," he said in his low, cultivated voice. "Mr. Tatterton is strolling on the beach, but your grandmother is in her suite."

Jillian was shut away in her rooms in that glorious mansion that had again retreated into silence almost as deep and thick as a grave.

She sat as I'd seen her sit many times before when she was less than happy with herself, cross-legged on her ivory sofa, wearing another of those loose-fitting ivory floats that was trimmed this time with peach lace.

The sound of the door opening and closing as I entered made soft clicking noises that seemed to wake her from some deep meditation. The spread of solitaire cards on the coffee table before her was precise, even, the cards in her hands held loosely, forgotten. Her unfocused blue eyes turned to gaze at me almost sightlessly. As Jillian stared at me, almost with fright, I tried to smile. If my appearance had shocked her, hers shocked me even more.

Her complexion now was cracked porcelain, unhealthily white. And as she stared at me, I was appalled at the disorientation in her eyes, at the way she wrung her pale hands, at the way her hair hung about her face, unclean and uncared for.

Only as I turned away so she wouldn't see my distress did I see sitting in a distant corner, quietly making lace, a woman in a nurse's white uniform. She looked up to smile my way. "My name is Martha Goodman," she informed me. "I am very happy to meet you, Miss Casteel. Mr. Tatterton told me that you were due back any day."

"Where is Mr. Tatterton?" I asked, directing my question to her.

"Why, he's off prowling on the seashore," she answered in a very thin, small voice, as if she didn't want Jillian's attention drawn to her presence in the room. She stood up to point the direction, and I turned to leave.

Jillian jumped to her bare feet and began to twirl around and around, making the wide skirt of her garment flare out. "Leigh," she called in a lilting, childish voice, "say hello to Cleave for me when you see him next! Tell him sometimes I am almost sorry I left him for Tony. Tony doesn't love me. Nobody has ever loved me, not ever enough. Not even you. You love Cleave better, you always have . . . but I don't care. I really don't care. You are so very much like him, nothing at all like me except in appearance. Leigh, why do you stare at me like that? Why is it you always have to take everything so damned seriously!"

My breasts rose and fell in heavy gasps. I backed out of the room; her insane laughter followed, shivering the air.

When finally I reached the door, I couldn't resist taking one more glance at her; I saw her framed before her arching bay windows, the sunlight pouring through her hair, silhouetting her slender form through the transparent film of her long, loose dress. She was old, and paradoxically she was young; she was beautiful and she was grotesque; but more than anything, she was insane, and she was pitiful.

And I walked away knowing I intended never to see her again.

On the rocky shore of the beach I strolled where Troy had never wanted to walk at my side, so afraid he'd been of the sea and its portent. There were rocks and huge boulders feet higher than I was, and walking here wasn't easy. At that time I, too, had been terrified of the sea with its relentlessly pounding surf, its towering high waves that crashed on the shore and made of human time but a pinch of sand.

Bits of gravel slipped into my shoes, and soon I took them off and ran to catch up with Tony. I planned to stay only an hour or so. For I had a destination in mind now.

Rounding a curve in the beach, I came upon him suddenly. He was standing on a high pile of boulders, staring out over the sea, and it was with some difficulty that I climbed to stand beside him. I told him what I planned to do.

"So you will return to Winnerrow," he said dully, without turning his head. "I have always known you would go back to those godforsaken mountains that you should hate so much you should never want to see again."

"They are part of me," I replied, brushing dirt from my feet and legs. "I always intended to go back and teach there, in the same school where Miss Deale used to teach Tom and me. There aren't many teachers who want that poverty area, so they'll take me, and I'll have my chance to carry on the tradition started by Miss Deale. My grandpa Toby is expecting me to stay with him while I teach. And if you still want to see me, I'll spend some time here with you. But I don't want to see Jillian again, ever again."

"Heaven," Tony began, and then he stopped and just stared at me with so much pain in his eyes. I tried

414

to deny the twinge of pity I felt when I noticed the hollows under his eyes, and the dark shadows. He was thinner, less than elegantly dressed. His trousers, which had been so sharply creased before, had no creases at all. It was obvious the best years of Townsend Anthony Tatterton were behind him now.

He sighed before he asked, "You didn't read about it in the newspapers?"

"Read about what?"

He sighed deep and long, still staring out to sea. "As you know, Troy has been flitting about the world. Last week, he came home. He seemed to know you were gone."

My heart jumped. "He's here? Troy is here?" I was going to see him again! Troy, oh Troy?!

Tony smiled crookedly. The kind of smile that twisted my heart and made it hurt.

His shoulders hunched to shorten his neck, and still he stared out to sea, forcing me to glance that way to find what his eyes kept watching. And with some difficulty I saw a wreath of flowers bouncing on the waves far out in the ocean. Golden glints of sunlight on the deep sapphire water made it exceedingly beautiful. The flower wreath was just a tiny, bright speck. Again my heartbeats quickened. The sea, always the sea had chased Troy. A sudden weight formed in my chest.

Tony sighed with the cool wind that blew always from the ocean. "Troy returned home very depressed. He was happy to hear that you and Jane and Keith had been reunited. But he was approaching his twenty-eighth birthday. Birthdays always depressed him. He believed, sincerely believed, that thirty was his cut-off day. 'I hope it's not a painful illness,' he said a few times, as if that disturbed him more than anything. 'It's not that I'm afraid to die, it's only the road to death that terrifies me, for sometimes it can be so drawn out.' You have two more years, I kept reminding him, if your precognition is true. If it is not, you have fifty, sixty, or seventy. He'd look at me as if I knew nothing. I stayed close by just to see him through, fearing something would happen. We used to sit in his rooms and talk about you, and how strong you were when you cared for your brothers and sisters after your stepmother and your . . . your father went away. He told me that during the past semester he used to visit your college and hide on the campus just so he could see you.

Again his eyes swiveled to the sea. And by this time the wreath had disappeared, and I was scared, so terribly scared.

"I'm telling my story knowing you still love him. Please indulge me, Heaven. To take Troy's mind off that dreaded birthday, I planned a party to last over the weekend. I made everyone promise not to leave him alone for one second. There was a girl there that he had dated once or twice. She'd been married and was divorced. The kind of laughing, bright, and breezy girl I thought would lift his spirits, and perhaps help him to stop thinking about you. She had all kinds of tall tales to tell, about the celebrities she'd met, and the clothes she'd bought, and the huge mansion she was going to build on her own South Sea island . . . if only she had the right man to live with her. And she looked at Troy then. He didn't seem to see or hear her. No woman likes to be ignored like that, and that's when her humor ended. She became derisive, ugly acting. Finally Troy could bear no more of her taunts, and he jumped up, and left the house. I saw him head toward the stables. I didn't want him to go there, and if this idiot girl hadn't raced to follow me outside, I would have caught up with him in plenty of time to prevent what he did. But she seized my hand and she teased me about being my brother's keeper.

"And when I finally got away, Troy had saddled Abdulla Bar, according to a stable boy, and on horseback Troy raced through the maze, over and over through the maze. It was not a place that a sensitive horse liked and soon he leaped the last hedge hurdle, driven insane by the twists and turns of the maze he'd never been in before—and the horse headed for the shore!"

"Abdulla Bar . . ." I repeated, the name almost forgotten by this time.

"Yes, Jill's favorite stallion. The one nobody but her could ride. I saddled my own horse and rode to catch up with him, but the wind here on the shore was wild. Ahead of me about a hundred feet, a sheet of trash paper flew into Abdulla Bar's face. He reared and whinnied as if terrified, and he whirled about and ran straight into the ocean! It was crazy to sit on my horse, who refused to run into the wind, and watch my brother fight to bring that crazy horse back to shore! The sun was red and low on the horizon behind us . . . and the sea turned to blood . . , and then both horse and rider disappeared."

My hands fluttered to my forehead and hovered there. "Troy? Oh no, Tony!"

"We called the Coast Guard. All the men at the party put out in the boats I have, and we searched for him. Abdulla Bar swam back to shore with an empty saddle, and then, toward dawn, Troy's body was found. He had drowned."

No! No! It couldn't be true.

He went on, wrapping my shoulders with his arm and pulling me against his side. "I tried desperately to find where you were staying in Maine, but I never was able to. Every day I have held my own small memorial service for him, waiting for you to return, and say your own goodbyes."

I thought I had cried all the tears I could cry for the love I'd had for Troy. Yet, as I stood there and gazed out to sea, I knew that throughout my life I would cry many more tears for him.

Time passed as I stood with Tony and waited for that floating wreath to reappear. *Oh, Troy, years we could have had together! Almost four years that would have given you a fair share of life, and love, and normalcy, and maybe then you would have loved life enough to have stayed!*

I was numb now, blind with tears I didn't want to share with Tony. On the walk back to the mansion I said goodbye to Tony quickly, though he clung to both of my hands and tried to force from me the promise that I'd return again.

"Please, Heaven, please! You're my daughter, my only heir. Troy is dead. I need an heir to give purpose and meaning to my life! What good is all of this that we have accumulated through the centuries if our line ends now? Don't go! Troy would want you to stay! Everything that he was is here in this house and in his cottage that he left to you. He loved you . . . please, don't leave me here alone with Jill. Please stay, Heaven, please, for my sake and for Troy's! All that

you see around you will be yours. It's your legacy.
Take it if for no better reason than you can pass it
down to your children."

I tugged my hands away. "Why you can go anywhere you want without Jillian," I said ruthlessly,
stepping into my fine car. "You can hire help to take
care of her, and not come back until she is dead. You
don't need me, and I don't need you, or the Tatterton
money. You have now exactly what you deserve—
nothing."

The wind fanned my hair. He stood and watched
me drive away, the saddest-looking man I'd ever seen.
But I didn't care. Troy was dead and I had graduated
from college, and life would go on, despite Tony, who
needed me now, and Jillian, who had never needed
anything but youth and beauty.

# Twenty-three
## *Revenge*

I WAS GOING BACK HOME, BACK TO WINNERROW. AT last it was time for me to put the past to rest, and to become that person I always wanted to be. For I knew now that our childhood dreams are often the most pure ones; I wanted more than anything to follow in Miss Marianne Deale's footsteps, to be the kind of teacher who could give a child like me a chance in life, who could open up the world of books and knowledge that provided a way out of the narrowness and ignorance of the hills. And it was not really hard to risk my Tatterton legacy—for I was no longer a scumbag Casteel, cowering on the fringes of society. No, I was a Tatterton, a VanVoreen, and even if I planned never to tell anyone in my family the truth of my parentage, still, I was now ready to confront the man whose love I had needed so desperately as a child, who had denied me so relentlessly and brutally. For I didn't need him at all now. And I wanted him, and only him, to know just who I was.

It took me three days to drive to Winnerrow, and on the way I stopped in New York City, at one of the best hairdressers, and did something I'd wanted to do for years. All my life I'd wanted my mother's silvery blond hair color. All my life I'd been the dark angel, betrayed by what I had thought was my Indian Casteel hair. Now I would be the true, bright, shining angel, the rich girl from Boston who no one ever looked down on. I emerged from that salon a different woman—a woman with shining, silvery blond hair. No, I wasn't a Casteel anymore. I was my mother's true daughter. And I knew that to at least one man I would no longer appear to be the Heaven Leigh Casteel he hated—no, he would see how much like Leigh I was, he would finally understand how much he loved me. I would be a Heaven Leigh he loved—for at last he would see in me his beloved Angel.

Grandpa almost didn't know who I was when I first arrived at the new cabin in the woods. He seemed almost afraid when he first saw me, as if a ghost had truly come back from the dead. It was then I realized that if he ever really did catch sight of his "Annie" he'd probably have a heart attack. "Grandpa," I said, hugging his frightened, rigid body, "It's me, Heaven. Do you like my hair?"

"Oh, Heaven child, I thought ya was a ghost!" he heaved a mighty sigh of relief. And when I told him I was coming to live with him he was overjoyed. "Oh, Heaven chile, ever'body comin' home at once. Ya know Luke's circus is comin' to town next week. All the Casteels comin' back to Winnerrow. Ain't it grand tho!"

So, I wasn't the only Casteel come back to show

who I was now. Now I could get on with my plans much sooner than I expected. Now I knew just what I had to do.

The circus was all that people in Winnerrow talked about. They stood on street corners, and in the pharmacy, and in the beauty shop and barber shops, and cluttered the one and only supermarket with their many speculations on whether or not it was "Godly" to attend a circus where so many performers wore so few clothes. Everyone was so busy with the circus, they barely had time to gossip about me and my white Jaguar driving through town.

I was busy that week before the circus was due to arrive—busy making the cabin as cozy and pretty as possible, busy washing an old dress that had to be carefully bleached so it would turn truly white. Then the dress had to be ironed, and I'd had no experience ever with handling an iron, even the best new one that money could buy. It just so happened that the day I was setting up the contraption called an ironing board, Logan dropped by to bring Grandpa his weekly supply of medications. He sucked in his breath when he saw me. "Oh," he said, looking uncomfortable, "I almost didn't know who you were."

"You don't like it?" I asked lightly, determined to keep my distance.

"You look beautiful, but you looked even more beautiful with your own dark hair."

"Of course you'd say that. You like everything as God gave it to us. But I know nature can be improved upon."

"Are we going to start off again fighting, and over such a silly thing as the color of your hair? I quite honestly don't care what you do to your hair."

"I didn't think you really did."

He set down his bundle on the middle of the kitchen table, and looked around. "Where is your grandfather?"

"He's down the hill, bragging about Pa and his circus. Why, you'd think Pa had become the president of the United States from the way he's carrying on."

Uneasily Logan stood in the center of the kitchen, looking around, obviously not wanting to leave yet. "I like what you've done to this cabin. It seems so cozy."

"Thank you."

"Are you going to be staying awhile?"

"Maybe. I'm not sure yet. I've filed my application at the Winnerrow's school board, but so far I haven't heard a thing."

I began to try and iron my dress. "You didn't marry Troy Tatterton, why not?"

"It's not really any of your business, is it Logan?"

"I think it is. I've known you for many years. I took care of you when you were sick. I loved you for a long time . . . I think that gives me a few rights."

It was several minutes before I could say thinly, with tears in my voice, "Troy died in an accident. He was a very wonderful man who had too many tragedies in his life. I could cry for all he should have had, and didn't."

"What is it the super-wealthy can't buy?" he asked, with a certain mocking tone in his voice, and I whirled to confront him, still holding my iron in my hand. "You're thinking as I used to think, that money can buy everything, but it doesn't and never will." I turned and began to iron again. "Will you please leave now, Logan? I have a thousand things to do. Tom will be staying here with us, and I want the house to be perfect in time for his arrival—I have to make it feel like home.

For the longest time he stood behind me, so close he could have leaned forward and kissed my neck, yet he didn't. I felt his presence, almost as if he were touching me. "Heaven, are you going to find time in your busy schedule to fit me in?"

"Why should I? I hear you are as good as engaged to Maisie Setterton."

"Everyone is telling me that Cal Dennison returned to Winnerrow just to see you!"

Again I whirled around. "Why are you so eager to believe anything you hear? If Cal Dennison is in town, he's made no effort to contact me, and I hope never to see him again."

Suddenly he smiled. His sapphire eyes lit up and made him seem a boy again, the boy who used to love me. "Well, it's nice seeing you again, Heaven. And I'll get used to your blond hair, if you decide to keep it that way." And then he was turning and walking out the back door, leaving me staring after him, and wondering, wondering.

As the day of the circus dawned, Grandpa was so eager to see his youngest son and Tom that he was almost hopping with excitement as I tried to knot the first tie he'd ever worn. He grouched and complained and said I was worse than Stacie, who was always trying to make him look like what he wasn't. "Ya kin't do it, Heaven chile. New clothes won't do it . . . jus' get ya gone. I kin brush my own hair!"

It was my intention to make him look like a gentleman as much as possible and to show all those pseudo-snobs in Winnerrow that even Casteels could change. Grandpa was wearing, also, the first real suit of his life. I tucked a colorful handkerchief in his pocket, fiddling with it for a few minutes, while Grandpa itched for me to get on with it.

"Why, durn iffen ya ain't gone an' made me look like some big city gent," he proudly said, eyeing himself up and down in the full-length mirror that had been ordered for the bedroom that I was using. He preened like a bird in bright plumage, touching tentative fingers to his hair, the little he had left.

"You be careful with yourself, Grandpa, until I'm dressed."

"But I don't know now what to do wid myself."

"Then I'll tell you what to do. You won't go farther from this house than the front porch, and don't start whittling or you'll cover your good suit with sawdust and shavings. Sit in one of the rockers next to Grandma, and tell her all about what's going to happen today. And sit there until I come out, ready to go."

"But Annie's not gonna want to stay here widout us!" he said in shrill objection. "Luke's her son, too."

"Then Grandma will go with us." He smiled when I said that. He touched his withered old hand to my face. "Yer gonna dress her up fancy, too?"

"Of course."

Grandpa stared at me almost struck with awe, and then teary wonder came to his eyes. "All yer life ya've been a good girl, chile Heaven. The best kind of girl t'have."

Oh, oh, it hurt more than I'd ever expected to be complimented by someone at this place in the mountains where no one had ever loved me enough.

"Now don't go farther than the front porch until I'm ready," I warned him. "If you get yourself dirty we'll have to begin again from the beginning—and that means the bathtub."

He shuffled away, mumbling to himself about the number of baths taken in this house, and all that water wasted.

That night I wore a thin, blue summer dress and matching blue sandals. I was saving my white dress for the second night, when the circus performers would be more at ease and perhaps able to pay more notice to the audience. The first night all the Casteels would display themselves to Winnerrow. The next night I would show my true self to Pa. My jewelry was real, and I knew I was a fool for wearing it to any circus, but I figured nobody would know it from costume junk, unless they too owned the real thing.

When finally I showed up on the front porch, ready to go, Grandpa was having a terrible time keeping Annie from getting nervous. "She looks pretty, don't she, Annie," he said, looking pleased even as he looked troubled whenever my fair hair drew his attention.

After we had Granny "dressed to kill" I still wanted Grandpa to sit up front with me, so I could show him off to all the snobs in Winnerrow who thought Casteel men didn't know how to look like gentlemen.

"But I don't wanna leave my Annie sittin' back there alone," he complained.

"She wants to lie down and rest, Grandpa, and there isn't room for her to do that unless you move up here beside me."

Once I had him persuaded it was his duty to let her rest when she wanted to, he moved to sit beside me. And that's when a big, happy grin broke out on his craggy old face. "What kind of auto ya got here, Heaven chile? I neva in my whole life rode so soft! Takes t'bumps like they're flat. Why, gosh durn iffen it don't feel like we're home in bed!"

Slowly, slowly we drove down Main Street in Winnerrow.

Heads turned on Main Street. You bet they turned.

Eyes bulged to see the Casteel scumbags riding in a custom-designed Jaguar convertible. And if there was one thing every country person knew about, it was automobiles. For once in his life Toby Casteel found dignity and sat straight and proud, only turning to whisper back to his wife after we'd left Main Street behind us.

"Annie, wake up now. Did ya see 'em starin', did ya? Ya didn't sleep through it, did ya? Weren't it somethin', though, t'way they eyeballed us, weren't it? Why there ain't nobody who's got it betta than us, not now. Why this Heaven chile of ours has gone t'college an' come out wid all that money can buy. Neva saw t'likes of what education kin do, neva did."

I'd never heard Grandpa say so much before, even if he didn't know what he was talking about. The money that had bought this car had been Tony's, not any money earned by me.

It took us more than an hour to get there, I drove so slowly, but eventually we did arrive at the circus grounds just beyond the city limits.

Three large tents were up, and many smaller ones for the side show. The huge middle tent impressed me with its bright colors, its many flags snapping smartly in the wind. People from five counties had flocked to see the circus, where Luke Casteel would stand high on a platform and spiel out his talk. As Grandpa and I strolled in, heads turned to stare, and I overheard their whispers. "That's Toby Casteel, Luke's father."

Grandpa and I had hardly had time to adjust to having so many eyes stare at us, when a slender woman wearing bright red came up from behind, yelling like a bull moose all the way. "Stop! Wait up! It's me, yer sista, Fanny!" And before I had the time to brace myself, Fanny hurled herself into my arms with her overly enthusiastic greeting.

"Oh holy Jesus Christ on the cross, Heaven," she screeched loud enough for a dozen people to turn around and stare, "ya sure do look good!" Fanny hugged me several times before she embraced Grandpa. "Why Grandpa, neva saw ya lookin' so citified before! Why I hardly know ya, when ya usually look so old and crummy."

That's the kind of compliments Fanny always knew how to give. Double-edged ones. Her red dress had large white polka dots. It fitted so tight it seemed painted on. Gold bracelets laddered up both of her tanned arms. Her black hair was parted in the middle and caught behind both her ears with large white silk flowers. She looked, indeed, like a fine exotic cat wearing the wrong colors.

Fanny stood back to stare at me. Her dark eyes gone frightened-looking. "Ya scare me, ya really do. Ya don't look like yerself no more. I bet ya look just like yer dead ma. Don't it frighten ya some t'look like somebody dead an' buried?"

"No, Fanny. It makes me feel good to look like my mother."

"Neva could understand ya, neva could," she mumbled, then grinned shyly. "Don't hold no grudges,

Heaven, please. Let's be friends. Let's go an' watch Pa, an' ferget t'past."

Yes, I thought I could do that tonight, for Grandpa, and for Tom whom we would meet later. Tomorrow night, the past would rise again.

"Got rid of ole Mallory, I did. Second I knew he married me only so I'd become his brood mare, I brushed him off, fast, fast. Kin ya imagine that man thinkin' I'd have his baby, when I already got one? I told him straight out I weren't gonna ruin my figure so when he kicked t'bucket, I couldn't get no young fella. An' ya know what? It made him mad. He asked me what t'hell did I think he married me for but t'have his babies . . . Lordy, he's already got three grown ones."

She threw me a sly smile. "Thank ya fer tryin' t'buy my baby back that time. Knew ya couldn't do it. They wouldn't sell my beautiful Darcy fer all t'money t'Tattertons got stashed in their vaults."

I sighed for having played her fool. Nothing the Reverend Wayland Wise had said to me about myself had made me feel good. I was only too afraid he was right.

From time to time as we made our way toward the center tent, Fanny turned to hug Grandpa, before she lavished me with more affection. "Ole Mallory pays me a pretty alimony, but heck, it ain't no fun t'have money if ya don't make nobody jealous. Heaven, let's ya an' me show these hick dummies jus' what money kin do. I got me a nice big house on one hill ova there," she said, pointing, "an ya build on t'otha side of t'valley across from where I'm buildin'. Then we kin holler an' ya-hoo t'each other when t'wind is right."

It was an amusing idea for a circus day.

It was fun being with Fanny when she was happy, and I could forget, when laughter and happiness spun all around me, all that had gone before. It wasn't Fanny's fault that she was what she was, any more than it had been Troy's fault that he'd been what he was. And maybe there were excuses to be made even for Tony, if I would let myself forgive him—but he had robbed me of Troy. To show Grandpa the time of his life gave me great joy. Again and again he told me how much fun he and Annie were having.

"But we don't wanna wear her out," he warned around dusk, when the lights came on, and even larger crowds flocked in to mingle with the others. His bent legs began to falter, and soon his steps became a mere shuffle, and he began to pant breathlessly.

We were late when we reached the platform where Pa would have been giving his spiel. Already the main tent was packed, but Tom had sent us tickets, and in the nick of time the three of us made our way to three of the best seats under the main tent. Just as we sat, the band struck up a bright and lively tune, and soon, from between curtains that were drawn wide open, out of the wings and into view paraded a short row of Indian elephants in gaudy costumes, with pretty girls riding on their backs. Grandpa puffed out his chest when he saw Pa strutting center ring with his microphone, his voice cutting through the music as he introduced each animal and rider, and telling of the wonders yet to come.

"That's my Luke," shouted Grandpa, nudging Race McGee, who sat next to him. "Ain't he a good-lookin' man, ain't he though?"

"He sure don't take afta ya, Toby," answered a man who had gambled many a possession away playing poker with Pa.

By the time the show was half over, Grandpa was at such a pitch of excitement I feared he wouldn't live long enough to see the end. Fanny was almost as bad. She squealed, screamed, applauded, and from time to time she jumped up and down so much her bosom almost fell out of her low neckline. I wished to God she knew how to sit still and not make such a show of herself, but a show was what Fanny wanted to make. And she succeeded.

When the big cats slunk into the center ring to do their stunts to the command of the lion tamer I began to get nervous. I didn't enjoy the act. The big cats, made to do silly things like sitting on pedestals, embarrassed me. I kept looking for Tom and didn't see him. I wished the clowns would go away, they kept blocking my view with their foolishness, distracting me from what I most wanted to see.

And then I saw Logan.

He wasn't even watching the lion act; he was staring across ten feet of bleacher benches loaded with people, gazing at me with the worst glowering frown. The moment our eyes met he hid that expression and briefly saluted. Seated next to him was the prettiest auburn-haired girl I'd ever seen. It took me four or five glances to recognize his companion as Maisie Setterton, Kitty's younger sister. Oh, oh, he *was* seeing her a great deal.

"Heard tell Logan's got himself engaged t'Maisie," whispered Fanny hatefully, as if she could read my thoughts. "Kin't see what he sees in her. Neva could stand natural redheads wid their pale skins that splotch so easily, an' neva heard of no redhead who wasn't loud-mouthed an' mean, even fake ones."

"Your mother was one," I absently answered.

"Yeah," mumbled Fanny.

Again she smiled over to where Logan sat next to Maisie, and her flirting smile quickly changed into a sharp look of anger. "Look at that Logan, actin' like he don't even see me, when he does, when he'd have ta! Why I wouldn't marry up wid no stuffy, serious no-fun man like Logan Stonewall iffen he were t'ask me on his bended knee, an' there weren't no otha men left alive on this whole earth but Race McGee." And here she laughed right in Race McGee's livid, fat face.

Soon all the acts were over, and still we hadn't seen Tom, only Pa. The crowd began to thin out, and Grandpa, Fanny, and I made our careful way to where Tom had told us he'd be waiting, but I didn't see him there. Only a tall, thin clown in an outlandish costume stood near the tent where the stars of the circus dressed. I stumbled over one of his huge, green shoes with yellow polka dots and red bows to tie them on.

"Excuse me," I said, stepping around his size-thirty shoes; then he was tripping me up again, and I whirled to snap at him. "Why don't you keep your feet out of my way?" That's when I saw his green eyes.

"Tom . . . is that you?"

"Why, who else is so clumsy, with feet so big?" he asked, pulling off his wild red wig and smiling at me. "You really look great, Heavenly! You really do!—but I wouldn't have known you if you hadn't told me about being blond."

"And what about me?" yelled Fanny, flinging herself at him. "Ain't ya got no sweet talk fer me, yer favorite sista?"

"Why Fanny, you're exactly as I knew you always would be, hotter than a firecracker!"

She liked that.

Fanny was in a wonderful mood. She pouted to hear Pa had already gone back to the hotel where his wife and son were staying and hadn't waited to see us. In a small tent chamber that reeked of rancid makeup and powder and greasepaint, Tom removed his makeup and changed into street clothes, while Fanny regaled all of us with stories I'd not heard as yet.

"Ya gotta come an' see my place!" she said several times. "Tom, ya gotta make Pa come, too. An' his wife an' little boy as well. It ain't no good havin' a pretty new house wid a swimmin' pool an' everythin' brand new an modern if nobody that's family don't come t' see it."

"I'm beat, really beat," said Tom, trying to smother a yawn, even as he assisted Grandpa to his feet. "And just because the show is over doesn't mean all the work is done. All this ground litter has to be cleaned up. All the concession stands have to be scrubbed down to pass health inspections. The animals perform half-hungry, so they'll want to eat. The performers themselves have to unwind, and I'm in charge of most of that . . . so I'll be seeing you tomorrow, and maybe then I can look at your new house, Fanny. But why the heck would you want to buy a house here?"

"Had me my reasons," Fanny replied sulkily. "An iffen ya don't come with us t'night, it's gonna tell me like a punch in t'face, that Heaven is t'only one who counts in yer life . . . an' I'll hate ya, Tom, hate ya fereva, if ya do that t'me."

Tom went along with us. Fanny's new, contemporary-styled home sat high on a hillside, directly across from the mountain where the log cabin was; however, the valley was too vast to look across, though when you hollered down into a valley, it carried far, far.

"Gonna live here all by myself!" stated Fanny emphatically. "Not gonna have no husband, no live-in lover, an' no boss of no kind. I'm not eva gonna let myself fall in love—I'll just make 'em love me—an' when I get tired of 'em—out they go. Just before I'm forty I'll snag me some rich fella an' keep him around fer a companion."

Fanny had her life plan well worked out, which was more than I could say for myself. Two Great Danes were soon freed so they could romp and play with Fanny, who had never really liked any kind of animal. "Gotta have vicious dogs like this now that everybody knows my ex sends me a bundle each month," she explained. "Every blasted man I hire is out to skin me!"

"Who would have ever thought Fanny Casteel would wind up living in something like this?" Tom said, as if to himself. "Heavenly, is this anywhere near as grand as Farthinggale Manor?"

What could I say without hurting Fanny's feelings? No, all of Fanny's house could have been fit into one wing of Farthinggale Manor. And yet, this was a house to live in, to feel cozy in, to know every nook and cranny of.

I sauntered around, looking with interest at all the photographs hung on her walls. I stared to see Fanny at some beach with Cal Dennison! When my eyes swung to confront hers, she smiled wickedly. "Jealous, Heaven? He's mine now, anytime I want him, an' he's not so bad, 'cept when he's around his parents, then he's got no spine at all. Sooner or later I'll brush him off when he bores me one too many times."

By this time I was exceptionally tired. I wished, and not for the first time, that I hadn't let Fanny persuade me to come here.

Yawning, I stood up to go, and that's when I found out the real reason why Fanny had returned to the Willies to live. "I see Waysie every once in a while," she unexpectedly threw into our conversation. "He said he'd be more than appreciative iffen I'd let him come fer visits once a week or so. An' he's gonna bring my lil Darcy t'see me. I've already seen her twice. An' she's so pretty. Of course sooner or later everybody in Winnerrow will find out jus' what's goin on . . . an' that's when I'll have my revenge. Ole lady Wise is gonna cry through many a night, many a night."

Not for the first time I felt an overwhelming dislike for Fanny flood through me. She didn't want Waysie. She didn't really want Darcy. She just wanted revenge. I felt like slapping some sense into her. But Fanny was so drunk she fell when she lost her balance, and when I strode out of her house, she was screaming that she'd get even with me for all I'd done to rob her of self-esteem. And there she was at age twenty, once married and once divorced, hating me because no man had ever loved her enough . . . not even her own pa.

I guess Fanny and I had that in common.

Caught in some deep compulsion, the very next night I went again to the circus, this time dressed in the filmy white dress I had cleaned and ironed so carefully. This time I went alone, without Grandpa and Fanny. Once more I sat amidst the hot, sweaty crowd that had come to see their "hometown hero"— Luke Casteel, the new owner, the mesmerizing barker. Only tonight was a bit different. This time Pa's pretty young wife Stacie was there, nervously wringing her hands when Pa strode into the arena, spieling out his long introductory speech without hesitation or flaw. So why was she nervous? He was a magnificent and powerful man, radiating sensuality. All about me the women and girls stood up to cheer and yell, and some threw flowers and scarves. I saw my brother Tom, who had aspired to becoming president, reduced to a frolicking clown all because Pa had to have what he wanted, despite what Tom wanted.

I thought of Our Jane and Keith and Fanny, who had been made into what she was as surely as I'd been molded by fate into what I was. And the words of the good Reverend Wayland Wise came flooding back into my brain: "You carry with you the seeds for your own destruction, and the destruction of everyone who loves you . . . an idealist of the most fatal kind—the *romantic* idealist . . . born to destroy and self-destruct!"

As my own mother had!

Doomed, I felt doomed. Just as Troy had felt.

Over and over again the good Reverend's words played in my brain, until I felt my planned confrontation with Pa was stupid and wrong and would only end up hurting me. Quickly I stood and blindly made my way out of the stands. It didn't matter that people yelled at me to sit down and stop blocking their view. I had to get away. It didn't matter that the lions were running in the center ring cage, quite out of control. Pa stood ready with pistol and rifle just outside the cage door that he had unlocked, while inside the cage the lion tamer tried to bring control to cats that weren't paying him any attention. "It's the new lion confusing all of them!" some man yelled. "Tear down the banners! It's the fluttering that makes the new one nervous."

I should never have come back to the Willies.

I should have let well enough alone. I paused about ten feet from the cage, wanting to say goodbye to Tom, who was hovering just behind Pa, before I headed back to the cabin where Grandpa was snuggled down with his ghost wife.

"Tom," I called softly, trying to draw his attention.

Tom, in his baggy clown costume and greasepaint makeup, ran closer to snatch at my arms and hiss, "Don't say anything to Pa, please, please! He's taking the guard's place for the first time tonight cause he showed up drunk. Please, Heaven, don't distract Pa."

But I didn't have to say anything. Or do anything.

Pa had seen me.

Me, with the lights overhead shining down on my silvery blond hair, wearing the very dress my mother had worn the first time he'd seen her standing on Peachtree Street—the expensive and frail old white dress with full, fluttery sleeves and skirt. The dress that I had carefully washed and ironed, and lightly starched. The prettiest dress in my summer wardrobe. And I had to wear it . . . tonight for the first time. Pa was staring at me, frozen, his dark eyes wide. Step by step he was advancing toward me, away from the lion cage and the tamer who needed his attention.

Something happened then that took me by total

surprise. Into Pa's stunned and astonished eyes jumped a shot of pure exhilarated, disbelieving joy. My heart raced in painful response. As I stood there undecided as to what to do, I felt the full, long, white sleeves of my summer dress fluttering upward, caught in some errant evening breeze that blew through the tent opening.

At last, at last, Pa was glad to see me! It was in his eyes! At last he was going to say he loved me.

"Angel!" he cried.

He stepped toward me, arms outstretched; his rifle slipped from his fingers, and the pistol he'd pulled from its sheath fell silently into the sawdust.

Her!

It was still my mother he was seeing!

As it would always be her he saw, never me, never me!

I turned and ran.

Breathless and crying, I paused just outside the main arena. Behind me the tumult began. The screams! The roars! The cries of people gone crazy! Trained animals gone wild! Now I was frozen. I heard the shots and half turned. My hands fluttered to my forehead and pressed there.

"What's happened?" I asked two men running out of the tent.

"The cats have the tamer down on his back and are mauling him. Casteel's attention was averted and they were safe enough t'make their move. Then that stupid clown with the red hair picks up the rifle, pockets the pistol, and enters the cage himself."

Oh, my God, Tom, Tom!

The frantic man shoved me out of the way and ran on.

Someone else picked up the story. "All those crazy cats piled up on the lion tamer, and Luke's son ran braver than any man I ever knew, straight into the cage, trying to save his friend's life. Then Luke saw what was happening and he went in to save his son. God knows if anyone will come out of this alive!"

Oh, my God—my fault, my fault!

I didn't care about Pa, of course I didn't. Pa deserved anything he got.

But caring about Tom made me run faster than I had ever run before, tears streaking my face.

A terrible infection set into the deep claw wounds on Pa's back. Two days passed while I lay on the bed in Grandpa's log cabin, forcing myself to believe that that man in the hospital trying to hold on to his life deserved what he'd gotten, had asked for it long ago when he decided he had to join the circus life.

Just as Fanny in her new house was setting herself up for a day of reckoning with the town folk who had always despised her; for you couldn't go through life striking out right and left without someday bringing down your own house of cards.

Tom had been mauled much worse than Pa; he'd been first in the cage with only a pistol thrust in his baggy pants, and a rifle that he'd managed to fire once before a cat reached out with a mighty paw and clubbed the gun from his hands. And Pa had rushed in to seize the rifle and kill two of the cats, but not before he was mauled considerably.

And the worst of it was, it was Tom who died, not Pa. Tom, Tom, Tom the best of all the Casteels. Tom who had loved me. Tom who had been my companion, my other half. Tom who had given me the courage I needed to persevere and to wait for the day when Pa accepted me as his daughter.

The newspapers made Tom into a hero. They spread his smiling photograph from coast to coast, and the life story that had been Tom's was told for all to read, and somehow, they made it seem brave, not pathetic.

Only when I knew that Pa would live did I have the courage to break the news to Grandpa about what had happened to Tom. Grandpa couldn't read newspapers, and Grandpa didn't like colorful news broadcasts when he could listen all day to weather reports on the radio while he whittled. His knobby old hands paused, then loosened their grip on the tiny elephant he was carving to complete the jungle chess set he'd started long ago at Logan's request.

"My Luke is gonna live, ain't he, Heaven girl?" he asked when I finished. "We kin't let Annie suffa anotha loss."

"I called the hospital, Grandpa; he's off the critical list now, and we can go to see him."

"Ya didn't tell me, Heaven chile, did ya, that Tom is gone? Tom kain't die when he's only twenty-one . . . Oh, I neva did have much luck in keepin' my boys around me."

In the hospital I allowed Grandpa to go alone into the small room where Pa lay completely swathed in bandages from head to foot, peering through one tiny eyehole. Shaken, I went to lean against a wall. I cried, cried for so many things that could have turned out differently. I felt so alone, so terribly alone. Who would love me now, who? And almost as if God heard my question, arms tenderly slipped around my waist, and I was pulled backward against a strong chest, and someone's head pressed down on mine.

"Don't cry, Heaven," crooned Logan, turning me around to take me into his arms. "Your father is going to live. He's a fighter. He's got a lot to live for—his wife, his son, and you. He's tough. Always has been. But he's not going to be so handsome anymore."

"Tom is dead, don't you know that? Tom is dead, Logan, dead!"

"Everybody knows that Tom died a hero's death. His entrance into the cage diverted the lions, who were mauling the lion tamer, who had four children, and he's alive, Heaven, alive. Now say something to your pa."

What could I say to a man I'd always wanted to love, but couldn't? What could he say to me now, now when it was far too late for words that might have brought us together. And yet he was staring at me. Through that small eye opening I could see the sadness in that single eye, and his hand, bandaged and bound, made a small awkward gesture, as if he'd reach for me if he could.

"I'm sorry," I managed to whisper. "So sorry about Tom." I wiped at the tears that began to slide down my face. "I'm sorry about everything that went wrong between you and me!"

I thought I heard him mumble my name, but by that time I was running out of the hospital. Running out into a day that was blazing hot, and flinging myself at a metal lamppost, I wrapped my arms around it and really bawled. How was I going to live without Tom in my life, how, how?

"Come, Heaven," said Logan, striding up with Grandpa stumbling beside him. "What's done is done and we can't undo it."

"Fanny didn't even show up at Tom's funeral," I sobbed, glad that he could easily pull me into his embrace and forgive me for so much.

"What does it matter what Fanny does or doesn't do?" he asked, tilting my teary face upward and staring gravely down into my eyes. "Weren't we always happiest when Fanny was out of sight?"

As he stood there in the bright sunlight, how sensitive and caring he appeared, like Troy in some ways. I bowed my head against his chest and tried to stop my tears, and then we were walking, all three of us, toward the car.

"You were wrong when you said I didn't need you," said Logan when we were halfway home.

The whispering in the leaves, the songs of the wind in the grass, the wildflowers that scented the air with sweet perfume did more to heal me than any words could. Everywhere I looked I saw the green of Tom's eyes, and when I faltered in decisions, I heard him speak in my mind, encouraging me to go on, to marry Logan—but to leave the hills and the valley as soon as Grandpa was gone.

We laid my grandpa to rest on the sixteenth day of October, laid him to rest beside his beloved wife Annie. We stood all in a single row—the Casteels, Pa, Stacie, Drake, Fanny, and every resident who lived in Winnerrow. It had been Tom's bravery, and not my wealth or my education or my clothes and new car that had won their respect.

I bowed my head and cried just as if Grandpa had really been flesh of my flesh. And before we walked away from that gravesite, Pa reached out and took my hand. "I'm sorry for a lot of things," he said in a kind of low, soft voice I'd never expected to hear from him. "I wish you great success and happiness in whatever you decide to do. And I hope more than anything, that every now and then you'll show up at our place."

Funny, only now could I stare at the man I'd thought I'd hate forever and not feel anything.

I didn't know what to say. I could only nod.

In a lonely, huge house another father waited for me to return. I knew as I stood on the hillside and looked around that someday I'd go back to Farthinggale Manor, and by that time I would be neither a Casteel nor a Tatterton.

By then, from the soft way Logan was looking at me, I knew he'd go with me, and I'd know for sure I was a Stonewall.